THE BUTCHER'S BLOCK

THE BUTCHER'S BLOCK

A Story about the Horrific Marine Battle for Tarawa

Day Three

James F Dwyer

Copyright © 2020 James F Dwyer
All rights reserved.

ISBN: XXXXXXXXX
ISBN 13: XXXXXXXXXXXXX
Library of Congress Control Number: **XXXXX (If applicable)**
LCCN Imprint Name: **City and State (If applicable)**

Dedication

This is probably the most enjoyable part of the book writing process…because this is where you get to say thank you to all the people who helped make this possible. Since this is my final book, this list will be somewhat different from the dedication that appears in Book 1 and Book 2…but it's just as important …because without them…this book would never have been written. So here goes…

I would still like to acknowledge my Father in Heaven…and His Son…Jesus Christ…who is my Lord & Savior…and His Holy Spirit…for all the wonderful blessings They have bestowed on me. Without my faith…I would have nothing… and I am still truly blessed beyond words.

The genesis of this book began when I was a little boy…when my younger brother…Bobby…was sick with leukemia. A young marine…whose name I do not know…learned about Bobby's illness and sent my brother a stuffed marine bulldog and a typed message addressed to M/Sgt (Honorary) Bobbie Dwyer.

The message read as follows: It has been brought to the attention of this command that you are a brave and obedient young marine. Bravery and obedience are taken as a matter of fact in the case of every marine. However, due to the degree that you have exhibited these qualities, we are privileged to award you the Good Conduct medal. The message was signed by John C. Smith, Maj. General, U.S. Marine Corps, Commanding. Bobby died a few months later…in May of 1968…and I never forgot that kind act. It was my first contact with the Marine Corps…and one that left a lasting impression on me. I would like to thank that marine…whoever you are…for making my nine-year old brother an honorary marine…and for sparking my first interest in the Marine Corps. Without you…I may never have written this book.

I would like to thank my father…a former FBI agent…and the most generous and kind-hearted man alive. My dad tried to enlist in the Marine Corps in 1944…but he was turned down due to his having asthma as a boy…so he became a Navy radar man and he served aboard the U.S. Navy cruiser Portsmouth in WWII. This man gave me a love for all things military…since he took me to my first war movie…and many others…and he paid for my subscription to the Military Book Club…and he took me to the Army-Navy game in 1973. It is because of my dad…who I love and respect…that this book was written.

The next group of men I would like to thank all served in the 2nd Division, U.S. Marine Corps and all were at Tarawa… and I feel a special connection to each of them…

Second Lieutenant Joseph Sexton…who grew up down the block from my dad in Brooklyn, New York…and who fought with the 1ˢᵗ Battalion, 2ⁿᵈ Regiment and lost has life in the battle. I first thought of writing a story about Tarawa as a way of honoring Joe…who never returned…and the little girl…his daughter…that he never got to meet. Joe's sacrifice was the inspiration for this book.

Corporal Robert George…who fought in the battle and experienced more acts of valor than he could count. Bob graciously took my calls and he spent several hours on the phone telling me what the battle was like, and he described everything he saw with such emotion and detail that I will never forget him. My only regret is that he did not get to see these books… as he passed away in Sacramento, California before they were finished.

Colonel Paul Millichap…was at Tarawa and I am the proud owner of his Springfield rifle…which was given to me by his daughter…Denise. Major Millichap was the Second Division's Ordinance Officer at the time of the battle and he was paid the highest compliment possible…when retired Colonel Ed Bale… who led his tanks ashore as a first lieutenant on the western end of Betio Island on Day One of the battle…told me over the phone that he was a great officer. Denise's kindness and love for her father…and mother…who was one of the New Zealand war brides that I wrote about in Book 3…helped motivate me to start writing my story again.

Without the inspiration of these four men above…a Navy man and three Marines…all members of the greatest generation… and their families to motivate me…I might never have written this story.

I would like to thank my mother…who never complained when her boys came back to the house coated in dirt and sweat… after spending an afternoon playing war…and for letting me hang those World War II models from the ceiling in our bedroom…a simple act…but one that let my imagination run wild and encouraged my love for the military. Without my mother's love, guidance, and willingness to sacrifice for her children…I would never have made it to West Point…which gave me the foundation I needed to write this book. My mother is one of a kind…and her love for our Country…which she received from my Irish grandmother…who was born in County Tipperary…motivated me to write this book.

I will always be indebted to Sergeant Colin Jackson of the Atlanta Fire Rescue Department…who told me that I needed to finish what I had started so many years before. Just get something done, he told me. Well, I listened to his advice… and Book One…and Book Two…and now Book Three are done.

And last but certainly not least…in fact, the most important of all save for the Father, Son, and Holy Spirit…is my wonderful, patient wife, Meryl, who has kept the house operating while I was working on my three stories…especially the second one…which was finished while I was incapacitated with a torn Achilles tendon. My wife has done everything I have asked of her…without complaint…and there is no better person to be with when the chips are down. She was gracious in letting me read long passages from my story to her…even though she had better things to do…so I could see how they sounded, and to show her that I was a good writer. She gave me confidence to keep going…and I love her for spoiling me. She is my treasure and without her love, compassion, and encouragement, I may never have been able to finish any of these books. And Meryl's position in the order is perfect… since Jesus told us…those who seek to be first must be last… and a servant to all. Meryl fulfills these words to the letter…which is why I put her right where I did. Thank you, Darling…I love you!

There are several other people who I thought about as I wrote my stories…and I would like to take the time to mention them here below…since they motivated me and kept me going:

Colonel Edward Lewis Bale, Jr. who passed away on December 21st, 2017. I had the honor of both emailing him and speaking with him on the phone several times…and he told me that I had done a fine job in capturing the essence of the battle.

Corporal Kenneth Schauble…who was related to my Mother… and who was killed in action on June 6th, 1968 while serving as a rifleman in E Company, 2nd Battalion, 26th Marine Regiment, 3rd Marine Division in the Republic of Viet Nam. Even after all these years, I can still remember the sadness that descended over our family at the news of his death…nearly a month after my brother passed away.

James F Dwyer

Brigadier General Robert L. Scott Jr...West Point Class of 1932...and fighter pilot and ace with the Flying Tigers in China during WWII and who wrote the story, "God is My Co-Pilot." I met General Scott at a West Point dinner in Atlanta many years ago...and I will never forget raising a toast to his wingman...who was shot down and killed during a mission they were on in China. He also sent me two letters which I treasure to this day. General Scott passed away on February 27th, 2006...and I like to think that he would've enjoyed reading my books...since he fought in that war...and that he would have enjoyed my depiction of a fighter pilot in action.

Father Vincent R. Capodanno, MM...a Catholic priest and Maryknoll Missionary...who won the Congressional Medal of Honor while serving as a U.S. Navy Chaplain with the U.S. Marine Corps. Known as the Grunt Padre, Chaplain Capodanno was killed in action on September 4th, 1967. I used his prayer card as a book marker...and I believe it has blessed my work as a result.

I would like to thank the other six members of Station 25... my station mates...for their patience and encouragement as I worked on my story. It is an honor to serve with men like these...who are willing to risk their lives for the citizens they do not know...and to a man...will be running towards the fire when others are running out.

Acknowledgements

The formulation of this book began many years ago...when I first discovered military books...while I was suffering through seventh grade detention in our junior high school library...in 1970. Over the last fifty plus years or so, I have read hundreds of war books... both fiction and non-fiction alike...and I have watched every war movie...the latest one being the remake of the 1970's classic: Midway...that came across the airwaves or was shown in a movie theatre near where I lived at the time. Many of the battles and the men involved in them were very interesting...but Tarawa stoked my imagination the very first time I read about it. This happened when I was in junior high school...because I can remember spending time in our local town library investigating Tarawa in a Marine Journal that listed details about marine battles of World War II. All these years later, I can still remember the feeling I had when I saw the name of Second Lieutenant Joseph Sexton with a KIA listed next to his name in the battle-deaths index for the battle. This young officer had grown up right down the street from my father in Brooklyn, N.Y. and seeing his name brought the battle to life for me…since my father remembered seeing him walking down the street in his dazzling marine uniform when he was home on leave during the war. Then…without realizing it…my father mentioned something that changed my life. In talking about Joe…my dad said how sad it was to see his wife…a girl who had grown up directly behind my dad's own brownstone…pushing a baby carriage up the street with a little girl inside. That little girl was Second Lieutenant Joe Sexton's daughter…and he never got to see her…nor she him…since he was killed fighting for his Country in the battle for Tarawa. Even at that young age, I swore that I would do something…someday…to honor that man and the little girl who would spend the rest of her life without her father.

That goal never really left me…and I remember the first time I tried to do something about it. I was in my early 30's and I began writing a movie script about the fight for Tarawa in a small apartment in New Milford, New Jersey. I didn't get very far…but I had made my first attempt at fulfilling my dream…and that's what counted at the time. That spark would reignite almost fifteen years later…when I decided to write a book about a military figure that I thought a younger audience would find interesting. I was going to call it, "A Marine Lieutenant at Tarawa," and I wanted to model my book after the Hardy Boys series by Franklin W. Dixon. These were the very first books that I had ever read as a kid…and I loved them. If I was successful in this first endeavor…I planned on producing a series of books like it…using different characters in different branches of service to describe the battles that were fought in World War Two. I was hoping that they would generate the same level of excitement in the young boys of today that I had experienced when a new Hardy Boys book hit the shelf in our local department store. With that in mind, I began writing the story about my lieutenant…and I found the exercise very exciting. Without realizing it, I had stumbled back into my real calling…the one that had been lying dormant for so many years. So, I continued to write…giving life to my marine lieutenant…and before long I realized that my simple story had morphed into something far more sophisticated than a simple child's story and I was now writing for a more mature audience. And in the process, I found out…most importantly…that I really enjoyed writing. I have spent the last sixteen years working on this story…writing when the urge hit me…putting it off when it didn't. Had I not become a firefighter after 9-11, my story might have been finished earlier…or maybe not at all…but life has a funny way of interrupting our pursuits at times…so my endeavor has taken a little longer than I anticipated…but Book Three is now finished as well.

The story you are about to read is the third in a series of three books about the battle for Tarawa….and it deals with the actions that took place on the third…and last…day of the battle…and the men involved in them. As you will see…I have tried to arrange the books in chronological order…but some scenes…out of necessity…will take the reader back to the actions of the day before…and to the first day of the battle too…and to places other than the island of Betio. I have attempted to capture the battle through the eyes of the marines who fought there…and to some degree…through the eyes of the brave Japanese soldiers who fought there as well. To this end, I have created my own cast of characters who will experience as much of the battle as possible…while rubbing elbows with the actual marines who fought the battle. I have tried to stay as true to the real story of Tarawa as possible…and I relied on the superb books below to assist me in this regard:

Utmost Savagery
The Three Days of Tarawa
By Colonel Joseph H. Alexander USMC (RET.)

Tarawa
a legend is born
By Henry I. Shaw, Jr.
Battle Book No 8 of Ballantine's Illustrated History of World War II

Tarawa
20-23 November 1943
A Hell of a Way to Die
By Derrick Wright

Bloody Tarawa
A Narrative History with 250 Photographs
By Eric Hammel and John E. Lane

ONE SQUARE MILE OF HELL
The Battle for Tarawa
By John Wukovits

We Were Going to Win, or Die There
With the Marines at Guadalcanal, Tarawa, and Saipan
By Roy H. Elrod

TANKS IN HELL
A Marine Corps Tank Company on Tarawa
By Oscar E. Gilbert and Romain Cansiere

Tarawa
Too young to Vote
By Robert L. George

tarawa 1943
the turning of the tide
Praeger Illustrated Military History Series
By Derrick Wright

Mantle of Heroism
Tarawa and the Struggle for the Gilberts, November 1943
By Michael B. Graham

The U.S. Marine Corps in World War II
The Stories Behind the Photos
By Steve Crawford

James F Dwyer

War in the Pacific
Pearl Harbor to Tokyo Bay
Edited by Bernard C. Nalty
Technical Advisor Russ A. Pritchard

About the Author

James F. Dwyer is a 1980 graduate of the U.S. Military Academy at West Point. While a cadet, he attended the U.S. Army Paratrooper School at Fort Benning, Georgia and earned his jump wings in the summer of 1978. He also served in the U.S. Army as an armored cavalry officer in the 2nd Squadron of the 9th Cavalry Regiment at Fort Stewart, Georgia from 1981 until 1984. After leaving the Army, he worked as a trader on Wall Street for nine years before leaving for Sandy Springs, Georgia where he worked as a stockbroker for another nine years with A.G. Edwards & Sons. He left the financial world after 9-11 and became a firefighter with the City of Atlanta Fire Rescue Department at the age of forty-six. He has been with this department for sixteen years and is currently assigned to Station 25 in the Cascade Heights section of Atlanta. He also worked as a part-time firefighter for seven and a half years with the Sandy Springs Fire Rescue Department from 2007 until 2015. He has been married to his wife, Meryl, for twelve years and they have three dogs and a cat at home in Acworth, Georgia. He and Meryl belong to Freedom

Church, a non-denominational Christian church in Acworth and on Sundays he participates in a bible study program for inmates at the local jail. This is the final book of a three-part series about the battle of Tarawa.

Notes/Corrections/ Clarifications

In doing my research for Book Three, I came across several errors or inconsistencies in Book One and Book Two. These errors are noted below:

1. The M 4 Sherman tanks at Betio did not have a loader's hatch which was mentioned on page 321 of The Slaughter Pen. At the time, there was only one hatch on the top of the turret… and this hatch was above the tank commander's position. Later versions of the Sherman tank did have this second hatch…over the loader's position, however.
2. The exterior radio/communications box on the M4 Sherman tank that was mentioned on page 321 of the Slaughter Pen did not exist on the tanks that served on Betio Island. This device was added to later versions of the M4 tank as a result of the action on Betio Island.

3. The tank landing that is depicted on page 161 of Annihilation Beach needs further clarification. The scene mentions four LCMs trying to land on Red 2...and that the LCMs then backed off and headed for Red 3. These LCMs were carrying Stuart Light tanks...not the Sherman tanks that the scene seems to indicate. Two of these LCMs then veer off and try to make a landing using the right side of the pier. The two tanks that were lost in this scene were Stuarts...not Sherman tanks. Also, the scene mentions one tank running into a shell hole...and that the crew then drowned inside. Evidence indicates that this was a Stuart tank...since no Sherman tank crewmen were listed as having drowned as a result of their tanks running into shell holes off the beach at Betio. PFC Bob George states that he saw dead tankers floating in the water on Day 4 in his book, "Too Young to Vote," which would indicate that several tank crewmen that served in the Stuarts were killed after their tanks became stuck in the water.
4. The two Sherman tanks that arrived on Red 2 on page 162 of Annihilation Beach were not part of the action mention in point 3 above. How these two tanks arrived on Red 2 is better described in Book Three, however.
5. The tank landing on Red 1 that is depicted in pages 163-164 of Annihilation Beach is more accurately described in Book Three.

The Butcher's Block

6. The rank of the marine that stays behind with Private Grasso at the seawall is incorrectly listed as a private first class on page 312 of The Slaughter Pen. Since it was Private Hennessey that stayed behind, the rank should have been noted as a private instead.
7. It is stated on page 312 of The Slaughter Pen that Sergeant Varner has eight men with him at this point. This is an error. At this stage, he only had seven men with him.

Preface

On December 8th, 1943 Private David S. Spencer…having survived the three-day ordeal that was Tarawa…wrote home to his family:

You've probably read the papers about Tarawa so I won't bother to tell you all about it. God and your prayers must have pulled me thru because I came close to being killed several times. I've got two bullet holes in my jacket that is evidence that if I'd have been running a little faster I would have got it in the heart.

Then…on December 12th, he wrote again:

Tarawa made me a very good Christian and church-goer. It seems as if I look forward to Church to thank God for my life and the fact that all of you are well & happy. I believe all of us that came back from Tarawa can safely say that Death had us by one hand and God the other and God was a little stronger.

A little later he added: *I'll never understand or stop being grateful why my life was spared while other boys around me were being taken. I guess our prayers were answered.*

A young lieutenant who commanded a machine gun platoon on Tarawa wrote home about the men in his platoon:

After the battle was over I spoke to my men and gave them my heartfelt congratulations. It was the most important incident in my life. I couldn't say much, the words just seemed to choke up, but each and every one understood. My men followed orders bravely and did their respective jobs magnificently. Each is a hero in his own right. I am proud of them…they may not have rank, prestige or background, but they have greater substitutes—guts, bravery and honor in facing death's danger. To me these traits are outstanding and will bring this war to an end…Those that did not return fought like men and met their end bravely. Not one flinched, nor did they show any signs of pain. Theirs was the satisfaction of another job well done, one that would bring peace on earth closer to their loved ones. I find comfort in my prayers for them, in a comrade-in-arms' duty to carry on, and the honor of having been with them in our common cause.*

*Both letters were taken from ONE SQUARE MILE OF HELL THE BATTLE FOR TARAWA pages 236-237 by John Wukovits

Introduction

Life feels eerily different for a man who has been in combat...and especially so if he has walked away from it physically unscathed. For that lucky man...the survivor...the one who somehow beat the odds...every experience in life thereafter, no matter how insignificant, will be savored...will be cherished...will be appreciated. For every soldier, marine, sailor, or airman who has experienced the ugliness of war...who has looked death in the eye...who has seen blood shed...knows all too well that the precious gift of survival is not bestowed on every participant during a battle. This was certainly the case for the men of the Second Marine Division who were still alive on Betio Island on the Monday morning of November 22nd, 1943. These men could look around in any direction and see the carnage that had transpired after two full days of vicious combat on the small, two-mile-long island. Yet they were still there...and they had survived...somehow.

The marines had been fighting their Japanese counterparts who were stationed on Betio...the vaunted *rikusentai* of the Special Naval Landing Forces. And these Japanese warriors were defending their island ruthlessly...since it was their home...and the marines were trying to steal it from them. The evidence of the Japanese willingness to fight to the end...until death even...to protect it...was everywhere in sight. Behind the marines lines, out in the cove and along the shoreline, were the scattered relics of the vehicles that had brought the marines into the island...the LVT-1's and LVT-2's and Higgins boats that had been hit by uncannily accurate Japanese shore fire. Some of them were still burning...their twisted remains issuing ugly, black smoke that drifted skyward...marking the point of their farthest advance. Many still contained the broken bodies of the marines who had ridden in them...their lives snuffed out by a direct hit from a mortar round or a burst of machine gun fire that had ripped their vehicles apart. Others...the ones that had been hit by larger weapons... by the anti-boat cannons...had simply vanished in the blink of an eye. It was if they had never been there at all. The rest...the ones that had been holed beyond repair... had simply sunk...taking everything to the bottom with them. The only sign that they had once existed was an oily patch of water and the random military items that may have floated up to the surface above them.

As depressing as these sights were, they were nothing compared to the horrible scenes that had dotted the shoreline and narrow beachhead for the past two days... where well over four hundred dead marine bodies were packed into fifteen hundred yards of space. Most gruesome of all, if there were such a thing, were the bodies of the men entangled in the barbed wire fencing that the Japanese engineers had strung in the water some fifty yards from the beachhead all around the island. Rigor mortis had taken affect quickly after these men had been hit and some of them were now frozen in gruesome contortions with their arms outstretched as if they were still alive and calling for help. The seaweed that was draped all over them told the men ashore otherwise...that these men were no more alive than the wire that now held them in its tight embrace.

Closer in...in the shallows and on the beachhead itself...dead marines...or what was left of them...were scattered about as well. These men had been killed either singly or in groups while they were trying to exit the amtracs that had made it to the seawall...or they had been killed while wading in from the reef that had so effectively blocked their Higgins boats from reaching the beach. Finally, scores of men had also been killed as they tried to advance inland...moving beyond the seawall...to knock out the hidden Japanese emplacements that had been wreaking havoc on the marine landing teams all along. Evidence of the how far the marines had advanced could be determined by the line of marine dead in the sectors where they had tried to break out...a grim reminder of the cost for leaving the beach. Farthest forward...in the Red Beach Two area...marine bodies could be seen lying in the open on the tarmac of the main airstrip that made the island - code-named *Helen* - a valuable target in the first place.

Thus, the marines of the Second Division who were still alive on the morning of D + 2 for the battle of Tarawa had no illusions about how hard or dangerous it would be to complete the task that lay ahead of them. They had firsthand knowledge of the bloody cost that two days' worth of fighting had produced all around them. Yet despite the carnage, a glimmer of hope had emerged among the men that was hard to resist. It was a feeling that the worst that could've happened had already happened…that somehow the setbacks and stalemates of the last two days were now behind them. Incredibly, a new day…a day of possibilities…a day of victory…was just now dawning.

Chapter One

"Hey, lieutenant!" a voice, low but loud enough to be heard, cried out plaintively...breaking the silence that had descended over the group for the last eight hours.

First Lieutenant Robert Hackett was dozing...not really sleeping...so he stirred when he heard the marine call out to him. "What is it, Wykoff? You see something out there or are you trying to ruin my beauty sleep."

Jeremy Wykoff, a private first class and driver in the 2nd Amphibious Tractor Battalion, smiled at the lieutenant's response. Even though the young enlisted man from Louisiana had not known the lieutenant very long...less than two days really...he still appreciated the platoon commander's sense of humor...and his ability to tell a good story. But more than that though, he appreciated the officer's competence as a leader...since the lieutenant had managed to keep most of the men around him alive…at least so far. Wykoff had a lower opinion of some of the other officers he had served under…just like most of other men around him did.

"Yes, sir. I think I saw somethin'. Out there on the taxiway. One of those guys that got hit trying to cross over isn't dead. At least not yet anyway. The Japs must have missed him when they machine gunned the others out there yesterday. I saw him lift his head up and then he waved his arm. I guess he thinks that some of his buddies are still over there on this side of the strip. Maybe he was trying to let them know he's still alive and that he wants someone to come help him. He must be hurtin' real bad or maybe he's delirious. I sure hope the Japs didn't see him."

The lieutenant looked over at Wykoff…and then he shifted his gaze to the taxiway to see if he could see the marine in question. "I don't see anything moving out there. You sure you saw it?" the lieutenant asked, hoping he was right and Wykoff was wrong.

Since it was now dawn and the sun had come up, the bodies of the men who had been shot down the day before were now plainly visible out on the taxiway… although they looked like dark green lumps instead of human bodies to the lieutenant.

"I know what I saw, lieutenant. My eyes weren't playing tricks on me. I got real good eyesight. The boys back home who I hunt ducks with love to have me along since I can see a duck a long way off when no one else can."

Now the man positioned to the left of the lieutenant and one to the right of Wykoff began looking too… since they could hear the conversation. And they quickly passed the word down the line in each direction so that before long all fifteen men, plus the lieutenant, were straining to see if they could spot the marine who might still be alive. Private Hall, who had been shot in the forehead the day before, was not looking. He was quite dead...the unlucky recipient of a bullet that had been fired at their group by the Japanese across the way.

"I think Wykoff is right. I just saw some movement too. Look closely. One of those guys is moving ever so slightly. I think he's trying to drag himself back to our lines." This time it was Sergeant Tom Endres who was lying all the way at the left end of the line. He crawled slowly over to where the lieutenant was...checking on each man as he passed by. "Whatta ya wanna do about it, lieutenant?" the veteran squad leader asked pointedly, knowing there was no good answer to his question.

"There's not much we can do, sarge," the lieutenant answered quickly, and then added, "the Japs still have us outgunned by a country mile. For all I know they could've brought up a few more machine gun teams during the night...to really seal off the taxiway and the airfield triangle from us. I'm not gonna risk an attack against that position with just fifteen men so we can save one man who might end up dying anyway. We'd probably lose three men just trying to get to the taxiway alone...so it just doesn't make much sense. At least not to me."

"I agree," Endres stated, knowing the decision the lieutenant just made was one of the toughest ones a leader in a combat situation must make. Now all the others were staring at the two of them, wondering whether the lieutenant would order an attack to try to rescue the downed marine or not. Sensing their concern, Sergeant Endres looked at the group and shook his head to indicate that no attack would be made...that no rescue attempt would be attempted...and then he crawled back to his position. The men relaxed immediately at the news since they knew all too well the cost of mounting such an operation...that some of them would not have made it back. And yet some of them still felt guilty over leaving the wounded man out there to his own devices.

Since there was nothing they could do to help him, Hackett and his men watched intently now as the unknown marine made his own desperate attempt to reach safety. The man was going slow given his condition, but his progress was steady, and he continued to inch his way towards the northern side of the taxiway. As he got closer and closer, everyone's spirits soared higher and higher too...and some of them could not contain their enthusiasm. "He's gonna make it. By God, he's gonna make it," one man drawled out. Another said, almost with reverence, "Of course, he's gonna make it, you dumb SOB. The man's a marine...and there's no quit in a marine." The staccato bark of a machine gun from the Jap side of the taxiway crushed their hopes in one fell swoop however as the wounded man was stitched across his back by a string of bullets...leaving him just as dead as the other men who were splayed out on the tarmac of the taxiway around him.

"Damn Japs," one man seethed, "they let him get all that way and then they finished him off. Like it's a game to them. I bet they're all laughin' about it over there."

Another man, one of the other strays who was not in Hackett's own platoon, was just as distraught. He yelled out, "We just gonna sit here and let them do that to one of our own?"

PFC Feeney, who was nearby, looked over menacingly and said, "Shut up, Miller. We'll get our chance to pay them back…just not now. Don't do anything stupid like takin' a shot at them since that'll just bring heavier fire down on us. Be patient for now and just trust the lieutenant…he knows what he's doing."

PFC Bobby Miller…a member of the 2nd Platoon of E Company…glared at Feeney and was about to curse him out, but the man next to him reached over a patted him on the arm. "Just let it go, Bobby. Feeney means well," Private Clark Glass…who was in the second platoon with Miller…advised.

"Feeney is just a private in my book, Glass," Miller said, his Irish temper rising. "He thinks he can shoot his mouth off now that the lieutenant has made him a PFC. He'd better be careful from here on out…or I'll put him back in his place so fast his head'll spin."

"Ahhh…let it go, Bobby boy. Clark's right. Feeney's a good man. Irish, too…just like you. And he means well," Private Danny Thompson added…the third and last member of the second platoon who had stumbled in beside Hackett's men on D Day.

Miller looked over at Thompson…and then at Glass…and said, "Oh, all right. I'll cut Feeney a break. But I hate what the Japs did to that guy out there. They're animals…and I'm gonna kill every single Jap that I can get my mitts on."

Glass…who had risked his own life in rescuing Miller from drowning on D Day…glanced over at Thompson and said quietly, "Thanks, Danny. Old Bobby can get crazy at times and he's hard to rein in when he's riled up. Thanks for backing me up…you really helped settle Bobby down. You're destined for stripes down the road since you seem to be one of the few guys who can get Bobby to back off when his Irish temper kicks in."

Thompson took the compliment in stride…and he winked at Glass…and then the three platoon mates settled back…to see what would happen next.

Corporal Johnny Ingunza, an F Company brawler of noted distinction among the 2nd Division men, glanced to his right and grunted at the sight of Private Hall's helmeted head lying serenely on his M-1 rifle. Then he looked over at PFC Wykoff and watched as Wykoff tapped his index finger rhythmically against the trigger of the BAR that he was gripping ever so tightly. Wykoff had borrowed the weapon from Private Marty Poffineger and he had put the weapon to good use in the firefight yesterday. So far, Poffineger had not asked for the weapon back. At least not yet anyway. Poffineger…and the three other men under PFC Harry Mornston…were positioned several yards behind Wykoff so they could defend against a Jap flank attack that could come from the vicinity of the huge airfield apron and the string of aircraft revetments that were built along its northern edge. Since nothing had materialized from that direction to challenge Hackett's men during the battle yesterday...or during the first hours of daylight now... Wykoff felt justified in hanging on to the BAR a little longer.

Wykoff continued to glare at the Jap position across the way...and then he shifted to the left slightly to get a better firing angle on them. "Easy does it," Ingunza whispered, his gravelly voice easily carrying across the few feet that separated the two men. "No one wants to get at those lousy Japs more than me...trust me. I'd trade a crate of whiskey...good whiskey too...not that lousy, watered-down stuff they sell at the slop chutes...for the chance to spend two minutes in the ring with any one of those murderin' jokers across the way. Maybe two crates of whiskey even."

PFC Wykoff shook his head in affirmation and seemed to relax...but deep inside...where feelings can hide...his anger over what the Japs had done to that wounded marine would linger far longer than this one battle.

Once the tension among Hackett's men dissolved, they settled into the same routine that had taken place the morning before...checking their weapons and passing out what little food remained among them. There wasn't much...since most of the men had removed their heavy packs long ago and left them by the seawall. They did this so they could move more nimbly and save energy...but this choice had come with a price...and they were dealing with it now. However, even though they were hungry, the lack of food didn't bother them all that much. While food was important, it was not their main priority. Water was. At this stage of the battle, some of the marines were becoming seriously dehydrated... since they had been fighting in the intense heat of the equatorial sun for two days on no more than two canteens worth of water. Luckily, some of the men had been more judicious and disciplined in their water consumption than some of their thirstier buddies were, and they were able to share what little they had left with their dry-mouthed companions.

Lieutenant Hackett was one such man. Despite being just as thirsty as the others were, he still had some water left. He reached down and withdrew one of the canteens from his web belt and threw it over to his runner, PFC Gino Petraglia. The runner caught the canteen in mid-air and twisted off the top as quick as he could, his thirst beyond control. He took a small sip and capped the canteen just as quickly though, worried that his thirst would get the best of him. Then looked over to PFC Feeney, who was just as thirsty, and he threw the canteen over to him. Feeney was more deliberate in removing the top...hoping the lieutenant would notice his discipline despite his thirst. He took a small sip and then underhanded the canteen back to its owner. "Thanks, sir," the battlefield-promoted private first class said, "I'm sorry I don't have any left myself. I shared a lot of what I had with the other guys yesterday. I guess I wasn't too concerned about having nothing left. I should have been."

"That's okay, Feeney," the lieutenant responded. "Lesson learned, right."

"Yes, sir. I guess there'll be plenty more of these islands we'll have to attack...and they'll be just as hot

I imagine. I won't let my canteens get empty so fast ever again." Feeney nodded to the lieutenant and then winked at Petraglia who was nodding his head as well. Then Feeney added, "I don't know what's worse...the lack of water out here...or the horrible smell of all these dead bodies. I'm dyin' of thirst...but I think the smell is getting to me worse now. I've never experienced anything like it. I bet it can drive a man crazy if he's exposed to it long enough."

With that, the lieutenant reached up to his nose and withdrew some cotton from one of his nostrils. "Here you go, Feeney," he said, and laughing, he threw the cotton ball over to him. "I couldn't live with myself if you killed yourself over the smell...especially since you gave me one of your own cotton balls."

"Stole is more like it," Feeney corrected the lieutenant good-naturedly.

"I like to think that I confiscated that material," Hackett countered, "for the good of the Marine Corps. That's why I'm an officer...and being an officer hath its privileges."

"Yeah, officer privilege is exactly what it is. I get it, sir. Us enlisted guys have gotten the short end of the stick more than a few times with some of the other officers in this battalion. They really believe in their officer privileges...believe you me."

Hackett was comfortable with the tac the conversation had taken because he knew that Feeney was not talking about him...that he wasn't the type of leader that he was referring to...and it was good to let the enlisted men vent every once in a while.

The lieutenant believed in and practiced servant leadership instead. It was a concept he had been exposed to while he was taking mandatory religious courses at a parochial school in Brooklyn, New York. The idea of serving others...even if it diminished your own image and prestige...appealed to Hackett for some strange reason...and he had put it to the test at the Naval Academy...which he attended right after high school. There was not much he could do as a plebe...other than help his classmates from getting hazed...since plebes were the lowest form of life at the Naval Academy.

The opportunity to lead others finally came when he was placed in charge of other midshipmen after his long plebe year was over...and especially so on the football field...when he was named the co-captain of the team after excelling as a defensive back. His success on the football field had enabled him to apply this style of leadership to its full effect since his coaches had labeled him a born leader and his teammates swore that they would follow him anywhere. It would have been easy to take advantage of or abuse this type of adulation...becoming arrogant towards those who put him up on a pedestal so often. And it could have made him very selfish and egotistical...becoming consumed with enhancing and promoting his own abilities. But he chose to lead differently...and the football team rallied to his call. In elevating those around him, the team gelled, and victories began piling up. His leadership strategy influenced others to do the same...to mimic him...and it all culminated in a glorious victory over the Army football team in November 1940.

The Butcher's Block

After graduating in spring of 1941, Hackett headed to the Marine Corps instead of the Navy, and he was commissioned a second lieutenant instead of a naval ensign. It was a decision he never regretted...and the young officer had tried to apply this style of leadership to those under his charge ever since. And now it was paying dividends for the men who were lying beside him.

The lieutenant shook his canteen...checking to see how much water was left. He heard a sloshing sound and without taking a sip, he placed the canteen back in its pouch and snapped the cover closed. Then he checked his watch for the first time that day. It was coated in dust, so he wiped the face clean with his right hand...which was bandaged with a filthy field dressing that he had put on almost twenty-four hours ago. His hand had been hit by a sliver of shrapnel from the same exploding mortar round that had also killed two members of a machine gun crew who were not far away from Hackett when it hit. These men had decided to stay and fight with Hackett...even though they had landed on the wrong part of the beach. Their decision to remain...instead of heading off to find their own unit...had cost them their lives...and Hackett had not forgotten it.

"What time ya got, sir?" Petraglia asked, watching him.

"It's zero seven hundred, boys...or close to it. I haven't been winding this old watch like I should be. Too distracted, I guess. It might be a few minutes off... who knows?"

Chapter Two

Lieutenant Hackett's watch was exactly right...and the time it showed...0700 hours...signaled the start of a three-pronged marine attack that took place on the morning of the third day of the battle for Betio Island. The attacks had been planned the night before...after the arrival of Colonel Merritt "Red Mike" Edson...the Second Division's Chief-of-Staff...to Colonel Shoup's command post on Red Beach Two at 2030 hours. It hadn't taken Edson quite as long to get in as it had taken some others before him...since the fire along the pier was beginning to slacken for the first time since the landings had begun some thirty-six hours earlier. Luckily, some enterprising or quick-witted pioneer officer had had the presence of mind to hang a thick rope all the way in from the end of the pier to the boat slip near the beach and this contrivance had allowed the movement of everything...both in and out...to speed up immeasurably. And two jeeps...each towing a 37mm cannon behind it...had made it ashore as well now. They had raced down the pier in the dwindling twilight to the cheers of the marines who were carrying supplies in from the end of the pier, and from the wounded who were being towed back out on rafts beside them.

Once ashore, Colonel Edson found the CP easily... since it was close to the shoreline...and he could see Major Culhane, a noted yeller and Colonel Shoup's operations officer, gesticulating wildly as he faced a young officer who already looked worn and ragged.

"Go back and tell Major Hays that we are doing everything possible to get him more support. I know what he's up against over there and we should be able to send you guys some tanks as soon as those lights get in," he said affirmatively. Then he put his hand on the young officer's shoulder and spoke softly...which was out of character for him. "Look," he said, "that *Pocket* has been bedeviling us since we got here...and if Major Hays can knock it out, it would be really helpful to us. Hopefully, you boys in the First of the Eighth can get the job done tomorrow morning."

"We'll do our damndest, sir, that's for sure...or we'll die trying...just like this morning when we came in," the young officer stated confidently. He turned on his heel and left without saluting...since snipers were still active in the vicinity around the command post.

"Is it that rough, Tom?" Edson asked, overhearing the conversation between the major and the lieutenant.

"Welcome to Betio, sir," Major Culhane said, and pointing, added, "and, yes, it is that rough. Colonel Shoup is right over there."

Colonel Edson looked over and saw Colonel Shoup sitting against the outside wall of the bunker that was part of the CP. The bunker was perfectly situated to provide cover from any Jap fire that might come from the airfield triangle area...which was only a hundred yards away to the south. "Is he okay?" Edson asked.

"It's his leg, sir. We got caught in a mortar barrage comin' in and he took some shrapnel in one of his legs. It's been bothering him but he's trying to act like it isn't. Plus, he's exhausted. I don't think the man's really slept since we landed. But then again, who has, right."

The colonel walked the short distance to where Colonel Shoup was seated. He could see that the colonel had his head resting on his arms...which were supported by his knees...which were drawn up close to him. His eyes were closed too...so he couldn't see Colonel Edson standing in front of him. But, somehow, Colonel Shoup sensed the senior officer's presence and he slowly lifted his head and looked up at the colonel.

"Don't get up, Dave," Colonel Edson said reassuringly.

Colonel Shoup stood up gingerly, nonetheless. "Glad to see you made it in safe and sound, sir," he said tiredly.

"Glad to be here, Dave," Edson replied truthfully. "How's the leg?"

"Oh, it's okay, sir. Thanks for asking. Just a little present from a Jap mortarman. Could've been worse," the commander of the marines on Betio replied just as honestly.

"So, are you up for a briefing on what we got goin' on here?" the colonel asked, but it really wasn't a question...and Colonel Shoup knew it. And with that, Shoup began filling in the new commander of the marines on Betio with the conditions on the island and what they were up against.

Chapter Three

Colonel Merritt "Red Mike" Edson was already a legend in the Marine Corps well before the battle for Tarawa. Born in Vermont in 1897, Edson graduated high school in 1915 and then spent two years at the University of Vermont...but he dropped out of college when an assignment for the Vermont National Guard, of which he was a part, sent him to the Mexican border. When that duty was completed, he returned to the university and spent another year at school before leaving yet again when he joined the Marine Corps Reserve. Getting a degree was obviously not high on his priority list...but being a soldier was...and Edson was soon commissioned as a second lieutenant in the Marine Corps in October 1917. His timing seemed to be perfect, for the United States had entered the Great War to end all wars in April 1917, and before long, over two million men were fighting the German Army under the command of General John Pershing. But...despite being sent to France...Lieutenant Edson would not be one of them. His unit - the 11th Regiment - did not see any combat. They were held in reserve instead, so the young Edson missed his first opportunity to "*see the elephant.*" This did not deter his aspirations for a career in the Marine Corps however, and he stayed on...even though many others left. In three years, he became an important member of the national, award-winning Marine Shooting Team in 1921. Then, sensing the future importance of aerial warfare, Edson applied for flight training in 1922 at the Pensacola Naval Air Station, and he had his wings by the end of that year. Edson showed even more promise when he attended the Company Officer's Course at Quantico, Virginia in 1925... and he received the highest score of any officer who had ever attended the course until that time.

Promotion to captain came in December 1927 while Edson was aboard the *USS Denver*...a cruiser that was operating off the Central American coast. As the commanding officer of the marine detachment on the ship, Captain Edson had one hundred and sixty men under him...and he trained them mercilessly. The hard work paid off and he eventually led the men ashore to fight in the Nicaraguan Banana Wars from February 1928 until mid-1929.

It was during this time that Edson acquired his famous nickname...Red Mike...since he had stopped shaving, and he grew a distinctive red beard instead. He and his men also fought in twelve engagements with the rebels in the Nicaraguan jungle and it was here that he won the first of the many medals that he would accumulate over his distinguished career. For his heroics in one battle, he was given the Navy Cross, which is the Navy's second highest award...and only eclipsed by the Congressional Medal of Honor. The citation read in part, *"His exhibition of coolness, intrepidity, and dash so inspired his men that superior forces of bandits were driven from their prepared positions and severe losses inflicted upon them."* For added measure, he was given the Nicaraguan Medal of Merit with Silver Star by the very grateful Nicaraguan government to commemorate his outstanding service.

With the *"elephant"* met and conquered, Captain Edson returned to the United States and he served in a variety of positions before returning the marine shooting team once again. This time he served as both the assistant coach and then the head coach...and his team went on to win several national titles while he also participated as the acting captain of both the pistol and rifle teams.

An interesting assignment for Edson came shortly after his promotion to major in February 1936...one that would serve him well in the years ahead. From 1937 until 1939, Major Edson served as the operations officer with the 4th Marine Regiment...which was based in Shanghai, China. This duty was particularly beneficial because Edson was able to observe Japanese military operations up close since Japan had invaded Manchuria in 1931...and then China itself after the Japanese Army staged the Marco Polo Bridge incident in July 1937. All-out war ensued between the two countries, and Major Edson had a front row seat to see how the Japanese Military would conduct itself in a war against a vastly larger, but unprepared, opponent.

The Butcher's Block

Promotions came quicker for Major Edson once the drums of war began beating between the Japanese and American governments over their differing policies for the Pacific region. Edson made lieutenant colonel in April 1940...and then colonel in May 1942...after he had established the 1st Marine Raider Battalion. This was a new type of unit in which the marines were all volunteers and they were trained to operate behind enemy lines with little support...if any at all. They also received extensive weapons training and they became experts in hand-to-hand fighting...which they would likely experience while serving as pirates in enemy waters.

Colonel Edson's first combat in World War Two started on August 7th, 1942 with the dual invasions of Guadalcanal and Tulagi Island under Operation Watchtower. Acting in concert with the 2nd Battalion, 5th Marines, Edson's Raiders were tasked with clearing the small island of Tulagi of the four hundred or so Japanese soldiers who were mainly holed up in a bunch of caves on one side of the island. During their first night on the island, Edson's men experienced the first *Banzai* charges in the Pacific war...a phenomenon that the marines would face again and again in future battles right up to Iwo Jima. Edson's men, along with the 5th Marines, held the line all through that long night...and by daybreak they were exhausted. The fighting had been incredibly tough...so tough in fact that the Raiders and the 5th Marines ended up needing help from the 2nd Battalion, 2nd Regiment to finish the job of eradicating the Japanese from the island the next day.

Once Tulagi was secured, Edson and his Raiders transferred over to Guadalcanal...and it was on the *Island of Death* that Edson's heroics and battle savvy reached their pinnacle. With the marines of the 1st Division under General Vandergrift hanging on to their perimeter for dear life, Edson's battalion of raiders and two companies of paramarines from the 1st Marine Parachute Battalion were assigned to hold a long ridgeline that ran directly south from Henderson Field for one thousand yards. The ridge had been barely noticed at this point...by the marines and the Japanese alike... and it was basically unoccupied when Edson's force began digging in along its barren spine and slopes.

Like their American counterparts, the Imperial Japanese Navy admirals headquartered in Rabaul considered Guadalcanal a do-or-die proposition as well... and they committed all their resources into recapturing its strategic airfield...the sooner the better. To that end, they sent Major General Kiyotaki Kawaguchi and five thousand troops of the 35th Infantry Brigade into the fight via the *Tokyo Express*. Once ashore, the veteran Japanese general consulted his maps and decided that the best way to defeat the marines was to break through their perimeter along an exposed coral ridgeline that was known as Lunga Ridge. It was aptly named...since its entire length ran right beside the wide Lunga River to the west. And, coincidentally, it was the exact same ridge that Colonel Edson was now defending.

The Japanese general then came up with a complicated plan to accomplish his goal: he would launch his attack from the south...deep within the jungle...and he would split his force into three separate wings...with each wing attacking the ridge from a different direction. This would force the marines...who were already outnumbered...to split up and weaken their defenses. Kawaguchi also chose the date for the battle: 12 September 1942. And if everything went according to plan...and with a little luck thrown in as well...he would be toasting his victory over the marines with a cup full of *saki* on Henderson Field on the morning of the 13th.

Like most of the Japanese leaders at the time, Major General Kawaguchi had underestimated the mettle of the men his soldiers would be facing at Lunga Ridge... and the mettle of the man who was commanding them. That, and the fact that his plan began to unravel from the start, doomed him and his men once the battle commenced...but he almost pulled it off. Instead of attacking in a coordinated effort, Kawaguchi's three wings ended up arriving at their jump off locations at different times and thus what should have been a one-day affair ended up being a battle fought over three separate days...from the 12th until the 14th. This allowed Colonel Edson's men to fight off three separate attacks instead of one monumental one...and his men were able to hold on despite the overwhelming odds against them. In the end, Colonel Edson's eight hundred and forty men had turned back nearly five thousand of Kawaguchi's men while losing only one hundred of their own. In the jungle and on the slopes of the ridgeline, Edson's men counted out almost eight hundred and fifty enemy dead...about the same amount of men the marines had in the battle itself.

Once the battle was over, Kawaguchi's battered survivors melted back into the jungle from whence they had come...disorganized and despondent...with no gains to show for their efforts. And it was the fiery marine commander who had seemed to tilt the balance of the fight against them. Throughout the three-day engagement, Edson had seemed to be everywhere at once...physically rallying his men when they were being overrun...calling in artillery to blunt an attack here and there...inspiring his men to fight on despite the odds...and challenging them to never give up or give in. As a result of his determination and coolness under fire during the Battle for Bloody Ridge...or Edson's Ridge as his men liked to call it...Colonel Edson was awarded the Congressional Medal of Honor...the highest award a soldier can win for performing heroically in combat.

Colonel Shoup had no problems turning the command of the battle over to the division's chief of staff that night. In the first place, Colonel Edson simply outranked him. Shoup, who was just thirty-eight years old, had only been a colonel for a short period of time, in fact. On the other hand, Colonel Edson, who was forty-six, had been promoted to his rank almost a year and a half prior to that. And despite his many years of service, Shoup possessed a very limited resume when it came to combat experience...while Colonel Edson was sporting a Congressional Medal of Honor and two Navy Crosses - he had received his second Navy Cross for his actions on Tulagi - to boot.

Shoup had started the Betio operation out as a mere lieutenant colonel while serving as the operations officer of the 2nd Division. In this critical position, he was intimately aware of all the plans and aspects of the operation...since he had planned it right along with Major General Julian Smith, the Division Commander. But fate had intervened when the original Assault Combat Team Commander, Colonel William Marshall, suffered a medical emergency shortly after the division had conducted its two practice landings at Mele Bay on Efate Island in the New Hebrides Island Group after leaving New Zealand. Word leaked out that Marshall had suffered a heart attack from the stress of trying to organize and coordinate all the tentacles of such a massive operation. But there were others who believed that the colonel was just overwhelmed and not up to the task...and thus he had simply bowed out gracefully. Whatever the reason, it worked to the benefit of Lieutenant Colonel Shoup... since he was promoted on the spot to the rank of colonel by Julian Smith himself...and then he was handed the job of commanding the Division's Combat Team Two that would be attacking Betio in the coming days ahead.

And so far, Colonel Shoup had performed wonderfully in his new role. But the situation on Betio was about to become even more complicated than it already was...since yet another regiment was being thrown into the mix as well. And it was this development...the addition of the Sixth Regiment...that would really change the complexion of the battle in the marines' favor.

"So is Jones on board yet?" It was Colonel Edson...and he was asking...in a sort of shorthanded way...if the 1st Battalion, 6th Regiment, which was commanded by Major William Jones, had made it ashore in one piece.

"Yes, sir, they're in. The entire battalion too. For the first time we've been able to get the whole lot in without a single loss...as far as I know. This is significant, sir," Shoup responded confidently.

Colonel Edson smiled at the good news too...but only for a quick second...and then he turned serious again. "How about our artillery? What's their status?"

"Rixey's been able to get all twelve of his seventy-five's in finally. He's got them set up and ready to support whatever we...uhh...you...decide," Shoup answered crisply.

"And Shell?" Colonel Edson was asking about the whereabouts of Lieutenant Colonel George Shell's 2nd Battalion, 10th Artillery Regiment. They were equipped with twelve pack howitzers too...just like Rixey's 1st of the 10th was.

"I've sent orders out to Colonel Hall already. I told him to land the eight guns that were assigned to him on Bairiki Island as soon as possible. And I've directed Colonel Holmes to shift the four guns that we had assigned to Jones' First battalion over to Bairiki as well. I told Shell to start pounding the eastern tail as soon as all twelve of his guns are set up. When that will actually happen though is anyone's guess...given the difficulties we've had in finding transportation for everything around here."

"That's good...real good," Colonel Edson said. "You've done an incredible job out here, Dave," Edson added, "and General Smith is grateful for all the work you've put in to get us this far. We couldn't have done it without you."

"Thank you, sir," Shoup replied evenly...knowing there was still a long way to go before the battle would be over.

"The Second Regiment is all yours...if you still want it," Colonel Edson offered.

"Of course, I want it. I'd feel mighty guilty handing those boys off to someone else. Don't get me wrong, sir. There are plenty of officers out here that are just as qualified...more qualified than me even...to take over the job of leading the Second. But how could I do that to them after what they've done for me during these last two days. It just wouldn't sit right with me...now or ever. So, the Second is mine."

"Then that settles it...you got it," Edson proclaimed. "Now go get that leg of yours looked at before it starts giving you some real problems. The Second will be waiting for you as soon as Doc Brukhardt gives you a clean bill of health."

"Aye aye, sir," Shoup answered affirmatively...and Colonel Edson smiled for the second time that day...which may have been a personal record for him...according to those who knew him best.

Chapter Four

Two key actions took place during the second day of fighting on Betio that finally swung the battle in favor of the Marine Corps. The first of these occurred when Major Michael Ryan led his orphans in an attack down the length of Green Beach on the northern end of the island. Using two tanks and the accurate fire of two destroyers cruising just off the beach to shield their advance, Ryan's men reached Temakin Point around noon and signaled that the coastline on that side of the island was finally secure. This meant that reinforcements could now reach the island without being fired on...an incredibly important event.

Word of Major Ryan's pivotal achievement reached Major General Smith on the USS *Maryland* well before Colonel Shoup caught wind of it at his CP on Red Beach Two. This strange circumstance occurred because Colonel Shoup's headquarters was still hamstrung by the lack of a functioning communications net between his own HQ and the units that were on the ground around him. This radio nightmare had bedeviled the operation from the start, and it had not been solved to any degree by noon on D + 1. Thus, all communications with Green Beach and Major Ryan were still being funneled through the USS *Maryland*...and then relayed to Colonel Shoup on Betio itself.

Taking advantage of the plum that had suddenly dropped in his lap, Major General Smith radioed the commander of the 6th Regiment, Colonel Maurice Holmes, the following message: *Land one LT immediately south half Beach Green. Suggest column of companies. Our troops now hold shallow beachhead to cover your landing. Pass through covering force, attack to east and seize west end of air strip, prepared to continue the attack immediately. Boat third LT and prepare to land it in close support of first...Tow rubber boats.*

Colonel Holmes wasted no time in responding to the order from his commanding general. Since the message mentioned *rubber boats,* Holmes assigned the mission of landing on Green Beach to Major William "Willie" Jones and his 1st Battalion...who were aboard the attack transport ship, USS *Feland*...or APA 11...which was steaming northwest of Green Beach with several other ships of the transport division. Holmes knew that Major Jones was the best man for job since he had trained his men extensively in the use of rubber rafts... or LCRs...which stood for landing craft, rubber in military vernacular. The rubber boats had been designed with river crossings in mind...but Jones believed that they could handle a rougher ocean environment as well. To prove his point, Jones and his men had logged a lot of training hours aboard their LCRs out on the open seas...and they seemed to do just fine. The only problem they encountered had to do with the small, gasoline-powered engines that were attached to the rear of the rafts. They found out that these engines were basically unreliable...that they would conk out when they became saturated with seawater...which seemed to happen more often than not. In fact, Jones' men spent so much time in their LCRs that they had taken to calling him, affectionately, "The Admiral of the Condom Fleet."

Soon after the landing order came in, the *Feland* sheared away from the rest of the transport group and headed for the reef off Green Beach. Unloading began around 1400 hours and Jones and his men had nearly completed the transfer to their rubber boats when the operation hit a snag. The captain of the *Feland* suddenly received an urgent message to cease unloading so close to the reef...that some unidentified danger was lurking nearby. Incredibly, Jones and his men were forced to climb back up the landing nets and reboard the *Feland*. The transport ship then pulled back almost twelve thousand yards from the reef and the unloading process began yet again. Since they were now so far away, Jones asked for...and got...a slew of Higgins boats to pull his fully loaded rafts back to the reef. From there, the First Battalion men paddled the final one thousand yards to the beach without the loss of a single man along the way. Shortly after that, an amtrac carrying supplies for the battalion hit an underwater mine as it headed in from the reef. The explosion was so powerful that the amtrac rose completely out of the water and it flipped onto its back...killing the entire crew save one man. Danger...it seemed...was always lurking nearby...just around the corner...no matter how safe or sound the situation appeared to be.

Colonel Shoup was both thrilled and frustrated at the same time when he learned that Jones' battalion had made it into Green Beach in one piece. Thrilled since he had another thousand marines or so on the island... ones who had all their equipment and gear with them... and at a location where they could really do some damage to the Japanese who were still holed up along the southern coastline. Frustrated since the whole operation had taken nearly six hours to complete...way beyond the time frame that he had envisioned when Major General Smith had ordered Jones' men in. Now, with daylight fading, Jones had his men settle in instead. This allowed them to get organized for the day ahead...and it prevented the most dreaded mishap of all...friendly fire accidents...from occurring between his men and Ryan's orphans who were now encamped around them.

While there would be no attacking or seizing the northern end of the airstrip that night, the successful landing of Major Jones's unit on Green Beach represented the second key action of the day...and it would have dire implications for the Japanese defending the southern shoreline on the third day of the battle...on D + 2.

Chapter Five

"Ya hear the good news, sarge?"
"No...what good news do you have now, Flock?" Platoon Sergeant Roy asked...genuinely interested... since Sergeant Flockerzi was pretty reliable when it came to scuttlebutt.

Sergeant Eugene Flockerzi was the First Platoon's Right Guide Sergeant...which made him second in command to the man he was talking to. "I heard from a guy down the way that he saw a fresh battalion just come in all by its lonesome. He thinks it's one of the battalions from the Sixth Regiment...although he couldn't say what battalion it was."

"Oh, that's what that was," Roy replied...seemingly disinterested in the same event that Flockerzi found so exciting.

"You mean you saw them too," Flockerzi asked, somewhat bewildered.

The Butcher's Block

Roy, Flockerzi, and the other twelve men he had left had been fighting up and down the Green Beach hornet's nest since they had landed on the Bird's Peak on D Day...almost thirty-six hours ago. And as part of Major Michael Ryan's Orphan Force, they had participated in the D + 1 dash to the southern coast that had freed up Green Beach for first time since the landings had begun. Now, to consolidate his hold on Green Beach, Major Ryan had placed Roy's group in a position that overlooked both the Green and Black Beaches alike... since it was close to Temekin Point itself. "I want you to use the revetment as the center of your position and you are to hold the trench networks that run alongside it as well." The major then pointed off towards Black Beach One...which ran down the southern coastline from Temakin Point and said, "If the Japs are gonna hit us, the attack will come from the southeast over that way. That's where they're strongest now...so keep a good lookout," Ryan stressed to Roy one last time before heading off to position the other units that he had under his *ad hoc* command.

Platoon Sergeant Roy could easily see the bright blue waters off Green Beach from his position on Temekin Point...and thus it was by chance that he had spotted Major Jones' force coming in late that day.

"Yeah, they came in using what looked like rubber rafts. I've been in the Corps a long time, but I don't think I've ever seen those things bein' used before...even on the *Canal*. It would be the First Battalion though...no matter what regiment it was." Roy was pointing out that the first battalion of each regiment had always been tasked with training with the rubber rafts...even though most officers in those units believed the tactical use of rafts was highly unlikely.

"Rubber rafts, huh," Flockerzi said, adding, "I don't think I've ever seen them either. I bet they'd make a great fishing boat though."

"What do you know about fishing," Roy asked skeptically. "You wouldn't know a bass from a trout...or a barracuda from a swordfish probably."

"Okay, so you're right. I don't know a whole lot about fishing. I guess I should stick close to home and only comment on the things I know something about...right. Like building construction for instance."

"You're wound too tight, sarge," Roy said lightly, "I was only kidding."

"Wound too tight? Of course, I'm wound too tight! Who wouldn't be after what we've been through these last two days," Flockerzi pointed out defensively. And with that, Flockerzi ran his hand over one of the logs that made up one of the sides of the revetment in which they were sitting. The revetment had three sides of equal length and it was shaped like a squared off U...with the open side facing directly south. The big entrance...or exit...depending on which way you were headed...made coming and going very easy. "The guy that made this little gem certainly knew what he was doing. This thing could withstand just about everything the Navy threw at it

The Butcher's Block

except a direct hit by a fourteen-inch round...and it looks like one of them hit nearby." Flockerzi had observed the outside of the revetment when Platoon Sergeant Roy and the others had come up to it several hours ago...and he had noted the ugly scarring on the coconut logs from all the shrapnel that had impacted against the three-sided structure.

Roy, Flockerzi, and the two runners...both privates first class...were now relaxing inside the revetment while the rest of Roy's men had taken up positions in the narrow trenches alongside it. Both runners were napping at the time...their gentle snoring creating a rhythmic backdrop to the conversation the platoon sergeant and his platoon guide were now having.

"I wonder why they built this thing here of all places. Generally, revetments of this type are used to house aircraft...but we're a good six hundred yards away from that airstrip apron at least," Sergeant Roy wondered.

"That's an easy one," Flockerzi replied, sounding confident. "It was used to house a tractor. Look around... and what do you see. Nothin' but stumps. The Japs cut down all the coconut trees in this section of the island for their building projects...and they used the tractor to haul the cut logs around the island. I bet it's probably sittin' out on that airstrip somewhere. They could've used it to move disabled aircraft from one place to another as well. There are plenty of roads around here which would have made gettin' around pretty easy."

"You bet, huh," Roy responded. "You tryin' to sound like Staggs with the betting!"

"You think Staggs made it, sarge," Flockerzi asked, wondering if the ace card player had somehow beaten the odds and was still alive somewhere on the island.

"Good question," Roy answered. "He could be still alive...I guess. If anybody was gonna make it through this hellhole alive, you know Staggs would be the one. That guy had uncanny luck...in cards...and everything else for that matter. You know I always heard that our commander, Colonel Shoup, was a good card player too. I wonder who was better...and if they ever played against one another."

"Played against one another?" Flockerzi asked skeptically. "Are you kiddin'? What officer is gonna risk his reputation against a shark like Staggs. Not one...that's for sure. And you know I'm not one of those guys who walks around criticizing everything our officers do. Yeah, we all know there's a caste system in the Marine Corps...but I'm fine with it if the officers keep to themselves and leave us alone. Remember that jerk captain we had on the *Canal*...Turlinger. What an ass he was. Clean uniform and shiny boots all the time. Thank God he was relieved before we hit the beach over here. That idiot would've cost us a lot of lives if he were still around...that's for sure."

"I try to remember the good officers I've served with...like Shoup...and Carlson...and a bunch of others I've run into along the way. And our own lieutenant... for that matter. Lieutenant Hackett is one fine officer. He's probably gonna make captain right after this operation is over...if he's still alive. I'd like to see him make general someday, too. Hopefully, he's still out there somewhere…and leadin' the rest of the platoon…and killing Japs left and right. The jerks? Well, those guys are always gonna be there too…so why waste time worrying about them," Roy pointed out.

"That's a pretty good philosophy you got there," Flockerzi said, mulling the idea over in his head. "I think I'm gonna try that one…to keep a positive attitude," he added for good measure.

"That's the spirit, good 'ol Flockerbee. Don't let anything get ya down. Life's too short to waste your time worrying' about things that are out of your control." Roy had used the platoon guide's nickname…Flockerbee…that the men in the platoon had given him. It was a combination of his last name and the Seabees…which was a Navy unit that specialized in building and repairing stuff…like the airfield on Guadalcanal…and the one here on Betio.

"Life can be short around here…that's for sure," he agreed…knowing that Platoon Sergeant Roy had a far deeper intellect than his tough exterior portrayed.

Roy was about to say something else, but PFC Larry Rickard suddenly came awake and cut him off. "Are you two going to keep jabberin' through the rest of this campaign…or do I have to go outside and risk getting my butt shot off with the others out there, just so I can catch a little shuteye?" Rickard was hoping his desperate plea for silence would carry some weight and he wouldn't have to get up.

"Thanks for reminding me that you two yard birds have had enough of a break as it is," Roy answered right back. "Now take your sorry butts outside and have

Sergeant Varner send two guys back from his squad so they can get some rest. He'll probably send Reisman and Nelson back if I know Varner...since those two were up all night fighting off that Jap suicide squad that hit our lines last night. They gotta be crapped out by now. So, get goin' you two...and don't let the door hit you in the ass as you leave," Roy added for good measure.

PFC Rickard got up stiffly and stretched his arms out wide. He yawned deeply and then kicked his buddy, PFC Lerman Mudd, in the leg. "Get up," Rickard intoned mildly, "we gotta sit watch outside now."

PFC Mudd scrunched up his face and ignored the kick. Then Rickard leaned down and pulled on his uniform shirt to get his friend's attention. "Let's go, Lerm... rise and shine, buddy," he said, speaking more forcefully now.

"Oh, okay," Mudd finally drawled in a thick Southern accent. Mudd was a Kentuckian and a horse lover...as all Kentuckians are.

"That's right, Lerman," Rickard continued, "time to saddle up. We're needed outside to stop those evil Japs from taking over the world."

"I'm a comin'," Mudd said slowly. He reached over and grabbed his rifle and checked it quickly to make sure it was clean. Mudd loved his guns as much as he loved horses...and he was fastidious about keeping his weapon spotlessly clean. He then stood up and they sauntered out without saying another word to one another.

Flockerzi watched them leave and shook his head. "That's what I love about the Corps, sarge. Who would've thought that a Philadelphia city slicker like Rickard would have anything in common with a country boy from the South like Mudd? If the two of them met in the street they'd probably hate one another...yet stick them in the Corps and they become the best of friends. Ain't it just crazy?"

"That it is, 'ol Flock...that it is," Roy agreed reverently...since he loved the Corps just as deeply as Flockerzi did...and probably more so...since he had long considered it his only true home.

Chapter Six

One of the men that Platoon Sergeant Roy and Right Guide Sergeant Flockerzi had been talking about...Corporal Timothy Staggs...the inveterate gambler...was quite alive in fact. But he was about as far away from them as he could possibly be. Unbeknownst to either Roy or Flockerzi, Staggs was lying in a shell hole that had been blasted into the sand by one of the many 5-inch shells that a Navy destroyer had fired in support of Major Henry P. "Jim" Crowe's 2nd Battalion, 8th Regiment on D Day. Crowe's men had landed on Red Beach 3...which was located on the eastern side of the main pier that served as a boundary line between the Red Beach 3 and Red Beach 2 beachheads. Later, at the behest of Colonel Shoup, the 3rd Battalion of the same regiment had also landed on Red 3 as well...and Major Robert Ruud's battalion had met even fiercer resistance that Crowe's men had earlier.

The Butcher's Block

How Corporal Staggs had ended up amid Major Crowe's men on Red Beach 3 was a long story...but one that was very similar to what so many other men had experienced once the landings commenced. According to the plan, Corporal Staggs should have been over on Red Beach 2 by now...since the company he was part of was scheduled to land in the first wave there. But just like on Red 3, the Japanese *rikusentai* defending Red 2 had put up so much fire that the landing waves approaching the Red 2 beachhead had been completely wrecked. All semblance of order was lost...and unit integrity... which was so critical in waging a successful attack...had been destroyed. Units landed in a helter-skelter fashion and many men ended up on the wrong beachhead as a result.

By all accounts, Staggs was quite lucky to be alive. His amtrac, nicknamed *Widow Maker*, had been hit by several anti-boat shells before it had even reached the beach...and the corporal had been blown out of it. The men on the amtrac who had survived the hits, including First Lieutenant Hackett, his platoon commander, and Sergeant Tom Endres, his squad leader, had spotted him lying on a coral outcropping not far away. No one had gone over to check on him though, since Hackett and the rest were still under fire and Staggs appeared to be dead. Before long, Lieutenant Hackett had decided that the best course of action was to get the rest of the men into the beach, and Staggs was left there as they made their way towards Red 2 on foot.

It wasn't long after Corporal Staggs regained consciousness that he met Private Rolf Jorgenson. Jorgenson had seen Staggs apparently struggling in the water and he had come over to help him. Staggs claimed that he wasn't in any kind of danger at all...except for the Jap machine gun fire that continued to lace the water around the two men. Then Staggs made the wild claim that he had been looking for his rifle along the cove floor instead...and that he had found it in the three feet of murky water in which they were standing. Jorgenson thought the man might have actually gone crazy...but he didn't say so at the time...since Staggs was wearing the chevrons of a corporal...and most of the NCOs that the young private had met in his brief time in the Marine Corps seemed to be missing a gear or two. Then the two men had watched in horror as an entire squad of marines was gunned down in the water beside them. At that point, Jorgenson, who was an extremely mild guy given his size, lost his patience and he started to walk off in the direction of the long pier. Staggs...though still groggy...looked around at the mayhem taking place in the cove, and he came to his senses quickly. Calculating the odds in his head, the gambler quickly decided that his best chance of survival lay with the big private...so he grabbed the private's arm, and they made the journey to the pier together.

Staggs had never seemed to stop talking as the two men made the dangerous trip to the island...and by the time they got to the base of the pier, Jorgenson had begun to think that he had gone crazy...instead of the other way around. Along the way, Staggs had made Jorgenson explain how he had acquired his two nicknames...and then the corporal had spoken in depth about how the law of averages statistically supported their chances of survival...which made Jorgenson feel much better. Then, incredibly, they had caught an actual glimpse of the assault commander as he was heading into the island in an amtrac that drove right past them.

An astute Japanese mortarman located somewhere on Red 2 had spotted the very same amtrac however, and he began to pepper it with mortar rounds. With their path along the right side of the pier now blocked with incoming mortar fire, Staggs decided that the left side of the pier would provide a safer passageway to the island. So, he and Jorgenson climbed up the right side of the pier...using its coconut-log trestles as handholds... and then jumped down to the other side. The corporal's intuition proved correct...and before long the two marines were splashing their way ashore onto Betio Island...safe and sound...their joint odyssey finally over.

However, at the base of the pier, they ran into a young lieutenant who had been assigned the crappy job of serving as a traffic cop. Instead of allowing the two enlisted men to join their regimental buddies who were fighting for their lives on Red Beach 2, the lieutenant told them that they were needed on the left side more. The young private pleaded with the lieutenant to let him join his own battalion...the First of the Second...on Red Two...but to no avail. The lieutenant stuck to his guns and stated that he had his orders...that the Eighth Regiment was in trouble too...that they had been shot up real bad trying to reach Red Beach Three...and they needed men just as badly as the Second Regiment did. And orders were orders...and that was that.

Corporal Staggs had stepped in and finally broken the stalemate between the young officer and the even younger enlisted man. Like Jorgenson, Corporal Staggs wanted to head over to Red Beach 2 too...so he could be with the men from his own unit...the 2nd of the 2nd. But Staggs also appreciated the necessity of following orders just as well. With that, the corporal stated that he understood the officer's predicament...and that he would obey the young officer's order...even though he didn't want to or like it very much. Now Jorgenson, chastened by the corporal's calm acceptance of the situation, agreed to go too...at least until the whole messed up situation could be sorted out. The relieved lieutenant happily agreed to the compromise....and the two enlisted men nodded to young officer and they left... heading east...not west...like they had wanted.

This was how the two men...Corporal Staggs and Private Jorgenson of the 2nd Regiment...ended up fighting with the men under Major Jim Crowe's 3rd Battalion, 8th Regiment on Red Beach 3.

Corporal Staggs and Private Jorgenson were both awake. In the intense heat, neither one of them could think of napping. Jorgenson had thrown up a while ago...puking right there in the hole. "I think I got heat stroke." He had managed to eke out the words between retches.

"Throw that crap outta the hole," Staggs said, "it looks disgusting...and the smell is worse."

"I'm too tired to scoop it up, Staggo," Jorgenson replied weakly, "this sun has zapped all of my strength. Can you do it for me?" The private had taken to calling the corporal *Staggo* that morning...and Staggs had not corrected him...so he kept it up.

"Oh, what the hell," Staggs replied nonchalantly, "it can't smell any worse than those dead marines over by those amtracs do. During the second day, the tide had begun to recede so some of the dead who had been lying in the water were now lying on the dry beach apron... fully exposed to the baking sun. Most of the bodies had begun to swell already...and some had even split their uniforms open as a result. The ensuing smell was almost mind-numbing...since there were nearly three thousand other dead bodies lying about by then as well.

Without another word or thought about it, Staggs scooted over and threw some sand on the pile of puke. Then he picked the gooey mess up with Jorgenson's entrenching tool and he had flung it out over his head... so it would land somewhere behind him.

"What the hell!" It was one of the two marines who were lying in a nearby shell hole...not far from the one that Staggs and Jorgenson were in. "Who threw that?" the voice cried out angrily. Since Staggs and Jorgenson had shared some of their C rations with the same two men the night before, Staggs didn't feel quite as guilty as he probably should have about bombarding them with Jorgenson's ex-meal. "I guess I should have yelled out, 'Incoming!' when I threw that," he yelled over... hoping to appease their neighbors.

"That would've been nice," the man yelled back as he scraped what remained of the sandy puke from his lap. "You got anything left to eat?" he asked, hoping Staggs would share whatever he had left…if he did…as a peace offering.

"Nothin' left over here…we ate the last of our rations last night. We're in the same boat as you fellas are now," Staggs answered back.

"Well, that was real nice of y'all boys to share what little you had with us last night. Me and Andre here will hopefully find a way to pay y'all back before it's too late," Corporal Todd Wilbanks said in return, the puke bombing apparently forgotten.

"Whatta you mean by too late? Too late for what?" Staggs shouted back, concerned.

"Before the two of you get yourselves killed…or we get killed first. Whatta y'all think I meant," Wilbanks said sternly. "The way I see it," he continued, "it ain't very likely the four of us are just gonna waltz off this island together like. I've seen too many guys gettin' killed in all sorts of ways to be foolish enough to think that we're special cargo. You catchin' my drift now."

"Oh yeah, I hear you…loud and clear. I wouldn't bet on that one myself…and I'm one good-bettin' SOB," Staggs responded dourly…while believing all the while that it would be Andre and his buddy who was doing the talking that would get it first…not him and Jorgenson. Then he added, "I didn't catch your name, friend? And who are you with?"

"I'm Corporal Todd Wilbanks…and the guy sharin' this foxhole with me is Sergeant Andre Owens. He's not much of a talker as you can well see...or hear, I guess. We're with the Eighteenth Regiment...F Company. We're attached to the Two Eight...in direct support of them. We were pioneers to begin with...part of the shore party detail...until we lost all our gear comin' in. Now we're in the demolitions business...and we're supposed to be experts at it...at least that's what we've been told anyway."

"Welcome to the party, Mac," Jorgenson said weakly.

"Well, I'll be. My partner over here is gettin' real salty-like in his old age," Staggs yelled over, laughing. "He just called you, Mac," Staggs said to Corporal Wilbanks... who laughed at the euphemism just like Staggs was. "He's not doing so well right now. We think he may have heat stroke...or close to it. It's gotta be nearly a hundred degrees if not more out here."

"I hope he doesn't," Wilbanks cautioned...knowing full well the dire effects that heat stroke could have on an army in the field. With that, Wilbanks scrambled out of his own foxhole and dove into Staggs' and Jorgenson's hole...almost landing out top of Staggs himself.

"You tryin' to kill me before a Jap sniper gets a chance to," Staggs said, dusting himself off.

"Nah...the Japs can have you all to themselves. Just stick your head up for a little while and you'll find out. It's that salty boot that I'm worried about," Wilbanks said, pointing at Jorgenson's prostrate body. Wilbanks then slid over to Jorgenson and said, "Let me take a look at ya, kid. I grew up and still live in South Carolina...just outside of Charlestown. At least I did before the war started. A lot of my kin we're around during the Revolutionary

James F Dwyer

War…and I became a Revolutionary War buff as a result. I look for and collect artifacts…you know…stuff left behind by the soldiers back then. Sometimes I find interesting things…like a rusty musket…or musket balls…or a button or two. I've found plenty of those. I've been to all the battlefields around there…you know…places like the Cowpens, Kings Hill, and Camden, of course. I've studied the battles that were fought there…and the other big ones that were fought up in the Northeast…at places like Saratoga…and Yorktown…and Bunker Hill…and Monmouth…to name just a view. Which concerns me… since a lot of men were killed at Monmouth…both British and American alike. And heat stroke was what did a lot of those soldiers in during the battle that day. A lot of people think that most of the casualties in that war were probably produced by musket ball wounds from rifle fire…or shrapnel wounds from cannon fire maybe. Some even think that there were a lot of bayonet wounds too… from all the charges the two armies did…but not many men died that way to be honest. What got most of the men killed was illnesses and diseases like smallpox…and sometimes conditions like heat stroke. Heck, the Brits and the Americans lost nearly a hundred men between them to heat stroke alone at Monmouth, since the battle was fought on one of the hottest days in June. And it was supposedly one of the hottest summers they ever had on record in Jersey. We can only imagine what it must have been like to be wearing those heavy cotton uniforms in weather like that. But fightin' in this heat can't be too far behind it, I guess. They didn't have much water to drink either…just like us." Wilbanks than reached down and

The Butcher's Block

touched the private's forehead…to see how hot his skin was. "Not too bad," he said, reassuring both Jorgenson and Staggs at the same time. "He's still sweating…which is good sign. It's when the skin gets really dry that the body's in deep trouble. I don't think, Mac here, is in that kinda condition just yet."

Both Staggs and Jorgenson smiled at Wilbank's remark…and then Staggs said, "How'd you become an engineer…or pioneer? You seem to be more like a corpsman?"

"Never had any real interest in medicine of any kind really…but I have always liked building things…so I signed up to be an engineer with the Corps. Nothing more than that really. I'm good with my hands…can build just about anything. But not good enough to be a surgeon by any stretch. I learn best by just watching someone do something…and then I do it. I'm no good at school learnin'… that's for sure. I just know about heat stroke since it played a big role in the battle for Monmouth. Other than that, I would never have known about it. Here's something else interesting about that war. Did you know that General Washington was almost killed the year before the battle of Monmouth was fought…at a place called Brandywine Creek…near Philadelphia? Seems a British officer…a Scotsman by the name of Patrick Ferguson…had a bead on General Washington. He was supposedly the best shot in the British Army…and he was using sniper tactics when sniping wasn't an accepted way of waging war. Instead of shooting him on the spot, Ferguson demanded that he should surrender instead. Well, Washington and the staff officer he was with ended up galloping away, and

Ferguson just let them go. He said their backs were to him, so he never fired a shot at either one of them. And he could've gotten off a lot of shots too, since he was carrying a repeating rifle that he had developed on his own. He had our dear old General Washington dead to rights...but this Scotsman never took the shot. He later said that he thought it was unbecoming of a soldier to shoot down someone...especially an officer...who was so vulnerable."

While listening to Wilbank's tell his story, Staggs noticed that Jorgenson had raised himself up to hear the corporal better. *That's a good sign*, he thought, *he must be feeling somewhat better to do that.*

Wilbanks noticed it too...and he gave a subtle wink to Staggs and said, "He's gonna be just fine." Then he finished up by saying, "Something tells me that if the same thing were to happen out here...if some Jap sniper had our Colonel Shoup in his sights...he wouldn't let the colonel off the hook...no matter how vulnerable he looked. We're playing by a whole new set of rules out here...or maybe it's a lack of rules now? Whatta you think?"

Staggs glanced over at Jorgenson and then back to Wilbanks. "We discussed the same sort of thing as we were making our way into the island. We came across two dead marines...and realized that some good Samaritan had secured the men's bodies to one of the pier's trestles. You know...so the bodies wouldn't sink or float off...never to be seen again. We thought it was a pretty nice thing to do...given the fact that there were so many dead bodies out there. I mean where do you start. When does your humanity kick in, right? Whoever the guy was, he must have said to himself, "Somebody'll appreciate what I did for these two marines...whoever they are. And some families back home won't have to suffer...never knowing what happened to their sons or brothers at Tarawa."

"Amen to that," Wilbanks stated firmly.

"So, are the Japs experiencing the same feelings? Are they just as human as we are? I mean I saw a guy who pulled the gold teeth out of the Japs' mouths with a pliers on Guadalcanal."

"What if the Jap was alive...just wounded like," Jorgenson asked, horrified. "I mean they weren't always dead, were they?"

"The guy also carried a thirty-eight with him in a shoulder holster. I think his dad, who was a cop back in Arkansas, sent it to him. He'd just shoot the Jap in the forehead if he thought his patient was still breathing."

"I sure hope he doesn't become a dentist after the war," Jorgenson said...apparently worried over the prospect.

"Is that guy any worse than the worst guy the Japs have?" Staggs held his hands up in surrender...showing that he did not...or could not...come up with a sufficient answer to the age-old question that plagues men who must go off to war and condition themselves to kill others, so they won't be killed themselves.

"War's a dirty business," Wilbanks said, "and even dirtier now than it has ever been. Maybe I think like that since I'm in it now. Every guy who has ever gone off to war has probably felt the same way...that the war he was fighting was the dirtiest there ever was."

"This stuff is way too deep for me," Private Jorgenson said suddenly, now sitting up. "If I have to kill somebody...to save myself or someone else...then I guess that's what I'll do. It's not something I ever thought I'd have to do...to take another person's life...but here we are. I just hope and pray that God understands and that He'll forgive me for whatever I end up having to do out here."

"Amen to that," Wilbanks said again. No one else said anything for a while...each man thinking his own thoughts...before Wilbanks spoke once more. "I've been feeling guilty...since I've let my faith slip a little over the last few years. Now here I am calling on God to save me. I feel like I owe Him a big apology...since I took Him for granted in a way. I hate feeling like a hypocrite...but I do. I have been praying that He'll forgive me kinda like Mac over there has been praying...that He'll understand what he and I have to do."

Corporal Staggs said nothing...but he too was wondering if the God he had been brought up to worship would ever forgive him as well. He looked over to Jorgenson...as if for moral support...and Jorgenson nodded back.

The private remembered the conversation that they had had as they were coming in...when the private revealed that he had experienced some sort of miracle in the cove. Jorgenson knew beyond a doubt that God... or one of His angels...had saved him. That the voice he had heard was real...and that the presence he had experienced was genuine. And the more he thought about it, the more he realized that it wasn't a question of God forgiving him for what he did. He had been taught since he was a little boy about the deep love God had for him...and Jorgenson had never questioned it. And suddenly...like a bell being rung...or a light coming on...the dilemma he had been struggling with was solved...his prayers answered. It became crystal clear to him now: God would never desert him. All he had to do was love God right back...just like King David had done all his life...and everything would turn out just fine.

"Do you guys realize that you haven't taken the time to introduce yourselves to me yet. What if Andre wants to know who the heck I've been talking to all this time. What am I supposed to tell him?" It was Wilbanks breaking the ice once again.

"You tell Andre that you've been talking to the two greatest guys in the Second Regiment...besides Colonel Amey, of course. He's the best there is...and ain't nobody gonna even come close to him for being the best marine in our regiment. As for me...I'm Corporal Timothy Staggs...E Company. And this guy next to me who's gettin' real sunburned is Private Rolf Jorgenson. You can call him, 'Clutch' or 'Hutch', since he answers to both nicknames. And he's from the First Battalion...which makes us bosom buddies, I guess."

"I'm in C Company," Jorgenson cut in, "and Staggs wouldn't know that since he's never bothered to ask me. And the next greatest marine to Lieutenant Colonel Amey is my platoon commander...Second Lieutenant Joe Sexton. I'd follow him anywhere...anytime. I hope he's doing ok...since I still haven't seen hide or hair of him...or anyone else in my platoon...or company...since I jumped off our Higgins boat yesterday morning."

"So, you two guys didn't even know one another before yesterday?" Wilbanks looked perplexed at the thought...but this sort of thing was happening all over the island. Strangers before the landing...and now friends after the landing...and all fighting to save one another. "At least me and Andre are from the same platoon. We came in with our lieutenant...First Lieutenant Bonnyman. He's the executive officer of our unit...and he's a great one, too. We know he's still alive...since he's sitting in a shell hole just a little way over. He's wearin' that helmet with the two stripes on the front. That indicates he's part of the shore party section...not a captain."

"I guess we've been lucky when it comes to our officers then. Some guys I know hate theirs," the private said gratefully.

"Give it time," Staggs said to Jorgenson sadly, "and you'll see. You stay in long enough and you'll end up hatin' some of them too. The Corps doesn't have the market cornered on good officers...trust me. But it seems that the great ones are truly great."

"Well, good 'ol Bonnyman has been in the thick of the fighting since we've landed. He led several attacks yesterday against that big Jap installation that's been blocking our way off the beach. And he's been tellin' us that another attack is gonna take place sometime tomorrow. We're just not sure when...but he said he'd let us know when the time is set."

"Well, good luck with that," Staggs said thoughtfully.

"Yeah...I hope you guys are able to knock that thing out. We watched F Company get hammered yesterday when they tried to assault it. It seems like it's almost impregnable so far," Jorgenson said, adding his two cents to the conversation.

"And it has been...so far. But Lieutenant Bonnyman is gonna solve that problem once and for all tomorrow. He's been loading us up with explosives and flame throwers and he keeps tellin' us that we're gonna see that thing get blown to kingdom come...or he'll die trying to do it at least."

"We sure hope he's right...since we'll be the next guinea pigs to take it on if he fails," Staggs said sourly. The idea of attacking that monstrous fortification had been troubling him all morning...and now his fears had been confirmed yet again. An attack was being planned and there was nothing he could do to stop it.

Corporal Wilbanks clapped his hands, signaling that their meeting was over. "Thanks, guys, it's been fun," he said, and added, "let me know if there's anything we can do for you. We're always ready to help."

"Hey, before you head off...tell us what your buddy, Andre, is like? Is he French or somethin'?"

Wilbanks laughed out loud. "Why would you think he's French?" he asked incredulously.

"Because of his name...Andre. That's a French name where I come from," Jorgenson explained innocently.

"As I said earlier, Andre's last name is Owens. That's as American as you can get. He's from Texas...near Dallas...and he's a tax-paying republican through and through. He claims that he was a cowboy at one time... and then he said he worked as a fireman. That's what he was doin' when the war broke out. A lot of us engineer types are a little older than you younger gyrenes.

We joined up...just like you young bucks did...out of duty and love for our country. Only difference is that we're longer in the tooth than most of the guys were supporting. Heck...I'm twenty-seven already...which makes me ancient around here. I'm just glad the younger ones aren't calling me Pops yet. I wouldn't stand for that... even though it's sorta true. But back to Andre. So, he doesn't talk all that much...but when he does talk, it's usually to argue about the reasons we're in this war. He hates the president. I know that for a fact. You mention Roosevelt's name around him, and he'll tell you that it was Roosevelt's democratic cronies who led us into this fight. He thinks the president knew it was comin'...that Roosevelt let the Japs bomb Pearl Harbor so we could enter the war against Japan...and then Germany. He thinks he did it to get our economy going...that the stupid programs he and Eleanor came up with...like the New Deal and the Civilian Conservation Corps...were a complete waste of money and manpower. Other than that though, he doesn't really have much to say. Oh...and he's the best damn engineer I've ever worked with...by a long stretch. Knows the building-side of the business inside and out. Probably had to in civilian life if he was gonna be a good fireman. I guess it helps to know how the building is made if you wanna put the fire out, right. Did I mention that he hates the president?"

"Geez...I'd better not talk to him then," Jorgenson said, "my dad voted for President Roosevelt at least three times while I was around...and he'll probably vote for him again in the election next year. That'll give President Roosevelt four terms if he wins that one too. The guy's gotta be doing something right to get reelected like that. Most people that I know up in Wisconsin voted for him, too."

"If you do get him mad...like saying you hope Roosevelt stays our president forever...then just offer him a cigar...and that'll tie him over. He likes cigars...like all republicans do. He says he's gonna open up some kinda place that just sells cigars when he gets back home."

"Just cigars?" Jorgenson asked, mystified. "How can a store like that survive? Could there be enough money in just selling cigars?"

"I can see that," said Staggs, mulling the idea over in his mind. "I always enjoyed smoking a cigar when I was gambling...especially when I was winning. And my dad like to smoke one on our porch...after we had dinner."

"I guess it'll be like a liquor store," Jorgenson theorized. "There are plenty of those stores around...especially in my town...so maybe it could work," he added, warming to the idea.

"Andre says he's gonna call it a 'smoke shop' or 'cigar shop' or something like that. Them republicans are always thinkin' of ways to make money, aren't they?"

"Somebody's got make the dough...or we'll all be on the bread lines again," Staggs said, remembering how tough it had been when the mines his dad had worked in were forced to shut their doors every so often.

"Andre says, 'Yeah, we make the money, and then the democrats in Congress come up with new ways to tax us, so they can spend it.' He says that he's better at spending his own money on what he wants than some bureaucrat is with our tax dollars. And Andre says there's no incentive for the bureaucrat to spend it wisely...unless he can skim off the top and get rich in the process." Wilbanks shook his head in dismay. "That's part of the reason I came over here. If I had to listen to him badmouthing our president one more time, I was about to kill myself. You gotta give it a rest sometimes, no?"

"I was never that interested all that much in politics...even if my folks were. I just considered them all crooks basically. Doesn't really matter what party is stealin' from your pocket, does it?"

"Well, we're just glad you came over...no matter what the reason," Staggs said, and he reached down to his cartridge belt and took out a canteen. He shook it to make sure it had enough water left, and then he tossed it to the other corporal.

"Make sure to give some to Owens...with my compliments. Tell him my mom voted for Hoover in the Thirty-Two election...and Alf Landon in Thirty-Six. I remember those two elections. And my dad would've too...if he'd been alive to do it. You can't blame this war on my family either. He'll like that."

"Like it...he'll love to hear that. He might even risk a sniper's bullet to come over and shake your hand. And by the way, thanks for everything." Wilbanks was about to dash across to his own hole when he stopped suddenly. He looked back at his two new friends thoughtfully, and then said, "And God bless you guys!"

The situation on Red 3 had remained mostly static...to a degree...throughout much of D + 1...and Major Crowe had used the downtime wisely. The first project he accomplished was to reconsolidate the units that had been torn apart on D Day. Throughout the day, men who had been fighting elsewhere finally stumbled in... trying to locate their parent units. As soon as they came in, Crowe had his staff and line officers separate the men into two separate groups: the first group was comprised of the men from his own battalion...and the second one was made up from the men in Major Robert Ruud's battalion. Then the men were placed back with the other men from their own units who were already there...and under their old leaders...if their own leaders were still around. Tragically, so many casualties had occurred among the officer and senior NCO ranks that some of the line companies were now being led by green lieutenants...platoons by buck sergeants...and squads by corporals or privates first class even. It was by no means ideal, but that was the reality of the situation, and the men just adapted to it.

Major Crowe then realigned the areas of responsibility for each of his battalions...since the 3-8 under Ruud... and his own 2-8...were now under his control. He assigned the area to the northeast...where the Burns-Philip wharf and the two-story, sand-covered bunker were located... to his own 2nd Battalion, 8th Regiment. Their job that day, under Major Bill Chamberlin, the battalion's executive officer, was to keep the Japs from advancing further west down the northern coastline...and right into the heart of the Red 3 beachhead. This was a tall order... since the Japanese leadership on the tail of the island still had a sizable force of men they could utilize if they wanted to wage a full-fledged attack against that part of the marine perimeter. Luckily, Chamberlin could call on the two destroyers out in the lagoon for direct fire support if such an attack were to materialize. Plus, the Sherman tank, *Colorado*, was still there as well...even if its ammunition was low. And lastly, Chamberlin had a platoon of the 18th Marines...the pioneers who had become engineers...at his beck and call. These marines would blow up the obstacles that were blocking the 2-8 marines from advancing off the beach...if...and when... the decision was made to advance off the beach. Satchel charges loaded with TNT and flamethrowers would be their weapons of choice in accomplishing this dangerous mission.

After he finished shoring up his own battalion area, Major Crowe turned his attention to Major Ruud's sector of action. This job...while daunting...wasn't as hard as it once seemed since two majors were available to carry out whatever orders Major Crowe had for the 3rd Battalion. Not only was Major Ruud still alive...but his executive officer...Major Stanley Larsen...had managed to survive as well. Larsen had spent most of D Day out near the end of pier trying to organize the flow of supplies into the Red 3 beach area. He had been somewhat successful in this endeavor...but by D + 1, he managed to get himself inland, and he hooked up with Major Ruud. Finally in the game ashore, Larsen was able to take some of the heavy load off Major Ruud's shoulders as Ruud tried to push his battalion out of the beachhead on Red 3.

Major Ruud's battalion continued to grow as more and more of Ruud's men emerged from the shadows, and this added strength gave Major Crowe more latitude of action than he had had previously with the 3rd Battalion. Instead of just holding the narrow strip of beach along Red 3, Major Crowe gave Ruud permission to expand the Red 3 beachhead by advancing inland from the area that was bordered by the boundary line between Red 3 and Red 2...which ran dead south from the pierhead...and the taxiway apex area that sat just to the southeast of the pierhead. This part of the airfield complex was located almost dead center on the island... and it was the area where the two taxiways converged on the northern coast. To some of the planners, it looked like a rounded-off diamond sitting on the parrot's gut... while others saw it as a large, rectangular-shaped slab of concrete not far from the end of the pier.

Ruud's new goal then was to occupy and hold as much of the central portion of the airfield triangle as possible...and to that end, he began ordering his men to swing left and south after crossing the dangerous taxiway and apex that sat right in front of them. And to their credit, the 3-8 men accomplished this task... but they were not able to get as far south as the men under Sergeant Melvin McBride or the men under First Lieutenant Aubrey Edmonds had on D Day. But on Betio, something gained was definitely better than nothing gained…and Major Crowe was quite pleased with the 3-8's effort and accomplishments on D + 1.

The expanded beachhead had finally given Major Crowe some breathing room…and with a little luck…another good push from Ruud's men might cut Betio in half. But this was just wishful thinking on the afternoon of November 21st…since Major Crowe was mainly worried about the Japs breaking through his perimeter along the northern shoreline from the east. Rather than overextend his lines, he had Major Ruud hold up where he was and dig in…thus consolidating the gains in the airfield triangle area. This would also enable Major Ruud to attack the Japanese in their flank if they tried to stage an attack down the northern coastline. He also called for naval gunfire and air support and before long, large naval shells were smashing into the Japanese lines east and south of his battalions. When the battleships, cruisers, and destroyers were done, the Navy's F6F fighters went to work…strafing and bombing the same area that the Navy's guns had just obliterated. The destruction wrought by these two arms was telling…and there would be no Japanese attack against the Red 3 lines that night.

Chapter Seven

Will these fighter planes ever go away? Jinzo Yoshizawa wondered to himself while watching the sun sink lower and lower in the distance. The Japanese seaman was sitting in the driver's seat of the small, three-man Type 95 *Ha-Go* Light tank that was parked outside the building that served as the island's command post. Yoshizawa looked up yet again and saw another American Grumman F6F Hellcat fighter diving towards them...its engine screaming.

The heavy F6F Hellcat was bigger and faster than the plane it had replaced...the valiant F4F Wildcat...which had served so reliably over the skies of Guadalcanal. Marine fighter pilots like Major Joe Bauer and Captains Joe Foss, John L. Smith, and Marion Carl had become aces flying the Wildcat...but the F6F was an even better killing machine with its six fifty-caliber M-2 machine guns in the wings compared to the Wildcat's four.

The Hellcat that Yoshizawa was concerned with was flying in the direction of Takarongo Point…which was nearly two thousand yards away at the eastern tip of the island. As it neared the bottom of its dive, the plane's wings lit up as its six fifties began firing in unison. The ground behind the two-story, concrete building erupted in small explosions as the bullets cut a deadly swath down the spine of the island. This time the pilot's aim was better…and he hit a fuel storage dump that had been missed by the other pilots in his squadron. As the drums of aviation gasoline exploded in a ball of flame, the pilot, Lieutenant, Junior Grade William "Wild Bill" Basnett, from Fighting Squadron 9 of the USS *Essex*, pulled back on the stick and circled around to inspect the results of his final gun run. He smiled when he saw the fire and thick, black smoke boiling up from below…confirming that he had hit his target. What he wasn't prepared to see were two Japanese soldiers who came running out of the conflagration…engulfed in fire. Basnett watched as the men ran about ten yards and then collapsed in a heap…obviously dead…their blackened remains smoldering away. *Better them than some marines down there*, he thought grimly, and he leveled off and headed back to the USS *Essex*…one of the several aircraft carriers that were supporting Operation Galvanic.

"Wake up, Kanji." Seaman Yoshizawa heard the heavy metal door bang shut and knew that Petty Officer Koshio, the tank commander, was headed their way.

The Butcher's Block

"Oh, leave me alone," Seaman First Class Kanji Kubo replied...the irritation in his voice quite evident.

"No...get up. Koshio is here. The meeting must be over."

Kubo was sitting against a palm tree that stood about five feet away from the front fender of tank. He had been sleeping but the sound of the door's hinges squeaking had woken him just as surely as the loud *whaanngg* the heavy iron door made when the Japanese *rikusentai* who was detailed to guard it slammed it shut.

Koshio had to walk just a few feet to reach his tank... since it was parked right behind the concrete-reinforced entranceway he had just left...and underneath the concrete stairway that led to the rooftop of the two-story building. As he rounded the corner of the entrance, he spied his assistant gunner laying against the coconut tree. *At least he's awake,* Koshio thought angrily. The petty officer walked over to where Kubo was sitting and stared down at him. "You know you are not supposed to be sleeping...or out of the tank for that matter," Koshio stated...his patience with the man finally running out. "I gave you strict orders to remain in the tank when I left. Why did you disobey me?"

"Because I was baking in there...like a loaf of bread... that's why. At least you got a break from the heat while you attended that meeting of yours inside the command post," the assistant gunner of the tank replied condescendingly. "And what are you going to do to me anyway? Transfer me to the infantry?"

"You know I would never do that to you, Kanji. For some reason...one I'll never completely understand myself…I like you. What would our crew be like without you? You keep me on my toes, so I'll keep you around," the tank commander replied, changing his tact.

"Don't do me any favors," the assistant gunner grumbled, and then added, "so how did the meeting go? Is the Navy on the way or are we going to fight to the last man?"

"Yes, what did Commander Horii tell you, Tadashi? Are we going to receive help…or are we on our own?" Yoshizawa asked, still hoping that a miracle was possible.

"All Commander Horii could tell those at the meeting is that the Navy is still trying to decide whether they should sortie out of Truk and engage the American Fleet."

"Still trying to decide?" Kubo seethed. "By the time those ships leave the harbor, we'll all be dead over here. Even if they win the battle, we'll never know it." The desperation and anger were evident in the assistant gunner's voice.

"Why is the Navy not coming," Yoshizawa pleaded. "Don't they know what's happening here? Certainly, Commander Horii has explained our predicament to them. The Americans keep landing more and more men. We have killed some of them…but it doesn't seem to be enough. At some point, there will be more of them on the island than us. Don't they understand that back at Truk? They've got to come."

"Commander Horii is an experienced officer. He understands our situation…and he has conveyed our needs to our leaders in Truk. If they choose to come… then they will come. If they cannot come…for whatever reason...then they will not come," Koshio stated emphatically. "In either event, we will continue to act like the trained sailors we are, and we will continue to fight to the very end. Until our last breath...if necessary."

"I am willing to do that...just as long as I don't end up burning to death," the driver said...deadly serious. "Don't forget that you made that promise to me, Tadashi."

"I have not forgotten, my dear friend. I will protect you. Never doubt me on that," Koshio replied, just as serious.

"That is a very patriotic speech," Kubo replied, "but you and I both know that we are doomed. Some of the others do too. This afternoon I heard that several men are planning to commit *hari kari* already. They think the battle is lost and they will not be taken prisoner."

Petty Officer Koshio knew the men Kubo was talking about. Around one in the afternoon, Koshio had received orders to move his tank a thousand yards to the east...towards Takarongo Point...to defend against a possible marine landing along the northeastern coastline. Apparently, someone using a rangefinder located near the Point had spotted several ships cruising in that direction...and the alarm had been sounded. The tank had left as soon as the order was given...but it took over an hour to reach their destination. The reason it took so long was that the tail of the island was pockmarked with shell holes from the naval bombardment that had taken place in the early morning hours of D Day...and from the subsequent shellings that were delivered by the two destroyers out in the cove. And then the American warships and marine artillery units had begun blasting the area all over again around noontime of D +1... which made it risky to move in any direction. But the tank eventually made it through...after dodging the shell holes and incoming naval shells and artillery fire... no worse for wear.

Looking skyward, Koshio had Yoshizawa pull the tank into a small stand of coconut trees that sat about a hundred yards off the beach. *A perfect spot,* he thought wisely, since it would hide the tank from any snooping American fighters that might show up overhead at any moment. Plus, he could use the tank's 37mm cannon and machine gun to full advantage...since he could see up and down the beach for two hundred yards in either direction.

Yoshizawa shut the tank down immediately, and all three men wasted no time in climbing out...since it was so hot inside the tank. The shade offered by the trees was comforting to say the least...and it wasn't long before Yoshizawa was napping against the base of a tree.

"Pretty nice, huh," Koshio said to Kubo...who was sitting cross-legged in the sand.

Kubo looked around and said, "Sure is." Even with the shells exploding in the background, he could still hear the tank engine clicking rhythmically as it cooled... and the sound of the waves as they gently washed up on the beach. "I wish the Americans had just bypassed the island and left us all alone. We could've survived on our own for quite a while...if we had to. Probably until the war was over even. There's more than enough fish to go around...and those chickens we had were wonderful egg-layers."

The Butcher's Block

"Who could ask for more, right," Koshio said, agreeing with his assistant gunner. Neither man said anything for a while...both lost in their own thoughts. Then the petty officer said softly, "I guess it just wasn't meant to be though," as if talking to himself.

"No...I guess not. Just wasn't meant to be," Kubo said sadly...capturing the petty officer's sentiments to a T.

It wasn't long before several *rikusentai* who were stationed in the bunkers that dotted the area came over to inspect the tank...and the men who manned it.

Petty Officer Koshio was leaning against one of the trees when they came over and he walked over and introduced himself to them. "And that's Naval Seaman First Class Kanji Kubo sitting over there," he said, pointing to him, "he's my assistant gunner on the tank. He fires the machine gun we have." The newcomers nodded in Kubo's direction and then one of them asked, "What about him. Who is he?" The man was pointing at Yoshizawa...who was still sleeping against the base of the tree...apparently dreaming about something since he moaned occasionally.

"That's our driver...he's Naval Seaman Second Class Jinzo Yoshizawa...who I would introduce you to...if he were awake, of course."

The men then introduced themselves as well...and explained that they had been sitting in their bunkers for the last two days...and they had missed most of the action. "The bigger guns down on the Point are having all the fun," one of the men said, obviously a veteran and the leader of the group. "We don't field anything big enough to reach the enemy that landed off to our left. Their boats were out of range for our machine guns...but we squeezed off a few rounds just the same."

"Have you seen any action?" one of the younger ones asked eagerly.

"Yes, we have," Koshio answered with flair. "We were stationed near the cove yesterday morning and we hit several landing boats with our main gun as they tried to land. Our rounds aren't big enough to sink any of them but we certainly damaged enough of them. I saw several hits myself. After a while, we were called back to the command building. We've been out of action since then though."

"You were stationed at the command building?" the leader asked, jumping back into the conversation.

"Yes," Koshio answered, "we've been sitting right outside of it. We have been guarding it for the last twenty-four hours. It's boring duty for the most part...if you don't mind the shelling."

"Is the rumor true then...is Admiral Shibasaki really dead?" the man...an ensign...asked, very concerned.

"I can't say for sure...since I haven't seen the body," Yoshizawa lied. "I heard the rumor too...but it may be just that. You know how these things start. Someone who wants to sound important starts spreading false information...and before long the entire island is believing it...even though it isn't true."

"I've seen that same thing happen hundreds of times over the years. I hate rumors," the ensign said with contempt.

The Butcher's Block

"Plus, how could Admiral Shibasaki be dead if we are still winning. It seems to me that the reason we're doing so well is because of the brilliant tactical decisions he is making. So, I don't believe he is dead…no." While he was saying this, Koshio noticed that Kubo had been having a private conversation with one of the other men who had settled down beside the assistant tank gunner. They were talking very quietly…so none of the others could hear them.

"That is wonderful news…the best we've had in a while," the veteran ensign said, relieved. "We're stuck out here all by ourselves and don't really know what to think. Thank you for sharing your thoughts with us." Then he bowed stiffly to the petty officer and he led his men back to their bunkers in the distance.

"What were you talking about, Kanji" Petty Officer Koshio asked innocently.

"The man I was talking to is second in command to the one you were talking to. He was saying that their leader has his head in the sand…that he doesn't want to face facts…since the rest of them know that the island is all but lost. They can see it with their own eyes…just like I can. Some of them are even talking about killing themselves before the Americans get the chance to do it. He said that some of them have been practicing putting the muzzles of their rifles in their mouths while putting one of their toes on the trigger. Those that don't want to do it that way are going to use their grenades to blow their bellies open. They were very serious, Tadashi," Kubo explained earnestly. Then Kubo placed his hand on Koshio's shoulder and looked him directly in the eye.

"You shouldn't have lied to him either. That was wrong, Tadashi...even though you thought you were helping him. The truth is always better...even when it leaves a bad taste in your mouth. Personal integrity is a rare commodity...more valuable than gold. Shibasaki is dead...and you know it...just like we do. Giving that man false hope was wrong...but I will forgive you since I know your heart was in the right place."

"Thank you, Kanji," the petty officer said humbly, "it is a lesson I swear I shall never forget." Koshio then turned away...so his assistant gunner would not see him wiping the tears away.

Kanji Kubo smiled for the first time in a long while...pleased with himself. It was a moment that he would never forget either...since he had addressed his own tank commander by his first name. Twice even. And that was something he rarely did...if ever...with anyone.

In the end, no landing had been made or attempted even...and eventually the tank and its crew were sent back to defend the command post once again.

Chapter Eight

Crawling through scorching-hot sand was a torture of the worst kind...but it paled when compared to the pain that Petty Officer Saburo Okagi was experiencing on the left side of his body. Yet he continued to crawl...since it was his only way of getting where he needed to go. *Don't think about it...just keep going,* he kept repeating over and over, trying to ward off the sharp pain that kept shooting up his left leg...like a lightning strike. Luckily, the pain in his left hand had begun to dull somewhat as time had passed...and now he was using it to claw his way forward...even though he was missing two fingers and part of his thumb. His left leg was in far worse shape though...since it had taken the brunt of the hand grenade explosion inside the bunker. The blast had blown most of his calve muscle off...exposing his tibia and fibula bones underneath...and his thigh was a tattered mess as well. These wounds, as bad as they were, were no longer bleeding, however. Instead, they had been bandaged tightly…thus preventing further blood loss…and this gave him a fighting chance at survival.

Petty Officer Okagi could still remember the magnificent job his eight men had done at repelling the enemy with their machine guns on D Day and D + 1. The two bunkers they had been manning were part of a larger bunker complex that had been built into and behind the seawall that ran along the northeastern part of the curve of the cove area…the part of the island that looked like the neckline and upper breast of the parrot on the marine maps. In the overall defensive scheme, Okagi's two bunkers were located on the eastern flank of the main complex. This positioning enabled them to provide a deadly crossfire against any head-on attacks against the main complex… but it also left them somewhat open to an attack against their own right flank. Okagi had understood the tactical deficiency in their positioning right from the start…since he was a veteran of the failed Guadalcanal campaign…and he put his men to work to nullify it. He had his men dig deep…and then go deeper still…knowing that these bunkers would have to withstand not only rifle and machine gun fire…but also artillery and naval gunfire, and…most deadly of all…aerial bombs. For added protection, he had his men use the largest coconut logs available…and before long his bunkers resembled small, underground forts…just like he wanted. Lastly, he encouraged his men to camouflage their bunkers so they couldn't be seen until you stumbled right into them. The building project had taken the entire summer to complete...and when the invasion finally hit...Okagi and his men were confident they could defeat anything the marines could throw at them.

Okagi and his men had cheered wildly after they survived the devastating naval bombardment on D Day morning. And then came the deadly fighters and bombers after that...and they had survived them, too. With their confidence soaring like the rising sun, Okagi and his men then watched in awe as the marine landing craft began approaching their island. Some of the men thought they looked like little, black beetles on the surface of the water...while others saw them for the deadly vehicles they were. Showing incredible patience and discipline, Okagi had his men hold their fire until the tracked vehicles had crossed over the reef. Doing so not only improved their accuracy...since their targets were closer by several hundred yards when they finally opened fire...but it also gave the marine drivers less time to react.

By the end of that first day, Okagi's men had taken a slew of landing craft under fire...and Okagi was certain they had destroyed more than a few of them in the process. While a small contingent of marines may have landed to their front, Okagi was still confident that he and his men had obeyed Admiral Shibasaki's standing order to the letter of the law. Since his arrival on the island several months ago, the admiral had been stressing to the garrison on Betio...and to anyone in Tokyo who would listen...that the only way to defeat an enemy landing force was to destroy it at the water's edge. To that end, the defenders of an island must inflict maximum damage on the enemy while the invading force is still inside their landing craft...not after it has landed. And as far as Petty Officer Okagi could tell, he and the other *rikusentai* around him on Betio had done just that...which would have made the Admiral very happy.

Petty Officer Okagi looked up and realized he was making pretty good progress...given the circumstances. His original plan had been to head for the tail of the island once he left the confines of the bunker, but he changed his mind when he heard the steady drumbeat of weapons being fired from the cove area. *Our boys must still hold that ground,* he thought proudly. Instead of heading east...or to his left...he decided to see if he couldn't sneak into the cove defenses that were up ahead...just off to his right...or to the west. And the more he thought about it, the more sense it made. It was a far shorter distance to travel on one hand...and his thirst was beginning to drive him crazy...even though he had had some water to drink a little while ago. *This heat will kill me before I can reach the tail...so the cove it is,* he decided wisely.

The water that was sustaining him now had come from a canteen that had been given to him back in the bunker...and it had been a godsend. And that canteen, now empty, had been discarded a few hours ago. But

Okagi knew that he would never forget the man who had given it to him....or the other man who had bandaged his wounds for him either. These men...whoever they were...had saved his life. And if he was lucky enough to survive the war, he'd probably spend the rest of his life wondering why these two men had done anything for him in the first place.

Private Johnny Scott didn't know what to think when he finally saw Petty Officer Okagi squirming around...except that the man was badly wounded...and certainly not dead. The first time he had looked inside the bunker, he had counted out five bodies...and these men were all dead. Then he had gone off to check on Private First Class Cohen...who had been wounded in the shoulder during the attack on the second of the two bunkers that Scott, Cohen, and Sergeant Endres had knocked out. Thinking he had heard a strange sound, Scott returned to the bunker and inspected the interior more closely...and that's when he spotted something moving. Looking closer, Scott could see the body of another Jap soldier...one that he had missed on the first go-around. This Jap was lying hidden against the back wall...and he was still alive...since he was trying to roll over. The effort was obviously too much for the man since he eventually gave up, and he just laid where he was. Then the Jap had let out a muffled moan...since he was terribly wounded along his left side.

Private Scott lifted his rifle up and pointed it directly at the Jap soldier's head. *Better safe than sorry,* he thought grimly, since he had heard story after story in boot camp about how wounded Japanese soldiers had refused to surrender or be taken prisoner on Guadalcanal. Instead, these sneaky Japs would hide grenades under their bodies, and they would blow themselves up when an unsuspecting marine went over to check them out. In this case, the marines' sense of fair play had worked against them. But the naive marines learned quickly from these disheartening experiences...and they adjusted their tactics accordingly. Now they were fighting a different kind of war. Theirs was a dirty war...one in which the old rules of decorum and restraint were thrown out the window. A war in which they would show their enemy no quarter...ever again...and none would be asked.

Petty Officer Okagi remembered coming to in the bunker...and then staring at a figure in the doorway. It was obviously a marine....since the man was very big physically. He looked to be about the same height as Okagi...who was tall by Japanese standards. In fact, the petty officer was one of the tallest men...if not the tallest...of all the Japanese on the island. The marine was also pointing his M-1 rifle at his head...which was never good. Okagi remained still though...anticipating the final shot...yet feeling no fear or regret. As a Christian, Okagi had made his peace with God long before he arrived on Betio Island...and he was quite certain that

The Butcher's Block

he would be staring at the *Pearly Gates* as soon as the rifle was fired. But the shot never came...the marine having simply lowered his weapon instead. Incredibly, the marine then came over to him and cradled him in his lap. Then the marine spoke softly to him...the sound of his voice strangely soothing. Okagi felt no animosity in the man at all...only mercy. Then the marine began yelling words that Okagi could not understand...but his voice sounded desperate.

Sergeant Tom Endres could not believe what he was seeing. He had been briefing Lieutenant Hackett on Private First Class Cohen's condition when he heard Scott yelling from inside the bunker. Leaving Cohen to the lieutenant, Endres approached the bunker and looked inside. Even though it was hazy, Endres could still see the private kneeling by the back wall...holding a wounded Jap soldier in his lap. Endres...who was holding his Thompson Submachine gun against his hip...told Scott to drop the Jap and to get away from him...immediately...but Scott simply pointed to the rank tabs on Jap soldier's shirt and implored Staggs to spare him. "He's wearin' chevrons... so he must be an NCO...just like you, sarge," Endres remembered Scott saying...or words to that effect. As if that fact was going to change his mind from doing what he had to do. Then he yelled at Scott again...only louder and more forcefully this time. Endres warned the private that the Jap might be holding a grenade...and that he could kill both of them with it. Incredibly, Scott had argued that point too...saying that the Jap would've killed him already...had he really wanted to.

Private Johnny Scott thought that he was one of the luckiest marines alive when he learned that he was going to be assigned to the first squad of E Company, 2nd Marine Regiment. Having recently arrived in New Zealand after graduating from boot camp on Parris Island, Scott was still brimming with pride over securing a billet with the vaunted 2nd Marine Division. Scott also knew that the division was in the process of resting and recuperating after the hard fighting it had participated in on Guadalcanal...one of the islands in the Solomon Islands chain.

When a staff sergeant from the Replacement Depot had asked him if he had any preferences about what unit he would like to go to, the private had said, "Yes, sir. I would like to be assigned to the First Battalion in the Second Marines."

"Any particular reason," the administrative sergeant asked, and added, "and don't call me sir. I'm not an officer. I'm a staff sergeant. I work for a living."

"Yes, sir. I mean sergeant...sorry. We had to call everyone 'sir' in boot camp, sorry again. I certainly realize you're a staff sergeant, of course," Scott answered defensively, his train of thought now broken.

The staff sergeant waited for Scott to speak, but the private didn't say anything. Instead, he just kept staring at the sergeant.

"So, you do have a reason for wanting to go to the First Battalion...or you don't?"

"Yes, sergeant, I do," Scott replied...and he continued to stare at the sergeant.

"Well, are you going to share that reason with me, private, or is it some kind of military secret?" the sergeant replied, exasperated.

"Oh...I didn't realize you wanted to know the exact reason. Sorry, sergeant. I just thought you wanted to know if I had a reason for going to the First. Which I do...since I just said I did."

"So, what is it," the staff sergeant replied, "if you don't mind telling me."

"Oh, I don't mind telling you," Scott said, "why would I?"

"It would appear that you do...since you've been sitting in that chair for over two minutes now and I still have no idea why you want to go to the dang First Battalion," the sergeant countered, and he held up his hands in mock surrender.

"Are you sure it's been two minutes, sergeant? It feels longer...more like three or four minutes...maybe five since I sat down," Scott countered.

"Are you serious, private? We're debating over the amount of time you've been sitting here now? Are you always so argumentative," he asked, perplexed.

"I wouldn't characterize it that way. I would call it a discussion more than anything else," Scott said, adding, "why you would think otherwise is beyond me."

"Listen," the sergeant barked, "all I wanted to know is why you wanted to go to the First Battalion in the first place. You said you have a specific reason for wanting to go there...but for the life of me I don't seem to be able to get you to tell me why you want to go!" The sergeant's voice had gotten louder as he spoke...and several men sitting at other desks now looked their way.

"Everything okay over there?" The question came from a sergeant who was interviewing another young marine at his desk across the aisle. He pushed his chair back and stood up to get a better look.

"Everything is fine...go back to doing what you were doing...we're fine over here," the staff sergeant stated emphatically. Then he looked back at Scott and said cheerily, "So...you wanna go to the First, huh."

"I sure do, sergeant," Scott replied just as enthusiastically. "And the reason I want to go is that a buddy of mine from New Hampshire is going to the First. We shipped over together...after spending boot camp together. He's from Nashua too...just like me. But I didn't know him that well. But I do now! His name is Gerdis...Private Paul Gerdis. He said he got his orders yesterday. Do you remember placing him?"

"No...I don't. But why didn't you just tell me that in the first place?"

"All you had to do was ask," Scott replied jauntily.

"Well, I'll tell you what," the sergeant said smoothly, "since you've been so cooperative this whole time. I've decided that I am going to do you a big favor."

Private Scott started smiling now...sure he was headed to the First. "My friend will be really happy you did this for us."

"I'm sure he will," the sergeant said ruefully, "I'm sure he will!" Then the sergeant stamped his assignment papers, slid them back into the file, and said, "Here you go, kid. Welcome to the Second Battalion...you earned it!"

Private Scott was depressed as he made his way over to the 2nd Battalion Headquarters...since he didn't know a soul in the unit. But not all was lost, since he was in the 2nd Regiment at least, which meant that his buddy was still nearby. Then his luck had changed for the better... since he was told to head over to E Company...and that's when he ran into the company first sergeant.

"My name's O'Toole...Mike O'Toole...but you can just call me 'First Sergeant' if that's alright with you," the big, beefy man said.

"That's fine by me," the young private replied nervously.

"Good...then we're off to a great start. Ya got your file with you?"

Private Scott handed him the folder he was holding in his hand and the first sergeant opened it up. He hummed as he scanned its contents...and then handed it back. "I see you did pretty good on the rifle range. Sharpshooter's badge. Not expert...but still damn good. No disciplinary charges to speak of. That's good too. The last thing I need is a brig rat. I got enough headaches as it is. Just keep your nose clean and jump when your squad leader tells ya to. And I can tell by looking at you that you are in good shape...so I'm gonna do ya a favor."

"Oh...I don't need any more favors, First Sergeant. Trust me on that one," Scott said innocently.

"Here's what I'm gonna do. Since it looks like you work out a lot...I'm gonna stick you in Sergeant Endres' squad. He's a beast...a gym rat...probably like you are. He's got the First Squad in Lieutenant Hackett's First Platoon. I'll square it away with Hackett, so you'll get the First Squad. Your platoon sergeant is a hard charger named Roy. You'll like all three. They're as good a leadership team as we got in the whole battalion...if not the regiment. And our company CO is Captain Ring. The captain is a good leader...I just wish we saw more of him. I think he's bucking' to make major, so he spends a lot of time up at Battalion. In any event, you hit the jackpot with this assignment, kid."

"Thank you," Scott said genuinely, "that's the first luck I've had since I got outta boot camp. I think I'll celebrate it with a big glass of milk. You know...good for the muscles and all."

"Celebrate with whatever you want, kid. Just don't get too drunk on the Aussie beer they serve out here. It's got a kick to it. And that reminds me...your assistant squad leader may end up being a guy named Staggs. Do not...I repeat...do not...gamble with that guy. He's got ice water in his veins and a mind like an adding machine. If you gamble with him, you'll end up like all the other guys who try to take him on...broke and lonely...since you'll be sitting in the barracks with no dough in your pocket. These New Zealand lassies have become accustomed to us Yanks having lots of dough to spread around. And woe to the man that doesn't have any cash in his pockets. He may just as well stay in the barracks...since he's not gonna attract any of the ladies...that's for sure."

"Thanks again," Scott said, picturing the bars and the New Zealand girls in his head. "And I'll definitely remember your warning about Staggs...since I'm not that good a gambler to begin with."

"Okay. Now one last thing. You may hear the boys talkin' about someone they call, 'Tough as a mule.' Well, as you can probably guess, that guy is me. 'Tough as a mule O'Toole' is what they affectionately call me. I don't mind, really. Just don't let me hear ya saying it to my face, of course. I'm a nice guy and all, but I do believe in military decorum...along with the rules and regulations...and I enforce them with an iron fist. Got it."

"Yes, first sergeant. I got it. Loud and clear," Scott answered smartly...yet thinking all the while that the guy resembled a grizzly bear far more than a mule.

"Well then, go ahead and head over to your platoon...they'll be expecting you," O'Toole ordered...and he turned on his heel and screamed for the company orderly to get him a hot cup of coffee.

Sergeant Endres had a temper...and everyone in his squad knew it. They also knew that Endres usually handled his disciplinary cases with his fists...if it came to that...in lieu of paperwork...which he found too time consuming. And no one had ever seen a private disobey one of Endres' orders...even a small one...and live to tell about it. So Private Scott...who revered his squad leader...knew when to hit the brakes when it came to arguing with his hallowed squad leader. Yet Scott could also push Endres' buttons when the mood struck him... which wasn't very often for his own sake.

That is why Sergeant Endres was staring at Private Scott with eyes that burned like hot coals in a fire. He simply couldn't believe what he was hearing now...to go along with what he was also seeing in the bunker. And as Private Scott continued to argue with him...over a stupid Jap no less...the sergeant's face began to turn beet-red...even darker than the color of his bright red hair. Then Scott watched as Sergeant Endres lowered the Thompson from his hip and leveled it right at the private...center mass. Scott quickly realized that the sergeant might shoot him and the Jap too...just to prove a point. The shaken private got the message...and laid the Jap soldier gently to the ground. Then he got up and left without a word...all the while dreading what was about to happen in the bunker behind him. The sudden rip of his squad leader's machine gun told him all he needed to know.

Sergeant Endres had taken the lives of more than a few men by the time he landed on Betio Island. In fact, he had become used to it while serving on Guadalcanal... where the killing of Japs had become routine after a while. And by noon of D + 1, Endres had added to his total...*so why was one more wounded Jap meeting his demise a big deal,* he wondered. Strangely, Private Scott had tried to protect the man for reasons Endres could not or did not want to fathom at the time...or so he thought anyway. Then, after growing tired of the debate, Endres had ordered him out. *That way the young marine won't have to watch me kill a man in cold blood,* he thought coldly. Deep down, Endres wasn't worried about the legal implications of this act, since he had seen plenty of guys do the exact same thing on Guadalcanal. *So, no big deal, right.*

With no guilt at all, Endres leveled his Thompson at the man and prepared to fire away. As he did so, the wounded Jap tugged at something around his neck until it broke free. *Probably holding up some kind of heathen talisman,* he thought wryly, *or maybe his dog tags...or whatever the Japs wear to identify themselves.* Pausing on the trigger, Endres looked more closely...trying to see what was dangling from the man's hand. And then it hit him...like a ton of bricks. *I can't believe what I'm seeing,* he thought, *how can that be?* Incredibly, the wounded man was holding up a cross that was hanging from the chain that he had worn around his neck. Then the man said something that Endres could not understand...since it was probably in Japanese...but in his heart, Endres knew the man was saying, "Jesus," over and over again.

In an instant, Endres pictured his own mother standing on the porch of their home in Long Island, New York. She had tears in her eyes...since her fourth son, Tommy, was shoving off to join the Marine Corps...just like her older son had before him. "Look, son," he remembered her saying, "I don't want you to worry about your father and me while you're gone, okay. We'll do just fine. Your little brother is going to be here...at least for a little while. I have a feeling he's going to follow your footsteps too...just like you did with your brother... as soon as he meets the age limit. Don't worry about him either...you trained him well...and he'll turn out just fine...like you did. Now there is one thing I want you to do for me while you're gone, okay."

"Sure, ma, what is it? You know I'd do anything for you. What is it that you want?"

"I want you to wear this medal, Tommy. It's a medal of Saint Sebastian...you know...the soldier's protector. My brother...your uncle...wore it in the last war and he said it got him out of a lot of trouble...that Saint Sebastian saved his life many times over there in France." Then she took the medal out of her pocket, kissed it, and handed it to her fourth son. He looked at it and noted that it was made of bronze...so it had a nice brown shine to it. The image on it showed a man tied to a tree...with deadly arrows protruding from his chest. "He died a martyr for the Lord," his mother said reverently. "He was a Roman soldier who refused to deny Jesus...and he was killed for his faith," she added...while making the sign of the cross.

Tommy draped the medal over his head, and it settled over his chest. "I will never take it off," he promised.

"And remember...no matter how bad things get over there...I want you to maintain your dignity...and your soul. Never do anything that will dishonor you or our family. Don't turn into an animal, okay," she told him.

"I won't let you down, ma, ever. I promise," he replied earnestly.

"I know you won't, son. Don't let God down either." Then, leaning forward, she kissed her son on the forehead.

"I love you, mom," Tommy said.

"I love you too, son." Then his mother turned and walked quickly back into house...so her fourth and favorite son wouldn't see her cry.

Okagi was convinced that he was going to die...for the second time that morning. But everything seemed to change when he had torn the cross from his neck and held it up for the marine to see. Then he had spoken some words that he had not said in a long time. The man called on Jesus...his savior...to save him somehow. "Lamb of God," he kept on repeating...hoping for a miracle. And he got one...when the marine with the machine gun fired off a burst...that hit the wall above him. *He missed me on purpose,* he thought joyously. *Jesus must have answered my prayer!*

Endres pulled the trigger...but he aimed high so he would purposely miss him. *I can't let Scott think I've gone soft,* he thought. And then he did something else that really surprised him. He reached down to his belt and removed a canteen that still had some water in it. "It's not much, but it's better than nothing, right. Use it in good health," Endres said, wondering if the man would know what he was saying. Then he saluted him...since he was an NCO like himself...and he left the man to his own devices.

The son of a bitch killed him, Scott seethed, as Endres rounded the bunker...his Thompson still smoking. But Endres did not see Private Scott...since he was hiding behind a coconut tree that had been blown over during the naval bombardment that had blanketed the area the day before. The private watched his squad leader cut around the corner of the bunker...making a beeline to the lieutenant...who was still kneeling beside PFC Cohen. And that's when he made his move. Scott dashed back to the bunker and scrambled inside...unseen. Then he got the shock of his life...since the wounded Jap was still lying where Scott had left him...but now he was gripping a canteen in his good hand. *Well, I'll be...Endres must've given it to him,* he thought, as his anger drained quickly away. Then Scott made another decision...which would end up helping the Jap NCO just as much as Endres' gift of precious water would...and he pulled two dressings out of a pouch on his web belt. Rushing over to the wounded man, Scott quickly wrapped one of the dressings as tight as he could around the man's injured thigh. Then he wrapped the torn calve up too...but the dressing was so long that there was some leftover. Scott took out his knife and cut the excess off...and then he used that part to wrap up the man's injured left hand. *I'd a made a good corpsman,* he thought proudly, admiring his work.

Then he patted the wounded man...who had drifted off into unconsciousness once again...on the shoulder and said, "Good luck, old timer. I hope ya make it." His mission of mercy now over, Scott got up and peaked out of the bunker entranceway. Luckily, Sergeant Endres was still occupied with the lieutenant on the side of the bunker...and with Cohen too...so he wasn't looking his way. As a result, Sergeant Endres never saw Private Scott dash out of the bunker...and he would spend the rest of the battle thinking that his act of mercy had gone unnoticed...just like he wanted.

Chapter Nine

Corporal Tom Bosco was lucky to be alive...and he said so...to the marine...Private Roger Wieland... who was sitting in the foxhole on Red 2 with him. "I bet it was that baptizing I got back on the *Sheridan* that saved me," Bosco theorized, remembering the ritual that had taken place on the tail of the transport, the USS *Sheridan*, APA 51. "I mean I was already baptized and all bein' Catholic," the corporal explained to the private, who was listening offhandedly, since he was more concerned with Japs infiltrating their position.

"So, why did you get baptized again then?" Wieland asked skeptically, all the while scanning the torn-up ground that lay beyond their foxhole.

"Cause I just figured it couldn't hurt, right," Bosco answered, looking to the private for some sort of reassurance. "I mean I was just a baby when I got baptized the first time, so I don't remember much about it. And then it hit me back on the ship...what if it didn't take... you know...that first one I got. So, I just went ahead and let the chaplain baptize me again. And it felt great."

"Well, I got baptized when I was twelve," Wieland said stalely, and added, "I don't really remember it bein' a big deal...but everyone else made out like it was. I belonged to a Methodist Church that my family had attended for years. I guess it was kind of expected of me to do it...so I did it. So, who performed the ceremony? The Catholic chaplain?"

"No. Chaplain Willard...the Protestant one did it. He got permission to seal up the drainage holes on that observation turret on the aft of the ship. Then he had some guys fill it with five-gallon cans of water. It took a little while but eventually the turret became sort like a tub...which was perfect for baptizing in. There were over fifty guys waitin' in line to get dunked. Even some of the swabbies joined in too. I guess they're just as worried about gettin' sunk as we are about gettin' killed on the island. Anyway, I said, 'Aye aye, sir,' after the chaplain made his speech and under I went. And when I came back up, I felt like a new man. Which is what you're supposed to feel like, since you got all your sins washed away, right?"

"I don't really understand the whole process," Wieland offered, "I guess I should have paid more attention to what our pastor was talking about when he gave of all those sermons. I believe in God in all, don't get me wrong. You know that old saying, 'There ain't no atheists in foxholes'? Well, it's true. I said more than a few prayers while I was on the *Canal*...asking God to protect me. But I'm definitely no authority on religion and faith...that's for sure."

"Well, gettin' baptized again sure made me feel better...and I have a feelin' that I'm here now because I did it," the corporal stated emphatically.

"Good for you," Wieland replied dryly, "now we just gotta hope that those Japs out there that wanna kill us are all heathens. Hopefully, none of them ever got baptized...or believe in Jesus either. Otherwise, we're really screwed."

Corporal Tom Bosco and Private Roger Wieland were both members of C Company, 1st Battalion, 8th Regiment...and while they were not in the same platoon...they still knew each other...having met while the 2nd Marine Division was resting and recuperating in Wellington, New Zealand. Like so many other men, Bosco and Wieland had run into one another on one of their many trips into the city...ostensibly to meet girls...but also to drink...which was becoming the two favorite pastimes of the 2nd Division marines. And with their faith discussion now over, Bosco began reminiscing about the drinking and dating forays that they had embarked on back in New Zealand...as a means of staying awake.

"So, Wheels, whatever happened to that girl you met...Donna. Wasn't that her name," Bosco asked. Bosco could picture the girl that Weiland had met in his mind: she was blond and very pretty...and smart... which gave her personality a sort of cutting edge to it.

Bosco remembered her shooting down more than one hopeful marine who had approached her while she was sitting on a barstool in a restaurant that had become a very popular marine hangout. And then Wieland had swooped in and swept off her feet...or barstool...and the two had spent the rest of the evening talking and dancing....two activities that Bosco felt he was very good at as well. "Did you guys ever have a second date? I mean the two of you looked like lovebirds that night," Bosco asked, intrigued.

"We sure did," Wieland replied, "and a lot more after that too. We really hit it off...and we got married...right before we shipped out."

"Are you kiddin' me," Bosco shot back, "who was there...at the wedding?"

"We kept it real small...just her family. That's all. I have a feeling my parents are gonna want to kill me when I tell them what I did. They'll claim I rushed into things...like I always do...but there's something about this girl that I just know is right. Even if she's a little older than me...I don't care. I love her and that's that."

"Well, congratulations are certainly in order, my friend." And Corporal Tom Bosco reached over and shook the other man's hand. "Best to you and the misses," he said, smiling.

"And what about you? Did you ever meet anyone special," Wieland asked, turning the conversation back to Bosco...who Wieland knew was the cat's meow when it came to flirting and dating.

"Oh, I went on tons of dates...but I never really found anyone that could keep me penned up...like you did,"

Bosco answered back. He was silent for a second or two... as if thinking about it...and then said, "I'm probably destined to meet my wife back home...on Staten Island... where I'm from. It'll have to be an Italian girl anyway... or my parents will kill me too. Just as well though...since I really do love Italian women. It's their skin tone and eyes...and dark hair...there's nothing quite like them. I'm probably too jaded and picky when it comes to them too though...which is why I'm still single, I guess."

"The pickier the better," Wieland said, lending his support, "since you're gonna be with her for the rest of your life. I heard about one guy over in the Second Battalion that got married about a month after we got here...and then he had to ask for a divorce right before we pulled out. Supposedly, Major Crowe was going to deny him permission to get married in the first place...said it was too soon...or words to that effect. But he softened up...if that's possible for Major Crowe...and he let the guy go through with the marriage anyway. Looks like the major should've stuck with his gut instinct in the first place."

"Yeah, they'll be no divorcin' for me. Catholics get married and stay married. I don't know of anyone who got divorced in my old neighborhood back on the Island."

"I plan on staying with Donna for the rest of my life too...as long as she'll keep me. I just hope she won't mind moving to the States when this war is over. I mean I love New Zealand and all...couldn't find a more beautiful place on Earth...but it's still not the good old US of A, right."

"No...there's nothing like home," Bosco agreed, "nothin' quite like home...and I sure hope we both get back there, too. I guess we're gonna have to kill a whole lotta Japs along the way though...before we head back."

"It's them or us out here, buddy," Wieland stated somberly, "and I, for one, plan on makin' it back...hopefully in one piece."

"Amen to that," Bosco replied...hoping that Wieland would get to see his Donna once again...and that he would eventually find his Italian beauty waiting for him...just like he dreamed...back in America.

As members of the 1st Battalion, 8th Regiment, Bosco and Wieland had climbed down the thick, rope netting that was draped over the side of the *Sheridan* at noon on D Day...and they fully expected to make a landing within the next few hours...at most. However, due to the persistent communication problems that had plagued the invasion from the start, the men in the 1st Battalion were still boated in their Higgins boats fourteen hours later...just bobbing away in the rough waters outside the lagoon...waiting for orders to land. And when those fateful orders finally did arrive...at sometime around 0300 hours in the morning...the men in the boats had cheered...knowing that their stomach-churning odyssey was almost over. What these men did not know, however, is that one particularly important component of their landing plan had been left out...and this omission would cost the 1st Battalion dearly when they began their landing at 0615 hours on D + 1.

Major General Smith, the division commander, and his staff aboard the battleship, the USS *Maryland*, which served as the flagship for the invasion, were completely worn out by the time they finished compiling the landing directive for the 1st Battalion. And their exhaustion was well-earned...since they had spent the entire night of D Day and then the early morning hours of D + 1 trying to develop it. Amazingly, they had been forced to scrap two other complete landing directives along the way...before they finalized on this one.

In designing the third plan, Smith had relied on information that came from two sources since the invasion began: from the radio operators who were ashore...and from runners who physically delivered hand-written messages from the island's commanders or recited their messages verbally from memory to the leaders or staff on the ships. But both of these means were proving to be faulty at best...since the radio messages were spotty and fragmented in nature...and the messages the runners were carrying - both verbal and written - were usually several hours old by the time they reached the Division Staff out at sea.

Major General Smith had recognized the problem and its implications early on, and to fix it, he ordered his second-in-command, Brigadier General Leo "Dutch" Hermle, to go ashore on D Day at 1345 hours and assess the situation personally. He was to gather as much information as he could from Colonel Shoup in his command post and then head back out to the *Maryland*. With this key information, Smith could then make more prudent decisions to influence the direction of the battle...before things really got out of hand.

The Butcher's Block

The brigadier general, who was aboard the transport, the USS *Monrovia*...or APA 31...which had also carried Major Robert Ruud's Third Battalion, 8th Regiment into the battle, wasted no time in complying with General Smith's order. Hermle gathered a small staff of men around him and they quickly boarded a Higgins boat for transport to the island.

Unfortunately, Brigadier Hermle's efforts would be in vain however, since he never reached the island at all. His Higgins boat ran into the same intense shore fire that prevented so many other boats from landing...and Hermle told the coxswain to head for the pier...where several other Higgins boats were gathered. Upon pulling up, Hermle quickly saw some men haplessly milling around while others were ducking behind anything they could find to avoid the incoming Jap machine gun fire...which seemed to be coming from everywhere on the island. In addition, hundreds of boxes of all shapes and sizes were stacked on the end of the pier...their contents stenciled on their sides...and he realized that someone with some rank had to step in and get this gigantic mess organized. If not, the delivery of the supplies the fighting men needed most...like ammunition and water...would take too long...and lives would be lost as a result. Sensing that his duty was there, Brigadier Hermle jumped onto the pier and immediately began barking orders to anyone who would listen. Before long, order had taken shape and the supplies were moving shoreward...and just as important...the casualties were being placed in empty Higgins boats for a ride out to the ships and their waiting medical staffs.

Incredibly, when time was of the essence, the whole trip from the *Monrovia* to the end of the pier had taken Brigadier Hermle four hours to complete. And he had not been able to communicate with General Smith at all...so Smith just assumed that he was now on the island and that he was assessing the situation...as he had been ordered to do. Hermle, in a decision that many were to question, chose to conduct his business from the end of the pier instead...since pushing his way in to the island was fraught with danger. And this decision...which some would characterize as selfless...would end up causing friction between himself and his commanding officer... especially when General Smith finally learned of it.

But closer to home, to the men who were doing the fighting, it would have a telltale effect in the fight to come...especially for the 1st Battalion...who were still out in the lagoon...waiting for their orders to land.

Brigadier Hermle's D Day travails began a little while before he was ordered to the island...at around 1100 hours...when the slaughter of the 3rd Battalion began off Red Beach 3. From his perch on the upper deck of the *Monrovia*, he could see...just as well as anyone else could...that the Japanese shore defenses along the tail of the island had zeroed in on Major Ruud's landing team...since his Higgins boats were closer than the ones carrying the 1st of the Second over on Red 2. And their marksmanship and timing were impressive. Hermle watched several boats pull up to the coral reef and get hit immediately...the detonation of the Japanese rounds coming as soon as their ramps were dropped. At this point, Major Ruud sent a radio message to his Regimental Commander, Colonel Elmer Hall, who was in another boat by the line of departure that stated: *Third wave landed on Beach Red 3 were practically wiped out. Fourth wave landed...but only a few men got ashore.* Colonel Hall apparently never got this message, since he didn't respond to it...but Brigadier Hermle did. His response was: *Stay where you are or retreat out of gun range.*

The return message confused Major Ruud. Was the message a direct order from the assistant division commander...or was it an overarching suggestion. And did the assistant division commander want Major Ruud himself to hold off from landing further...or did he want Major Ruud to hold off landing what was left of his battalion assault force. In the end, Major Ruud chose to interpret the message liberally...and he applied it to both himself and the rest of his assault force. Major Ruud immediately cancelled any further landings and then he made his way over to the end of the pier...just like the order had stated. His trek into the island would have to wait.

In hindsight, Ruud's decision was very similar to what Major Schoettel did over on Red 1...and while it was somewhat controversial...it invariably saved lives... since the later waves of Ruud's landing team were not destroyed. This is what Brigadier Hermle had to have in mind when he sent the message in the first place. And to his credit, Major Ruud then exploited the opening... once it presented itself. He directed the marines in his follow-up waves to use the pier as a means of getting to the island...and thus they avoided being slaughtered by the Japanese shore batteries...as the earlier waves had been. And the remnants of his first waves were directed to use the pier as well...which saved an untold number of lives, too. Eventually, Major Ruud was able to make it ashore successfully and reunite with his men. But it had taken him several hours to get there...and it was... by then...late in the afternoon when he finally made the linkup. Luckily for him and his survivors, Major Crowe had taken the initiative and assumed command of what was left of Major Ruud's unit on Red Beach 3 in the interim...just like Major Ryan had done on Red Beach 1 when Major Schoettel failed to show up. Major Crowe wasted no time in placing Ruud's men in a ragged line near the small turning semi-circle just east of the pier-head...and his orders were simple: defend the pierhead to the last man...which was a tall order to say the least.

In the end, Hermle's confusing message...while well-intended...was endemic of all the hundreds of other messages that were being passed back and forth between those fighting on the beachheads and those doing the leading and decision-making from the rear area at the end of the pier...and all the way back to the *Maryland* itself. And it would continue to happen repeatedly during the battle...especially on D + 1.

"Ya think it's gonna be bad when we finally get in there," the green marine asked his squad leader, Corporal Tom

Bosco. The young marine's teeth were chattering...since he was chilled to the bone.

It was 0615 hours in the morning on D + 1 and the 1st Battalion had just received its long-awaited orders to commence the landing.

"I sure hope not," Bosco responded hopefully, while glancing at the smoke rising off the island in the distance.

"I'd fight a handful of hornets right about now...if that's what I had to do to get outta this boat. Yesterday I'm burning up...gettin' sunburned out here...nowhere to hide...and now I feel like I'm freezing to death. Makes you wonder if our uniforms will ever get dry again, don't it," the kid kept talking, obviously nervous.

"Ahhh, just relax, kid, it's a piece a cake. We'll probably just waltz in there and collect souvenirs...like *samurai* swords and such...stuff that these Navy swabbies will pay up for when we get back on the ships. We'll be swimmin' in cigarettes all the way to Pearl after it's over," he said, trying his best to relax the kid.

"That sounds good...but I don't smoke yet. Wasn't old enough to buy any cigarettes before I enlisted...and I guess I never developed a taste for it. I've tried to smoke... don't get me wrong...I'm not a baby...but I just choked and coughed after my buddy gave me one. He's over there," the young marine pointed across the way, "in boat number thirty-three...off our starboard side," and he stood up waved to the boat...hoping that his friend would see him.

"Did he see you," Bosco asked, knowing the answer.

"Nah...no one waved back. I guess they're all just as sick and miserable as we are," the private said dejectedly.

"Maybe he was just sleepin'. Some guys can do that...even in these slosh buckets," Bosco pointed out. "I knew I guy that could sleep anywhere...anytime...any place. Back on the *Canal*, this guy conked out when the Jap battleships came in and hit us with their big sixteen-inchers. Just hope you never have to go through one of those...it's a nightmare. The ground shaking and your teeth chatterin'...just like yours are now. Only it's caused by the shell's overpressure when it hits near ya. It's so strong some guys got concussions from it. They'd have blood running outta their ears...and they'd look at ya like they couldn't hear you talking to them...which...come to think of it...I guess they couldn't. We gotta pray that the Jap Navy stays where it belongs...up there at Truk...and leaves us alone."

"Oh, that's no problem," the kid said proudly, "I pray all the time. No atheists in foxholes, right," the kid said enthusiastically.

"That's what they say," Bosco replied evenly.

"So, what happened to the guy that could sleep through everything...did he make it off of Guadalcanal with you?"

"Nope...he didn't."

"Well, what happened to him," the kid pressed, when Bosco declined to elaborate on it.

"You really wanna know," Bosco replied cautiously...offering a warning of sorts.

"Of course, I do...so long as you don't mind telling me. I guess if he was a buddy of yours it might hurt to talk about it...but sometimes talking about things that bother you ends up helping more than it hurts," the young marine replied honestly.

"You're way older than your age, kid. At least in the smarts department, that is," Bosco said, giving the kid credit where credit was due. Since he was the kid's squad leader, Bosco knew his age...which was sixteen. How the kid had managed to enlist while he was that young was anyone's guess...and Bosco had never asked...and the kid had never elaborated on it...so everyone just called him kid and moved on.

"So, what happened?"

"Well, this guy heads down to the Mantanikau River to wash up. We did it a lot of times as the fightin' slowed down after the First Marines pulled out. And just like that, this guy decides to up and take a nap...right there on the riverbank. Even though the Japs were at the end of their rope, they could still put up a fight every now and then...so you still had to be on your toes. And we were still sittin' watches at night...and Washin' Machine Charlie was still flying over to bug us...so we were tired most of the time. And the heat and humidity just sap it outta ya too. So down he goes...right by the bank...and he curls up and goes to sleep...like he doesn't have a care in the world. Well, none of us paid him any mind...at least until we heard him scream. When we looked over to where he was, all we saw was a slimy trail in the mud that led down to the river. We never saw him again... we just heard that one awful scream...and he was gone. Well, about a week later, one of the boys that grew up in Louisiana somewhere south of New Orleans ends up killin' a crocodile for supper. And as he cuts it open, out spills what's left of Sleepy. It wasn't a pretty sight, trust me. We figured the croc spotted him on the bank and decided to make a meal of him...before we could of it. It's all in the timing, kid."

"Geeze...that sounds terrible," the kid replied...shaking again...but not from being cold.

"Well, there ain't any crocs or alligators where we're goin' so don't worry too much about it."

"Yeah...but there are sharks," the kid replied astutely.

"So, don't fall overboard, kid. It'll be much easier explaining to your folks back home that you got killed facin' the enemy bravely...than havin' to tell them you ended up in a shark's belly for breakfast."

"Oh...I don't have any parents, corporal," the kid said matter-of-factly, "I'm an orphan...that's how I was able to join up so early. I was raised in an orphanage just outside of Albany...in New York."

"So that's how you managed to pull it off," Bosco said, amazed.

"Pull what off," the kid replied innocently.

"How you got into the Corps so early," Bosco answered.

"Oh...that. Yeah, I guess I am a little young. The lieutenant doesn't seem to mind though. I just didn't think anyone really cared. Anyway, the nuns that ran the joint where I was knew the recruiting sergeant in town...and they told him I'd make a good marine. Maybe they knew somethin' that I didn't...or maybe they just wanted to get rid of me early for some reason...but I never gave them no trouble. I liked them in some ways...since most of them were kind to us...but some were hard on us too. They were a lot like our drills at Parris Island now that I think about it. Even so, I would've liked to have had parents though...but I never did...so nobody'll have to know how I got it. Don't worry about that part of the deal."

"But I'll know...and I don't want to have to tell my grandkids about two guys that ended up being killed by the offspring of Mother Nature, okay."

"Deal," the kid said thoughtfully...and neither man spoke again until their Higgins boat was heading towards the reef.

Neither Corporal Bosco, the kid, nor anybody else in the Higgins boat with them from the 3rd Platoon, C Company, First Battalion, 8th Regiment had any idea what they were about to face as their landing craft suddenly changed course and headed south...its bow now pointing directly at the island...and more specifically... at the Red 2 Beachhead. All they knew was that they had been crammed into a Higgins boat for the last seventeen hours...and that their nightmare was almost over. Every one of them had already thrown up...some more than once...as the boat had continued to rock up and down and then roll side to side for hours on end. Some of the men had even tried to urinate over the side...but this had proved to be an exercise in futility...so they gave up the effort. The only bright spot had been when the minesweeper, the USS *Pursuit*, had pulled up beside them in the middle of the night. In an act of kindness, the swabbies had offered to shuttle over coffee to them…which they gladly accepted. They had refused the offer of food, however, since most of them were still seasick…and the thought of eating food only made them feel worse.

The men in Bosco's boat had let out a resounding cheer when word finally reached them that the landing was on…just like the marines did in the other twenty-five boats that comprised the 1-8 landing team. And then their coxswain had deftly maneuvered the boat into its proper position in the first assault wave…which was a place of honor…or so Bosco said.

"Keep your eye on that control boat over there," Bosco yelled over the engine noise. "That's one of the control boats that are assigned to shepherd us in. It'll send a signal to let us know when to start in. The other one is at the other end of the line. They're job is to keep us in line and on track."

The kid looked over the gunwale and spotted the Higgins boat Bosco was talking about…and he could tell that it looked slightly different from the one they were in…and he asked why.

"Those two Higgins boats are much faster than the ones we're riding in. Their bow ramps were welded shut…so they can't drop 'em…and their sides are a little lower…to reduce their weight. They gotta be able to race around like greyhounds to keep us goin' where we're supposed to go."

"Wow," the kid said, obviously impressed. "How do you know all this stuff about them? The guys manning them are Navy guys…sailors, right?"

"Yeah, they're swabbies. I met one of their officers while I was eating up on deck one night. It was way too hot in the mess down below...and I took my chow up on deck...where it was a little cooler. I guess this Navy officer had the same thing in mind...since he was eating a sandwich right next to me. Well, we got to talkin' and the whole time I'm thinkin' that I recognize this guy from somewhere. And even though he's an officer and all, he's not pulling any kinda rank on me. He's just talkin' to me man-to-man...which doesn't always happen with officers...whether they're in the Navy or the Marines."

"I ain't never talked to no officers," the kid replied, "other than our platoon commander...and even that ain't too often."

"Well, then this other officer comes over...another lieutenant...and the guy I'm talkin' to introduces me to him. He says, 'Lieutenant Flethcher here is my CO,' and he sticks out his hand and I shake it. Then he says, 'And who do I have the privilege of talking to?' So, I pipe right up, 'Corporal Tom Bosco, sir. I'm a squad leader with the Third Platoon of C Company.' And he says right back, 'Well, nice to meet you, Corporal Bosco. Me and my friend here are going to be leading you boys into the beachhead when we get to Betio. I'm the Boat Group Commander and the man you were talking to prior to my arrival is Lieutenant Eddie Heimberger. He's my salvage boat commander. If any of your boats break down or get hit on the way in, Eddie here will be over like a jack rabbit to help you out. If you need repairs, he'll repair it...or if you need refueling, he'll refuel you. And if you need rescuing, Eddie, here is going to be your lifeline. But you probably know him by his stage and acting name, right.' And I say right back, 'Of course,' even though I don't. And then he sticks out his hand and goes, 'Nice to meet you, Corporal Bosco, I'm Eddie Albert.' That's when it hit me...I was talkin' to a Hollywood star! And then he goes even further and says, 'My boat is number thirteen...how's that for luck, right? Just keep an eye out for good old number thirteen if you are in any kind of trouble and I'll do whatever I can to help you out.' And I say, 'Thank you, sir,' and he goes, 'Hey, I'm only a junior grade so don't go overboard with the rank, okay.' And just like that, the two of them take off and head on up to officer's country. Quite a story, huh?"

"Wow...no wonder you know all about them boats," the kid replied, while looking around to see if he could see good old number 13 out there somewhere...but the boat was at the other end of the line from where their Higgins boat was located. "I was gettin' worried that we might get hit on the way in...but I'm not all that worried now. Thanks for tellin' me that story. With Eddie Albert out there lookin' out for us...how bad can things get, right!"

What the kid didn't know was just how bad things were about to get...since the 1st Battalion under Major Lawrence Hays was quickly approaching one of the most well-defended beachheads in the entire Pacific War: Red Beach 2. And the reason it was doing so was

The Butcher's Block

the result of yet another series of the cataclysmic communications breakdowns and miscues that continued to bedevil Major General Smith and his staff well into early morning hours of D + 1. And sadly, it involved his assistant division commander...yet again.

That the 1st of the 8th was finally landing at all was a minor miracle in itself...since the Division Staff had already scheduled it to land two times before that. But neither of those landings had taken place...since the orders to carry out the landings never reached anyone of consequence to make them happen.

The 1-8's first landing had been drawn up during the afternoon hours of D Day itself...and it had been born out of desperation...since Major General Smith and Colonel Edson were so worried about the future of the two battalions under Major Jim Crowe on Red Beach 3.

Despite the spotty communications coming in from the beaches, Smith and Edson still had a pretty good sense of how bad things were all across the island on D Day morning. At one point, a message came in from an unidentified sender that stated bluntly: *Have landed. Unusually heavy opposition. Casualties seventy percent. Can't hold.* And then, at around 1330 hours, both Smith and Edson had listened in on two radio transmissions that came in from the Red 1 beachhead. Both messages painted a dire picture of the precarious toehold that the marines had curved out on Red 1...and they summed up the seriousness of the conditions ashore. The first message came in from Major Schoettel's air liaison officer. He was riding in the same Higgins boat as Schoettel was and his message stated succinctly: *Cannot land because of heavy fire.* And the second message came shortly thereafter. This one was from Major Schoettel himself, and it was just as depressing: *CP located on back of Red Beach One. Situation as before. Have lost contact with assault elements.*

At this point, Major General Smith....known for his gentlemanly and scholarly demeanor...lost his control. Grabbing the microphone from the petrified Navy radioman, General Smith addressed Major Schoettel directly...trying to light a fire under his subordinate commander. He stated in no uncertain terms: *Direct you land at any cost, regain control your battalion and continue the attack!*

Then he turned to his taciturn chief of staff and barked out, "Edson...where's Hermle located?"

"He's on the *Monrovia*, sir," Edson shot right back.

"Get a message to him right now. I need him to get in there and find out just what the hell is going on. Tell him to find Shoup's CP and figure out if Shoup is in over his head. He's a good man. But we may have put more on his plate than he can handle now. From the way it looks, we may need to put two more battalions ashore to stabilize the landings. That's two more to deal with than the original three that we first gave him. Plus, I need to know if we can hold on to Red One and Red Two with what we already got...or do we need to start thinking about getting the Sixth ready too. And I'm deeply worried about Red Three as well. Crowe will do everything

The Butcher's Block

he can to hold on to it...but that's the area where the Japs will hit back first."

Colonel Edson continued to listen attentively to the general...but while doing so, he subtly nodded to another officer who was standing in the wings. This man caught the nod and dashed out of the room without saying anything. "I agree completely, sir. I think the Japs will mount an attack from the tail end of the island, too. Shibasaki's not gonna sit by idly and let us take this island from him without putting up a fight. And that's where he's got the most men probably...since we haven't hit him there yet. Crowe...even with Rudd backing him up...could be overrun if we don't do something fast."

"Exactly," General Smith replied, "so get the staff working on getting the First of the Eighth ready. Let Colonel Hall know as well...so he has a head's up, too. With all the communications problems we're encountering, the sooner he knows the better."

"We'll send the orders out right away, sir," Edson answered confidently. Then he added, "I'm thinking that the best place for the First of the Eighth to go in is along the tail somewhere. Do you agree, sir?"

"It's just what I was thinking. We must do it there. That's the only way we will be able to take the pressure off Crowe...God bless him."

"I do want to point this one important aspect out though, sir. If you don't mind," Edson asked permissively.

"You've got the floor, colonel," Smith answered right back, "I count on your input at all times. Helps keep me honest, right," the general said agreeably. Everyone knew that the two men had a great working relationship...that each man complimented the other...and that they made a great team as a result.

"Thank you, sir, I appreciate that. Here's what I'm thinking. If we send the First of the Eighth in there...if we have them hit the tail...which I think is the correct decision...we do run the risk of losing them too...maybe more so. The other battalions have taken tremendous casualties getting in...but at least they had one another for support...if nothing else. The Eighth will be hitting that tail all alone though. With nobody on their right or left for help. It could be another blood bath. Are you ready to accept those losses...if it plays out that way?"

The general was silent for a while...thinking about the implications of the decision he was about to make. Then he said crisply, "I am, colonel. War's a nasty business. Lives are lost...sometimes in vain, even. But I believe this move must be done. It may cost us the lives of all the men in that battalion. But if we don't do it...if we just sit around waiting for a better...safer...opportunity elsewhere...that decision could cost us, too. I am making this decision, as tough as it is, because I think, in the end, that it may save the entire operation. If the Japs hit Crowe with any kind of force...and he caves...well, then they could just keep going and chop us up piecemeal as they head down the northern coastline. It must be done."

"And so, it will be, sir," Edson said emphatically...the admiration he felt for his commanding general never greater.

The Butcher's Block

"Pack your sea bags," Brigadier General Hermle said confidently to the men gathered around him. "We're heading in. I just got an order from the General Smith. We're to go to the island and contact Colonel Shoup. The general needs some eyes and ears in there to find out just what the hell is going on. This will be a short trip...hopefully...so I will be taking only a small contingent with me. The rest are to stay here...on the *Monrovia*...and monitor the radios and continue to pass whatever messages you receive from the beaches on up the chain."

"Who will you be taking with you, sir?" one of his staff members asked, hoping he'd be picked.

"I'm going to take you, Paul, and Tom, too," the brigadier said, "I knew you'd wanna be part of my little expedition. Am I right?"

"I wouldn't miss it for anything," Major Paul Millichap, the division's ordinance officer replied eagerly.

"Or me," Captain Tom Dutton, a supply officer chimed in...and both men shook hands...celebrating their luck at getting picked for such a great assignment.

"If I have to spend one more second on this miserable rat magnet, I just might kill myself...and save the Japs the trouble," Major Millichap threw in...just in case his boss was thinking about changing his mind.

"Well, you probably won't have to worry about rats when we get ashore...just land crabs. Can you handle those?" the brigadier joked, enjoying the camaraderie of the moment.

"Paul's already killed about five rats on the *Monrovia*, sir," Dutton chimed in, "so those crabs better watch out!"

"And one of those rats was so big, I think it might have been the ship's mascot, for all I know!" the major added, spreading his arms out wide to show how big the rat had been.

"I certainly hope not, Paul. All I need is to have the captain of the *Monrovia* waging a complaint against me… or against one of our marines who are aboard his lovely ship. Up until now we've had a wonderful relationship with these guys…even though they are Navy and all. General Smith will jump down my throat if that firebrand Harry Hill finds out about it…and I've managed to keep my nose clean all these years…which is why I made brigadier. Don't go messing up my winning streak," the general warned easily.

"Is Admiral Hill that bad?" Millichap asked, suddenly concerned that the rat elimination program he had waged so effectively aboard the ship could end up having some unforeseen and unwanted repercussions.

"They call him 'Handsome Harry' to his face… but behind his back…he's called 'Blowtorch' since he's scorched more than one junior officer who bucked him," the brigadier shared.

"Oh, boy," was all Millichap could eke out.

"Well, you'd better get used to standing before the mast, Paul," the brigadier continued, "since you're married now. Colleen is one tough cookie…just like my wife is…and you'll be on the receiving end of more than one ass-chewing…so get used to it."

"I'll remember that," the major said astutely…and he smiled at the memory of his wedding on New Zealand. He had met and married his wife, Colleen, in July. It had been a whirlwind affair and Paul was still beaming over being so lucky that the wedding had been approved so fast. He had Brigadier General Hermle to thank for that...and the brigadier had been an honored attendee at the wedding as a reward.

"Well, enough small talk, gentlemen," the brigadier said, clapping his hands. "Let's mount up and do what we've got to do. I got this message at thirteen-forty-five...and I want to be on that island by fifteen hundred...at the latest. General Smith isn't someone you want to keep waiting. I hope you had your lunch... since I doubt we'll have much time to eat anything over the next few hours. We're gonna be real busy," he added.

"Aye aye, sir," both Dutton and Millichap sang out in unison...and they dashed below to gather the weapons and gear they would need for the journey ahead.

"We've got a problem," Colonel Edson said dryly.

"What now," General Smith murmured...the bad news seemingly endless. He glanced over at the ship's clock and it indicated 1700 hours...the afternoon almost over.

"We just got a report from that Kingfisher we sent up earlier...to keep tabs on the Eighth. Well, the pilot was over the island...and he's reporting that a unit was in the process of landing along the pier at 1548 hours. He thinks it was the First of the Eighth," Edson replied evenly.

"Is he sure," Smith demanded.

"Who's sure of anything out there today, sir. He's claiming it was in his radio message...and that is all we have to go on for now."

"But how could that happen? No one ordered them to land yet...least of all along the pier. Our plan has them hitting the tail at 1745...which is forty-five minutes from now. And then they were going to attack westward...to link up with Crowe...just like we talked about. Is Hayes just freelancing now...landing where he sees fit? Have we lost total control of this operation? Does Colonel Hall know about this? What does he have to say?"

"We've queried him, sir, but so far we haven't received anything back from him. As far as we know, he's still on the *Monrovia*...so he should know something. It's just these damn radios...nothing seems to be working out there. I'm keeping a detailed log of all the radio problems we have run into out here...and I'm going to see if I can't get to the bottom of what caused it. It'll all be in my report. I'll have it ready by the time we reach Pearl... after the whole operation is wrapped up."

"That's fine...but it isn't any help to us right now," the general seethed.

"I know that, sir. The boys are doing everything they can to bring order to the chaos that seems to be part and parcel of everything that is going on out here. Damndest thing I've ever seen."

"So, what can be done about it...now...while the pan's in the fire?" the general demanded.

"We've got them plotted on our maps now...right by the pier...where the Kingfisher pilot saw them go in."

The general leaned on the table on which the large map of Betio Island had been laid. It had several colored markers on it to indicate the different units and their locations on the island. He studied it carefully... and saw that there were now six battalions operating on Betio. This meant that there should have been nearly six thousand men ashore...if the operation had gone smoothly...which it hadn't. How many men were actually on the island was still a mystery at this point...given all the casualties...but there were certainly way more than the original plan had called for. And thus, he made his decision. "Have we heard from Hermle yet? He must have made it to Shoup's headquarters by now. It's been over four hours since I ordered him over to the island."

"Nobody's heard from him either," Edson said tiredly, the constant flow of bad news slowing him down as well.

"Well, get a message to him. I want him to set up the Division Forward Command Post on the island itself now...and to take command of the fight. I love David Shoup...but he's not trained to handle six battalions. Plus, Colonel Hall has probably landed with the First... and he outranks Colonel Shoup by a good twenty years. That'll cause some problems too...so let Hermle take over the reins for now. Let's see what he can bring to the party, no?"

"I'll send out the message immediately, sir," Colonel Edson replied...and he walked away...the general still staring at the map of the island…and shaking his head in disbelief.

"Has General Smith been appraised of what Colonel Shoup needs?" the brigadier was shouting to be heard. He was crouched at the end of the pier and talking to a marine officer who appeared to be in charge.

"Your guess is as good as mine, sir," the officer answered casually. Then the two men ducked again… as machine gun fire hit the wooden boxes that were stacked in haphazard fashion near the end of pier.

The brigadier pointed to the major and the captain who were beside him and he said, "These two men just came back from the island…and it seems that Colonel Shoup is asking for more ammunition and water. Are you telling me that you don't know that as well?" Hermle then pulled the major over and said, "Tell him, Paul."

Major Paul Millichap was sopping wet…since he and Captain Dutton had just slogged their way back out to the end of the pier. Since the pier was too dangerous to walk on, they had just sloshed though the water alongside it…just like everyone else was doing…the healthy and walking-wounded alike. The two men had stopped for a second near the middle of the pier to let a marine who was pulling a raft loaded with wounded pass by. Both men heard the gentle moaning coming from the raft…the plaintive sounds unmistakable…even out here…where the sound of battle never relented.

The Butcher's Block

Millichap...out of curiosity...had looked over at the raft and he saw sights that would haunt him forever. Some of the men had received nominal wounds...such as a gunshot wound to the leg or arm...and they appeared somewhat normal...a splotch of blood indicating where the wound had occurred. But it was the other men...the more badly wounded...who left a mark on the major. One man had been shot in the face...and his whole cheek and eye on the left side were missing. Some corpsman or his buddy had tried to wrap his head with a dressing...to stem the flow of blood...but the marine was delirious...and he kept pulling the dressing away...which exposed the horrible looking wound. Another man had been hit in his shoulder area...and his whole arm was gone...while another was sitting up...and staring listlessly at the stumps that used to be his legs...as if trying to make them reappear. The worst though was the marine who was lying near the edge. He had been hit in the abdomen...and his intestines had fallen out of him. Someone had pushed the mess back into the body cavity...but they kept falling back out...and the trailing end of them had then fallen over the side of the raft. Millichap watched in fascination as a small school of brightly colored fish swam behind the raft...darting in and out...nipping at the intestines that were dangling in the water. *Thank God I haven't eaten*, was all he could think of as the raft continued on its way...the fish enjoying their evening meal.

Upon reaching the end of the pier, they spied the brigadier immediately...since he was one of the few men who seemed to be doing anything out in the open...instead of ducking under cover.

"The two of us just came back from Colonel Shoup's CP. He says he needs ammo, water, and medical supplies desperately. Forget about everything else for the time being. Just get me more ammo, water, medical supplies is what he kept telling us...over and over so we wouldn't forget it...ammo, water, and meds."

"Has anyone been able to raise the *Maryland*?" Hermle asked the pioneer officer...who had taken over the stevedore duties on his own.

"I have no earthly idea, sir," the officer answered... the frustration in his voice unmistakable. "It's only me out here...and I don't have a radio. These Higgins boats keep comin' in and dumping what they have on the pier and then off they go. I decided to take charge...to see if I could get some of these supplies into the beach. I just keep grapping any empty-handed marine who comes by and I hand him a box of whatever I think is useful. But I'm just one man, sir."

"I understand," General Hermle replied, understanding the officer's plight. Then he turned to Dutton and Millichap and said, "This is where we're needed. I've sent two messages over the radio letting General Smith know that I'm here...and that the pier is under heavy fire. Until I hear otherwise, we're going to camp out right here. This is where we're needed most. It seems Shoup can handle things ashore just fine...if he gets the help he needs. And we're gonna get him that help...and more ammo and water and medical gear...right, boys."

"Yes, sir," Major Millichap and Captain Dutton said together...and the three men began the impossible task

The Butcher's Block

of trying to organize the supplies that kept piling up in the dumping ground at the end of the pier.

"Sir, are you awake?" It was Captain Dutton...and he was shaking Brigadier General Hermle's leg. Hermle was sitting on a small stack of boxes and his back was resting against another pile that had been stacked behind him. There were also boxes piled up on each side, so it resembled a U...with the opening facing the lagoon and the reef beyond. The little fort offered some protection from the constant machine gun fire that laced the area around the end of the pier and from the mortar rounds that had been exploding with regularity for most of the night.

"Yes, I'm awake, Dutton. I was just resting my eyes. It's too noisy for anyone to get any shuteye out here. Whatta you have," the brigadier asked...shaking the cobwebs from his brain. "What time is it?"

"It's oh three hundred, sir. Sorry about the time. But it's important. Colonel Shoup says that he needs the First Battalion, Eighth to land on Red Two tomorrow morning. He said that it is imperative that the First come in along the pier...on the right side. That's the best and only way to get a battalion in here without it getting slaughtered. That's word for word, sir. He's hoping we can get this message out to the *Maryland* in time to make it happen."

"Okay, Dutton, well done," the brigadier said, and added, "this is critical. We've got to get this message through somehow."

Major Millichap looked out into the lagoon and said, "Why don't we hop on a Higgins boat and get over to that destroyer out there. It's gotta have a working radio, no."

"If I could, I'd promote you to lieutenant colonel, Paul," the brigadier said, complementing his brilliant idea.

"I'll hail a boat," Dutton said, joining in eagerly.

"Good. Let's get one over here quickly. The sooner I get that message out, the quicker they can start getting the details of the landing worked up."

But the process of commandeering an empty Higgins boat took time...as everything seemed to in and around the beaches of Betio. Two hours later, the three officers were finally boarding the USS *Ringgold*...the very same destroyer that Private Whitey Thompson...a wounded man from Lieutenant Hackett's platoon...had boarded earlier in the day.

"Are you serious," General Smith stammered...trying to control his temper...which rarely surfaced.

Colonel Edson had just presented the commanding general with a radio message that had come in from the *Ringgold*. "I can't believe it myself...but it seems to be our lot that everything we try to accomplish out here will go for naught," the colonel replied, stifling a yawn.

"So, let me get this straight...have patience with me...cause I'm trying to sort it all out in my own mind...just to make sure I haven't gone batty. We learn from our Talk-Between-Ships communications suite at midnight that the First Battalion is still roaming around out there beyond the reef. And this unit has not...I repeat...has not...made a landing at the pier like we were led to believe. Instead, these guys have been circling around the whole time in their landing craft...which are like bobbing corks out there. And that was nearly sixteen hours ago...since it's now almost zero four hundred in the morning. Are you tracking with me on this so far, Edson," the general said mechanically...without a trace of emotion.

"You've got the timeline down perfectly, sir," Edson responded dryly.

"And now you're telling me that Brigadier General Hermle...who should be running this show...is telling us that Colonel Shoup wants the First of the Eighth to land on Red Two. So, from this message, I'm led to believe several things. First...that Hermle is not running the show...Shoup is."

"Correct."

"Second...that our plan to defend Crowe by attacking the tail is kaput. That's not going to happen...which is what we've been working on for the last several hours. All that meticulous coordination we laid on with the Navy to make this go down has been wasted."

"Again...correct," Edson said...and several staff members who were standing around just looked at the deck...no one wanting to make eye contact with the general.

"And three...now we must drop everything and start working on a plan to get the First into Red Two...like Shoup wants."

"Correct."

"Fourth...It's a little after oh five hundred in the morning and Shoup wants the First ashore by oh eight hundred. Which leaves us about two hours to gin up an effective landing plan."

"Correct, sir," Edson stated deferentially.

"Edson," the general stated firmly.

"Yes, sir," he answered right back.

"Make it happen. Do whatever you have to do...but make it happen."

"On it, sir," Edson replied...now energized...feeding off the general's strength and passion.

"And get Hermle off that damn destroyer and get him over here...now!"

What Major General Smith and Colonel Edson did not know...or the men of the First Battalion either... was that Brigadier General Hermle...in his haste possibly...had neglected to transmit the most important part of the message that Colonel Shoup had conveyed to Captain Dutton. Colonel Shoup stated emphatically that Major Hayes' men were to land on Red 2...which he got right...but what the brigadier omitted...for whatever reason...was that the men were to come in along the pier...where it was proven to be safer. Brigadier General Hermle's message from the Ringgold stated: *0513: From ADC (on RINGGOLD): Shoup desires 1/8 to land on Beach Red Two.* And this simple admission precipitated another dreadful scene on the morning of D + 1.

The Butcher's Block

There was little to do on Corporal Bosco's Higgins boat except wait. The coxswain had done a wonderful job of cutting the throttle at just the right time...so the boat glided right up to the reef. There was a slight bump as the bow nudged the coral outcropping...which was visible now...since the tide had gone out slightly...thus exposing more of the reef than on D Day. "Ramp's goin' down. Get ready to debark," the coxswain screamed... and then all hell broke loose.

—◈—

The first indication that the landing was in trouble was when the boat next to Bosco...the one carrying the kid's friend...took a direct hit the second its ramp hit the coral reef. In a flash, the entire boat disintegrated... along with the thirty-one marines in it. One second there...the next second gone. And then the other boat beside them detonated as well. This time nearly half the men in that boat were killed...while the rest became casualties in one form or another. Thinking their boat was next, the men tensed up as a group...dreading the moment the ramp hit the reef. "Oh, God help us," one marine pleaded, capturing the thoughts of the rest of the men in the boat. Then a melodic sound captured everyone's attention despite the noise of the explosions happening outside the boat. Mesmerized, the men stared at the revolving hand crank near the bow as the chain securing the ramp was let out. A loud smashing sound echoed as the heavy steel ramp crashed into the reef, but thankfully, no incoming shell found the men or the boat. "Let's go! Everybody off," the coxswain screamed from behind his shield...knowing that the boat became an easier target the longer it sat motionless. The marines hesitated for a second or two...but then their training kicked in...and they knew what they had to do. Overcoming their fear, the men jumped into the water beside the boat. Luckily, it wasn't too deep... so the men gained their balance quickly and then they scrambled over the reef. Once in the lagoon, the going became even more dangerous...as the men seemed to be under fire from all four points on the compass.

"Was it like this on Guadalcanal?" the kid asked, stunned by all the violence taking place around him.

"Hell no! The *Canal* was a cake walk compared to this!" Bosco yelled over the noise of the bullets smacking the water around them.

"So, I'm cuttin' my teeth on a good one then," the kid said proudly.

"You're a veteran now, kid," Bosco said, "just like the rest of us, old salts."

"That's good to know, corporal," the kid said, "but I only care what you think."

Bosco looked over at the kid...who looked calm and collected...despite the noise, death, and destruction that was taking place around them. A quick glance back at the reef revealed several more boat explosions...and Bosco watched in horror as six men cartwheeled in the air after their boat was hit by a large caliber shell. "Stay close to me, kid," Bosco warned. "It's gonna get rougher the closer we get to the beach...and no sense for us to get separated after we've made it this far together, right!"

The Butcher's Block

"You point the way, and I'll follow...to hell if necessary," the kid replied...and Bosco marveled at the guts the kid was displaying...despite it being his very first action.

"Okay, kid, just do what I do, and we'll make it in there. If you see me duck, then you duck. If you see me head left...then you head left. If I stop, you stop. Got it," Bosco advised.

"You and me...we make a good team...don't we," the kid said proudly...and the two of them kept on...one dangerous step at a time.

Two battalions of marine infantry - the 2-2 and the 1-2 - had already tried to land in the exact same place on D Day that Corporal Bosco, the kid, and the rest of the nine hundred men of the 1-8 were now heading for...and both of those battalions had met the same fierce resistance that Bosco's battalion was meeting now.

Colonel Shoup was understandably furious...since he had specified that he wanted the 1-8 to land near the pier on Red 2...not several hundred yards west of it. The route the 1-8 was taking took them right into the teeth of the *Pocket*...and Hayes' battalion was paying a dear price for this egregious error.

Shoup and the rest of his staff ashore had tried to lend them aid by planning attacks in two different locations on Red 2...and by having Lieutenant Colonel Rixey's pack howitzers firing in their support...but their efforts...while helpful...were just not enough.

At first light, the remnants of Amey's 2nd Battalion, Second…now being led by Lieutenant Colonel Jordon…had tried to attack southward…away from Shoup's CP…but their attack lacked punch and it quickly stalled for lack of organization and manpower.

At the same time, what was left of Major Kyle's 1-2 attacked southwestward to break away from the beachhead and shore up the 2-2's right flank in the area where the longer northwestern taxiway met the large, main airfield apron at the western end of the island. Unfortunately, Kyle's men ran up against a nest of well-hidden Japanese machine gun teams and their supporting infantry who were defending the taxiway…and this attack petered out as well. In the end, only a small contingent of marines from Captain Maxie William's B Company and Captain William Bray's A Company was able to cross the taxiway…and this group became trapped in the area between the main airstrip and the northwestern taxiway.

So, the First was basically on its own as it tried to land on the Beach Red 2…and a slaughter ensued.

"Let's head left," Bosco advised, "it seems safer!"

"Whatever you think is best, corporal," the kid replied, and added, "you've done a great job so far. Can't say that for the rest of 'em though."

Bosco took the kid's hint and glanced behind him…and saw scattered groups of marines trying to make it in…just like they were. But these groups were taking casualties…since men were keeling over as they got hit…while Bosco's squad had hadn't lost a man…yet.

Bosco, the kid, and the ten others who made up Bosco's squad saw two lines of what looked like little pyramids in the distance…off to their left…and they made for them. What they had spotted were two parallel rows of twenty-five tetrahedrons each that the Japanese pioneers had constructed to impede any tanks from getting ashore in that area near the pier. The two lines were about a hundred yards long each and about one hundred yards to the right…or west of the pier. A gap of nearly one hundred yards separated the two rows…and most of the objects were exposed at this point…since the water was only about one foot deep there. Each tetrahedron was made of concrete… so it wasn't going anywhere…and they were about three feet wide at the base and three feet tall…but it tapered off to only a foot wide near the apex…which made the top appear pointy. The same configuration…only much longer…was laying off the entire southern half of Green Beach…and a single line of them shielded almost the entire southern coastline as well…except for Black Beach 1 and 2…which were located along the southwestern corner of the island. The little pyramids had not been visible on D Day…when the tide was higher…but they were exposed now since the tide had receded during the early morning hours of D + 1.

Bosco picked out one near the middle and knelt behind it. As the others came up, he yelled out, "Spread out! Don't bunch up! We'll wait here for a second or two… to catch our breath…and then we'll head up to that next line up there. We'll wait again…just to see if one of those Jap machine gunners has us in his sights. If the way is clear…then we'll try to reach that sunken tank lighter next. That seems to be some type of gathering spot," Bosco said, planning their moves in advance.

Bosco's assistant squad leader, a marine from Southern California, and a corporal like Bosco, nodded that he understood...and then his head exploded...leaving a pulpy mess on top of his shoulders. The rest of the man's body fell forward and hit the tetrahedron with an audible thud. Then it slid down the pyramid...leaving a reddish smear of blood in its wake...and fell into the water. The water turned a pinkish color immediately and the men looked terrified...since he was the first of their group to get hit...and to die for that matter.

The kid watched the scene without a trace of emotion...neither fear nor revulsion at the grizzly sight that took place within with an arm's length of where he was kneeling. "I heard that bullet zing right past my ear," he said to Bosco, who was right beside him, and then added coolly, "I can't believe it got him and not me."

Bosco looked at the kid with amazement once more... and then replied, "You don't hear the one that gets ya, kid."

"Then I sure hope I keep hearin' 'em pass me by... so long as they don't hit anyone else, that is," the kid answered back, his confidence never wavering.

Corporal Bosco sensed the timing was right and he said to the others, "Okay, let's make for that next set of tetrahedrons. Everybody ready," and he dashed off without waiting for an answer...with the kid not far behind him. Both men made the hundred-yard trek safely... and they splashed down behind another set of concrete pyramids. But none of the others had followed...their fear getting the best of them now. The other nine men had remained where they were...the one-hundred-yard gap looking like a thousand yards to them now.

They had just watched one of their own get hit...and killed in a horrible way...and it had affected them significantly...even more than Bosco thought it would...and his men were frozen in place...unwilling to move.

Bosco glanced back, saw what was happening, and said to the kid, "Stay here. I'm gonna go back and light a fire under their butts. This type of thing happened on the *Canal* every once in a while. Don't worry...they just need some encouragement...and if that doesn't work... then I'll put a boot up their butts. Sometimes that's what it takes."

"Who's worried," the kid shot back as Bosco slogged his way back to the first line of tetrahedrons.

Bosco could see the terror in their faces as he approached them, but that wasn't going to deter him. He knew what he had to do. This time he stood in the open though, knowing that a show of bravado goes a long way in these situations. "Men," Bosco barked out, "I know you're scared. That's perfectly alright. Everyone is out here. But we got our duty to perform...and we are marines...which makes us better than any fighting force in the world. And the rest of those guys comin' in after us need us to get in there and go toe-to-toe with those Jap bastards and kill them. Now who's comin' with me? Lemme see a show of hands!" The corporal looked hopefully from man to man... letting his eyes settle on each one for a brief second...and then...slowly but surely...he got the response he was hoping for. First one man...then the next...and then two more...and then the last five all put their hands in the air.

"That's the marine spirit, boys!" Bosco shouted...and this time the rest of the squad made the trek over.

It took a while, but Bosco and his ten-man squad finally made it ashore...a miracle given how many other squads had taken severe losses...in some cases nearly sixty percent or more. Coming in near the boat basin, Bosco pointed to several vacant foxholes and told his men to jump in...since they were exhausted from their journey. "Sit tight," he said, "I'm gonna see if I can find someone in charge who can point us in the right direction." Looking around, he spotted two men sitting in a foxhole all alone...about sixty yards down the beach to his right...on the beach side of the seawall...and one of them was waving him over. "I'll be right back," he added, "make sure you're all here when I get back. I don't want any souvenir hunting!" On the way over to them, Bosco noticed scores of marines just lying around...apparently just as tired as his boys were. Several bullets passed by...the high-pitched *ziiinnnggg* sound unmistakable...so a Jap sniper was obviously still alive somewhere in the area...but none of the shots hit him and he made the quick trip over unscathed.

"How are things," Bosco said happily to the two men...and both slid over to give him a spot to sit down inside the foxhole.

The Butcher's Block

"You won't last very long out there," one man said dryly. "That Jap sniper isn't the greatest shot, but he gets someone every once in a while, so I'd climb in if I were you."

"Thanks for the invitation," Bosco said, jumping in.

"I'm Bob Sherrod...and this is Bill Hipple...we're both combat correspondents," Sherrod said, extending his hand.

"And I'm Tom Bosco. I'm a squad leader in C Company...First of the Eighth. Nice to meet you guys," Bosco replied, taking his hand...and then shaking hands with Hipple as well. "So how goes it," Bosco asked, the introductions over.

"Not good, I'm afraid," Sherrod said sadly, "this is worse...far worse than yesterday!"

"I came in with the Second of the Second yesterday," Sherrod explained, "and it's been hell all along. But watching you guys get shot to pieces was hard to take."

"Tell me about it, bub. That was the longest seven-hundred-yard-long walk I'll hopefully ever make in my life. I lost my assistant squad leader out there. Had his head blown off."

"What was the man's name?" Sherrod asked, taking out a notebook from a kit bag he had beside him. "Johnny Cook. He was a corporal."

"And where was he from," Sherrod said, writing the man's name into the book.

"Temecula, California. I've never been there...but Johnny said it was beautiful."

Sherrod wrote that down too...and then he asked Bosco if he had any more casualties.

"No, that's it. We only lost one man making it in."

"You were luckier than most," Sherrod said, and pointing out to the reef, he added, "take a look."

Bosco glanced over his shoulder and took the visage in...and it was truly horrible. Closest to them, laying in the shallows were a group of marines who had been shot down coming in on D Day. They hadn't made it all the way to the beach though...and their bodies had lain in the surf all night long. They were still holding their rifles...as if they were going to use them...and they had started to sink into the sand...which was now covering most of their lower bodies.

The grim scene reminded the corporal of pictures he had seen of the scores of Japanese soldiers who had been killed during the battle of the Tenaru River on Guadalcanal...the first big battle the marines had fought there. The pictures...taken by the marines the following morning...showed hundreds of Japs laying in their death poses along a sandbar that they had used the night before to attack the marine lines. During the night, the tide had run out however, and in doing so, it had pulled the Jap bodies deep into the sand. In some places, only heads were showing...while others had just a head and shoulder sticking out of the sand. It looked like the earth had tried to gobble up the Japanese dead...and the pictures had left a lasting impression on Bosco.

Now the same grisly scene was playing itself out all over again...only this time it was the marines who were being gobbled up by the beaches of Betio as the tide had gone out.

Further out, scores of marine dead were now laying fully exposed on the dry coral flats. The day before these men had been laying in nearly three feet of water...but the water level had dropped so significantly that these dead were now visible...for all to see. "There must've been over three hundred dead men out there when dawn hit this morning...and you guys must have added something like another two hundred more to that total," Sherrod stated coldly.

"What about all these other guys I saw lying around in the sand as I came over here," Bosco asked, sounding kind of aggravated. "Are they wounded...just takin' a break...or what?"

"Dead too," Sherrod answered quickly, "just as dead as the ones out there on the shelf."

"All of them are dead?" Bosco asked skeptically.

"As dead as they're ever gonna be. The wounded are being patched up as quick as possible...by the corpsmen and docs alike...and they get taken out on the rafts or anything else that they can get in here that'll float. The wounded are long gone...those men in the sand are definitely dead."

"My God," was all Bosco could reply.

"I never thought I'd make it in alive to be honest with you," the combat correspondent Sherrod revealed. "It was so bad yesterday. Coming in along the pier is what saved me. And the first thing I see is a dead marine laid out next to an amtrac. Welcome to Betio, right. Well, who do I run into but Major Crowe. Old Jim was as cool as ice. Never saw the man get flabbergasted…not once. And guys were being shot down all around him. Then I worked my way over here late in the afternoon. And I ran into Bill on the way. We had a reunion of sorts…just happy to see one another alive…much like you marines do when you link up with guys you thought were lost."

Hipple, following the chronology, nodded in agreement. "I was right beside Lieutenant Colonel Amey when he got it yesterday morning. Machine gun opened up on us. It killed him about fifty feet from the water. He was so close to getting in. Whatta shame. Everybody liked him. I figured Bob knew where he was going so I stuck with him. And here we are."

Seeing that Hipple was finished, Sherrod continued, "Then I run into some guys…a mortar crew…and I asked them where I could find the headquarters for the Second…and they pointed right over there…to that foxhole. So, I head over there…and there is Colonel Jordan and two staffers sitting in the foxhole…just underneath the seawall…for protection. I asked the colonel if Major Rice…the battalion XO…had made it in but he said he hadn't seen hide or hair of him…nor anybody else. Jordan thought he might have been knocked off too…or possibly wounded. In any event, they handed the whole rotten package to him...even though he's just an observer...and nobody knows who he is. Talk about a raw deal!"

"So, that's the Second Battalion's HQ...right over there...in that foxhole?" Bosco asked.

"Yup...the one surrounded by all the runners and radiomen...that's it," Sherrod acknowledged, pointing to the foxhole just fifty feet from where they were sitting.

"I'll be...I wonder where the First of the Eighth is going to set up...if Major Hays does make it in...that is," Bosco murmured.

"Probably somewhere around here...at least initially...I'd think," Sherrod postulated, "since Colonel Shoup is set up just inland of here too...over by that big pillbox just a little way inland from here."

Corporal Bosco stood up to look over the seawall and said, "Oh yeah, I see it."

"Don't stay upright too long, buddy, trust me," Sherrod warned...and just like that a shot went whistling by. "Told ya so," he said.

"They're in the trees," Hipple theorized. "Only way they could see us down here." And he pointed to various trees still standing in the wood line up front. Most of their tops were still covered in palm fronds so the theory was possible. "Several guys have come by claiming they killed snipers hiding up in the tops. They said the Japs are tying themselves in, so they won't fall out when they're shot. That way they can be a disturbance even after they're dead, I guess. Crafty little devils," Hipple added.

"The Japs did it on the *Canal* so why wouldn't they do the same thing here. They don't seem to mind sacrificing themselves if they can kill one officer. I guess they figure our officers are just as important as theirs are."

"Makes sense," Sherrod said.

"Let's hope nobody tells them the truth though. Let 'em keep targeting the officers…that's what they get paid for, right," Bosco said…and his comment caused all three of them to begin laughing…which was a nice break from all the sadness they had witnessed recently.

The sounds of aircraft engines suddenly drew their attention skyward…and away from the macabre scene on the flats and along the beach in front of the seawall. Looking up, the three men could see several F6F Hellcat fighters in the distance…winging over. Their target was the British Government-owned *Niminoa*…the interisland tramp steamer that had been run aground on the reef by its master, Edward Harness, after the Japanese invaded the Gilberts. When the Japanese found the *Niminoa* scuttled, they had blown its oil tanks up as a way of preventing the few whites who were left from escaping the atoll. But Harness outfoxed them by hiding his sextant and a small, twenty-foot motor launch from the inquisitive eyes of the invaders. And when they left to inspect some other islands, Harness and several others…including a young British RAF pilot named Luke Howarth…made their escape. In an incredible display of seamanship, the group sailed their way to the island of

Suva...some thirteen hundred miles away to the south... and freedom.

<hr />

Pilot Officer Howarth was from Liverpool, England... and he had become an ace during the Battle of Britain... having downed five German ME-109 fighters and one twin-engine Heinkel HE – 111 bomber in air-to-air combat. Looking for more adventure, he had volunteered for duty in the Far East in late 1942. His request had been accepted...since there was a pilot shortage in that theater...but...to his chagrin...he was assigned to fly Consolidated PBY Catalinas out of Port Moresby, New Guinea. He took the change in stride...which was his nature...and made it work...since he was still flying... which he loved to do. His new duties included searching for Japanese surface vessels that were operating off the north coast of New Guinea...and looking for Allied service members...both pilots and seamen alike...who were lost at sea.

Howarth had flown close to fifty missions before his luck finally ran out, however. On the outbound leg of a long reconnaissance mission to the northwest, his plane lost not one...but both...engines...and he was forced to ditch the plane in the ocean. Sadly, his copilot and nose gunner were killed in the crash...but five other crew members were lucky...and they made it out alive. Unfortunately, only one life raft had been salvaged though...so there was little room for the six survivors...two of whom...the radio operator and the navigator…were severely wounded. Lost at sea with little hope of rescue…the men eventually lost hope…except for Howarth.

The first two men to die were the ones who were badly injured…the lack of fresh water and their wounds conspiring against them. That they had lasted that long…thirteen days…was a miracle in itself. And then one of the waist machine gunners had given up. He decided to drink seawater to quench his thirst…and within several hours he had gone crazy. He dove off the raft that night…saying that he had seen an ice cream parlor below them. The last thing he mentioned before he left was that an attendant was serving scoops of ice cream to whoever wanted some…for free…and he wanted to get some…so off he went.

The next one to go was the ventral…or belly…gunner. He simply gave up the fight…and Howarth and the flight engineer had found him lying dead in the raft as the sun broke over the horizon a few days later.

Several uneventful days had passed by after that…with Howarth and the flight engineer existing on no more than rainwater and an occasional flying fish that inadvertently landed in their raft. And then, on the twenty-eighth day…horror hit…when the flight engineer was taken. He had been exhibiting malarial-like symptoms for a few hours…and at one point, he leaned over the side of the raft…to retch up what little fish was still inside his stomach.

Then, out of nowhere, a large shark had lunged up and grabbed him. The shark's razor-sharp teeth sank into the flight engineer's shoulder and the beast simply dragged the weakened man out of the raft. The shark was probably a tiger...since a school of them had been trailing the raft for quite some time. But it was also big enough to have been a great white...and it had happened so fast that Howarth never got a good enough look at it to identify it with any amount of certainty.

The flight engineer screamed in agony as he tried to fight the monster off...but all his efforts failed... and the shark eventually won out...pulling the man completely under...never to be seen again.

Pilot Officer Howarth was now all alone...and though he felt like giving up a times...he never did. Instead, he occupied his time by thinking about two key topics: his family back home...where his wife and two boys were waiting for him...and about all the wonderful meals that he had eaten over the years.

Those thoughts kept him going...and on day thirty-one his prayers were answered. Unbelievably, his raft had drifted hundreds of miles to the northeast...and he landed on a small island in the Tarawa Atoll. Word of his landing spread quickly through the rest of the islands... and before long...Mister Harness had arrived with his tramp steamer...the *Niminoa*...to pick him up.

Mister Harness and the other Tarawa escapees...which were a mixed bag of British, Australian, and New

Zealand expatriates…went on to become the famed *Foreign Legion*…and they provided the Marine generals and the Navy admirals with keen insight and invaluable information into the tides and weather conditions that the U.S. forces would be encountering when they attacked the Gilbert Islands under Operation Galvanic.

Pilot Officer Howarth returned to flight duty after recuperating from his long ordeal…but he went back to flying fighters…which was his first love all along. He added three more kills to his credit…shooting down a Betty bomber and two Mitsubishi A6M Zero fighters…before his P-40 Kittyhawk was shot down over the northwest coast of New Guinea. He survived this crash too…like he had with the Catalina…and he eventually made his way back to friendly lines with the aid of some head-hunting tribesmen who hated the Japanese more than they wanted to see Howarth's head on their lodge pole. A well-deserved rest followed…and Howarth eventually made his way back to England…where he finished out the war.

"They're after the *Niminoa*…that small, rusting steamer out there to the left of the pier," Sherrod said pointing to the small boat that was resting on a portion of the reef.

"Yeah, they had that thing marked on the maps," Bosco agreed.

"Well, the Japs put men on that boat prior to the landings, and their machine gun fire really tore into us as the first waves came in."

"So that's where that fire came from," Bosco realized. "I thought we were taking friendly ship fire...but now it makes sense. We were getting hit from the right flank...and then from behind when we came in...and it was those Japs on that boat that must've been firing on us. Now it makes sense."

"So, the Japs must've got more men on it during the night. It's still a thorn in the side of the guys coming in so Shoup must've called in the fighters to deal with it," Sherrod guessed.

And he was exactly right.

Up above, Lieutenant, Junior Grade Basnett looked down at the small target and test fired his six fifty caliber machine guns. The bucking of the weapons in the wings told him that they were armed and ready. Up ahead of him, Lieutenant, Junior Grade Eugene Valencia did the same thing and then rolled over on his left wing to make his gun run. Basnett, his wingman, followed closely behind...waiting until the small ship filled his gunsight...and then he pressed the trigger in the stick with the index finger of his right hand. The six fifties exploded all at once...causing the fighter plane to slow somewhat...or so it seemed. The tracers that were mixed in with the regular bullets marked out a phosphorus path that led right into the steamer...starting a small fire aboard the vessel.

"I poured it on that time," Basnett proclaimed proudly over the radio to his flight leader.

"I'm pretty sure I hit something too," Valencia said, and added, "but you got a fire going on your first pass. Good shooting, partner!"

"I went in extra low that time...to make sure I did a good job. Those boys out there in the water are depending on us to help them...and I would've slammed my plane right into that crummy hulk if I had to," Basnett stated forcefully...and Valencia smiled...knowing his wingman would have done just that to help out those desperate marines in the water below them.

The fighter pilots made several more firing runs until their guns were empty...all four hundred rounds in each gun expended...and then they headed back to their ship and home...a job well done.

Within minutes of their leaving, the battleships *Maryland* and *Colorado* fired several salvos from their sixteen-inch main guns and what was left of the *Niminoa* was obliterated...the deadly thorn in the marines' side finally removed.

Before long, Sherrod, Hipple, and Bosco noticed a group of twenty or so marines making their way in from the reef...weaponless.

The Butcher's Block

"Their Higgins boat must've been hit while they were still a good ways off from the reef," Sherrod speculated, staring at the marines drudging up the beach.

"What makes you think that?" Hipple asked.

"None of 'em have any weapons. They ditched them when their boat went down in deep water. You do what you gotta do when that water is over your head and you're sinking fast. Everything that's not tied down gets jettisoned...no matter how important ya think it might be. Survival is a strong instinct," Sherrod explained, his reasoning sound.

As the men got closer, Sherrod yelled over to them, and the leader came over and fell to his knees... exhausted. The other men just laid down in the sand... struggling to catch their breath.

The ominous sound of several mortar rounds arcing in caught everyone's attention...and they all looked up to see if they could spot the incoming rounds above them. Within seconds, four powerful *crummppphhhs* came rumbling in from the left......down by the pier... but the impact was far enough away that they didn't have to worry about being hit by any shrapnel from the rounds.

"That was a mortar...eighty-one millimeter...by the sound of the detonations," Bosco said knowingly. "The Japs used them on the *Canal* a lot."

"Yup. The Type Ninety-Seven. A good weapon. Or it could be one of those seventy-millimeter howitzers they got. Intelligence determined that the Japs had four of 'em on the island. They're wheeled...so they can move them around. Not static...like a lot of their heavier stuff...which is dug in solid," Sherrod pointed out, his tactical knowledge impressing Bosco.

"That would be the Type Ninety-Two...also good...but not as good as the Ninety-Seven," Bosco countered...trying to impress Sherrod now. "Or it could be one of the fifty-millimeter knee mortars the Japs like to use...they have hundreds of them on the island. Intelligence probably didn't inflate those numbers," he added for good measure.

"It's actually a grenade launcher...the M Eighty-Nine...but we call it a knee mortar because it's got a rounded base plate. If a Jap tried to fire it off his knee, he'd end up with a busted leg...since the force would blow his knee threw the back of his pants if he tried to fire it that way." Sherrod was really on a roll at this point...but they had run out of mortars to name at this point. Then he said, "Thankfully, the Japs are low on ammo for whatever the heck they're using on us...otherwise they'd be firing more rounds at us. Since they're not...they must be low on ammo," Sherrod said astutely.

"Why's that?" Bosco asked...not willing to trust Sherrod's intuition just yet.

"With so many marines packed into this tight a spot along the beachhead? I'd be throwing those rounds over every two minutes if I had enough of them to do it. We'd be takin' casualties left and right from those mortars...if they applied them right. It's a deadly weapon...whatever size round is comin' over."

Then the marine who was kneeling got up off his knees and stood up. He wiped his uniform to knock the sand off it and said, "That was one hell of a trip, but we made it."

"Welcome to Betio," Hipple replied, "the choice cabins are spoken for...but we do have some berths available in steerage if you'd like. But if you keep standing up like that...we might have to cancel your reservation."

The sergeant, still standing, glanced around and said eerily, "Snipers?"

"Yup," Hipple replied, "and they love newcomers who stand around in the open...begging to get shot."

The sergeant quickly knelt back down and replied, "We'll take whatever rooms you got, mister. The fee's no problem...so long as you'll take some wet cigars instead of cash money."

"I believe the proprietor of this establishment will accept those terms," Hipple said agreeably...while pointing to Sherrod.

Sherrod then stuck out his hand while the sergeant reached into his shirt pocket and produced two cigars. "We'll have to break them in half so we each get a piece if that's alright."

"I accept your offer," Sherrod said...and the sergeant broke the cigars in half and distributed the three sections to Sherrod, Hipple, and Bosco.

"Thank you," Bosco said, "it's been a while since I had a cigar...even a wet one."

Sherrod, holding one of the halves in his hand, said, "Anything's better than nothing."

"Well, enjoy them while they last. They were my last two," the sergeant said dejectedly.

Sherrod and Hipple put theirs in their shirt pockets…hoping they'd dry out…but Bosco stuck his in his mouth…savoring the taste.

"So, we noticed you guys comin' in," Sherrod stated, "and we were wondering where your weapons were. Wanna share it with us…since we're curious about it."

"Don't mind at all," the sergeant answered unabashedly. "Our boat got hit by one of those guns the Japs got on the tail of the island…at least that's what I think happened. The shell hit the aft part of the boat…and killed the coxswain straight away. Nothin' was left of him…or the stern…and we sank immediately. We were still about a hundred yards from the reef…and the water was nearly ten feet deep when we went over the sides. Only lost one man. I saw him struggling with his pack… like we all were. Everybody else got theirs off…he didn't. I wish I could've helped him. Nice kid, too. Well, when you strugglin' like that…you just get rid of everything… so that's why we came in empty-handed. Nothing more to it than that."

"You were right," Hipple said to Sherrod…acknowledging that his theory was indeed correct.

"Yeah," the sergeant noted, "and then the strangest thing happened. Like I said…we were over a hundred yards away from the reef…and in ten feet of water. Most of us were good swimmers…luckily…but still…ten feet of water is damn deep. So, we're bobbin' on the top…like corks in a bathtub…and we were making good progress. The guys that were havin' trouble were being helped by the better swimmers…and we made it to a point where most of us could finally stand on our own. But we're dog tired. Trying to swim in these uniforms ain't for the faint of heart is all I can tell ya. Then, this Higgins boat comes outta nowhere and stops beside us. I think I'm seein' things...or that I'm dreamin' cause this guy leans over the gunwale and asks if we need help. He wants to pick us up and take us back to the transport. Then he tells me that he's saved a lot of guys that were in the same fix as us. But I told him no, that we'd be real pleased if he'd go back and pick us up some weapons instead. I told him that we were heading in no matter what the cost...that goin' back to the transport was not an option. But we'd be much obliged if he showed up with some rifles and a few BARs. He says okay...and then off he goes...cutting through those waves like a hot knife through butter."

"That was nice of the guy to stop though. He obviously didn't follow through on what you wanted...since you came in empty-handed," Hipple pointed out.

"Well, we didn't really give him too much time to fulfill our request. To be honest, we didn't want to sit on that reef any longer than we had to...since it was like being in a shooting gallery...and we were the targets. So, we hit the reef and just kept goin'. That fella might have come back with a boatload of weapons for us...who knows. But we were long gone by the time he would've gotten back to us."

"So, his boat was pretty fast?" Bosco asked... wondering.

"I'll say. It looked like it was a special Higgins boat that the Navy came up with," the Sergeant replied.

"Did it have a number on it?"

"Yeah...it did," the sergeant said in reply to Bosco's question. "It was number thirteen...which I thought was kinda eerie. Who wants to be running around out here sportin' a bad luck number like thirteen...especially on a day like this," the sergeant answered.

"You know who that was...the guy that was commanding that boat?"

"I know the guy looked familiar somehow...I just can't put my finger on it," the sergeant answered...his face scrunching up in thought...trying to picture the boat commander's face and why it had looked so familiar to him.

"That was the actor...Eddie Albert...you were talking to. He's a Hollywood star. Don't that beat all!" Bosco said triumphantly.

"Well, I'll be...me...talkin' to a big mucky muck like that. I knew I had seen that face somewhere before. I just couldn't place it."

"Now you know," the corporal stated matter-of-factly. "You can tell your grandkids that you met a famous actor in the war!"

"I just might do that...if I make it off this island alive. And I'll make sure I watch more of his movies too...at least the good ones!" the sergeant said...and he ran back to his men to tell them the good news!

Chapter Ten

"I gotta get back and check on my men. It's time we got back in the war...and did some Jap killing...or we'll never get off this island. I gotta locate my company first and let them know we're alive and ready to fight," Corporal Bosco finally said. "It was real nice meeting you guys. I'm glad you called me over. It's nice to know we've got some guys out here who are willing to follow us gyrenes around and tell the people back home what's really happening. Maybe you'll help them understand why a bunch of guys aren't going to be making Thanksgiving dinner anymore," he stated...feeling a genuine admiration for the job the two correspondents were doing...and that they were doing it voluntarily.

"We're glad you stopped by too...nice to get a real mud marine's perspective on things," Sherrod replied...appreciating the corporal's pat-on-the-back complement.

"Good luck, son," Hipple added...and he shook Bosco's hand...as did Sherrod.

"See ya in the funny papers," Bosco joked...and he jumped up and headed towards the pier...where his men were dug in. *I hope they got some shuteye while I was gone*, he thought somberly, *cause things are about to get dicey again...once our CO knows we're alive!*

A strange feeling overcame Corporal Bosco as he made his way back to the pier...which worried him. *This happened to me once before...on the Canal*, he thought. At the time he had brushed it off, but later the feeling returned...a dark premonition of sorts. Other veterans he knew admitted later on...in late night bull sessions back on New Zealand...to having the same types of experiences...and the outcomes had rarely turned out well.

And sure enough...later that night...a marine in Bosco's squad had been killed accidentally...or so they thought at least. The young private in question had acquired a Jap officer's pistol somehow. It was never determined whether he actually found the prized weapon on a dead officer himself...after one of the many engagements that they had participated in...or if it had been given to him by someone else. But the pistol had discharged that night...and the private's body had been found by Bosco the following morning. The private had a gunshot wound to his head...and he was still holding the weapon in his right hand. Bosco had questioned his squad mates about it...but nothing had come of his inquiries. The private had been a likeable kid sure enough...and he had shown no signs of cracking...which led Bosco to believe that it was nothing more than a freak tragedy. And the incident had been dismissed...and...after time...all but forgotten by the other men in the squad. But Bosco remembered it...because of the feeling that had accompanied it. And now he was having one of them again...and he sped up his step... hoping all the while that his instincts were off this time... that nothing would come of it.

"I'm gonna go see what's goin' on up at Shoup's headquarters," Robert Sherrod, the combat correspondent stated to Bill Hipple. "I guess it's time that I got back into the reporting business as well. I can't sit here on my butt all morning. My job is to report...so that's what I'm going to do. Plus, it's what my bosses back in New York are paying me for...and the stories I'm after aren't gonna fall in my lap...so off I go," he added, while looking at the tops of the trees up ahead. "I hope the snipers are distracted," he said, swallowing hard.

"Good luck, Bob," Hipple replied, "and if you don't make it...can I have your kit bag?"

Sherrod glanced down at the plain, green cloth bag he was using to carry his notebook and papers in and said, "This thing?" in surprise.

"Yeah...that," Hipple replied. "I've had my eye on it since we met. Good carrying case. I've been stuffin' my papers in my gas mask case…but it isn't working out so well."

"What did you do with your gas mask," Sherrod asked, patting his own gas mask holder that was dangling around his neck by its strap.

"Oh, I threw it away. Didn't think the Japs were going to be gassing us out here," Hipple replied, his logic making sense to Sherrod now.

"I'm gonna hang on to mine all the same," Sherrod replied, and scrunching up his nose, he added, "if the smell gets any worse around here, I might just put mine on and wear it the rest of the time we're stuck here."

"Stuck here?" Hipple snorted.

"I know…no one stuck a knife in my back and made me come here. I get it…this was all my doing…just like it was yours," Sherrod laughed. "Next time I'm asking for a combat bonus though," Sherrod stated dryly.

"Let me know what those paper pushers back in New York say to that…so I can ask for more dough from my employers at the AP," Hipple joked back…enjoying the banter.

"Well, time's a wastin'," Sherrod said, tapping his wristwatch…and he glanced once more at the treetops. "Ready…set…go," he yelled…and he jumped out of the foxhole and leaped over the seawall and dove behind a log for protection. When no sniper's shot came, he got up and dashed the rest of the way to the CP for Regimental Landing Team 2.

The Butcher's Block

"Welcome aboard," Colonel David Shoup said, recognizing Sherrod immediately. "Things turned out pretty much like I thought they would when we had our discussion back on the *Zeilin*, huh," the colonel added, smirking.

"It looks like you had it pretty much nailed down, colonel. Although we have no way of confirming it, I think your estimate for the casualties the Japs would take as a result of the naval bombardment were right in the ballpark."

"What did I say they were gonna take anyway... refresh my memory."

"You said that the Japs would lose something like seven hundred men out of three thousand to the incoming shellfire. That seems fairly accurate given the amount of fighting that has taken place over the last day and a half."

"Yeah, but that three thousand figure I threw out there was a low-ball estimate. I knew there'd be more here. The five thousand or thereabouts estimate I came up with using the number of latrines the Japs had was far more accurate."

"No one else saw that one, colonel, that's for sure. Counting the number of asses per latrine was sheer genius...if I don't say so myself," Sherrod acknowledged, laughing.

"That kind of logic makes me a good poker player, son," Shoup replied, "and the ability...and willingness to take risks. You'll never find a good gambler that isn't willing to roll the dice at times. You can take that to the damn bank."

"That's why I don't gamble," Sherrod replied somberly, and added, "for a little while...back on D Day...it looked like the Japs had pulled a royal flush right off the top of the deck."

"It did at that...and they made it awfully tough for us...the little bastards...but now it's starting to look like they were bluffing with that flush. Now it's starting to feel like all they had was two pair...and not very high either. We're starting to receive good news from Ryan over on Red One. I hope he can keep it up and capture Green Beach for us. That would really help," Shoup replied...and then a major strode right up and interrupted their conversation.

"Sir," the major begged, "there are a thousand damn marines back there on the beach, and not one will follow me across to the airstrip."

Colonel Shoup just stared at the major...not saying a word. Then it hit him...the officer was the same officer who had come in not long ago...with virtually the same complaint. The last time it had been a single Jap machine gun that was holding up his men's advance... and Shoup had thought his motivational speech had done the trick...since the major had left inspired. But it had obviously lacked staying power...since the major was now back.

Then another officer came over and offered him advice...thinking it might help. "I had the same trouble. Most of them are brave men, but some are yellow." Then he nailed it, saying, "I recall something a very wise general once told me. 'In any battle,' the general said, 'you'll find the fighting men up front. Then you'll find others who will linger behind or find some excuse to come back. It has always been that way, and it always will. The hell of it is that in any battle you lose a high percentage of your best men.'"

Then Colonel Shoup put his hand on the man's shoulder...to steady him...and added, "You've got to say, 'Who'll follow me? And if only ten follow you, that's the best you can do, but it's better than nothing.'"

Like before, the major seemed to buck up...and he thanked the colonel again and left...to mount yet another attack across the taxiway.

"It's not only the privates that need leadin'," Colonel Shoup said, turning to Sherrod, who had watched the whole exchange.

"Leadership's a rare quality, sir," Sherrod agreed wholeheartedly, "and on places like Betio, you really find out who has the gift. There's no mistaking who the real leaders are out here...where it really counts."

Colonel Shoup looked at the correspondent with a gleam of admiration...and then said, "Remind me to never gamble against you, Sherrod. You're too damn smart!"

The scene near the end of the pier was terrible...and it would have stood out anywhere else...except on Betio.

Corporal Bosco lengthened his stride in an effort to reach the end of the pier quicker...all the while hoping that he'd see his men seated where he had left them. As he got closer though, he could not only see...but feel... the desperation of the men up ahead of him. Corpsmen and marines were moving about...lifting debris off bodies that were scattered about...and checking them to see if they were alive. "What the hell happened," he asked a man passing by who was shaking his head.

The man stopped abruptly and looked Bosco in the eye. "What ya think happened? The damn Japs hit us with a bunch of mortar rounds. It looks like they were after that mortar team over there...and they got what they were after. Did you know them?"

"The mortar guys you mean?" Bosco responded.

"Yeah, them," the marine...a gunnery sergeant... answered right back.

Bosco kept looking around the hive of activity, trying to spot his own squad.

"So, did you know those guys...who they were? Or what outfit they were with?"

"No. I'm looking for my own squad. I brought ten ashore with me two hours ago at most...and I left 'em here...to rest up," Bosco replied.

"Well, the Japs had that mortar team targeted to perfection. I guess you lob over enough rounds and one of 'em is gonna get a lucky hit. There were explosions going off everywhere for a second or two. I don't know how many rounds the Japs sent our way. Then, all at once, the whole mortar pit went up in a fireball. One of the Jap rounds detonated right in their hole...blew them and their mortar ammo to smithereens. Nothin' was left of them...or the guys who were unlucky enough to be positioned around them. A bunch of guys were hauled off to Doc Brukhardt's hospital over there. Some of your guys may be there. There's also a bunch of dead stacked by his bunker too...under the ponchos. I hope they're not among them."

The corporal looked over at the bunker that the gunny had pointed to...the one housing Doc Brukhardt's hospital...and he said, "Thanks," as he ran over to see what he could find out.

The inside of the bunker was dimly lit...making it hard to see. Bosco closed his eyes for a second so they could adjust to the darkness...and then he saw them. One of his men was on a stretcher...and he was bathed in blood. The other was being operated on by the doctor himself...and he too was covered in blood...as was the doctor.

Bosco stood fast as the doctor continued to work on his man...watching and hoping that he could save him. Then, suddenly, the doc stood up straight and said, "Take him away, Dempsey. There's nothing we can do for him anymore. He's dead. Give me the next one." His tone was emotionless as he signaled the corpsman, Pharmacist Mate 1st Class Greg Dempsey, to remove the man's body from the piece of plywood that was serving as an operating table. "Come on, let's go," he ordered, "we haven't got all day."

Dempsey, who was worn out too, called outside and two marines ran in and carried the body outside...where it was placed beside several others already there.

Bosco could sense their exhaustion and he could see it in the look of their eyes. Doc Brukhardt, and his chief assistant, PhM1 Dempsey, had been working on badly wounded men for over thirty hours straight and though they were worn out, they weren't giving up.

Two other corpsmen beside the doctor then reached down and lifted Bosco's man onto the sheet of plywood that was laying across two sawhorses so the doctor could get a good look at him. "How you doing, son," Brukhardt asked softly...and the marine smiled and said, "Oh...not too bad, doc. Thanks for askin'. I hope you can save that leg of mine. It feels better than it looks."

Dempsey then leaned over and cut the man's trousers away with a knife...exposing the mangled knee and thigh. Doctor Brukhardt poked around the torn flesh and said, "You're lucky today, my boy. No damage to the artery that I can see...and the bone's intact. I think your wish is gonna come true and you'll get to hang on to this leg of yours."

"Oh...thanks, doc," the man said...and then he made eye contact with Bosco...who was still standing quietly off to the side. "Hey," he said, lifting his arm up to point at Bosco, "that's my squad leader over there."

Doc Brukhardt looked up from his work and nodded to Bosco. "He's one of yours I take it?"

"He is, sir," Bosco answered quickly. "So was the other one...Swales...who just died. He was about as tough a marine as you'll ever find. Everyone was in awe of him…including me. Damn Japs had to use a mortar to get him…only way they coulda done it. I just can't believe the Japs got him."

"What killed him was a piece of shrapnel…and it hit his heart…so there wasn't much I…or anyone…could have done for him. It's amazing that he was even alive when they brought him in," Brukhardt explained.

"His heart…the biggest part of him…that figures," Bosco said.

"Your other man is going to be just fine though."

"Can I talk to him?"

"I don't see why not," Brukhardt answered, motioning the corporal over.

"Hey, Jack," Bosco said…and he grabbed the arm of his friend…Private First Class Jack Harper. "How's it going?"

"Never…better, Tom," Harper eked out over the pain.

The doctor noticed Harper grimacing and said soothingly, "Son, I wish we had some morphine to give you…but it looks like an error was made in the loading process for the ships. Unfortunately, the morphine syrettes were loaded first…instead of last…so it has taken a while for them to be off-loaded. Navy ingenuity, right," the doc said, trying to downplay an egregious error in planning. "But all is not lost," he added, and then he reached down and pulled out a bottle of brandy from a bag underneath the table. "Take a swig of this," Brukhardt said, smiling. "This'll take some of that pain you're feelin' away. It's medicinal brandy…the best thing I've got next to morphine."

The marine looked tentatively at the doc…and then at his squad leader.

"Go ahead and take it, son," the doc said, smirking, "it won't bite you."

"Oh…I'm not worried about that…trust me, sir," Harper answered.

"Go ahead…take it, Jack. You earned it," Bosco said agreeably.

"Well, here goes then," Harper said, taking the bottle from the doctor. He glanced at the bottle, noted its maker, and said, "Good stuff, this. Down the hatch!" He lifted the bottle and took a good swig and then coughed. "Thanks, doc," he said, and he laid back down.

"Can you tell me where the others are," Bosco asked, hoping Harper was in the mood to talk.

"Swales and me were together. Some of the other guys were sittin' around us…just catchin' some shuteye… or resting. Harvey and Stephenson were over with the mortar guys. They were brewing up some coffee…and you know how Harvey loves…loved…his coffee."

"Good 'ol Cryder sure did love his cup of Joe in the morning. I don't think I ever saw him start a day without one in his hand…or when we were training…no matter what the weather."

"And then Stephenson finds out that one of the mortarmen is a bronc rider like himself…from Texas no less. So, the two of them were jabbering away about horses, saddles, belt buckles, and whatever else cowboys talk about. And everything seemed just fine until those shells started hitting all around us. There wasn't any of us that didn't get hit as far as I could tell…and Harve and

Stevey...well...when that mortar pit blew...there wasn't anything left of them."

"The kid...what about the kid...did he get it too...along with the others?"

"I can't rightly say for sure," Harper said, trying to remember if he had seen him get hit.

"Okay, rest easy now, Jack," Bosco said, patting his arm. "I'm gonna check outside and see if I can find anyone else. If I don't see you again...if you get evacked out while I'm gone...you take care. And I'll link up with you after the operation is over."

"There's a plan," Harper replied...and he closed his eyes as Doc Brukhardt began working on his leg.

"I got it from here on out," the doc said to Bosco. "I'll take good care of him."

Bosco nodded his thanks to the doctor...who had quickly turned back to his work...and left the bunker. Turning left, he saw another line of marines who had ponchos draped over them...too many to count. There was a chaplain's aide kneeling among the bodies...and he was praying over them and then removing their identity tags. He glanced up at Bosco and said, "Looking for some of yours?"

"I am...and they would have just gotten here. The mortar attack got 'em," he explained.

The aide pointed to a line of bodies and said, "They'd be among them. They were just brought in."

Bosco walked along the line, pulling the ponchos back from their faces. He found four more of his men there: Yoder, Owen, Long, and McDonald. Each one a warrior...and none of them would be going home. That left two unaccounted for.

The aide stopped what he was doing and looked at Bosco...who had stood back up...a sad look now etched on his face. "Did you find who you were looking for?" he asked softly.

"Not all of them. But I found four. These are mine," he said regretfully, pointing at four bodies arranged in a row. "All good boys," he added somberly.

"I'll say a special prayer for them...if you don't mind," the chaplain's aide...Tom Talley...stated.

"No...go right ahead. They'd like that...since all four of 'em got baptized back on the transport...before we hit the beaches," Bosco revealed. "I guess my squad had a revival of sorts...knowing that this could happen."

"Well," Talley said, "these boys are now in the arms of Jesus...and there's no better place to be. You be careful out there...and God bless."

"Thanks," Bosco said, and he made the sign of the cross over the four bodies...and then he glanced skyward...knowing his friends were now home with Jesus.

The corporal then made his way to the boat slip...where amtracs were pulling in to unload supplies and take the badly wounded out. Bosco looked the group over, and his eyes settled on one man...whose height made him unmistakable. "Casto," he yelled out, and the lanky marine corporal looked back...immediately recognizing Bosco's voice.

Bosco shuttered now...since Casto's face was swathed in bandages...as was his right arm. The corporal rushed over to him...and pulled him close. "Casto, buddy, you made it!" Bosco said happily.

"Hey, Tom," Casto said, sticking his good arm out...feeling for his squad leader. Bosco saw that he was looking over him...which was natural...since he was so tall...but also to Bosco's left...since he couldn't see him. "Looks like I'm headin' home for sure now," the BAR-man stated. "Didn't really wanna give up my sight to get off this island...but it sure beats bein' dead, huh," Casto pointed out.

"Don't worry about those eyes of yours," Bosco replied, "they're probably just sand blasted...and once they're cleaned up...you should be able to see just fine. That's my guess anyway. Those docs back on the transports are miracle workers too...so I wouldn't worry."

"Who's worried?" Casto answered. "Even if my eyes are gone...I'll just get a seein' eye dog and I'll train him to take me on my runs. I saw a guy who had his legs blown off on the way in...and I'll take losin' my sight over losin' my legs any day."

"That's the spirit, good 'ol Casto," Bosco said. "Nothing ever gets you down...that's why the guys love you."

"You just look after yourself. Hopefully, you'll make it through without a scratch," Casto said...and a corpsman came up and led him by the arm to a waiting amtrac.

"Good luck, Casto!" Bosco yelled out as the tall man was helped aboard the amtrac. When the amtrac was finally full, it backed up into the boat slip and then turned around. The driver then pushed the throttle forward, gunning the engine, and it seemed to leap ahead…heading for the transports in the distance. As he waved goodbye to a man who could not see, it dawned on Corporal Bosco that he had forgotten to ask Casto if he had seen the kid…and now he would never know.

Corporal Bosco's mind was racing. *Where is the kid?* he wondered. *Did he get atomized in the mortar explosion along with Harvey and Stevensen? Is that why I couldn't find him?* That was a possibility…sadly…he knew. *Or he could've gotten wounded and been takin' off before I found Casto. That made sense too,* he thought, *since there was no way that Casto could've seen him.* That might have happened too…and he was hoping that's how it had gone down…since it made him feel better. *I just missed him…that's all,* and tired now, he sat down in a foxhole near the end of the pier. He looked up at the boiling sun above and decided to shield himself from its rays…since he was getting sunburned on his neck. Looking around, he found some palm fronds that had been blown off a nearby coconut tree…and he pulled them over himself. *That's better,* he thought, feeling the difference immediately as the fronds deflected the sun's penetrating rays…and he quickly feel asleep.

"Hey, you, get up!"

Corporal Bosco stirred as he felt some sand raining down on him…and he peeked out from underneath the palm fronds. A pair of marine boondockers was all he could see now...and then one of the boots had reared back and kicked some more sand on top of him.

"You, there. In that foxhole. Are you alive?"

"Who the hell wants to know?" Bosco shot back.

"So, you are alive. Well, that's good. What's bad is that you're a coward. Now get out from under there and stand up like a marine...or I'll save the Japs the damn trouble and I'll shoot you myself!"

Who the hell does this guy think he is, Bosco thought? Aggravated now, he threw the fronds off himself and stood up...just like the guy had demanded. But he couldn't make the man out...since he was standing with the sun directly behind him. Even shielding his eyes with his hands didn't work...so he tried squinting. *No luck...but I'm still gonna punch this jerk in the nose and call it a day,* the corporal determined...since this man...whoever he was...had interrupted a pretty good nap.

"That's better," the gruff voice said, and Bosco jumped out of the hole to see who the offender was... before belting him. *Probably some mean-assed gunny...or a freshly barred lieutenant,* Bosco thought, picturing the man in his mind. *And this jerk is gonna find out the hard way that you don't kick sand on a guy who's tired...and sleeping...no less.*

"What were you doing hiding like that?" the man demanded to know.

In an instant, the enormity of the situation hit the corporal. "I...I...wasn't hiding, sir," Bosco stammered, "I was just taking a nap. I was tired...that's all."

Colonel Shoup looked the corporal up and down and determined that the man had answered him honestly. "Tired, huh. Well, we're all tired. But we got a battle to win. And we're not gonna do it taking naps…is that understood. Who are you?"

"Corporal Bosco, sir. Squad leader of First Squad, Third Platoon, C Company…First of the Eighth…sir. We got in a few hours ago, sir."

"I realize that, son," Shoup said, softening somewhat. "Where does your mother live?"

"My mother?" Bosco replied…not sure if he heard the colonel correctly.

"Yeah…your mother…you got one of those don't you? To tell you the truth, I've met some marines in my time that made me wonder if they really did have a mother. Tough bastards…the kind no mother would like."

"Yes, sir. I've got a mother…and she lives back in Staten Island…in New York," the corporal answered tentatively…not knowing where the colonel was going with this line of questioning.

"Staten Island, huh. I know it. Nice place…not really fond of the city though…way too busy for my tastes," Shoup answered.

"I didn't spend much time there…but I know what you mean, sir. The hustle and bustle…it wasn't for me either. I caught a bus outta the bus terminal on Forty-Second Street on the way down to Parris Island. That was good enough for me. I'm more of a country boy myself…even though I'm not from the South."

"You mean rednecks and peckerwoods, right. I'm from Battleground, Indiana and I like the country too. But some of these southern boys in our Corps are pretty damn nasty. You'd think they grew up without running water."

"A lot of them did, colonel," Bosco pointed out...picturing some of the boys in his company.

"Good fighters...don't get me wrong. I wouldn't trade them for anything. I guess I've become too refined over the years. I got too addicted to cigars and fine whiskey. Gotta be careful that you don't get too far away from the guys who actually do the fighting...and dying...which is why I came down here. I wanted to see for myself what the supply situation is like...and check out the aid station. We've got a lot of wounded men I need to see. But back to your mother. Do you think she'd want you crapping out... taking a break...when other men are dying up front?"

"No, sir. She wouldn't. She didn't raise no malingerer."

"I didn't think so. Where's your squad?" Shoup said... shifting gears...and he took the cigar he had been chewing on out of his mouth. He spit a small piece that had broken off out of his mouth and then stuck the cigar back in.

"All dead, sir, or wounded. Nobody's left...except for one I can't account for," Bosco stated...and he dropped his head...the sadness overwhelming him.

"What do you intend to do...now I mean," the colonel pressed.

"I don't know, sir, to be honest with you. I'm kind outta of the game for a while...I guess," the corporal replied...considering it now...for the first time.

"Well, go get yourself another squad," Shoup recommended, "there's plenty of men around here who are just waiting for someone to lead them."

"I don't know how to do it. And where would I find them," Bosco said...but his pleas sounded hollow...and he knew it.

"How and where? Look around. See all these men coming in along the pier. None of 'em have anyone to lead them. They come in and lay down...just like you were...happy to be alive. But they aren't doing me any good. I need men up front...killing Japs...or we'll lose this battle. The Japs have plenty of men left...and bullets too. So, you go over to one...and then another...and you keep going. And you say, 'Follow me.' When you've got a squad together, come up to my headquarters and I'll find a job for you. Deal," the colonel explained, and then added, "I gotta get going. But just remember...you're never out of the fight...you're a marine...and marines fight until their last breath...and then they fight a little more."

"Thank you, sir," Bosco said...and he watched the colonel turn and limp away. He was on his way to go see Doc Brukhardt...and share a good word with the wounded.

True to his word, Corporal Bosco did just that. He went out and found himself a whole new squad to lead...and it didn't take him very long to do it. With so many men coming in along the pier, he had more than enough to pick from...since so many of them had lost their leaders at one level or another. Some had lost squad leaders... others platoon sergeants...and still others their platoon commanders...and some all three...and they didn't know what to do. Within an hour, Bosco had gathered up ten men who were indeed willing to follow him...just like the colonel had said.

"Stay here," Bosco said to his new squad as he approached Colonel Shoup's HQ near the big Jap bunker just inland from the seawall. "I gotta see the colonel for a second," he added...and the guys' eyes got bigger...wondering what kind of pull a mere corporal had that he could walk up to the Landing Team Commander and have a discussion.

Colonel Shoup saw Bosco standing off to the side and went over to him immediately. "How'd it go," he asked...wondering if the squad leader had followed his instructions.

"A piece of cake, sir," the squad leader replied, "just like you said. All of 'em are from my battalion...the First of the Eighth. A few are from my company even...but most aren't. I can work with them anyway. A marine's a marine, right, sir. And now we're looking for a job...just like you said."

"How many did you find back there?" the colonel asked...wondering if the First of the Eighth was in as calamitous a state as he seen earlier along the pier.

"I found ten, sir. Not a whole squad...but ten's better than nothing, right!"

"That is great to hear, son. If I had a few more guys like you, this battle would be nearly over," Shoup said, his compliment sincere and genuine. Then he added, "Now go report in to your battalion commander…Major Hays. He's rallying your battalion just west of here…and I've assigned them the toughest job yet. They're gonna take on the *Pocket*…which has been a thorn in my side since D Day. It's gonna take a bunch of hardcases to break that damn position open…but Hays will have a better chance of doing it now that you're gonna join him."

"Okay, sir. We'll head that way…and we'll do everything possible to crack that nut for you. My mother would expect nothing less," Bosco promised…and he turned on his heel and left as the colonel was pulled away by another officer…to manage yet another crisis…which had become part and parcel of the life of the marine commander on Betio Island.

Chapter Eleven

True to his word, the corporal located his company... and he reported back to his platoon commander... who was still alive as well.

"Glad to see ya, Bosco!" the lieutenant said, beaming. "We thought you were dead."

"Not by a stretch," the squad leader replied, and added, "but I got me a new squad. The rest of my guys were killed or wounded earlier...so I formed a new squad. Do you mind if they stick with me, sir," Bosco asked.

"All dead...all eleven?" Lieutenant Anthony Dobson replied...shocked.

"No, sir. Not all dead. I have two wounded...and one missing. The others are dead."

"Okay...thank God you made it. Sure, you can keep these guys with you for now...since we're getting ready to move out. Are they all from the Eighth?" the second lieutenant asked.

"Yes, sir. All from the Eighth...unless they were lying to me."

"We'll get them sorted out later. Right now, the priority is to get the First moving. We're heading west... towards the area they're calling the *Pocket*. It's about two hundred and fifty yards away from here."

"Aye aye, sir. Just say the word and we'll go wherever you point us," Bosco said...embolden once again.

"We're glad you're back, corporal. I'm sorry about your men," Second Lieutenant Dobson replied...and then he scampered over to another squad to get them ready to go.

The area that Corporal Bosco and his new charges were resting in was just one hundred yards west of Colonel Shoup's CP...and it was just shy of the same ground that First Lieutenant Hawkins and his Scout Snipers had been working to clear the whole morning of D + 1. Shoup had given Major Hays the rest of the morning to rest and reform his battalion there...in relative safety... but by noon they were to move out...and clear the western portion of Red 2.

This was a difficult responsibility...and no small task...since this ground had been relatively untouched since D Day. The entrenched guns of the *Pocket* had prevented any marine units from landing there in force... and thus only a few small attacks...like Hawkins' valiant effort...had been attempted. And very little ground had been taken...since the entire area...as Hawkins and his men quickly found out...was literally honeycombed with Jap bunkers and pillboxes. It would take time and effort to take this ground...as Hays' men would soon find out...and gains would be measured in feet...not yards...as the day progressed.

"Don't do that," Corporal Bosco advised. "These Japs are shooting at anybody that moves...not just the officers."

"But I gotta piss," Private Roger Wieland moaned. Wieland was one of the men the corporal had found along the pier...and he had volunteered to come along the moment Bosco had approached him. Now he was squirming around in the foxhole...obviously distressed.

"Just do it here...in the hole...I don't care," Bosco advised, "but I wouldn't stick my head up like that...you're gonna get it shot off. There are snipers everywhere out here. This is worse than back at the pier. They were just shooting at officers back there...but here the Japs are targeting everybody...rank or no rank."

Wieland was beside himself now...and the longer he held off peeing the worse the pain in his groin got. "I'm not gonna pee right in here...we gotta lay in here...and it's unhealthy."

"Unhealthy...seriously," Bosco replied, not sure if his foxhole buddy was that serious.

"I'm a clean freak...always have been. And I would rather die than lay in my own piss," Wieland forced out...gritting his teeth for extra stamina.

"Well, I won't mind. I rather you did your business in here than out there...and have you get your fool head shot off in the process."

"I can't take it...any longer," Wieland said, leaning over at the waist, trying to squeeze his bladder closed. Then he straightened up and looked out of the foxhole...his head barely visible...to see if he could find a spot that was covered enough to offer some protection of sorts. "That'll do for now," he said, spotting a coconut log laying on the ground with some debris lying all around it.

Bosco watched him raise up just a little bit further... and then his head snapped back as if he had been hit by a punch. Wieland looked over at Bosco for a brief second...a look of confusion etched on his face...and then he fell backwards with a thud. A sniper's bullet had found its way right between his eyes...and the shock of it had caused the private to wet his pants...which was exactly what the fastidious private had been trying to prevent all along.

"Ah, hell," Bosco said sadly, but he didn't call for a corpsman...since he knew Wieland was already dead.

The rumbling of a tank in the distance got the attention of Corporal Bosco's men in a hurry. "Ours or theirs," was the question being asked by most of them...but no one knew for sure. Then...as the tank drew closer...one man shouted out, "It's one of ours...an M4...and it's headed our way."

The Butcher's Block

"Well, that should help loosen things up around here," Bosco said to no one in particular...since his foxhole mate was still lying dead beside him. He and his squad had just waged a failed attack against the brutal defensive system the Japanese had built to protect the Red 2 area...and they had been forced back to their original starting point. Bosco looked over at Wieland... whose expression of surprise had not changed in the two hours that he had been gone...and shrugged. Wieland didn't react though...since he couldn't...and Bosco just looked away...knowing that Donna was going to be sad when she got the news.

The tank that showed up on the afternoon of D + 1 to support the 1-8's attack against the Japanese defensive complex in the western half of Red 2 was nicknamed, "*Cobra*," since it was in Charlie Company of the First Marine Amphibious Corps' Medium Tank Battalion and all its tanks were denoted by a nickname that began with the letter C. When someone had asked the loader on the tank why the crew had named their tank that way, Corporal William Eads had replied, "I'm not sure why we came up with that name...other than that it had to start with a C." But the other crew members... the driver...the assistant driver...and the gunner...had felt it was most likely a reference to the deadly snake that could cause death almost instantaneously with one good strike...which is exactly what the M4A4 tank could do with its lethal 75mm main gun.

The Sherman tank *Cobra* was one of the tanks in the 2nd Platoon of C Company and the tank and the platoon was commanded by First Lieutenant Richard Sloat…a very likable Mississippian…who had been in the unit for several months. Sloat had three other tanks under him as well…and they were nicknamed: *Clipper*… *Cuddles*…*and Conga*. And Sloat's company commander was First Lieutenant Edward Bale…who commanded the tank *Cecilia*…which was named after his driver's daughter…and the other thirteen tanks in the company.

The M4A4 tank that the marine tankers like Sloat and Bale were using on Betio was built by the General Motors Corporation…and it weighed nearly thirty tons. It had two diesel engines that ran simultaneously in the rear of the tank…and it consumed diesel fuel…not gasoline. The crew members loved this aspect because a diesel engine was much safer than a gasoline engine was…since gasoline had a greater penchant for catching fire when an incoming round penetrated the engine housing. In another safety consideration, the tank had anywhere from two to three inches of armor plating to protect it from incoming fire…which the crew also loved. But what made it really useful…especially on Betio… was that its main gun fired a 75mm projectile…which was particularly good against the semi-underground bunkers that were located all over the island. Thus, the Sherman tank could do things that the smaller M3 Stuart tank…which was also seeing action on Betio… couldn't do…since it was armed with a puny 37mm cannon…whose rounds were having a hard time penetrating the bunkers ample defenses.

What the marines on the ground really needed was a tank with a punch...and that's exactly what they got when the heavy, lumbering M4A2 showed up...and countless marine lives were spared because of its participation in the fight.

Chapter Twelve

First Lieutenant Sloat had been lucky on D Day morning since all four of the LCM-3s…or Mike boats… that were carrying his platoon of tanks were still afloat. Unfortunately, Sloat had passed several other Mike boats that were part of the follow-up waves…just like his was…and they were already sinking. Hit by shore fire in deep water, these boats and their cargo…the lighter Stuart tanks… would be lost forever. It was obvious that the Japanese gunners had concentrated their fire on the boats carrying the tanks…since they were noticeably bigger than the Higgins boats that were coming in beside them. This made them a more lucrative target…and the Japanese gunners were punishing them appropriately. So Sloat had counted his blessings when all four of his Shermans splashed into the water and crawled across the reef unscathed.

The Butcher's Block

Although First Lieutenant Sloat's 2nd Platoon was slotted to land on Red 2...that's not where they ended up landing. To avoid the intense fire coming from the *Pocket* and the guns along the Red 2 beachhead, the LCMs carrying his four tanks steered eastward...toward the long main pier that poked out from the island. Looking for an entry point, the coxswains then spotted four other Mike boats disembarking a platoon of tanks to the left...or east...of the pier. The fours tanks in this group...*Cannonball*...*Colorado*...*Condor*...and *Charlie*...all belonged to the Third Platoon...and they were commanded by Second Lieutenant Lou Largey. His platoon was scheduled to land in the Red 3 sector in support of Major Crowe's 2-8...just like Sloat's platoon was supposed to land on Red 2 in support of the Lieutenant Colonel Amey's 2-2.

"Steer that way," Sloat yelled to the coxswain, "they seem to be getting in from that point. Let's do the same thing. We'll follow Largey's tanks in...and then we'll head over to Red 2 once we're ashore." The young man nodded his assent and rammed the throttle forward...causing the tank to strain against the chains that were securing it to the deck.

"Wait til the Japs get a taste of my seventy-five!" Private Henry Trauernicht...the tank's gunner...belted out...but no one heard him over the noise of the boat's engine...which was straining too...just like the tank's chains were.

"How are you doin' down there, Webb? Can you see anything through those periscopes of yours?" Lieutenant

Sloat asked his driver, Corporal Hestor Webb as they made their way down the left side of the pier.

"It's really hard to see anything out there, lieutenant," he responded over the intercom, and added, "being buttoned up is bad enough on dry land...but churning through this murky water is almost impossible. The lenses of the scopes get smeared with the stuff...making it difficult to see...so I can't tell if there are any holes out in front of us. I'm just headin' straight and hoping for the best."

"Okay, Webb, so far so good." Sloat then addressed the assistant driver, Private Jack Trent, who was sitting to Webb's right. The big, bulky transmission housing was positioned between the two of them...which made moving between the two positions difficult...but not impossible. "Help him out when you can, Trent. Your periscopes might be cleaner than his two are."

"You got it, sir. But mine are just as bad as Webb's," he volunteered, and added, "what about opening up our hatches...that's probably the only way we're gonna be able to see anything."

"Too dangerous. Keep 'em closed for now," the red-haired, former high school drama teacher from the state of Washington warned.

"What if we do fall in a hole, lieutenant? Are we gonna abandon the tank...or stay with it?" he asked, the concern in his voice obvious to all.

"I think our odds are okay right now. We're makin' headway...so the water level is getting lower and lower the farther we go. The XO did a test back at Hawke's Bay and we found out that the manual was right. The tank can handle a water depth of forty inches. Anything deeper than that gets dicey...and we run the risk of shorting out our electrical system...which will stop us dead. Our engines will actually keep running in deep water...for a little while...but the real problem is all that wiring we have down near the floor of the turret. That's our weak spot."

"Any chance we'll run into any of our Recon Scouts?" Trent asked. "They'd be a big help out here, sir," he added...wondering where they were.

"We only got twenty-two of them," the lieutenant explained, "and they're all slotted for the Red One Beachhead. They're leading the CO's two headquarters tanks and the First Platoon's four over on Red One...and then they're supposed to make their way over to us when they're done there. But I doubt they're ever gonna make it over here. With all this fire comin' at us, I don't see how any of them will survive over there...if it's anything like this. It'll be a suicide mission to get down in the water and walk ahead of a bunch of tanks. The Japs will figure out what they're doing and that'll be that. It looks like that part of the plan's gonna go belly up. We'll just have to do it on our own...and hope for the best."

Only three of Lieutenant Sloat's tanks were able to make it all the way into the beachhead. As feared, *Cuddles* had fallen into a unseen shell hole and she was now resting about one hundred yards from the beach and directly behind the amtrac that Major Crowe was using for his headquarters on Red Beach 3...dead in the water. Sloat's tank...*Cobra*...and the other two...*Clipper* and *Conga*...had come in safely though...despite all the fire that they drew while heading in...which may have helped the marines who were slogging their way in on Red 3 at the same time. Instead of targeting the infantrymen in the lagoon, a lot of the Japanese gunners had shifted their fire to the armored behemoths instead...since they saw the tanks as a greater threat to their existence on the island. This change in targets spared the lives of many of the marines in the water...since they were now free from the unrelenting machine gun fire that had been dogging them the entire way in.

The three surviving tanks of Lieutenant Sloat's platoon came ashore on Red 3 in the same spot that Lieutenant Largey's four tanks did before them...which was about one hundred yards east of Major Crowe's position. The tankers chose this section of the beach because there was a good-sized break in the seawall at this point... which allowed them to head inland without having to risk getting stuck on the seawall the way amtrac # 23 was down the beach to their right. Sloat then turned the three tanks to the right...and they drove down to the head of the pier...where an assembly area had been established for the C Company tanks by the Company's executive officer, First Lieutenant Kent. At around 1130 hours, Lieutenant Sloat was then directed to head further west...and to assist the forlorn remnants of the 1-2 and the 2-2 who were trying to expand the beachhead in the direction of Red Beach 1. But as soon as they got there...the marines turned them away because they felt that the area was too well-defended by the Japanese. Rather than risk losing the tanks in a vain attack against the prickly Red 2 beachhead defenses, the marines told them that they could do better by helping Major Kyle's 1-2 men who were trying to expand the beachhead out past the western taxiway and into the airfield infield... no small task on D Day.

"Hold up!"

Corporal Webb immediately pulled on the two breaking levers and the tank came to an abrupt stop as its treads dug into the sandy ground below it. A dust cloud billowed around the tank...hiding it for a second...and then it reappeared...as the dust settled. The two tanks behind it...one on its left...and the other to its right...pulled to a stop as well.

"You see somethin' out there?" the gunner asked... placing his eye over the periscope sight and looking for a target over the terrain in front of the tank.

"Yeah...we got a marine outside waving at us to stop," the lieutenant answered back. Sloat had spied him while he was sitting on the TC's folding seat and looking through the rotating periscope that was attached to the TC's split-opening hatch. Standing up, he pushed one half of the heavy hatch open and stared down at the man who quickly sat back down in his foxhole.

"Is everything okay, Mac," the lieutenant asked easily...while noting that the man already looked ragged, dirty, and tired despite coming ashore only four hours ago.

"It's staff sergeant," the NCO replied testily, "and no...everything isn't okay."

"Whatta ya got for me, sergeant?" Sloat replied now...respecting the formality.

"Well, sir, I don't think you wanna go much farther down the beach than this. This is the front lines and there's nobody friendly beyond this point...that I know of anyway. The Japs own it all...and they got the entire area laced with machine gun pits, bunkers, and pillboxes. And they're all tied in together with interlocking fires so you can't attack one without getting shot at by another one. You take those tanks of yours in there and you probably won't be comin' back out is what I'm tryin' to tell ya, sir."

"I understand, sergeant," the lieutenant said while glancing around...seeing only a few marines scattered about here and there. "How many men do you actually have with you over here, sergeant?"

"Only fourteen, sir. Japs got the rest comin' in."

Sloat noticed one of his men was wounded in the shoulder, so he asked, "Is that man in any condition to fight? We can take him with us if he's hurt badly enough."

"He's alright, sir. I tried to send him back once already and he came right back. Said there were too many guys wounded worse than him back at the aide bunker. We patched him up and handed him a forty-five. He's got one good arm and he'll use it if the Japs manage to get in close with us. Thanks for askin' about him. So, you are gonna head back...like I recommended?"

"I wish we could offer you some help...but I can't risk going in there if I won't have any infantry to back me up. One Jap with a magnetic mine is all it'll take to knock one of us out of action...and there's probably ten if not a hundred of the yellow bastards just waiting for us to drive in there so they can set one off against each of my tanks."

"Plus," the staff sergeant said, "your tanks are a big target and you're gonna attract a lot of attention over this way. I just don't have enough men to fight off a concentrated attack over here...so we're actually better off if you take your big bullseyes over to the airfield. I hear Major Kyle's men could use those tanks of yours over there."

A sudden flurry of machine gun fire came their way...and several 13mm rounds ricocheted off the hull of Sloat's tank. "I told you, sir. They mean business over here. The sooner you're gone...the better!" the staff sergeant yelled up at the lieutenant...who had ducked low behind the hatch cover for protection.

"I see what you mean," the lieutenant yelled back, "it's gettin' a little too hot over here...even for us tankers."

The last thing the lieutenant saw, before buttoning up, was the staff sergeant pointing inland...in direction of the airfield...and saying, "They're over that way. Good luck."

In quick order, the tanks slewed around and headed back to the assembly area near the pierhead to get new orders. When they pulled up, Lieutenant Kent was waiting for them and Lieutenant Sloat jumped down from the tank so he could hear what he had to say. And Kent confirmed that the tanks were indeed needed by Kyle's 1-2...just like the staff sergeant had suggested. "They're trying to punch their way across the taxiway just inland from the beach...go back the way you came...but don't go as far...and turn left. You'll run into Kyle and his men about a hundred yards in. Maybe your guns can help them get across," Kent said to Sloat.

"Okay, then that's where we'll go, Orrell," the 2nd Platoon leader replied, acknowledging C Company's executive officer.

Sloat turned back around and signaled that they were moving out again by circling his hand above his head. The two other tank commanders...Sergeant Baker and Sergeant Andrews...gave him the thumbs up indicating that they were ready to go. Sloat then climbed back onto his tank and slid into the turret through the commander's hatch. He then reached down and grabbed the hand-held microphone and said, "Let's go, Webb. We're going back the same way...only not as far. I'll tell you when to turn left. We're gonna try to get Major Kyle's men across the taxiway and maybe across the big airfield too...if it's possible." Sloat then radioed the other two TCs and told them that they were going to use an arrowhead formation instead of the file formation... where one tank was directly behind the other...on the trip out. "We're headin' into Indian Country, boys, and

The Butcher's Block

this formation will allow us to protect each other better. I'll take the lead. I want *Clipper* on the left...behind me. *Conga*...you take the right side...behind me. Watch our flanks...and make sure your targets are Japs and not marines. Everybody's mixed in where we're going, and the last thing we want is to kill some of our own men."

Both *Clipper* and *Congo* acknowledged the transmission and Sloat ordered Webb to move out...and then the flaw in the doctrine that the marines were using when it came to tanks and infantry reared its ugly head yet again. Instead of working in concert like they should have, the tanks and the marine infantry on Betio operated independently of one another...and this tactical error led to one setback after another...especially for the tanks...who were extremely vulnerable when traveling alone.

In Sloat's case, the three tanks turned around and headed west...again...and they had not gone very far when *Conga* drove blindly into a deep shell hole and got stuck...still within sight of the pier head. Unable to drive out, the crew decided to abandon the tank...for the time being...and they made their way back to Lieutenant Kent to inform him of their tank's condition.

After the loss of *Cuddles* and *Conga*, Lieutenant Sloat's platoon was now down to two operational tanks...the *Cobra* and *Clipper*...and they drove on in hopes of locating Major Kyle's men near the taxiway...*Cobra* first...and then *Clipper* in the rear. While heading that way, Private

Charles Mason...a former farmer from Oregon...and now the *Clipper's* gunner...was shocked when he saw two Japanese *rikusentai* try to disable the *Cobra* by shoving grenades into its engine housing at the rear of the tank. The two men had appeared out of nowhere...and they ran fearlessly up to tank...without concern for themselves. It took Mason but a second to process the scene in his head...and then he snapped to and reacted violently to their attack. Using his turret-mounted .30 caliber machine gun, Mason gunned the two men down...saving the *Cobra* from any kind of damage.

"Nice shooting, Charlie!" Sergeant Baker, the TC, shouted into the microphone.

"Once I got my wits about me and I realized what was happening, it was like shouting rabbits back home. It's them or us out here, Bake, right!" the excited gunner yelled back.

"Them or us. It's as simple as that," Baker agreed.

"I just don't wanna die out here...in this tank...on this miserable island. I'll kill as many Japs as I gotta to get outta here alive," the gunner added coldly.

"We do what we came here to do...and then we leave. If a Jap gets in the way, that's his problem...not ours," Baker, the tank commander, said...the conversation leaving no doubt about what the crew of the *Clipper* would do to survive.

The two tanks eventually located Kyle's men in the infield just past the western taxiway...and they tried to support them as best they could. The tanks maneuvered themselves out ahead of the marines...as their tactics dictated...and they began blasting any enemy positions that they could identify with their 75mm main gun...which was fired by the gunner...and the bow-mounted .30 caliber machine gun...which was controlled by the assistant driver. The two goliaths seemed to be making a difference...since the marines were cheering every time a difficult position was silenced by the blast of a tank's main gun. Sometimes it would take several rounds to accomplish the destruction of just one bunker...or a troublesome machine gun nest...since they were constructed so well...and then the tanks would move on to the next target.

Then, like before, a determined Japanese *rikusentai* decided enough was enough. Armed with a Type 99 *Hakobakurai* grenade mine, the sailor dashed out of his hiding spot and ran over to the *Clipper*...since it had stopped moving. Plus, it was sitting alone now...off the flank of the *Cobra*...all by itself...with no infantry nearby to protect it. The *rikusentai* held the mine against the engine housing and did not let go...since the four magnets that were attached to the bag carrying the explosive sometimes failed. If that happened, the mine would fall harmlessly to the ground and detonate when its time-delayed fuse went off. To prevent this, the suicide bomber remained in place...giving up his life to ensure a proper detonation...along with the destruction of his intended target.

The concussive effect of the mine going off in the rear of the tank was so strong that it knocked the *Clipper's* loader and radio operator, PFC Donald Pearson, completely out cold...and he fell to the floor of the tank... apparently wounded. Seeing that Pearson was down, Private Clifford Quine, the assistant driver, began wiggling his way up through the space behind his seat so he could enter the turret.

"What the hell was that?" the driver, Corporal Antonio Almaraz, asked, shaking his head.

"I think we got hit with a bunch of mortar rounds," the TC answered right back...thinking he had seen some explosions going off outside before the anti-tank mine had detonated and rocked his tank.

"Is everybody okay?" he asked.

"Pearson's laying on the deck," Almaraz replied, swiveling around and looking over his left shoulder. "I can see him...and he's not moving any," he added, still glancing back.

Sergeant Baker looked down from his perch on the folding seat...but it was so dark inside the turret that he couldn't see Pearson laying off to the side... his view also blocked by the breech block of the main gun. "Cliff...can you slide up there and check him out? I need to stay focused on what's going on outside, so we don't get hit again. Everyone check for fire...is anything on fire?"

"Already on it," Clifford answered from below... and he made his way through the small opening and stood up. "Pearson seems to be okay," he added, "he just seems to be knocked out. He's moaning...but I don't see any blood on him at all." Then Quine bent over to the ammo rack, picked out an armor-piercing round, and slid it into the empty breech. "AP up and loaded," he yelled across to the gunner. Private Mason never took his eye off the periscope...he just gave Clifford a thumbs up to signal that he heard him and was aware that the main gun was now reloaded and ready to fire.

"No fire...or smoke either, Bake," the assistant driver added, per the TC's last order.

"Ant...how's she handling? Is the engine damaged? Maybe we lucked out and that round didn't damage anything...other than knocking Pearson for a loop," the TC asked.

"Bad news," the driver said, " the dashboard is saying we've lost an engine. I'll cut it out immediately...and shift over to the good one. She's gonna be real sluggish... but she'll still move at least."

"Good work, Ant," the TC said, recognizing the great job the driver had done the instant he realized that one of engine's had been damaged. "Cliff...check the radios...see if you can raise anyone."

"Just a bunch of static on the radio," Clifford replied. He then changed the dial settings several times...hoping to hear some chatter on the net...but all he got was more static.

"Alright, no problem. Here's what we're gonna do. I saw an empty revetment not far away. We're gonna make for it and pull in there. Then we'll sit tight...until I can make sense of what is happening out here. I'll direct you there, Almaraz. Take it slow. We can't risk losing that other engine as well."

"It'll be hard maneuvering her with only one engine, Mace, but I'll get it done. Just don't have me make any tight turns...cause I'll break my arms trying to do it," the driver warned.

"I understand," Baker replied and Almaraz began inching the tank back towards the western end of the northwestern taxiway...per the TC's instructions.

"There it is. Directly ahead. Just pull in...nose first. If we can get a maintenance crew out here, it'll be easier to access the damaged engine with the rear closest to the exit."

Corporal Antonio Almaraz did as ordered...and he pulled the tank completely into the large aircraft revetment. He shut the one functioning engine down and then looked back into the turret and said, "Now what?"

"We wait...just like I said. And we stay buttoned up. I don't want some hero Jap tossing a grenade into an open hatch. If it gets unbearably hot in here...or we need new air...then I'll crack my hatch for just a second. That'll have to do for the time being. Everybody good with that," Sergeant Baker responded. It was the first time all day that he did not have to shout to be heard... since the deafening noise of the two engines were no longer a backdrop to every conversation he had with the crew.

"That sounds good to me." It was PFC Pierson...who had finally come to.

"Good to see you're feelin' better, Pierce," Sergeant Baker said...hearing him and then seeing him move around below him.

"Got a pretty good headache. Them sons-of-bitches! My mother wouldn't like them for that!" Pierson complained.

"Yeah, good thing she's not out here with us or those Japs would have hell to pay," the driver said...and everyone laughed for the first time since they had landed...a simple comment from the now-lucid loader finally breaking the tension that they had been under all day.

⸻⋆⸻

The *Clipper* did just what the TC said it would. It sat all night in the revetment...apparently unnoticed...since Japanese did not wage an attack against it. The men wiled away their time...dozing occasionally when the fatigue of D Day finally caught up with them. The rest of the time they shared quiet conversations...all the while listening to the sounds of the battle being waged around them...and hoping they'd be left alone. When the air became unbearable...Sergeant Baker cracked the hatch open...just enough to let some fresh air into the tank... and then he closed it...just like he had said he would.

At dawn, the crew decided to leave the tank where it was...since it would need a new engine to run properly... and they made their way back to the pierhead safe and sound. The trip back was uneventful...since no Japs had fired on them…and when they reached the assembly area, Sergeant Baker informed Lieutenant Kent about *Clipper's* condition while the rest of the crew joined the other tankers who were sitting in a huge shell hole for protection…awaiting further orders.

After realizing that the *Clipper* had been knocked out of action, Lieutenant Sloat ordered the *Cobra's* driver, Corporal Hestor "Buck" Webb, to head for the main runway. This was part of the instructions that each platoon commander in C Company had received prior to landing…and Sloat was fulfilling it to the letter. The only problem was that Lieutenant Sloat did not have a platoon to lead across the island…since the *Cobra* was the only functioning tank left out of his platoon of four tanks. Just like before, the *Cobra* engaged targets of opportunity…the tank firing on bunkers that were firing on it…and they knocked several of them out. But then the tank began to receive heavy return fire from several Type 88 75mm guns…which were potent and proven tank killers. The Type 88 was really an anti-aircraft gun…but just like the vaunted German 88…the Type 88 also excelled when it was fired horizontally at tanks…and the Japanese had already used them to knock out several tanks from Lieutenant Lou Largey's 3rd Platoon on Red 3. These guns were positioned further down the airfield…to the east…and their fire convinced Lieutenant Sloat to pull back to the infield triangle…where Kyle's men could offer the

Cobra a minimal amount of ground support...if nothing else. Lieutenant Sloat then continued to lend support to Major Kyle's men...shelling positions when they were pointed out...until late in the afternoon...when their ammunition began to run low.

As twilight approached, Lieutenant Sloat decided to hunker down beside the northwestern taxiway...only a few hundred yards or so to the east of the revetment that the *Clipper* was hiding in. And Sloat ordered the tank buttoned up as well...just like the *Clipper* was. But during the night, Corporal Webb decided to leave the tank. He didn't tell anyone he was leaving...and he slid out of the tank using the escape hatch which was located behind the assistant driver's seat in the floor of the tank.

And then tragedy struck.

"Who's missing?"

The three crew members still inside the tank...the gunner, the loader-radioman, and assistant driver came awake all at once. They looked around and then individually announced their presence to their TC...who had shouted down the question.

"Where's Webb? Did anyone see him go out?"

Their silence was their answer.

"Did he say anything to anybody? Was he acting crazy...in any way? Did he need water?" That question elicited a response. "We're all thirsty, lieutenant," the gunner, Private Trauernicht replied dourly. "Why we didn't carry more water is a mystery to me...when we got room for it." Then he added, "Someone with brains had to know how hot these tanks would get...that they keep all the heat in. Webb probably left to go find us some water. That's the only thing that makes sense to me."

"Probably went after some water, lieutenant," was all the assistant driver, Private Jack Trent had to say.

"Water...that's gotta be the reason," echoed the loader-radioman, Corporal William Eads.

"Henry," Lieutenant Sloat said, "crawl outside and see if you can see anything. Stay underneath the tank. You know what happens when somebody goes stumbling around at night. Just see if you can see him...that's all."

The gunner slid out of his seat and crawled head-first out of the small escape hatch...and slid up the nose of the tank and peeked out...looking in the direction of the taxiway. He didn't see anything...at least he thought he didn't...so he crawled on his belly to the back of the tank. Staying underneath it for safety, he scanned the ground and saw a dark lump not far away. *That could be him,* he thought, *or it could be a dead marine...or a dead Jap too though.* He crawled back to the hatch and stuck his head up into the body of the tank. "I saw somethin' out there. It looks like whoever it is was headin' back to the beach...so it could be him. I'm not certain...it's damn dark out there. But it could be him."

"Is he close enough to the tank where we could get to him?" Sloat asked.

"He's close enough. If I have somebody covering me, I could reach him. But I'll need someone to help me drag him back...if it is him," the gunner answered truthfully.

"Ok. Bill, you go with Henry. Take the Thompson with you...just in case. Trent and I will cover you from underneath the tank with the Carbine. If you do get into trouble...we'll use the smoke grenades we got aboard to cover you. I'd prefer to use them first...since our boys are behind us...but the Japs could be infiltrating all around us too...so just try to make sure it's a Jap you're shooting at instead of some scared marine."

"Aye aye, sir," Corporal Eads said...appreciating that the lieutenant was willing to leave the safe confines of the tank to cover their rescue attempt.

Then Eads got down on his knees on the turret floor and he slid out the escape hatch to join Private Trauernicht...who was already outside.

"The body's about twenty feet off the rear right fender," the gunner said to Eads...and the two crawled that way under the tank.

"At least the lieutenant is going to cover us," Eads said quietly, and added, "I was on a Stuart back on Guadalcanal before I got transferred over to the M-4's. The lieutenant on my tank back on the *Canal* would never leave it...just a gutless coward. I never saw him do a single thing to help us if it put his life on the line. Sloat's alright in my book," Eads said, while straining to see the body that Trauernicht had spotted.

"You see him," the gunner asked.

Eads shook his head no...so the gunner pointed directly at the body. This time Eads saw it...and said so.

The lieutenant and Private Trent crawled up next to them...and the lieutenant handed the Thompson sub-machine gun to the private.

"I'm no good with this thing," Trauernicht said glumly, and he handed it over to Eads, who took it without complaint.

"I got real good with it on the *Canal*. Practiced shooting down coconuts from the trees on the island. If we run into trouble out there, I'll handle it," Eads said confidently.

"Whenever you two are ready, we got you covered," the lieutenant said, more of an order than a suggestion.

"Ready," Trauernicht said.

"Ready as I'm ever gonna be," Eads responded...and the two crawled ahead...under the cover of darkness...to the body in the distance.

Trauernicht and Eads went slow...since time was not a factor. They would crawl a foot at a time...stop...listen...look...and then crawl some more. As they got closer, they could tell that the body was a marine...by his uniform...and a tanker...since he was wearing a one-piece, herringbone twill, mechanics coverall...the same type of uniform that Webb liked to wear. The man was laying on his stomach...and he looked dead. Eads rolled him over...and it was Webb...and he had been shot in the neck. Eads felt for a carotid pulse...and got one... so he knew that the driver was still alive...at least barely. He could also see a slight chest rise, so he knew the man was still breathing as well...a good sign...despite the circumstances.

"It's Webb," Eads whispered softly to Trauernicht, "and he's alive."

"Let's get him back to the tank as quick as we can. Maybe we can do something for him. You grab one shoulder...I'll grab the other...and let's just drag him back," the gunner suggested...and each man took a shoulder and they began to pull him back to the tank.

"Is it him," the lieutenant asked...still wondering why his driver had just up and left.

"Yeah...it's Webb...and he's shot in the neck," Eads huffed...tired from dragging a one-hundred-and-ninety pound man through the sand.

"Is he alive," the lieutenant asked skeptically.

"He sure is," Eads replied, "at least the last time I checked."

The lieutenant reached out along with Trauernicht and they helped pull him under the tank...and then they hefted him into the tank so they could get a better look at his wound.

"He's bleeding real bad," the lieutenant said, observing the jagged hole just above the man's collarbone. "Get me the first aid kit!" he ordered...and Eads pulled the kit from a box that was welded to the inside of the tank. He brought the box over to the lieutenant...and Sloat reached inside and found a thick dressing. He took it out and pressed it against the wound...hoping the pressure would slow the bleeding down. The dressing immediately turned deep red, indicating that the bleeding was progressing unabated...and the lieutenant just sighed...knowing what it meant. "It probably nicked his carotid artery inside...which is why he's bleeding so bad. Pressure won't stop it...so there's nothing we can really do...not out here." The lieutenant then looked at each man...trying to see if they understood what he had just conveyed to them.

"You wanna give him some morphine, sir, to ease the pain. We got some in here...in a syrette. It might make him feel better...if nothing else," Corporal Eads replied...understanding the situation.

"So Buck isn't gonna make it, sir," Trent asked, not realizing the severity of the driver's wound.

"I don't know how long he'll last," the TC said sadly, "I'm not God...but if you believe in Him...now's the time to start praying...cause Webb is in bad shape."

Trent slumped against the wall of the tank...now realizing that his buddy and mentor might not survive the night.

"I'm gonna need you to take over as driver...while Webb's down. You okay with that," Sloat asked the assistant driver...and Trent nodded that he would.

"Here's that morphine, sir," Eads said, holding the syrettes in his hand.

The lieutenant took them from him, and he injected Webb with one...and in time...another. Two hours later, unconscious Webb died inside the tank...in the company of his friends...who never found out why he had left the tank in the first place.

Just before dawn broke, the *Cobra* drove back to the assembly area and Corporal Hestor Webb's body was removed from the tank…and placed gently on the ground. In time, stretcher bearers showed up to carry him back to the area near Colonel Shoup's CP that had been chosen as a grave site…and his body was laid to rest in a grave that bore his name.

Back near the pierhead, Lieutenant Kent, the C Company executive officer, had organized a recovery effort to free the stricken *Conga*. He gathered the tank's own crew…plus some tank maintenance personnel who had nothing to do now…and some unattached marines…and he led them all over to the tank. Without orders or guidance, the team went to work on freeing the stuck *Conga* from the shell crater that it had fallen into earlier in the day. The men worked tirelessly for several hours during the night…digging a trench into the hole so that the tank could drive itself out under its own power. And in time, the *Conga* did just that…which was a tremendous accomplishment since it represented a triumph of the will and spirit of the men who had sought to free her.

Yet it was ever dangerous on Betio…no matter where you were…and as the tank was driving out…a sharp-eyed team of *rikusentai* took the tank under fire…and scored several hits with their heavy machine gun. Incredibly, one of the rounds found a soft spot right under the front shield and it exploded inside the turret...wounding both the gunner...Corporal Malcolm Garvock...and the tank commander...Sergeant Eugene Andrews. In short order, Lieutenant Kent ordered the gunner...Private Mason... and the loader-radioman...PFC Pearson...from the disabled *Clipper* to take their places...and both men headed over...eager to help out.

So...for D + 1 at least...the *Conga* and the *Cobra* would be ready for action once again on Red Beach 2.

Chapter Thirteen

"Can you make out the name of that tank?" Corporal Bosco asked...stretching his head up as high as he dared to see the tank that was coming up in the shallows behind them.

"It says *Cobra* on the side. Whoever painted it on should have made it bigger though...it's not like the Japs are gonna be able to read it," the marine beside him said, his eyesight somewhat better than his new squad leader's was.

"I didn't catch your name," Bosco stated, while looking him over. Bosco could see that the man was well-built...like he was...and about as tall.

"PFC Bob...Bobby...Klein. I'm from Chicago...since that's probably your next question," the city tough-guy wisecracked.

"You Jewish," Bosco asked. "Where I come from guys with the name of Klein are Jewish."

"If I said yes would it make a difference," Klein responded testily.

"Not a bit," Bosco replied, "unless you wanna it to be."

"Well, I'm not Jewish. I'm Lithuanian. My folks came over when I was a kid. I don't remember anything about the place…I was too young."

"I'm from outside New York City…Staten Island. Ever heard of it?"

"No. But that accent of yours gave you away. I figured you were from there…or Jersey maybe," Klein answered back.

"Are you Polish then…or Russian? Isn't Lithuania a part of those countries," Bosco asked, and added, "I never paid much attention to geography when I was in school…obviously."

"No…I am Lithuanian…not Polish…and definitely not Russian. Those countries have occupied my country at times throughout history…but we're our own people…with our own history."

"I get it. That would be like you asking me if I was Austrian…or French…even though my people were from Italy…right," Bosco said, working it out in his mind.

"Exactly," Klein replied, "now you know what I've been dealing with my whole life."

"Sorry," Bosco said, "I never thought of it that way."

"Piece a cake," Klein answered back.

"My name's Bosco. Tom Bosco. I'm a squad leader…or was…until yesterday. That's why I gathered you guys up. Colonel Shoup told me to get back in the game…and I told him I would…so that's why you're here."

"Shoup told you to do this? Our colonel...the guy who's in charge of this mess?"

"Yup...I ran into him yesterday...well, he ran into me yesterday actually," Bosco replied, correcting himself.

"I bet it's an interesting story...but why is that tank driving past us. We can use it right in front of us," Klein said, his attention now directed back towards the water. The two men watched incredulously as the tank literally moved past their foxhole and headed towards the boundary line between the Red 2 and Red 1 beachheads...where the *Pocket* was located.

The tank eventually stopped...about four hundred yards further down...and it began firing its main gun into area where the island curved inward to form the cove that represented the upper breast and lower neck of the parrot.

"Somebody must have figured out that whatever that tank is shooting at is a priority target. With all the rounds it's pumping in there, it must be having some effect," Bosco theorized...knowing how the chain-of-command worked.

"Have you seen the effort the Japs put into building these pillboxes and bunkers out here? If that's a high priority target, it's gonna take a lot more than one tank with a seventy-five to knock it out," Klein countered, and he shook his head in frustration.

Bosco wanted to answer...but he was suddenly very tired. The scorching sun was directly overhead now... and it seemed to drain the energy right out of the corporal. "I'm gonna catch some shuteye...if that's okay with you. Wake me if anything interesting happens…okay," he said…almost slurring his words.

PFC Klein just shook his head…and Bosco rolled over and quickly fell asleep.

Two hours passed by and Klein continued to watch the tank fire one round after another towards the *Pocket*…but around 1500 hours it ceased firing…and then swung around and began heading back towards them.

"Here it comes. Must be out of ammo," Klein said, observing the tank yet again.

Bosco stirred slightly from the nap he was taking…but he did not get up.

"Are you kidding me," Klein bellowed…and Bosco sat up quickly.

"What did I miss," he asked, shielding his eyes from the sun with his hand.

"If you had been watching that tank like I was…instead of napping…you would've seen it run into that crater out in water…and she's sinkin' fast."

Bosco swung around and looked down the beach and saw that the tank was out in the water…like it had been when he last saw it. Now it was sitting in a deep hole or shell crater canted slightly forward…and sea water was pouring into it through the driver's and assistant driver's hatches…which were almost under water.

"Why was the tank out there anyway? The driver should've stayed on the beach…coming and going!" Bosco stressed, mystified that the tank would risk moving ahead in the water like that without a guide to spot the holes like the one it had run into.

"Because of all the wounded and dead that are still lying out there on the beach...that's why," Klein informed him. Then he added, "And because the life expectancy of any guide would be zero. Plus, the angles were all wrong. The main gun on that tank couldn't hit anything except the Jap pillboxes along the seawall if it stayed on the beach...and we've already knocked those ones out. So, it stayed in the surf...where it could do the most good and engage targets further inland. It's all about the angles."

"I guess that makes sense. But now they've lost the tank," Bosco said dejectedly...and they watched as the crew of the *Cobra* began bailing out of the tank...one by one. Since the water wasn't too deep here, the men crawled their way in while under constant machine gun fire. As they neared the beach, the machine gun zeroed in on them...and two of them were hit, but they made it to the seawall...neither one willing to leave the other behind.

A marine sitting below the seawall scrambled over to the wounded tankers and said to Trent, "Lemme have a look ya." The man then removed the bloody utility shirt that Private Jack Trent...the newly promoted driver...was wearing and he cringed. "You got yourself a pretty nasty gash in your back," the marine said, examining the sides of the deep wound more closely.

"Yeah, it felt like a .50 cal got me...or something like that...since it knocked the wind outta me when I got hit.

I woulda gone under but Bill was there to help me make it in."

Eads...the loader-radioman...was looking at his own wounded arm...which wasn't quite so bad...but bad enough...and he nodded to Trent casually and said, "It was no big deal...you would've done the same for me."

In time, the two men made their way down the beach to the pierhead...where they were then loaded on a landing craft and evacuated off the island. Their next stop was the USS *Arthur Middleton*...APA 25...since its medical staff could provide far better treatment for the two tankers who...though wounded...were still alive.

Chapter Fourteen

First Lieutenant Kent made his way carefully back to the huge crater that was serving as the C Company assembly area near the pierhead and spoke to the tankers and maintenance men who sitting inside it for safety. "Listen," he said, "we finally got the *Conga* out of that hole it was stuck in during the night. But Sergeant Andrews and Corporal Garvock are wounded...and I need a TC and a gunner to replace them. Any takers?"

One marine raised his hand and asked, "What happened to them...how'd they get wounded. Isn't the tank not far from here...in a fairly safe place?

Kent looked at the man like he had two heads. "Haven't you figured out by now that nowhere is safe out here. As the *Conga* drove out of the shell hole it was in...it was taken under fire. Obviously, the Japs in the area were watching it and waiting for the perfect opportunity to fire on it. An incredible shot hit right under the forward gun shield and the round exploded inside…injuring both them. They'll live…but they're pretty shaken up and they're both on their way to the *Hayward*…where they'll get the attention they need. So that's that. Now I still need two volunteers. Anybody up for it?"

Private Charles Mason stuck his hand up in the air and said, "Me and Pearson here will do it, sir. We've been sittin' on the sidelines since our *Clipper* was put outta action…so we're free."

The lieutenant looked at the two men and smiled. "Thank you, Mason. Since you were the gunner on the *Clipper*, I'm assuming you'll take over those duties on the *Conga* as well."

"Aye aye, sir," Mason answered right back.

"Okay…but I still need a TC…and Pearson there was the loader-radioman on the *Clipper* if my memory serves me right, correct?"

"Yes, sir," PFC Pearson replied, "that was my position…but I don't have a problem bumping up to the TC seat. I've been at this game for a while and I'm confident I can handle whatever comes our way."

First Lieutenant Kent liked the man's confidence and said, "You got it then. The *Conga's* all yours. Now your mission will be helping out the boys from the Second of the Second who are still stuck in the airfield triangle out in front of Colonel Shoup's CP…which is right over there."

The men stared where the XO was pointing, and they could see Colonel Shoup and his staff moving around behind a large bunker...close to where they were now sitting.

"I never realized we were that close to the big brass," one of tank maintenance men said in awe.

"Well, that's them," the lieutenant said dryly, "and Colonel Shoup wants the *Conga* to link up with Lieutenant Colonel Jordan...who's moved up near the taxiway out in front of their headquarters. Jordan will give you more instructions...once you meet up with him."

"When are we supposed to go, sir," Pearson wondered.

"You're late already...so get on your horse and go find that colonel," the XO ordered...and there was no mistaking the urgency in his voice.

Pearson and Mason both looked at one another and without another word, they dashed off in the direction of the *Conga*.

The XO watched them go and said to the others, "Good boys those two...good boys."

"Here comes that tank we were promised," the Navy officer... Lieutenant Jay Odell... said...the relief clearly evident on his dirty face. The Navy lieutenant was one of the few surviving officers of Lieutenant Colonel Amey's original staff...and his job was to coordinate the actions of the naval aircraft operating overhead with the ground units down below.

"Make sure you signal him, so he knows we're over here," Jordan warned...the strain of the last two days clearly affecting him.

The lieutenant had already scrounged up a long piece of cloth for just this purpose and he was waving it over his head to attract the tank's attention.

The tank's driver must have spotted him...because it shifted directions suddenly and came rumbling up to the two men and rocked to a stop.

The hatch on top of the turret then opened up and PFC Pearson looked down at the colonel...who was shielding his eyes as he looked up at him.

"The *Conga* is at your service, sir," PFC Pearson said wittingly.

The lieutenant colonel looked at the man with a wary eye and said, "You're late. We were told you would be here by oh nine hundred. It's well past that. Any reason?"

"No excuse there, sir. We just got our orders and we headed over here as soon as we were released by our XO," Pearson answered back honestly.

"You're not an officer?" Jordan asked skeptically.

"No, sir. I'm just a lowly PFC," Pearson said unapologetically, "but I'm a PFC who knows how to command a tank...if that's what you're worried about."

"Nothing worries me anymore...not after what I've been through, son," the observer but now commander said wistfully.

"Well, that's good, sir. So, what is it that you want us to help you with," Pearson said, warming to the position of authority.

"I have a bunch of marines stuck in a large shell hole in the airfield triangle. They've been there since yesterday and a Jap machine gun has them pinned down. I need you to get them out of there...and

The Butcher's Block

anyone else you may run across when you get over there. Then you are to help the First of the Second who are down to the right of us. They are trying to make their way across the main airstrip to reach the Black beaches...but they've run up against the same resistance we have. They can use your help to get across...if that's possible."

"That's a lot on one plate...but I'll do my best to see that it gets done," Pearson replied positively.

The lieutenant colonel and the navy officer shook their heads in agreement and then Jordan said, "Okay... this is the way we're going to do it. I want that tank of yours to advance out in front of our boys and you will clear the area first...right up to that hole where the others are trapped. Then we'll come up later and join you. That's the way I want it done."

"Oh, hell no," Pearson replied...incredulous. "That's suicide, sir, and I won't do it!" he added adamantly.

Lieutenant Colonel Jordan looked stunned at the rebuttal...and he looked to the naval officer for support. "What do you mean, no? Of course, you'll do it. I'm ordering you to do it."

"You can line me up against a wall and shoot me... but this tank is not going out there alone. Again, it's suicide, sir, and I'm not gonna get my whole crew killed doing it," Pearson said, standing his ground.

"I just might shoot you myself," the colonel said, "for disobeying orders."

"Go ahead and do it...since it'll be quicker that way. You'll just save the Japs the problem," Pearson said back, calling his bluff.

"Okay…so do you have a plan of your own," Lieutenant Odell said, jumping into the argument.

"Yes, sir, I do. Here's what I propose. We go ahead of your ground pounders and clear the area…and keep the Japs pinned down. Then you have your men immediately come up to support us. Then we advance a little further…while your guys are keeping the Japs pinned down…and then you guys come right up after us. If we don't work together, the Japs will knock our tank out the minute they see us alone. One Jap with a magnetic mine and a death wish is all it takes to put us outta action. That's how we lost my old tank. One Jap…one mine…one less tank. And there aren't any more tanks on Red 2…we're it. So, you'd better be careful with us…and treat us like we know what we're doing. We need your men to come right up and protect us…or we die."

The air liaison officer looked at the colonel and said, "What he says makes perfect sense, sir. I say we do it his way and call it a day."

Lieutenant Colonel Jordan was too tired to argue the point any further…and he went along with the Lieutenant Odell's recommendation. "Okay. Now that that's settled, let's go to work then. Go free my men and then go help Major Kyle…and this day will be a victory for us. You okay with that?"

"I am, sir," the acting TC said proudly…and he pulled the TC hatch closed and ordered the driver to advance…just like he said he would do.

The Butcher's Block

In short order, the *Conga* was able to find the trapped marines. Over half a platoon of men were sheltering in a large shell hole that was just shy of the main airstrip...and a Jap machine gunner had the hole zeroed in perfectly so nobody could attempt to get out without getting killed. There were several dead marines lying inside the shell hole already in testament to the accuracy of the Japanese machine gunner...and he was looking for more marines to kill.

"Pull up between the shell hole that the marines are in and the airstrip," Pearson yelled into the microphone, "and let's see if we can find out where that machine gun is hiding."

The driver obeyed the TC's command and as the tank came to a stop, it was met with a torrent of machine gun fire. The bullets pinged off the exterior of the tank...doing no damage...and it sounded like hail hitting a metal roof to the crew members inside.

"Anybody see where that fire is coming from," the TC shouted...even louder this time to overcome the racket the Jap machine gunner was causing.

As the gunner swung the main gun around in the direction of the airfield, the machine gun fire stopped suddenly.

"Mace...did you locate the bunker that fire came from," Pearson asked excitedly.

"No...the bastard stopped just as I came around. But I got a trick up my sleeve that'll ferret him out. I'm gonna swing the gun back...and see what he does."

Sure enough, as soon as the main gun turned away from the area where the Jap gunner was located, the fire started back up. Mason then swung the gun back in the direction of the machine gun fire and it immediately stopped...just like he figured it would. "Okay...let's play this game one more time...and then I'll fix his ass," Mason said confidently...and he swung the gun and turret away one more time...only slower. The turret hadn't rotated nearly as much when the *rikusentai* opened fire again...just like the last time. What the Japanese machine gunner didn't realize...and what Mason was counting on...was just how fast the tank gunner could swing the main gun back around while using the gunner's handle that electrically controlled the rotation of the turret and the operation of the main gun. Mason timed it perfectly...and he swung the gun back around quickly... catching the Jap off guard. Looking through the gunner's periscope, Mason saw a flash coming out of a small aperture in a pillbox only twenty-five yards away. "Got 'em," the gunner stated proudly, "he's right over there... and he's about to get a taste of his own medicine." Mason then lowered the main gun a slight degree and he lined up his sights right on the small hole where he had seen the gun flash. "This is gonna require a little finesse since that aperture is so small...but he picked the wrong tank to mess with," Mason said, his eye glued to the periscope.

"How big is the hole," the driver asked...trying to locate it through his vision blocks.

"It's only about six inches wide and four or so inches high," Mason replied, "but it's not gonna be small enough to save him...that's for sure." With one smooth movement of his left foot, Mason pressed the firing button on the floor in front of his seat and the tank rocked slightly as a high explosive round left the tube of the main gun. Mason yelled, "A perfect shot," as the round exploded inside the pillbox...and smoke and debris blew out of the opening...confirming his accuracy.

"That Jap isn't gonna give those marines any more trouble," Private Pearson commented from above...and Mason smiled...since he could hear the marines who had been saved cheering wildly outside.

―◆―

After successfully freeing the 2-2 marines and destroying several other pillboxes, *Conga* made its way further west...in order to fulfill the second part of its assignment...which was to assist the marines from A and B Company of Major Kyle's battalion in getting across the northwestern taxiway and main airfield. To get to them, the Conga headed west and took a route along the inside edge of the main airstrip...since it was relatively clear of trees and debris which could impede their advance. But this route also placed them in the sights of a *rikusentai* gun crew who were located in the area along Black Beach 2...and they were manning an old Type 41 75mm wheeled field gun. While this vintage-1908 cannon might have been out of date...it could still pack enough wallop to knock a tank out if it was firing the right ammunition.

The *Conga* had almost reached the area where the 1-2 men were holed up when the front of the tank took a direct hit from a high explosive round. The impact of the round forced the front of the tank off the ground... but it didn't penetrate its 3-inch armor plating.

"What the hell was that?" Pearson shouted...alarmed that they were under fire again.

"It had to be something big...probably a seventy-five millimeter," Mason, the gunner, said.

"You two up front okay," the TC asked, since the round had hit right in front of them.

Both the driver and assistant driver responded that they were okay...a little shaken...but no worse for wear.

"Anybody see where it came from?" Pearson shouted...swiveling his topside periscope around...trying to spot the enemy gun.

Then another round hit the tank...but it did no serious damage either...just like the first one.

Mason was traversing the turret around and looking through his periscope when he spotted a small dust cloud in the distance. "I got a possible sighting. Might be smoke from a fire...or a dust trail from the gun that just fired on us. I'm gonna put a round down there and see what happens."

"Fire when you're ready," Pearson said.

"Round's in the chamber," the loader shouted out.

"On the way," Mason yelled...and the round streaked out of the barrel as the breech block recoiled back inside the tank.

The loader then opened the breech and removed the expended shell casing...dropping it on the floor. Coughing from the propellant fumes that filled the inside of the turret, he reached down to a rack on the inside of the turret and grabbed another round and slammed it into the breech.

"Round's chambered," he yelled across to the gunner, and Mason gave a slight nod of his head in acknowledgement while keeping his eye glued to the periscope.

"Did you see that," he exclaimed, and added, "hot damn! I killed them all!"

"What happened," the driver asked, "I can't see a thing...too much dust."

"We fired at the same time. I saw another puff of smoke go up when they fired...but they missed us with their third shot. I saw it go past us. But my round hit that mountain gun and blew it up into the air. When it came down, it landed right on the crew. I saw the whole thing with my own eyes. They're all dead...crushed by their own gun!"

"Great shooting, Charlie," Pearson yelled down to Mason. "Now do you realize why I took the TC's spot and left the gunnery up to you. I knew you were much better at handling that seventy-five than I was."

"Thanks, Don," Mason replied, and he reached back and slapped Pearson's shin with his hand, and added, "we sure got it. That we did!"

The *Conga* crew didn't get much time to celebrate its victory sadly. With the field gun out of the way, the tank resumed its secondary mission and began moving in the direction where they thought Major Kyle's men were held up. After traveling a short distance, an errant mortar round…probably friendly…struck the rear deck of the tank around 1430 hours and damaged either one or both of its engines…which made the tank nearly impossible to drive.

Realizing that the *Clipper* had been parked in a revetment not too far away the night before, Sergeant Pearson ordered the driver to creep over the taxiway to their right and he had the *Conga* park just outside the revetment…within yards of the *Clipper*…which was still sitting abandoned inside.

The crew then abandoned the *Conga*…just like the *Clipper* had been…and the men ducked and dodged their way back to the C Company assembly area…tankless once again.

Had the *Conga* had better luck, it would have found the stranded men of Captain Williams' and Captain Bray's companies in the western corner of the infield triangle…and it would have accompanied them when they made their mad dash across the large, barren airstrip to the Black Beach shoreline. Then its firepower could have been put to great use at either end of the long tank trap that the marines had taken refuge in. But since the *Conga* was knocked out…and it never made it over that way…the 1-2 marines and Pharmacist Mate Tom Fumai had to ward off the Japanese attacks at both ends of the tank trap all by themselves…all during late afternoon and night of D + 1.

Chapter Fifteen

Private Reed Marcy scrambled down the tank ditch and took a seat beside the man who had been mentoring him for the past eleven hours. It was a little after 0300 hours and the man was slumped forward...with his chin resting on his chest...out from fatigue. At the sound of the man returning, he glanced up slightly, and then set his chin back on his chest. "Everything okay over there?" he mumbled, too tired to open his eyes to look at the young private again.

"I took care of it, Tom!" Marcy said proudly...but his enthusiasm and pride were lost on the corpsman.

"That's good, kid," Pharmacist Mate Fumai managed to get out...a small reward but one that carried a lot of weight for the private.

"Nothin' but a knife wound to an arm. The man next to him killed the Jap that got into their hole...but not before the Jap had sliced the other one's arm open with a bayonet. The guy in the hole with him...his name was Hughes...Rodney was his first name...said that they had heard something movin' out in front of them...and then some jabberin'...so he had thrown some grenades out that way and then they heard some moaning. Get this...Hughes said he was a professional ballplayer at one time...and that he put his good throwing arm to use. After the moaning stopped, this Jap comes charging out of nowhere and jumps in the hole with them. It surprised both of them...which is why the Jap was able to wound the other guy in the arm. He's lucky it wasn't one of those *samurai* swords the officer's carry or he might have lost the entire arm. PFC Hughes killed the Jap with his entrenching tool. Hit him right in the middle of his back with it...and probably severed his spine. Luckily, the Jap only nicked the other guy on the bicep...and it wasn't too deep...so I just put a dressing on it and called it a day."

"You use one or two dressings on it?" Fumai asked... tired...but still concerned.

"Only one. Just like you said. I know we're short."

"Well done. You'll make a fine corpsman someday," the corpsman replied...and the young Marcy beamed at the compliment. "Maybe the Japs'll leave us alone for the rest of the night so we can get some rest around here," Fumai added hopefully...and he laid back against the sloping side of the tank trap and quickly fell asleep.

Chapter Sixteen

Colonel Edson and Colonel Shoup had been working on a strategy to curve up the Japanese defenses on D + 2 ever since Colonel Edson had arrived at the CP at 2030 hours the night before...and the plan they devised was both complicated and ambitious...but eminently doable...since all the pieces of the puzzle were finally in place to make it happen.

The conditions on the island had drastically improved since 1700 hours, when Colonel Shoup had sent a message to the *Maryland* that identified the boundaries of the marine lines and an update on the conditions ashore. The message stated: *Situation at 4pm: Our line runs generally from the Burns-Philip wharf across the east end of the triangle formed by the airfield to the south coast and along the coast intermittently to a place opposite the west end of the triangle; then from the revetments north of the west end of the main air strip on to the north; another line from the most of the centre of Red 1 across the end of the island to the south coast west of the end of the main strip. Some troops in 227 dishing out hell and catching hell. Pack howitzers in position and registered for shooting on tail. Casualties many; percentage dead not known; combat efficiency - we are winning. Shoup.* The 227 referred to a gunnery target area designation that the artillery and the naval units were using for the eastern half of Red 1...which comprised the *Pocket*... which was proving to be one of the nastiest and resistive spots on the island.

When compared to previous messages that had been received by the Division Headquarters, this message was simply electrifying...and Major General Smith immediately passed it up the chain of command to show that victory was in sight. And then two more key events transpired after its reception...which further buoyed the hopes of everyone involved.

The first was the successful attack by the combined elements of the 1-2 and the 2-2 under Captains Bray and Williams that reached the southern shore near the eastern end of Black Beach 2. This effort was further strengthened when Major Kyle arrived along with C Company under Captain Clanahan...and Kyle assumed command from Lieutenant Colonel Jordan.

But what really changed the complexion of the battle was the successful landing of Major Jones' 1-6 on Green Beach later that evening. This really upped the ante...since this was the first unit which had landed fully intact...and most importantly...with all its demolition gear and flame throwers ready to go. These weapons were proving to be incredibly essential in defeating the enemy pillboxes, bunkers, and blockhouses that dominated the island's defenses...and the 1-6 was going to use them with deadly efficiency the following morning.

"Have you gotten through to anybody over there yet?" Colonel Edson asked...the irritation in his voice clearly evident.

A marine holding a microphone looked over at the colonel forlornly and said, "Nothing, sir. I haven't been able to reach Major Jones or anybody with him yet."

"Now you know what I've been going through for the last two days," Colonel Shoup said to his new commander. "I've had to resort to using runners to get the word over to Ryan...or we have to do a daisy chain and send the message out to the *Maryland*...and then they forward it on to them somehow...either by destroyer...or by direct radio contact. Sometimes the radios work...sometimes they don't. No one has been able to figure out why nothing is working correctly. Some say it's got to do with them getting water-logged...but that's a stretch in my opinion. Not every damn one of these radios was submerged in seawater...the odds of that happening are too great to contemplate."

"We experienced the same thing on the *Maryland*...you don't have to tell me." Then Colonel Edson looked around and spotted the man he was looking for. "Major Tompkins...I need you," Edson called out.

Major Tommy Tompkins...the assistant division operations officer...dropped what he was doing and hurried over to the colonel. "What can I do for you, sir?" he asked.

"I need you to make a trip over to the Beak for me. Find Major Jones. I have a message for him. I'll write this one down...so everyone involved gets every word of it correct. I am sick of half-assed messages going back and forth. There'll be no mistake about what I want done...unless you don't make it, of course."

"Which means that I've been killed...or badly wounded...so I couldn't pass the message on," the major pointed out astutely.

"Well, if you're badly wounded, major, at least make sure you get the message into the right hands so they can get it where it has to go."

"Yes, sir, that I will," Major Tompkins replied, and added, "but hopefully I won't get killed...and the message gets delivered."

"Either way, just get that damn message over there... or don't come back. It's oh four hundred...and I need it over there before dawn, so Jones has time to work out the details," Edson said back...and the colonel began writing out his message on a piece of message blank. When he was finished, he handed it to the major and said, "Now read it...just in case something ruins the message and you have to relay it verbally."

Major Tompkins read to the message to himself. It said: *1/6 attacks at 0800 to the east along south beach to establish contact with 1/2 and 2/2. 1/8 attached to 2ndMar attacks at daylight to the west along north beach to eliminate Jap pockets of resistance between Beaches Red 1 and 2. 8th Mar (less*

LT 1/8) continues attack to east. Edson, Commanding, 0400 hrs 22 Nov 43.

When he was finished reading it, he looked up and Colonel Edson said, "You got it all."

"Yes, sir. I understand what you want done," the major replied confidently.

"Okay. Explain it to me in your own words...just so I know you get it," Edson demanded.

"Well, sir, you want Major Jones at first light pass through the Three Two's lines near the southern end of Green Beach. Then the One Six attacks eastward along the southern shoreline to affect a link up with the units from the One Two and the Two Two. Major Jones will continue to attack eastward to affect a link up with the Three Eight to seal off the western end of island. I embellished a little, sir, if you don't mind. It helps me picture the plan better in my head."

"You explained it perfectly, major, just like I envisioned it. Okay, on your way and good luck."

"Sir, if I end up running into Major Ryan...do you want me to fill him in as well. I have it in my mind what you want him to do. Do you want me to brief him too?"

"What will you tell him...if you find him," Colonel Edson asked, intrigued by the ingenuity of the major.

"I'll tell Major Ryan that you want him to allow Major Jones to pass through his lines at the southern end of Green Beach at first light. Then you want him to secure the length of Green Beach so the Three Six can affect a landing there. After that's done, he is to look out for the One Eight. They'll be driving eastward from Red 2 towards him. I think that pretty much sums up what you want done there."

"It sounds like you had a hand in formulating this plan...did you?" Edson asked, amazed that the young major had been able to capture the aspects of his plan so perfectly.

"Well, I was helping Major Culhane put it together, sir. I'd be lying if I said I just came up with it on my own," Tompkins answered, happy that the colonel was impressed with his battlefield acumen.

"Okay...time's wasting. On your way...and good luck," Edson replied...and he patted Major Tompkins on the arm.

"Thank you, sir. I'll do my best. With my shield or on it, sir!" Major Tompkins answered...and Edson smiled at the Spartan reference Tompkins was using. Edson studied military history, too...so he knew that the last thing a Spartan wife would say to her husband who was heading off to war was that he was to do his duty and fight well for their home and country and return with his shield... or on it. Then, if he survived, he would return with honor...and holding his own shield. But if he was killed in the battle facing the enemy, he would be returned to her by his warrior brothers...with honor...and lying dead on his shield.

Major Tompkins placed the message in his shirt pocket and trotted off in the direction of the pier. Within minutes he spotted an incoming amtrac and he hailed it over. The amtrac driver spotted him right away and steered his way...coming to a halt in the sand a few feet away.

"What's your cargo," the major asked the crew chief... who was also doubling as the driver...since so many amtrac NCOs had been killed.

"We're carrying five-gallon cans of water, sir," the corporal answered. Then he pointed back behind him and added, "The officers who are running things at the end of the pier and down here told us to get this water in right away...that the guys really need water desperately."

"They're right. Okay, unload what you got and then I have an assignment for you and your crew."

The other two crewmen looked at the driver apprehensively and then back at the major...who continued to stare at the driver.

"What kind of assignment, sir. I mean I already got my orders. We're detailed to the pioneer section at the end of the pier...and they need us to bring supplies in... since they're running outta room at the end of the pier."

"You let me worry about that. I need to get over on Green Beach...and you're going to get me there. Understood," the major barked back.

"Aye aye, sir. It must be a pretty important mission you got," the corporal said, giving in to the officer's demand.

"It is. Now unload that water and let's get going. I wanna be there before dawn!"

The driver glared at his two crew members for but a second and then the water cans started flying out of the amtrac's hold...landing with a dull thud in the sand beside the amtrac. Meanwhile, the driver drudged down to the boat slip at the base of the pier and he tapped another officer on the shoulder. The man spun around and the two began an animated conversation…with the driver pointing in the direction of the Beak…and the marine officer pointing towards the end of the pier. Finally, the other officer walked up to the amtrac and confronted Major Tompkins. "What are you doing ordering this amtrac off on some crazy mission? This damn thing belongs to me…and it's going to do exactly what I say it does," the pioneer major said condescendingly.

Major Tompkins was caught off guard by the other officer's demeanor…since he was the same rank as the other officer. "I've got orders to take a message over to Major Jones on the Bird's Beak…and I need an amtrac to get me over there. I just picked this one since I saw it coming in," he replied defensively.

"Well, go find another one. This one belongs to me… as I said. And I need it more than you do. Getting those supplies off the end of the pier is priority number one for my section…and we need every amtrac we can lay our hands on to do it." The tall pioneer officer stood defiantly…his hands planted firmly on his hips…daring Major Tompkins to respond.

And he did. "Listen. My orders come from Colonel Edson…and I've got to get this message over there as soon as I can. If I can't get an amtrac…then I'll have to hoof it over there…which will take a lot longer. I would like to use this amtrac…if you can spare it."

Unfortunately, the pioneer major didn't budge an inch. "I don't care if God himself ordered you to do what you gotta do. This amtrac stays with me…so you'd better start walkin' if you intend on getting that message of yours over there on time."

The Butcher's Block

Major Tompkins looked past the major and didn't see another amtrac in sight…and his gut instinct told him that arguing his point with this man would be a waste of time and effort. The pioneer major had his orders…and he took them just as seriously as Tompkins took his. Without another word, Tompkins turned on his heel and left the big officer standing there…an image of arrogance. *Well, that certainly wasn't my David moment*, he thought sourly, since he had conceded defeat to Goliath in the battle for the amtrac.

It would take Major Tompkins nearly three hours to negotiate his way through some of the most dangerous ground on Betio…but he made it safe and sound to Green Beach. In doing so, he delivered one of the most important messages of the day…if not the entire battle…and one that would alter the outcome of the battle for good.

With Major Tompkins in route to the Beak, Colonel Edson then turned back to Colonel Shoup to discuss the second component of their three-pronged plan to defeat the Japanese forces on Betio. "Is Colonel Hall aware of what we want him to do?"

The colonel was talking about Colonel Elmer Hall… the 8th Regimental Commander…who had finally arrived on the island in the mid-afternoon of D + 1 to take over the duties that Major Crowe had been performing until his arrival.

"He does…and we're actually in radio contact with him…believe it or not," Colonel Shoup answered.

"So, how'd you convince him to let you keep command?" Edson wondered out loud…since Colonel Hall was nearly twenty years senior to Colonel Shoup. "He was the division's chief of staff before me…which means that he's long in the tooth. Did he fight you for it?"

"He showed up around fourteen hundred hours yesterday…and I think sitting in that Higgins boat all night and then having to fight his way to the beach really took a toll on him. So, I don't think he was really looking to take over the whole show when he got here. He knew that I had a good handle on things…where everybody is…who's coming…who's going…and he decided that I was the best man for the job. I give him credit for checking his ego and letting me keep it," Shoup explained.

"Elmer's a good man…no truck in him…and he made the right decision," Edson agreed…and then added, "so we're not losing anything now that he's in charge of the Eighth."

"Jim Crowe did a tremendous job over there on Red Three. Ran his own battalion and then got Ruud's organized too. I never really worried about our left flank to be honest…knowing that Jim was over there."

"He's a character that's for sure…I wish we had a hundred of him," Colonel Edson said seriously.

"So, Elmer knows the situation there. We need him to get the Two Eight to knock out that bunker complex just east of their lines…and then he's got to push Ruud across the eastern end of the airfield triangle to link up the One Two and Two Two under Kyle who are pushing east from their position on the southern coastline."

"Excellent...and like I said...Elmer's a good man... he'll see that it gets done." Colonel Edson then looked Colonel Shoup over...appraising him in a way...and asked, "So how did you fend Brigadier General Hermle off. We initially sent him to consult with you...but later on we ordered him to take over the whole show. We thought Colonel Hall was ashore by then...and that his presence would create a dicey situation between you and him...since you're so junior to him in rank. That obviously never happened...but why didn't General Hermle assume command? Do you know why?"

Brigadier General Hermle's failure to take command of the fighting units ashore on D Day had angered Major General Smith to no end...since there didn't seem to be any reason or explanation for why he hadn't done so. And Colonel Edson...as the commanding general's chief of staff...had been trying to piece it together himself...but he had struck out so far as well...since he had not been able to come up with an adequate answer to the perplexing question either.

"Well, when the general first contacted me...he was out near the end of the pier. At that point, with so much fire heading out that way, I just told him to stay there. I thought it was too dangerous for him and whoever was with him to try and make it in. I was honest...I didn't think they would get in alive...and I told him so. But the decision to stay there was his choice. Colonels don't give orders to generals...at least as far as I know. I guess he took my advice…since he never made any attempt to push his way in. Later, when I found out that he was still there, I sent a messenger out and I was pretty blunt about it. I told him that there were better places for a general to be…certainly not at the end of that pier anyway…and that he could better serve us by letting General Smith know the conditions we were operating under here on the island. I guess I should have used more tact…but tact hasn't always been one of my finer points. Am I in trouble?" Shoup asked bluntly.

"No. Of course not. At least now I know your half of the story. I never got to hear his end of it though. I left the *Maryland* before he made it back. General Smith is as angry as a hornet though. It won't be a pretty conversation when he finally gets back there. Smith is mild in a lot of ways…until you get him riled up…which Hermle has…right or wrong. We'll have to see how that one's gonna play out later, I guess."

With the riddle partially solved, Colonel Edson then walked over to the bunker that the CP area was centered around. He bent down and consulted a map board that was leaning against one of the several coconut logs that made up the wall of the bunker. He tapped the area of the map that indicated the *Pocket* and said, "That place… my God."

Colonel Shoup limped over and stood behind the taller Edson and glanced past his side to see what he was talking about. "Oh, yeah, the *Pocket*. Who would have envisioned that the border between Red One and Red Two would give us so much trouble? We haven't come close to shutting that area down yet. The Japs are dug in there so tight that it's gonna take demolitions and flame throwers to get them out. I've talked to some of the tankers from C Company and they tell me that they gotta pump round after round into some of these bunkers before they're knocked out. Their ammunition expenditure rate has been astronomical. And the *Pocket* and the ground approaching it is littered with these same bunkers and pillboxes. I lost one of my best officers over there...Lieutenant Hawkins...the platoon commander of the Scout Snipers...yesterday morning just trying to get to the *Pocket*. We just haven't had any luck there since most of our frontline units lost all their special weapons during the landings. We've finally got it isolated though...so it's just a matter of time now before it collapses too."

"With Hays hitting it from the east on Red Two...driving toward Red One...and the Third of the Second under Ryan hitting it from the west side...driving in the opposite direction from the Red One side...we should be able to neutralize it by the end of the day. Do they have enough men to actually finish the job?" Edson asked, apparently worried that the third part of the attack puzzle he had fashioned might take longer than expected.

"Hays is getting stronger by the minute. More and more of his men continue to dribble in. They took a horrible beating out there yesterday. They came in all alone...so all the Jap guns concentrated on just them...and the tide had gone out some...so the lagoon was dry in a lot of spots. His boys didn't have as much water to cover them on the way in as the other landing teams did. A double whammy…but they're ready to go now…thankfully."

"Okay…how about artillery support?" Edson asked…leaving nothing to chance.

"Rixey has all twelve of his pack howitzers ashore now…and they are all laid on to fire on the tail of the island. We only had five yesterday morning…but the other seven made it in throughout the day…another stellar effort. There's been plenty of them over the last two days…so many that I've lost track of all heroics that have been going on."

"What about the Second of the Tenth? Amuse me and refresh my memory. I know you probably told me where they're at…but one unit is starting to blend into another," Edson stated humbly.

"That's quite alright, sir. Culhane over there has been a big help. He's better at it than I am to be honest with you." Then Shoup stooped down and pointed to the small island that lay to the east of the tail of the Betio. "That's Bairiki Island…as you are aware. Well, we got some reports from our spotter planes overhead that indicated that they had seen Japs heading over to it when the tide was fully out around noon yesterday. That's their only escape route at this point…so I had Ray Murray land his battalion there around seventeen hundred. The island was basically secured the minute the Two Six landed…since there were only thirty or so Japs there at the time. They were killed when the bunker they were hiding in was hit by a Navy fighter. The bunker was also a gasoline dump apparently…and it exploded when the fighter's rounds hit it. Ray didn't lose a single man that I know of...quite a feat around here. Then I ordered Lieutenant Colonel Shell to land his battalion there too...and he made it in with all twelve of his seventy-fives by two this morning. He has his guns registered on the tail as well. Those twenty-four seventy-fives are going to be firing around the clock to neutralize the tail end of the island and prevent any reinforcements from trying to help the Japs that are trapped in the western end now. We've got them penned up pretty solid."

"Naval gunfire and air?" Edson asked sharply.

"At oh seven hundred, the Navy's going to unleash their fourteen and sixteen-inchers five hundred yards east of the Burns-Philip Wharf...where Crowe's men are dug in...and then they're going to walk their way eastwards and southwards to obliterate the entire tail right down to Takarongo Point. Then the Navy fighters and bombers will go in...for twenty minutes...over the same ground. They'll repeat the same process at zero eight thirty...and at zero nine thirty...and at ten hundred hours...which will make it nearly impossible for the Japs to move above ground east of airfield circle for several hours. That's the plan at least...but these damn Japs must have an underground tunnel network going on here...cause they always seem to be able to move men around...just when we think they can't."

"I never underestimate the Japs. I learned that a long time ago...over in China. They're tough...and they'll keep fighting as long as their leaders are there to lead them. If we can chop off the head of the snake though, then the body dies on its own pretty quickly." Colonel

Edson made a slashing movement with his hand across his throat...emphasizing the old adage.

"Maybe we've already killed Shibasaki then," Shoup theorized. "I am still wondering why the Japs didn't attack us with all their forces the first night we were here...or last night even. They've always done so in the past...but they broke that mold here. Some of the staff seem to think that they're having the same commo problems we are...so they couldn't coordinate a general attack. But I don't think Shibasaki would have overlooked that contingency...and he would have prepped his subordinate commanders to just do it on their own authority if they didn't hear from him. Anyway, we were damn lucky that they chose not to attack...whatever the cause was."

"I hope he's still alive...so I can personally shoot him myself when we capture the bastard," Edson seethed... making no effort to conceal his legendary hatred for the enemy.

"You might have to get in line on that one, sir," Shoup laughed, "if we're able to bring him in."

Edson tough demeanor cracked for an instant...and he laughed along with Colonel Shoup as he pictured the imperious Japanese admiral being led into their CP at the end of a private's bayonet. *That'd be a sight worth seeing*, he thought, but his intimacy with the Japanese culture told him that it would never happen. "No...if Shibasaki's still alive...he's probably thinking of committing *hari kari* by now. No Jap admiral is going to allow himself to be taken prisoner. Heck, I doubt we end up taking many prisoners at all here...you wait and see."

"Let 'em all go out by their own hand," Colonel Shoup replied callously, "I could care less. If it'll end up saving more of my boys, I'm all for it."

"Amen to that," Colonel Edson agreed heartily...and the two leaders settled back finally...knowing their plan had been fully disseminated to all the parties involved... which was all they could do. Now it was up to their subordinate leaders...men like Crowe and Ruud...and Kyle and Hays...and Ryan and Jones...who they trusted implicitly...to carry it out.

Chapter Seventeen

"That watch of yours says it's oh seven hundred...is that what you said, sir?" Petraglia asked, glancing skyward.

"Yup...or close to it...like I said," Lieutenant Hackett replied...glancing skyward as well. The two men...and everyone else in the lieutenant's *ad hoc* group...were looking at the sky above them...searching for the shells that were now screaming their way towards the tail of the island...down to their left.

Miles away...out to sea...the battleships and cruisers that were assigned to provide gunfire support to the Betio operation had begun firing their sixteen and fourteen-inch shells at precisely 0700 hours...just like the plan called for.

"I wouldn't wanna be on the receiving end of one of those monsters," Petraglia, the lieutenant's runner, said warily.

"Remember when we were back on Tulagi...and those Jap battleships and cruisers would sail down the Slot and sit there all night in Iron Bottom Sound and shell the guys over on the *Canal*. You could literally feel the shells leaving their guns all the way across the water."

"And they sounded like a freight train going over," Petraglia cut in...agreeing with his platoon commander. "I'm sure glad we got over there in mid-November. The Jap Navy never did shell us the way they did those First Division boys."

"No...our Navy and the Cactus Air Force had beaten them fair and square by then. Sinking all those Jap transports in the *Slot* really broke their back. We were sure lucky in that regard."

"I ran into some of those guys that had endured a few of those bombardments...before they left the island... and they said waiting for those Jap shells to hit was the worst feeling they ever went through. They kept saying how helpless they felt...never knowing if the next shell was going to blast them to kingdom come."

"I remember reading a newspaper article almost two and a half years ago about the *Bismark*...the German battleship that terrorized the British Navy in the Atlantic."

"Am I getting another history lesson, sir?" Petraglia asked...yet again.

"I wouldn't call it a history lesson...since the story I read was written in Nineteen Forty-One. This is more like a current events lesson...but you probably hated those lessons too, didn't you?" the lieutenant replied... knowing Petraglia all too well.

The PFC just shook his head in surrender…like he always did…and he motioned the lieutenant to keep going by waving his hand towards him…back and forth. "Come on…let me have it…since you're gonna tell me anyway."

"Well, this article was from a British newspaper…and the writer had interviewed a sailor from the *Hood*…which was the one the two British battleships that first confronted the *Bismark*…right after it broke into the Denmark Strait. This sailor was one of the three guys that survived the *Hood's* sinking…and he said that you could actually see and hear the shells heading their way when the *Bismark* began firing on them…the shells were that big…and the *Bismark* and the *Hood* each carried fifteen-inch guns. Most of our battleships out there are armed with sixteen-inchers…even bigger than the *Hood's* and the *Bismark's*.

"Only three guys survived that ship's sinking…out of what…fifteen hundred maybe?" Petraglia asked…genuinely interested…a rare moment indeed.

"The *Hood* had fourteen hundred sailors and officers aboard…fourteen hundred and eighteen to be exact…if you really are interested," Hackett answered, surprised that Petraglia had finally shown some excitement about a conversation they were having. "The Hood went down so fast that only three made it off alive. They weren't stationed down below…all those guys were killed instantly when one of the *Bismark's* shells hit one of its ammunition magazines amidships…and the *Hood* went down in less than three minutes."

"Didn't the *Bismark* get sunk later on?" Petraglia said, intrigued.

The Butcher's Block

"Yes, it did. The *Bismark's* opening voyage lasted only eight days...and she was sunk after she was cornered by a whole slew of British warships. But what really did her in was that her steering mechanism had been damaged earlier...by a perfect torpedo hit from a *Swordfish* torpedo plane. Talk about luck...and British bravery. Those Swordfish torpedo planes were two-winger jobs...hopelessly outdated by then...yet a squadron of them took on the *Bismark*...and one plane got a miraculous hit."

"How many men did the *Bismark* lose," Petraglia wanted to know.

"The British Navy picked up a hundred and ten survivors. They believe another two thousand men or so went down with the ship."

"That's a lot of men to lose in one day," the runner noted, and added, "I wonder how many men we've lost here...over the last two days?"

"That's a good question...but one we're not going to know until the battle is finished...and all the mopping up is done. It'll take a while to get everything sorted out...you know...who's missing...and whether they've been wounded and taken out to the ships...or if they were actually killed...if they can find a body. Trying to piece it all together will be difficult to say the least," the lieutenant pointed out ominously.

"I just hope I'm one of the living...that's all," Petraglia added, and he marked himself with the sign of the cross.

"You and me both," Hackett said hopefully...and just then the island's tail began erupting in explosions...too many to count at once.

The two men could feel the reverberations from the explosions…even though they were happening over a thousand yards from their position along the western taxiway.

"This must be the start of something big," the lieutenant said out loud…and the men on either side of him began looking around…trusting their officer's instincts. "Okay, everybody…keep your eyes open…and let me know if you see anything out there," he added cautiously.

"Aye aye, sir!" rippled down the line…and the men began scanning the ground all around them…looking for any sign of movement that might indicate something new was afoot.

Once again, it was the eagle-eyed Feeney who sang out first. "Got some movement off to our left rear, lieutenant," the battlefield-promoted PFC called out…alerting the lieutenant and the fourteen other men who were splayed out around him.

"Friendlies?" the lieutenant asked…since he had just swung around and was still trying to spot whatever it was that Feeney was seeing.

"Don't think so," Feeney answered quickly…since the men were wearing the tan and green uniforms that were emblematic of the *rikusentai* who were serving on Betio. But what Feeney also noticed, and what really gave them away, was that they were all wearing wrap-around leggings…which no marine would be using.

The Butcher's Block

Now the lieutenant saw them...and they seemed to be falling back through a series of trenches to occupy a new line of defense that was already set up about two hundred yards east of the *Pocket*.

There must be nearly a hundred of them, the lieutenant thought, *far too many for us to take on.*

"Are they retreating, sir?" someone said down the line.

"Not retreating," the lieutenant yelled out...so everybody could hear him. "They're establishing a new line of defense."

Then it became obvious that the lieutenant was right...since the enemy soldiers began disappearing one by one as they scrambled into a series of pillboxes that were hardly visible to the naked eye.

"There must be twenty bunkers and pillboxes over there...and that's just a small section of Red Two," Petraglia offered up...trying to make sense of what he had just seen as well.

"Did you notice how they're set up?" Lieutenant Hackett asked him...wondering if he had picked up on the tactical advantage they offered the defenders.

"How they're set up, sir? What do you mean?" Petraglia answered...missing the point.

"There's two lines of them...with about ten or so in each line...and fifty yards separating the two lines. And every one of them are mutually supporting. They don't sit on a straight line...they're staggered...so each one can fire in support of the other one. It's brilliant...and deadly for the guys that gotta attack them," the lieutenant explained.

Even though they were difficult to see, Petraglia could make out enough of them to see the point the lieutenant was making…and he realized that anyone trying to attack that section of Red 2 would be in for a real fight.

"Why do you think they exposed themselves like that, sir?" Petraglia asked…wondering the same thing that everyone else was.

"They must know something we don't, right. Until now, I hadn't seen a single Jap move around out in the open like that. They obviously did it for some reason. Let's hope it's because they're damned scared about what's coming down the beach toward them," was all the lieutenant could come up with to rationalize why the Japs decided to risk a move like that.

"I've only seen two Japs out in the open so far…in plain view…and that's after two full days of fighting. I shot both down near the seawall when you sent me on my first mission…the one where I met Colonel Shoup," the runner acknowledged. Then he glanced down and saw the two notches he had scratched into the wooden stock of his M-1 rifle at the time…confirming his kills. *I wonder why that was so important to do then,* he thought sourly, knowing that his enthusiasm for killing had since drained away…having seen too much of it in the two long days he had spent on Betio.

"Well, we should have an answer one way or the other soon enough…since they would only be doing it if they were desperate…at least I hope that's why they did it," the lieutenant said, summing up his take on the Jap move on Red Beach 2.

"So, what do we do now, sir?" his runner asked…wondering what the lieutenant had in mind.

The Butcher's Block

Lieutenant Hackett considered several options...and then responded, "We sit and wait...for now."

"Just sit and wait, sir?"

"Yup...just sit and wait...again. We got two groups of Japs on either side of us...and both groups are way too big for us to take on...so we sit and wait. I don't like it... but I gotta be able to bring somebody home alive so they can tell their grandkids what the fighting on Betio was really like. That's my plan...you happy with it," the lieutenant asked his runner.

"I like it, sir. Almost sounds like something like I would have come up with...don't you think. Maybe I should consider becoming an officer when this is all over," Petraglia answered happily.

"Maybe you should," the lieutenant quipped, "maybe you should."

The lieutenant and his runner didn't have to wait very long to get the answer to their question. Minutes after they saw the Japanese streaming back to occupy a new line of defense, a lone American tank came into view. This was not one of the big, rambling Sherman tanks that Hackett knew was supposed to be operating somewhere on the island by now. Instead, this tank was one of the smaller ones that had also been assigned to the Betio operation...and Hackett had seen this type of tank before...on Guadalcanal...a little over a year ago.

The tank clanking its way through the debris inland of Red Beach 2 was a Stuart M3A1 Light tank and it carried a crew of four men inside it: the tank commander-gunner… the loader…the driver…and the bow machine gunner… who also ran the radios. The tank weighed a little over fifteen tons when fully loaded…so it was about half the size of the larger Sherman tank…and it was armed with a much smaller main gun. Instead of the more powerful 75mm gun that the Sherman tank was using, the Stuart was equipped with a 37mm cannon…which would prove to be a drawback on Betio. The tank was also armed with three .30 caliber machine guns and two of them were controlled by the same crew member. The TC-gunner fired two machine guns…one of which was coaxially mounted with the main gun in the turret of the tank. The bow machine gunner controlled the operation of the ball-mounted, .30 caliber machine gun that was located just inside the right front fender of the tank…and he could swivel it around to fire up and down and in an arc out in front of the tank. The last machine gun was mounted to a bracket on top of the turret…so it was handled by the tank commander too…and it served as both an anti-aircraft weapon and an infantry-suppression weapon depending on the need at the time. The M3 was named after the famed Confederate Major General Jeb Stuart…who served as Lieutenant General Robert E. Lee's cavalry commander in the Army of Northern Virginia in the Civil War…which seemed analogous…since the tank was intended to serve as a scout vehicle…rather than a tank killer per say.

"Where'd that come from?" Petraglia asked…astonished that an American tank had been able to get ashore.

"They were supposed to land right after we did," the lieutenant explained. "They probably had as bad a time getting in as we did…maybe worse."

"It never dawned on me that we had those things with us," the runner replied…and added, "since I never saw them on any of the ships that were beside us. I saw amtracs loaded up…but no tanks."

"The big M Fours were loaded on that new landing ship we just got. There are only three of them in the Pacific…and none over in the Atlantic…so they are a big deal. The one that came here with us is the USS *Ashland*. The Navy calls it an APD. The D stands for dock. It's big enough to carry several LCMs inside it…which are already loaded up with their tanks. The APD comes to a stop and then it floods its well deck with water. It opens its stern doors and the LCMs pull out using a ramp…ingenious."

"So that's why I never saw any of those tanks…interesting," Petraglia said…trying to remember what the big APD looked like.

"You should've seen the Stuarts that were supposed to land on Red Two with us though," the lieutenant pointed out.

"Oh yeah. Why's that, sir," Petraglia asked…perplexed.

"Because the tanks that are assigned to support our battalion were loaded on our transport. They were down in the bottom of the hold. You would've seen them if you had bothered to get out of your bunk for just two minutes and looked around the ship."

"Sleeping is very important, sir. Don't blame me for looking out for myself," Petraglia replied defensively.

"Sleeping for twenty hours a day is not healthy...no matter what spin you put on it, Petraglia," the lieutenant answered back. "You only got up to eat and crap...as far as I could tell."

"Well, it was a boring voyage. Sleeping made the trip easier to take. And details never really concerned me...so the fact that those tanks were stored down below me doesn't strike me as being that important. The fact that one is here now is important though. I don't clutter my brain up with any more information than I got to... which makes me useful as a runner."

"This ought to be good...and why's that," Hackett replied...jesting his runner.

"Since my brain isn't so cluttered up with all that stuff you find so interesting, it's free to remember all the important stuff I have to relay up to higher when you send me off on one of those important missions of yours. That's why, sir."

The lieutenant stared at Petraglia with a blank look on his face...and then he said, "Oh, I didn't think of that. Keep it up."

"Thank you, sir," Petraglia answered slyly, "I intend to!"

Lieutenant Hackett and PFC Petraglia continued to watch the small tank snake its way through the debris that was littering the ground in front of it...choosing its path wisely. Every so often the tank would stop...back up...

and then head off to the left or right...obviously dodging a shell hole or some other obstacle that could disable the tank. At other times, the tank would pull up and the turret would swivel around slightly as the TC lined up a target. Then Hackett and Petraglia would hear a sharp *cracccck* as the gun recoiled...and a 37mm round was fired at whatever the TC was trying to destroy. Sometimes this process would be repeated again and again when a particularly tough target was encountered.

"How many of those tanks do we have," Petraglia asked...his eyes still riveted on the tank as it stopped once again.

"We should have fifty-four...plus some scout cars... but we got shortchanged. We only have thirty-six of 'em...and no scout cars. Those days are over. And these Stuarts probably won't be around much longer either. They were designed to fight the last war...not this one. They'll meet their demise here...just like the horse cavalry did in the First World War." The lieutenant then glanced around...and everyone in the group was watching the tank drama as well...just like they were.

"Do you know any of the officers in charge of them?" Petraglia asked, always amazed at how small the officer community seemed to be in the Marine Corps.

"Not a one. Strange isn't it. Lieutenant Colonel Swenceski is the CO...I know that much. But I do know some of the officers in the company with the M Fours...

but not many. Lieutenant Bale is the CO of the M 4 company. I do know him. Tankers are a breed all to themselves," the lieutenant answered.

"Swenceski...sounds like a good Polak boy. There were a bunch of Poles living up in Buffalo near where I grew up. Hard workers...and tough. As for the rest of them, I don't know any either," Petraglia said offhandedly.

"There's two companies out here with us. B and C Companies. They're in the Second Tank Battalion. Like I said...they only have thirty-six tanks between them... and each landing team was supposed to have a group of them coming in behind them to offer support. The landing schedule had them coming in ahead of the larger Shermans...and I guess that's one part of the plan that seems to have worked...or that tank wouldn't be here. Let's hope we see some M Fours too...and more Stuarts as well. It's nice to know that one aspect of the landing plan went off without a hitch," Lieutenant Hackett said, not knowing any better.

The Stuart tank that Hackett and Petraglia were watching was one of the seven tanks from the 2nd Tank Battalion that had been assigned to support the advance of the 1-8 in the early morning attack along the western section of Red 2.

The battalion had thirty-six tanks scattered aboard the transports when it got to Betio...and by D + 2 only twenty-four were left. The other twelve had been lost on D Day...when their Mike boats got hit by anti-boat fire as they were trying to land. Of the survivors, twenty-two Stuarts had eventually landed late in the afternoon and night of D + 1 on Red Beach Two…their journey to the island made more perilous and time-consuming by the depth of the water around the reef when they came in. The other two Stuarts had managed to land over on Green Beach…coming in right after Major Jones' 1-6 had landed. These two stalwarts from B Company had somehow survived the one-thousand-yard journey to the island…a distance twice as long as the ones that came in near the pier on Red Beach 2. And these two had worked with Major Jones' battalion at first…during the early morning hours…but they were now getting ready to assist Major Kyle's men as they tried to break out of their perimeter along the southern coastline on D + 2.

Chapter Eighteen

In designing the order of attack for his battalion, Major Larry Hays had to consider the width and length of the area that his battalion would be moving across on Red 2. Near the jump off point...which was only a hundred yards or so west of Colonel Shoup's CP...his three companies would be packed into a narrow front of one hundred and seventy-five yards. But as his companies advanced up the beach, the area widened out to a little over three hundred yards by the aircraft revetments that sat on the northwestern end of the main runway. To reach that point, his men would have to traverse nearly four hundred yards of devastated landscape...which would be a major accomplishment...given how well the ground was defended. Because of this layout, Major Hays decided to employ all three of his companies at the same time...in a line abreast formation...which would allow him to attack across a broad front in one swoop.

The Butcher's Block

He could have chosen to attack in a column of companies...but that would have limited his firepower...since only one company could have engaged the enemy at a time. And he was convinced that the best way to defeat the Japanese was to overwhelm them...and to do that, he needed to have all his weapons employed at once.

"Initially, we'll be attacking over ground that has been somewhat cleared already," he said to the company commanders who had gathered around him. Then he knelt down and pointed with his index finger at a spot on the map that was spread out on the ground in front of him. "We're here," he indicated, circling his finger to an area on the eastern side of Red 2. "The Scout Sniper Platoon was operating in this section yesterday...and Lieutenant Hawkins knocked out several bunkers...all by himself. This was a great start...but he couldn't get them all...and that's where we come in. We'll finish up what he started... but it'll get tougher as we advance down the beach to the west. Nobody has been over there as far as I know. And this dope is coming right from Colonel Shoup himself. These Japs have had two full days to dig in and get ready for us...so let your boys know that we're in for a fight."

The company commanders had also knelt down by now...so they could get a better look at the map. Within seconds, they were glancing at each other warily as they considered the ominous task ahead of them. "And I thought the landing yesterday was as bad as it could get," one of them said under his breath.

"Sir, we tried to push our way to the west a little yesterday...after the First of the Second pulled out...and we met fierce resistance. Are we going to have any help...

tanks...flame thrower teams...anything...when we make our move?" another CO asked.

"Yes, we will. We're gonna have seven Stuarts working with us. Two of them are from B Company...and the other five are from C Company. I'm going to give two to each of you and I'll keep one in reserve with me. Which leads me to the scheme of maneuver. I want B Company to advance down the beach...using the seawall to anchor your right flank. A Company will be next to them...in the middle. And I want C Company to take the left flank. Guide off the taxiway...but you can certainly push out if conditions permit it. B Company will get the two B Company Stuarts. It just seems easier that way. Our overall objective is to take the *Pocket*...the area around the cove that gave us so much trouble yesterday. We'll jump off at oh seven hundred...just like Colonel Edson wants. Any questions?"

No hands were raised...so there were no questions concerning the attack.

"Okay then," the major said resolutely, "go brief your platoons on what we're trying to accomplish out here this morning...and we set sail at seven. Best of luck to you all...and let's get some payback for yesterday." The major wore a mask of grim determination...the likes of which none of the officers had ever seen before...an ominous sign if there ever was one.

Looks aside, nothing could have prepared the men of the 1-8 for what lay ahead of them in the Red 2 sector... other than the horror of the landing itself.

The Butcher's Block

At 0700, the three companies fanned out and began advancing into the areas they were assigned...with the six Stuart tanks leading the charge.

And the Japs were waiting for them...just like they had been the morning before.

Major Hays and the men of the 1-8 had advanced only fifty yards or so when all hell broke loose. Machine gun fire laced their entire front...from one end to the other... and all three companies were forced to take cover...the men burrowing into the ground where there was nothing to protect them...or jumping into foxholes or shell holes when they were available. Luckily, the tanks were able to advance though since there were no anti-tank guns in this area...and their thin armor plating still offered a modicum of protection from the intense machine gun fire that had driven the marines underground.

Now the fight took on a rhythm of leapfrogging with the tanks and the marines that would last throughout the morning for all three companies. Each Stuart tank would advance a short distance in front of the marines in the company it was supporting...select a target...usually a pillbox or bunker...and blast away at its firing port with its 37mm cannon. The tank rarely knocked out a position with one shot alone...since the round its main gun fired was just too small to do much damage. But what the tank could do was neutralize the bunker or pillbox long enough that the marines nearby could assault it and knock it out themselves. But to get to it, they had to first dodge through a deadly hail of machine gun bullets that were coming from the other bunkers and pillboxes that were positioned nearby to support it. If they got close enough without being hit, the men would then approach the bunker from its side…since most of the firing apertures on the bunkers were facing the direction of the cove…where the landing craft would come from…and pummel it with grenades. And as the marines got closer still, the tank would then move on to the next bunker and take it under attack…while the marines then entered the bunker and cleared it out using grenades, rifle fire, bayonets, and K-Bar knives in close quarters combat with the Japanese who were still alive inside.

Once a bunker was finally knocked out, the deadly sequence would resume…as the marines who weren't wounded…or dead…would then make their way to the next bunker that one of the tanks was already firing on. It was a brutal and exhausting process…and before long the marine attack had ground to a halt.

"The tank's stopping again," PFC Klein stated…annoyed. "Is this ever going to end?"

"How would I know. It's probably got another target ahead of it…or something's in the way. What else would it be," Corporal Bosco responded…short of breath. "The TC must see something that we don't. Anyway…I can stand for a break. This is killing me," he huffed out…drained after slithering and dashing over the broken

The Butcher's Block

ground that made up the inland section of Red 2 to attack one bunker after another.

"This'll be our fifth...if we go after it," Klein replied... shifting gears...now sounding excited about the prospect of going after one more bunker.

"I just don't have it in me...I'm spent. Let someone else take a chance on this one," Bosco said truthfully.

"I'll go...just cover me...okay," Klein replied quickly... and he scampered out of the hole without waiting for a response.

As tired as he was, Bosco still trained his M-1 rifle out ahead of him...searching for a target to fire on...but he came up empty as PFC Klein continued to run in the direction of the tank. Then he watched as Klein skidded to an abrupt halt and looked desperately behind him... all the while trying to raise his rifle to a firing position.

What Corporal Bosco couldn't see...and what PFC Klein had stumbled on...was a deep, reinforced foxhole that held four *rikusentai*...and one of them was arming a Type 99 *Hakobakurai* grenade mine...the same type of mine that had crippled the Sherman tank, *Clipper*, on D + 1 not far away.

Klein had not only surprised the four Japs...but he was also quicker on the draw...and he managed to get several shots off with his M-1...before the sustained *ripppppppp* of a Jap machine gun found its mark. Klein's helmet suddenly flew off his head and several puffs of cotton fiber exploded out of the front of his utility shirt as several machine gun bullets tore through his back and mid-section...eviscerating him. Klein then fell face-forward, and his body tumbled into the foxhole beside the bodies of the three Japs that he had managed to kill with his rifle fire. Unfortunately though, he had missed the sailor holding the mine...who was amazed that he was still alive. But the sight of his three buddies now lying dead beside him galvanized him to make his next move.

Corporal Bosco was shocked when he saw Klein's body pitch forward and disappear from sight...and he immediately scanned the ground behind Klein to see if he could spot the location of the machine gun that had hit him. He tracked back about thirty yards and saw it...a small, rectangular slit in the middle of a mound of sand that was covered by a bunch of palm fronds. The TC of the tank must have spotted it as well...since the turret's main gun began swinging over in its direction...and within seconds, the gunner had fired several 37mm rounds at the hidden pillbox. Some of the rounds struck the sand around the firing slit and glanced off...but several other rounds hit the bullseye and went directly into the aperture...triggering a small fire as the ammo stored inside it lit off.

    Bosco then looked back to the spot where Klein had fallen and was surprised to see a *rikusentai* who was covered in blood suddenly emerge like a ghost from the ground and bolt off in the direction of the tank. Some of the other men in Bosco's squad spotted him too...and they took him under fire...just like Bosco was doing. But the Jap was extremely agile as he darted back and forth to escape their fire and they all missed their mark.

The young Japanese sailor clutched the anti-tank mine in his hands and closed his eyes. He said a quick prayer to the gods above…asking for their blessing over the mission he was about to undertake. When he opened his eyes back up, his three friends were staring at him solemnly…knowing what he was about to do. Then, out of nowhere, a marine had appeared above them and opened fire. Before they could react, the marine had killed his three buddies with his rifle…and then the marine had been hit as well…by a friendly machine gun nest that was only thirty yards away. Incredibly, the marine had then fallen into the foxhole with them…and the *rikusentai* placed the mine down and grabbed for his long-bladed, razor-sharp bayonet…which he had stuck in the wood flooring beside him. He clutched the weapon tightly and crabbed over to the marine…who despite his horrible injuries…was still breathing. The marine looked at him forlornly…in anticipation of what was coming…and closing his eyes, he said a silent prayer.

The *rikusentai* had no feelings for the marine…and had no intention of sparing him. Marines like the man lying in front of him had been trying to kill him and his friends over the last two days…and mercy was not an option as this point. Without a thought, the *rikusentai* plunged the bayonet into the marine's chest…aiming for his heart…and blood splattered him as he continued to stab the man until his breathing stopped.

That is for my friends, he thought grimly, *and for our Emperor too.*

Discarding the bayonet, he then crawled back over and retrieved the mine. He examined the cloth case and felt the explosive disk inside…and then looked at the four magnets that were attached around the case. *These rarely work,* he knew, and he set the time-delay fuse for half a minute and inserted it into the mine…figuring that he could reach the tank in less than ten seconds once he started running.

He slowly counted off fifteen seconds in his head… and then he got ready. At the twenty second mark, he dashed out of the foxhole and began weaving his way towards the tank…figuring that he would be taken under fire by the marines who were there to protect it.

Just like he thought, bullets began whizzing by him… but somehow none of them hit him. He clenched his jaw and kept right on going…a look of grim determination set on his face. Now he aimed for the rear of the tank… which was where the engine was…and the steel monster's Achilles heel.

I've done it! he thought joyously, and he pressed the mine firmly against the engine housing…which was scorching hot. *Don't let go now,* he told himself…and he held on for all he was worth.

Bosco couldn't believe what he was seeing. He had heard about the fanatical nature of the Japanese soldiers they were fighting…but now he was witnessing it with his own

The Butcher's Block

eyes. *This Jap is one of those crazy ones*, he thought, and for a brief second Bosco gave the man a grudging level of respect...given what he was doing. Even with all the marines firing at him, the Jap had managed to make it to the Stuart tank alive...and then he did the unthinkable. Instead of tossing whatever he was carrying unto the back deck of the tank and running away, this Jap just stood there...holding it...as rifle bullets continued to ricochet off the hull of the tank around him. And still, no one could manage to hit him. Then...in a split second...an explosion occurred...and the man ceased to exist...except for his legs...which were still standing there on their own...and smoke began to belch out of the back of the disabled tank.

When no one else moved, Corporal Bosco left the safety of his hole and cautiously made his way over to the tank. Using the butt of his rifle, he banged on the sponson box on the side of the Stuart...trying to get the attention of someone inside. When this didn't work, he removed his helmet and began banging away with it instead. Then the top hatch swung open...and the TC stuck his head out...looking around.

"Down here," Bosco yelled...and he banged his helmet against the side one more time.

The TC swung around and saw Bosco standing there and said, "Jeez, lighten up with that helmet. It sounds like someone is beating on a base drum inside...and it's already too noisy in there as it is."

"Sorry," the squad leader replied…and he put the helmet back on his head.

"What the heck just happened. My driver is telling me our engine is damaged. Did you see what happened?" he asked…and swung around in the turret to look at the damaged back end of the tank.

"A Jap sapper just blew himself up against the back of your tank. We tried to shoot him down, but he came out of nowhere…and he was just too fast for us," Bosco explained guiltily.

"That was the one thing that worried us the most. The Japs did it on the *Canal*…so we figured that they'd try to do the same thing here. Now we know…don't we," the TC said dryly. Then he yelled down to his driver, "Will she move at all?"

A voice from inside the tank yelled back up at him, "The control panel warning light is flashing…which isn't good… but it could be worse. She'll probably move…but if we push her too hard, the engine will seize up sooner or later."

"Okay. Let's turn her around and head back…and go slow. We can't risk breaking down out here," the tank commander…Sergeant Vince DeWitt…said to his driver… PFC Mike Connelly. Then he turned back to Bosco and said, "Looks like we're outta the game for the time being. A mechanic will have to look under the hood to determine how bad we're hit. Good luck the rest of the way."

"Thanks for your help," Bosco acknowledged…and the TC waved to him and dropped down inside the turret. Then a hand reached up and grabbed the handle on the hatch and pulled it forward. The hatch slammed shut with a resounding bang…and then the tank limped off in the direction of the pier...leaving a light trail of smoke in its wake.

"Did you see that?" Petraglia exclaimed as he turned to look at his platoon commander.

"See what?" First Lieutenant Hackett asked, raising his head up off his chest and glancing at the sun overhead. "I must've nodded off again. It's the heat...I can't seem to stay awake this morning. What did I miss?"

"A Jap just ran up to that tank and detonated a mine against the back of it...where the engine is located. He killed himself trying to knock the tank out."

Lieutenant Hackett looked over at the tank and saw some smoke wafting off its rear end as it turned around slowly and headed back east...towards the pier. "The guy must've succeeded...since the tank is leaving."

"I wonder if any of the crew got killed by the explosion," Petraglia thought out loud.

"Maybe not. If that Jap had put it against the turret, he probably would've killed the TC and the gunner. But the engine probably protected everyone inside. He might have given them a nasty headache...but I doubt anyone is dead," the lieutenant said, volunteering an answer. Then he yelled out, "Anyone see the name on that tank?" Since everyone had been watching it, the lieutenant figured that someone might have been able to identify it.

"It had *Claptrap* written on its turret...in big white letters," PFC Feeney sang out...no surprise.

"So, it's from C Company," Hackett said.

"How do you know that?" Petraglia asked.

"Because the tankers use piffy sayings or words that start with the letter of the company they are in to nickname their tanks. Someone in the crew comes up with a nickname he likes and then they all vote on it."

"Piffy?" Petraglia said, "Seriously?"

"Yeah…piffy. You know what that means, don't you?" Hackett replied…but seeing Petraglia's point in his choice of words.

"I know what 'piffy' means…but I bet the tankers wouldn't describe their nicknames as 'piffy', sir."

"Maybe you're right. So, they pick something that they can all identify with…like the name of a family member…or a funny cartoon character. Anything they can come up with that strikes a chord with all of them. Lieutenant Bale's crew named their tank, *Cecilia*, and another crew named their tank, *China Gal*, for instance."

"Lemme guess…Cecilia was a girlfriend or the wife of one of the guys in the crew, right?" Petraglia said, catching on.

"Not exactly. They named their tank after the driver's new-born daughter. His wife had her while we were in New Zealand."

"Nice," Petraglia replied. "What about *China Gal*? That sounds a little more creative."

"Well, that crew named their tank after a Chinese stripper in San Francisco. I guess the crew spent a lot of time…and money…at the joint where she was dancing," the lieutenant answered.

Petraglia looked at the lieutenant askance…and said, "Seriously?"

"I'm dead serious. I know Lieutenant Bale…and he told me that personally. We had a good laugh over it, too."

Petraglia considered the implications that the nickname *Claptrap* entailed, and he nodded at the tank in the distance and said, "I don't even wanna think about why those guys named their tank like they did."

"Maybe one of the guys likes to spread a lot of scuttlebutt…so they named it after him," Hackett replied innocently.

"Let's hope so," his runner added, shaking his head.

"Now, check this out," Petraglia said a few minutes later, gesturing wildly in the direction the tank had taken when it left the fight.

The lieutenant looked that way again and finally saw what had gotten his runner's attention. "They gotta be our boys!" the lieutenant exclaimed. "I wonder what unit they're with?"

"I don't care who they are…as long as they keep headin' our way," Petraglia responded happily.

Then the lieutenant yelled out, "Feeney!"

"On it, sir," Feeney yelled right back, and he took off without the lieutenant having to tell him what to do.

The last thing that PFC Feeney wanted to happen... happened. *I can't believe this,* he thought, but he understood it. *These guys have been told that the only ones out here are Japs...so they think I'm one*...which is why the marines that Feeney was trying to reach were shooting at him.

The marines of C Company had spotted the lone man scrambling his way over to them...and they just figured that he was another sapper on a suicide mission. The fact that he was wearing marine utilities didn't matter much...since the Japs had been known to swap their own uniforms for marine ones so they could infiltrate the marine lines. And as the battle had dragged on, several Japs in marine disguise had been killed near the pier...so the marines of C Company were taking no chances...and especially so after seeing the Stuart tank get blown up.

"Either that Jap is crazy...or he's actually one of our guys," Corporal Bosco said, yelling to the remaining eight men in his make-shift squad. "Hold your fire...and let's see what he does next."

The man they were watching then began waving a piece of clothing of some sort that was draped over a Thompson submachine gun.

"What is he waving?" another one of the new men yelled out.

Bosco squinted harder and said, "I can't make it out...but that's a Thompson...and no Jap is gonna have

The Butcher's Block

a Thompson all the way out here. Let the man in...but keep him covered if it turns out that I'm wrong."

Several of Bosco's men then began waving the man over...and before they knew it, PFC Feeney was sliding in beside Corporal Bosco.

"Thanks," Feeney said...breathless.

"How the hell did you get out here?" Bosco asked... astounded that a marine could be out here all alone and still be alive.

Feeney took a second to catch his breath...and then he said, "I'm PFC Feeney...Sean Feeney. I was a private two days ago...but I got promoted to PFC by my platoon commander. We're with the Second of the Second. E Company. We landed on D Day over there...and we fought our way over here yesterday. Who are you guys?" Feeney had pointed back towards the area where Red 1 and Red 2 intersected...in the area where the *Pocket* was.

"We? There are more of you?" Bosco replied, incredulous.

"The lieutenant's over there...and fourteen more... plus me. But we're not all from the Second. We lost a lotta guys on the way in...but we picked up a few stragglers along the way. D Day was a helluva day," Feeney answered.

"We weren't aware that anyone made it over here... on D Day or otherwise. I'm Corporal Tom Bosco...and we're with C Company...First of the Eighth. We landed yesterday morning...and we had a helluva time gettin' in too," Bosco acknowledged...understanding Feeney's plight.

"We watched your unit try to land yesterday morning. It didn't go so well...kinda like ours," Feeney replied... and he shook his head to indicate how bad the landing had looked from their perspective.

"Well, we're glad that you guys made it in, too. You're the first friendlies that we've actually run into out here in Indian Country. The rest of your unit...what's left of them...is supposed to be over by Black Beach now. They got over there yesterday...and we got this headache thrown in our lap. So, we're trying to seal off and destroy the area you guys just made it through...which is incredible. They're calling it the *Pocket* now," Bosco explained...knowing that Feeney and the men with him had been out of the loop for a while.

"The *Pocket*, huh," Feeney replied...reliving some of the gruesome scenes that he had seen as they had tried to make their way in past the *Pocket* on D Day. Then he added, "Well, it's about time I made my way back. I gotta let my lieutenant know what's up."

"Tell him to stay right there. We're advancing in that direction...and we'll link up with your guys in ten minutes or so. We're going to try and get as far as the aircraft revetments that are due west of you guys. They're gonna serve as our left flank boundary. So just be patient and we'll be there in no time."

"That'll make his day," Feeney beamed, and he dashed off in the direction he had come from to deliver the great news...still clutching the item that he had used to signal the men of the 1-8 that he was a friendly.

The Butcher's Block

"And he said to stay right where we're at…since they'll be over here in a few minutes," Feeney said, finishing up. "Can you believe it!"

The lieutenant was thrilled at the news…and he was also aware of its implications. "If they're trying to seal off the area they're calling the *Pocket* now…then they must have made gains elsewhere too…which could mean that we're close to rapping this thing up finally," he said…his intuition spot on.

Then First Lieutenant Hackett signaled Sergeant Endres, Corporal Ingunza, and PFC Mornston over so he could deliver the good news to them personally…and then they could pass it on to the men under them as well.

After they scrambled away, PFC Petraglia turned to Feeney and said, "So I'm dying to know…what was that thing you were waving to let those guys know that you weren't a Jap?"

"Oh…that," Feeney said…and he held it up for Petraglia to see.

"Your skivvies? You used your drawers to signal those guys," Petraglia said, horrified.

"What else was I gonna use. I took them off while I was lying trapped in that shell hole in front of them. I figured that they would know that no Jap would ever wave a white flag and surrender. They weren't as white as I had hoped…but they did the trick…I guess," Feeney said, admiring them…and he took his pants off and put them back on.

"Now I've seen everything," Petraglia replied...and then he smiled as he saw the 1-8 marines heading their way!

With the loss of one of the Stuart tanks that had been leading their advance, C Company began to bog down as it butted up against a new labyrinth of Japanese machine gun nests, pillboxes, and blockhouses...and the marines began measuring their gains in mere inches instead of the yards they had been gaining earlier. By noon, they had managed to push ahead another hundred yards...which still left two hundred to go...but C Company could go no farther...and a halt was called.

The same situation confronted both the A Company marines...who were attacking down the middle of Red 2... and the marines of B Company...who were attacking to the far right...along the seawall. They ended up employing their tanks in much the same manner as C Company did...with their tanks out in front of the marine infantry...and they did a commendable job. But after a while, both the A Company tanks ran into problems. One of them became immobilized when it ran into a deep hole and couldn't get out...while the other one was disabled when it got caught in a mortar barrage. Then one of the tanks with B Company experienced ignition problems... causing its motor to cut in and out...rendering it inoperable. That left only two tanks to help out across the 1-8's front...but the men had already realized that the main gun on the Stuarts was just not big enough to destroy a Jap position on its own. So, the marines began using their last two tanks to pin the enemy down...and then the infantry would advance forward and destroy the position with whatever weapons they had in their arsenal. The best weapons to do the job...as they soon found out...were satchel charges of TNT and Bangalore torpedoes...which were long metal poles that were stuffed with TNT as well. But there weren't enough of these game changers to go around...since so many of them had been lost during the landings. To make up the difference, the marines resorted to using their grenades and bayonets...weapons that were best suited for close-in fighting...and casualties began piling up as a result.

If anyone looks like he can win a battle...good old Edson sure does, Colonel Shoup thought as he approached his new commander.

"Whatta ya got for me, David," the older colonel asked...standing ramrod straight...his hands planted firmly on his hips. He was looking down the beach in the direction where the 1-8 was attacking...trying to get a feel for the ebb and flow of the battle.

"Major Hays says that he's run into a roadblock. His boys made it two hundred yards towards the *Pocket*...but he's taking serious casualties again...so he called a halt...for now. He's also sending those Stuarts back...the ones that can get back. He lost one to a suicide sapper...one got stuck in a hole...one's having starting problems...and another took a hit from a mortar. That leaves him with two…but they're basically ineffective. Main gun's not big enough. He wants to know if we have anything else we can send him," Colonel Shoup stated. "His runner is right over there…waiting for our reply," he added, pointing to a towheaded private first class standing off to the side.

"Has Freddie Smith's SPMs made it in yet?" Colonel Edson asked, referring to the armored M-3 half-tracks… or Self-Propelled Mediums…that were in the division's Special Weapons Battalion. This unit was under the command of Major Frederick Smith…and the SPM looked like a normal truck in that it had rubber tires up front…supporting the armored cab…but none in the rear. Instead, it relied on a metal track system…much like a tank did…to propel it where it needed to go. The SPM was also outfitted with a 75mm gun in the bed of the truck…which gave it the wallop that the Stuarts were lacking…but it was lightly armored, and its open cargo bed was susceptible to air bursts from enemy artillery fire.

"He's got several of them in so far," Shoup responded… his finger still on the pulse of the overall operation… even though he no longer commanded it.

"Okay, give him two of them and let's see if they can shake things up any. How about those M 4s? Do we have any of them available?" Edson asked.

"No, sir. We only have two left…and Crowe has one… and I gave the other one to Kyle." Then Colonel Shoup called the runner over and he went over the details of the message that he would take back to Major Hays. "Do you have any questions, son?" Shoup asked when he was done.

"No, sir. Not about the message anyway. That's pretty straight forward. But is there any water around here. I emptied out my canteens a while ago...and me and a bunch of others could stand to get our hands on some decent water," the PFC said innocently.

Colonel Shoup considered the young marine's request and pulled his own canteen out of its holder and handed it to the marine. "Take a swig on that," he said as a sly smile crossed his face.

"But that's yours, sir," the young boy answered... amazed that the colonel would be so generous with his own water.

"Down the hatch," the colonel replied.

The boy wasted no time in obeying the colonel's order...and he lifted the canteen to his mouth. Then he took a big gulp and swallowed it without a second thought. And then he coughed violently...almost spewing some of the liquid on the ground in front of the colonel. "What the hell was that," he managed to choke out...still finding it hard to swallow.

"That, my son, was some of the finest bourbon that will ever cross your lips," the colonel said as he slipped the canteen back into its pouch on his hip. "I hope you enjoyed it!"

"I did...very much...and thank you, sir," the young marine said hoarsely.

Then the colonel pointed to the beach and he told the boy that he could find the rest of the water he needed among the piles of supplies that were stacked by the end of the pier.

The boy thanked the colonel…nodded…and went on his way…still coughing…but very happy that the colonel had shared some of his special water with him!

Colonel Edson watched the interchange between the two…and laughed as the boy walked off…shaking his head. Then he looked at Shoup again and said, "Only two left out of fourteen?" The colonel sounded incredulous…but not shaken…as the conversation swung back to the business at hand.

"Yes, sir. The other twelve are out of the fight. They got knocked out one way or another…and none of them are coming back any time soon. We're gonna have to analyze our tank and infantry tactics when this is all over…along with a whole bunch of other mistakes that we made out here," Shoup pointed out sharply. "A lot of things that we took for granted never materialized…and a whole lot of things that we thought would never happen…did happen," he added matter-of-factly.

"General Smith and I are well aware of the many shortcomings that have taken place…and I for one am extremely proud of what we've been able to accomplish despite them," Edson said in reflex…but he was not troubled by Shoup's comment…since he knew it was true.

"Just so you know beforehand though," Colonel Shoup stated dryly, "I do intend to find out who was responsible for our communication failures…and then I'm going to shoot the bastard myself."

"I won't stop you, David…and neither will the general," Edson said easily…and both men laughed as they pictured the execution playing out in their own funny way.

"Even better than me delivering the coup d'grace…I'm gonna have him tied to a stake…with no blindfold…and I'm going to put the mess cooks on the firing squad. The SOB'll end up dying of a heart attack since none of the cooks will be able to hit him," Shoup said…trying to contain his enthusiasm over the idea.

"That sounds very appropriate…but I believe I have something even better. I would put him on Bairiki Island and tell him that a bombing mission is scheduled in ten minutes. Then I would hand him one of his own water-logged radios and tell him that the planes are monitoring a certain frequency…and that he can save himself if he can raise them on the radio. Then I would leave him there…him and his radio. What do you think?"

Colonel Shoup mulled it over for a few seconds and then said, "I love it. I guess you have a better imagination than I do…so we'll go with yours!"

"I thought you'd like it. Plus, we don't want to get the cooks mad at us for making them kill someone… no matter how bad the guy deserves it. Just remember this…an army always travels on its stomach. I think it was Napoleon that said that…and that little Frenchman was always right!"

"Except at Waterloo," Shoup countered. "He got that one wrong."

"You're certainly right there," Edson conceded, "but I bet they ate well despite losing the battle. Napoleon probably made sure of that at least."

"Probably so...probably so," Colonel Shoup replied...smiling now...the image of a large T-bone steak sizzling away in its own juices foremost on his mind.

With the seven Stuarts out of the picture, the momentum of Hays' attack quickly petered out since the marines were losing several men every time they tried to advance against a pillbox or machine gun nest in their sector. And the two hundred yards ahead of them held just as many...if not more...of the very same bunkers that the first two hundred yards did...so Major Hays wisely called a halt.

But when the two half-tracks that had been promised by Colonel Edson showed up...the attack got underway again.

Major Hays decided to employ them in front of A Company and B Company...since the Japanese defenses appeared to be more concentrated along the coastline...rather than inland by the taxiway where C Company was attacking. And like the Stuarts, the SPMs were initially successful...since the 75mm cannons they carried could knock out a small bunker or pillbox with just one shot. But as the attack progressed, the marines and SPMs were coming up against bunkers that had multiple rooms built into them...so they could withstand this sort of attack. Instead of registering one-shot kills like before though, the SPMs were now firing multiple times at these larger structures…and even then, they couldn't knock them out. The supporting marines would then be called up… just like before…and they would have to enter the bunker to kill the Japanese who were still holding on.

A deadly cat-and-mouse game then developed inside the bunkers: as the marine grunts would clear one room, the Japanese would retreat to another. The game would end when the rooms ran out eventually… and then marines and *rikusentai* would engage in hand-to-hand combat to settle the matter.

This approach took more and more time…and the SPMs were also using more and more rounds on each bunker…so their ammunition stocks dwindled as the attacks dragged on.

Then, one of the half-tracks got hit by machine gun fire in its front end and its radiator was damaged… which caused the motor to overheat. This SPM left the battlefield trailing a stream of smoke…just like *Claptrap* did a few hours earlier. Rather than risk losing the other SPM, Major Hays had it pull back as well…and thus the 1-8 was back to square one…with no armor support to help them as they tried to advance against the Japanese bunker complex in front of the *Pocket* on Red 2.

Major Hays sent his runner back to inform Colonel Shoup and Colonel Edson of their situation…that it was suicide to keep on attacking this way…and that he intended to stop yet again.

By late in the afternoon, the 1-8's advance resembled an arc around the *Pocket*…with the C Company marines having achieved the biggest gains. With less pillboxes and machine gun nests to contend with, they had been able to reach the aircraft revetments that bordered the northwestern end of the main airfield. A Company... off their right flank...had almost matched them in the amount of ground covered...but not quite. But B Company had run into a buzz saw near the seawall...and the fierce resistance the Japanese put up there stymied B Company's advance almost as soon as it started...so they gained the least amount of ground of the three companies. All in all, the 1-8 had gotten to within one hundred and fifty yards of the *Pocket*...and though they had not taken their prize...they had succeeded in cutting it off.

With the sun setting and the enemy noose tightening around them on D + 2, at least fifty determined Japanese staged a last-ditch effort to take back some of the ground they had lost to the marines on Red 2. The cornered *rikusentai* emerged from the protection of their bunkers and pillboxes and stormed the marine lines just inland of the seawall...but to no avail.

The marines of the 1-8 had been waiting for the Japs to resort to this sort of *banzai* tactic all along...and when it finally came...they were ready for it. Now the marines got to dish out the same kind of punishment that the Japs had been dishing out to them all day long...and they did so with a vengeance. Thirty caliber machine gun fire and rifle fire tore into the ranks of the *rikusentai* and most of them were leveled before they had gone fifteen yards. The ones that survived this initial onslaught and managed to make it as far as the marine line were then finished off by bayonets and butt strokes...and there were no recorded survivors as far as anyone knew.

While the wonderful news from Red 2 was not as significant as the 1-6's landing on Green Beach the night before, it was still a major breakthrough nonetheless... and Major Hays had every right to be proud of what his valiant men had been able to accomplish in the twelve hours of tenacious fighting on D + 2.

Chapter Nineteen

"Runner comin' in," Sergeant Flockerzi shouted...rousing the three men around him. It was first light on D + 2 and Flockerzi had drawn the last watch of the night...so he was awake when the marine came dashing in from the direction of the Beak.

"I'm looking for Platoon Sergeant Roy," the marine huffed out...winded from his circuitous jaunt from the north side of the island.

"That'd be me," Roy yawned, wiping the cobwebs from his eyes. The two runners...Mudd and Rickard... remained sleeping.

"Major Ryan wants to see ya up at his CP. Said he wants to discuss the day's plans with you, sarge," the boy said, repeating the same message he had already given to Captain Crain, First Lieutenant Turner, and First Lieutenant Kelly along the way. "I can lead you back... since you're my last stop," he added.

The Butcher's Block

"Did the major move his CP from where it was yesterday," Roy asked, adding, "I know where that one is."

The private looked over his shoulder towards the Beak and then back at Platoon Sergeant Roy. "Yeah, sarge. He moved it closer to the *Pocket*. I'll show you."

"Okay, let's go. The major doesn't like to be kept waiting," Roy replied, reaching for his shotgun.

"I didn't have any trouble gettin' here, sarge, but, occasionally, some Nip'll take a potshot at me as I'm makin' my rounds. A few diehards are still around...so keep a look out," the boy warned.

"You got it," Roy answered...and the two men headed back north towards the western side of the *Pocket*.

The meeting was already breaking up by time Platoon Sergeant Roy and the runner made it back to Major Ryan's new CP...but First Lieutenant Kelly hung around... since he wanted to clarify one more point before heading back to his men.

Major Ryan nodded to Roy as he entered the narrow, wood-frame building that had probably served as a Jap mess hall, but it was now serving as the major's CP. The building itself was damaged...with boards missing in several places...but the roof was intact...and that was all that mattered.

"I see you've decided to upgrade your quarters," Roy said casually.

"My status as a battalion commander warrants it," the major joked right back, and added, "plus, that sun'll be up in about three hours or so...and I'm already sunburned after two days out there. Irish skin tone...never could last very long in the sun."

"I know how you're feeling," First Lieutenant Kelly joined in...and he removed his helmet so the two men could get a better look at him. Despite the dust and grime that had accumulated on his body after two days of fighting, it was still easy to see that the lieutenant was very light-skinned...with freckles covering most of his face...and his head was topped with thinning red hair. "I'm as Irish as it gets...all four of my grandparents came from there."

"Well, I'm Scottish, but I never had a problem with the sun for some reason." Roy then took off his helmet to better reveal his dark complexion and a crop of short, dark hair to boot.

"Let's save the beauty contest for another time, gentlemen," Major Ryan said seriously...and Roy and Kelly put their helmets back on...realizing they had pushed the point too far. "Do you need something else from me, Kelly," the major asked, "I thought we were done."

"Sir...has any word come in about the whereabouts of our own units. I know what you have planned for my men this morning...but will we be able to link up with our own guys anytime soon?"

The major pointed to the map that was spread out on a table and said, "Your B Company is over here...just east of Black Beach Two." Kelly looked at the map and saw that the southern coastline of Betio was marked with two beachheads on it. The first...labeled Black Beach 1... ran from Temekin Point...which was at the southwest corner of the island...to a point seven hundred yards east of there. Then Black Beach 2 came next...and it ran another five hundred yards east down the coastline... ending near the tank trap that Captain Williams' and Captain Bray's men had taken cover in. "I was told that your company made it over there late yesterday afternoon. I imagine that Colonel Shoup is going to use the First of the Sixth to attack down the southern coastline to link up with them...since they're fresh. I'm still waiting on word from him concerning us. My guess is that he'll use us to attack the *Pocket* from our side...driving east. And if that's the case, I'll need you over here...with me. I can secure Green Beach with L and M Companies from my own battalion...but I need your boys to help me take out that *Pocket* with I and K Companies. If it doesn't play out that way, then I'll try to free you up as soon as I can so you can head over towards the Black Beaches. I won't keep you any longer than I have to...but if I'm right...I will definitely need your help to wipe out the *Pocket*."

"You're a hard man to argue with, sir," First Lieutenant Kelly said, "so you got us as long as you need us...until the very end if necessary."

"Thanks, lieutenant," Major Ryan replied, and added, "now let me explain what I need Sergeant Roy to do...so I can let him get back to his men too."

"You got it, sir," Kelly said crisply. Then he turned to Sergeant Roy and added, "Best of luck, sergeant. I hope we run into each other again when this is all over with... so I can beat you fair and square in that beauty contest we were just having!"

As First Lieutenant Kelly left, First Lieutenant Bale arrived. "You wanted to see me, sir," he said, pulling the wooden door at the end of the building back open. As he approached, the flimsy door slammed closed behind him…causing him to duck reflexively.

"Yes…thanks for coming over," Major Ryan answered. He then beckoned him over to the map table and added, "How was your night?"

"Not bad…given the circumstances. We were able to unload the rest of the ammo off the stranded tanks in the cove--"

"Were you able to get any more running? I can use another one of your tanks to help me attack the *Pocket*," the major asked, interrupting him.

"Well, sir, to be honest, I think I may have gotten my numbers mixed up when I debriefed you on Saturday night. Fog of war is what they call it. I think I got it pretty much straightened out in my own mind now since I've been able to talk to all the tank commanders that came in with me over here. You can only see so much when your buttoned up…and one tank starts to look like another…especially when you start taking anti-tank fire," Bale explained. The lieutenant then noticed Platoon Sergeant Roy and he nodded to him.

"There's more than enough fog around here to last a lifetime, Bale," the major agreed. "I'm still wondering if I've been able to account for all the units that are over here on the Beak. I might have missed one or two units…who really knows."

"I understand, sir. Trust me. I only had to worry about six tanks over here…and I still confused one with another during the landing. But here's the breakdown on my six. I lost *Cherry* coming in. She hit a shell hole and lost her electrical system. We're not going to be able to do anything with her where she's at. Then I lost *Count* and *Cougar* closer to the shoreline...as they were following me over to the Beak. Both of them drowned out...just like *Cherry* did. I put together a salvage crew under Platoon Sergeant Sooter and he has managed to unload all the tank ammo off those three over the last two days...so we're doing okay on ammunition for the time being."

"So, we have three left now? I thought we only had two that were operational yesterday?" The major then looked over at Sergeant Roy to see if Roy was as confused as he was.

"Bear with me, sir. I did get two tanks ashore on D Day. You saw them yourself. One was mine...*Cecilia*...and the other was *Commando*. *China Gal* didn't make it to the Beak on that first day. The breech block on her main gun got jammed somehow on the way in...so I had her remain on the beach near the Beak to see if we could get her fixed...and the crew was able to pull off a miracle. They worked through the day and got her fully functional that night...which is why she was able to lead your attack down Green Beach yesterday morning."

"So which ones were actually running yesterday? I thought we only had two...*Cecilia* and *China Gal*? And *Cecilia* couldn't use her main gun...only her machine guns. So, what happened to *Commando*? She would put us back up to three if my math is correct." It was obvious that Major Ryan was following the tank lieutenant's synopsis closely…since he had named all three tanks correctly.

"You're right, sir. *Cecilia* had her main gun knocked out by an incredible shot from a Jap tank that we encountered after we landed. The Jap round went right down her gun tube and damaged the breech block…a one-in-a-million shot if there ever was one. That same round also took out a chunk of her gun tube near the tip which made firing the main gun really dangerous…even if we were able to repair the breech block. That's why she only had her machine guns working yesterday. Well, *Commando* ended up destroying that Jap tank…and then she ended up getting hit herself…by a Jap anti-tank gun…and she was knocked out. She's sitting just south of us here…a few hundred yards away…abandoned."

"So, we're down to two again," the major said, following along as best he could.

"Unfortunately, no. We're down to only one tank now, sir. *Cecilia* did just like she was ordered yesterday…and she helped clear the inland side of Green Beach during the morning's attack. But sometime after that…during the afternoon…some officer approached the tank and asked the TC if he could help reduce some particularly tough emplacements that were firing on them from the *Pocket*. The TC didn't think he needed to contact me…and he agreed to help them out…but she had to go around the Beak and head east to do it. Once over there, she silenced two pillboxes on her own…but she eventually ran into a shell hole in the surf and couldn't get out. So, all I have left now of my original six tanks is *China Gal*...and I have another problem."

"Another problem?"

"Yes, sir. Another problem. And you're gonna have to get involved to solve it. Major Jones is saying that *China Gal* is going to be assigned to his battalion...not yours anymore. He told me to be ready to go by oh eight hundred...that we were going to support his battalion's drive down through Black Beach One and Two."

"He told you that?"

"Yes, sir. Not more than fifteen minutes ago. I told him that I had been supporting you for the last two days...and that I would have to hear from you first before I just up and left."

"And what did Major Jones have to say about that?" the major asked.

"He said that you and him were pretty close friends... and that the two of you would work it out."

"He's right...we are good friends. And we will work it out. But for now, you stay with me," the major said emphatically.

"Yes, sir," the tank lieutenant answered right back... and then he added one more thing. "By the way, sir. I just wanted to let you know about some of the brave work my boys did during the last two days. Not only did they retrieve all that ammo off their tanks in the cove... which were still under fire...and then lug it in...but several of them...LaPorte...Cobb...and Palmer to name a few...climbed up on the tanks and they've been firing the turret-mounted fifties all day long at the defenses in the *Pocket*. How they're still alive is beyond me. But they are...and I'm gonna put them in for medals when it's over."

"A lot of guys are going to be given medals for what they did out over here...but I'll make sure your boys get theirs...deal," Major Ryan replied...shaking his head in approval.

"Deal," Bale shot back, and turning to go, he said, "just let me know who I'm under today, okay, sir," and he left the building...the rickety door slamming shut behind him...just like it had when he entered.

"My turn?" Platoon Sergeant Roy asked sarcastically... looking around the empty room.

The major turned an evil eye towards the sergeant... and then smiled. "You earned that one," he said easily. "So, what am I to do with you and your men?"

"Well, that speech you gave Lieutenant Kelly certainly wasn't lost on me. On the other hand, Kelly had something like a hundred men with him on Saturday when we landed...probably less after yesterday. So, let's say he's got about ninety left. I have thirteen," Roy stated...his point inescapable.

"I understand." The major was pensive for a moment...and then spoke up. "Major Jones is going to have to pass through the ground you're holding down near Temekin Point. Go ahead and see if you can hook up with either him or his XO...and let him know that you'll be trailing behind him. I know you want to head that way...for the same reason Kelly did. The Second of the Second is over there...and Jones is going to link up with them sometime this morning...or afternoon. It just depends on how many Nips are left between that tank trap and Temekin Point...and how hard they're gonna fight to hang on to that ground. Either way, you'll be with your battalion by the end of the day. That sound good to you?"

"I couldn't have designed it better myself, sir. Thanks. I would've stayed with you if I thought you could use our help...but you won't be needing my guys to finish off the *Pocket*. Let your boys from the Three Two get all the credit for that one."

"Thanks, sergeant...I appreciate that. And thanks for all your help over the last two days. The Two Two was well represented on the Beak...and I'll let Colonel Shoup know it," the major said...and he meant every word of it.

Roy looked the major in the eye and said, "Sir, what you did here...holding onto the Beak...and taking Green Beach...were the keys to this battle. I wouldn't have wanted to serve under anyone else. Reserve officer my ass...you did better than any officer out here. And I for one am glad that I had the privilege of serving under you."

The major thanked the sergeant once more...and then he quickly turned away. "Now get outta here...and good luck finding the rest of your unit," he said quietly...hoping the sergeant had missed the tears that were welling up in his eyes.

Chapter Twenty

It was shortly after 0800 hours on D + 2 when the startled radioman turned to Major Ryan and exclaimed, "Sir...Higher's coming through finally!"

The major swung around and grabbed the headset that was extended to him. "Glad to hear you too, sir," he said beaming, "it's been a while!" Then he listened intently as Colonel Shoup began to explain what he wanted done over on Green Beach...nodding occasionally.

When the colonel was finished with that part of the day's plan, Major Ryan jumped in and said, "Yes, sir, I understand what you want done there. And yes, sir, I'll let him have the tank. We'll do fine without it. As for me, I plan on moving out as soon as possible as well...and I will attack the *Pocket* from the west," he said confidently.

"Negative, major. I want you to stay where you are. The One Eight is going to be attacking the *Pocket* from the east...and there's a good chance that you'll end up shooting at each other if you both attack it at the same time. Hold what you have...and let the One Eight handle this one. Your men have done so much...now it's time to give them a break. I'm gonna use the One Eight as my hammer...and you're going to be my anvil. Your mission is to secure that flank...and if the Japs up and run...then you finish them off. Understood?" the colonel radioed back.

The major had a solemn look on his face as he considered the order...wondering whether he should argue the point...but he finally acquiesced and radioed back, "Understood. Three Two to hold in place. Out." Then he handed the headset back to his radioman and summoned a runner who was standing off to the side. "Make your rounds. Let the companies know that we are not attacking this morning. We are going to hold on to what we have and let the One Eight have a crack at taking the *Pocket*. Tell the company commanders to continue clearing the ground around them and to eliminate any stragglers that are still left out there."

"Yes, sir," the young private answered and as he turned to go, he bumped into another officer who had just come into the room. "Sorry 'bout that, sir," he said apologetically.

"No problem, son. Go about your business," the major stated crisply.

"Stoddard!" Major Ryan called out, recognizing the man immediately. "What took you so long to get here?" he added, joshing the man that commanded Mike Company...the heavy weapons company of the Third Battalion.

James F Dwyer

"What a nightmare," Major Stoddard Cortelyou answered...and he took a seat on a long, wooden bench that had been pushed up against the wall of the building they were in. "Let's see...where to begin," he continued, and he took off his helmet and dropped it at his feet. "I rode in on Major Schoettel's boat...the morning we tried to land. Schoettel saw what was happening to the landing team and called a halt early on. He wouldn't let anyone else go in...said it was a slaughter. He was probably right...in hindsight. I was fuming though. We just rode around all that day...trying to get in...which was impossible since fire was coming from everywhere. We should've just pushed our way in...but he wouldn't allow it...so we just wasted several hours sitting out beyond the reef trying to organize what we had left of the battalion. Sometime after midnight, I transferred over to an amtrac that had come up beside us. I don't know if it was the right thing to do, but I just left the major with his headquarters group on that Higgins boat. I wanted in...and I wasn't going to waste any more time dilly-dallying around out beyond the reef. That amtrac headed right in and we all got off near the pier...no worse for wear. For the last two days I've been fighting my way over here. And I finally made it. Sorry it took me so long, Mike, but I tried my best."

"Well, now you're here. I guess you'll want to take over the battalion...since Major Schoettel is still missing. We both know you outrank me...so the battalion is yours if you want it," Major Ryan stated matter-of-factly.

"If you don't mind, I'd like a shot at it," the other major replied, knowing that Major Ryan would follow the proper protocol and relinquish his *ad hoc* command to the senior man.

"She's all yours, Stodd. And your M Company has been doing yeoman's work in your absence. You should be very proud of them," Ryan added...his compliment defusing the subtle tension of the moment.

"Thanks, Mike," Major Cortelyou said graciously, and he added, "George made it in...I know that much. He must have taken over for me. The boys love him...so I can see why they did so well without me." The M Company Commander was referring to his executive officer, Captain George Wentzel, who had made it in on D Day...along with many other M Company men as well. "I can't wait to tell him how proud I am of him...and the others who made it in too."

Major Ryan was quiet for a moment...remembering the chaos of D Day...and how Major Wentzel had helped clear the beaches by encouraging the marines beside him to head inland. Then he spoke. "Stodd...George didn't make it. He was killed two hours after he landed. A sniper shot him in the throat. He was standing on the seawall in full view of the Japs. He put his life on the line so we could get the beach freed up. The men were scared to death. Nobody wanted to leave the safety of the seawall. They were paralyzed with fear. And then George got up there and showed them all how it was done. They certainly must've loved him cause they pushed their fear aside and they started climbing over that seawall. First one man went...and then another. Then two more...together...for support. And then groups of men started heading in...since George was so brave. It was a sight to see...and then he was down. I'm sorry."

"Oh, good 'ol George. I'm glad he went down fighting. I'm gonna miss him," Major Cortelyou replied... wishing he had been there to see him in action.

"He's not the only one, I'm afraid," Ryan continued. "Carlton and Rixstine were killed too. And Cogdill and Hall were wounded. You only have one officer left... Lieutenant Estes. He's leading M Company now."

"Jack is the only one left of all my platoon commanders?" the M Company commander asked in disbelief.

"It was brutal over here on that first day. On one hand, Major Schoettel was right. It was sheer suicide trying to get in here on Saturday. And then we had to fight like hell to hold on to it. How we did it is still a mystery to me."

"Well, it was because of officers like you, Mike, that we're still here. There was a point when this thing could've gone the other way...and yet you pulled it off. I'm just glad I have something to take over...and for that...I thank you," the major said to his counterpart... who shed a tear for the second time that day.

Chapter Twenty-One

"It's working!" the young marine yelled out as the radio crackled beside him. It was 0815 hours on Green Beach and the radioman looked at his bleary-eyed, twenty-seven-year-old commander and smiled. "I knew I could get it working again," he said proudly.

Major Jones looked at him askance and said, "Did you raise one of those destroyers again?"

"No, sir! I got Colonel Shoup's headquarters! And he wants to speak to you right now!" The young radioman was having trouble containing his enthusiasm since he had been spinning dials for the last several hours...trying to raise anyone he could.

"Hand it over...and quick-like. Who knows how long we'll be able to talk to them before these damn radios start acting up again," the major from Missouri demanded...tired and a little irritable after having spent the last twelve hours getting his companies organized after they came ashore on Green Beach.

The radioman scrambled over and handed his battalion commander the headset…and then made a sign of the cross. "Ohhh, don't fail me now," he pleaded, hoping the precious connection would last longer than a few mere seconds before going dead.

"Jones, here," the major barked into the mouthpiece.

"Major Jones…Shoup here," the colonel answered, and Jones looked over at his radioman and mouthed, *it is him!*

The radioman mouthed, *I told you*, right back.

The colonel then went on to explain what he wanted Major Jones and the 1-6 to accomplish that morning. "Do you think you can get that done for me, Willie? And just so you know, Colonel Edson is in charge overall. He made it in last night. You'll be under my operational control for the time being however…attached to the Second Regimental Combat Team. I'll communicate directly with you as long as we can keep this connection open. Colonel Holmes and the Three Six should be landing shortly. We're working up plans for them now. I'll coordinate that with Holmes once he makes it in. Do you need anything from me?"

"Well, sir, as it stands right now, I only have two Stuarts over here with me for armor support. The whole company was supposed to be here…but only two were able to land last night…the surf was just too rough to risk trying to land the rest of them. I know Major Ryan has been using an M Four on Green Beach. I could really use that tank, sir. But Major Ryan wants it too...to help him take the *Pocket*. I might've overstepped my bounds though. I told the company commander...Bale...that you were going to assign his tank to my command earlier this morning. I shouldn't have done that without your authority."

"I've already told Ryan to give that tank to you," Shoup cut in...solving the problem.

"Oh...okay. We'll put it to good use. We'll be jumping off as soon as the tanks are repositioned...which is what they're doing right now. I'd have already started if we didn't have to wait on them. I hope to be linking up with the First of the Second by eleven hundred this morning. I'm gonna push my company commanders to meet my timeline. That'll give you some options for this afternoon, sir," Major Jones replied...relieved that he was getting that tank.

"One more thing...Major Tompkins is on his way over there to brief you. You already know what you need to do now. Just tell him to head back when he can. And good luck," Shoup said, ending the transmission.

Chapter Twenty-Two

One thousand yards away to the east, Pharmacist Mate 2nd Class Tom Fumai was staring at a line of twenty dead marines laying side-by-side near the middle of the tank trench near Black Beach 2. Some of the dead were covered by ponchos...while the rest were lying serenely in the open. With only so many ponchos to go around, it had been up to the corpsman to determine which marine warranted a poncho...and only those that were horribly...and depressingly...disfigured had gotten one. Fumai had kept another five ponchos off to the side...just in case...since the men were going to be jumping off to attack eastward at any moment.

"You think they would've learned by now," Private Reed Marcy said, staring at the group of dead as well.

Fumai looked at the young marine and frowned. "Learned what?" he asked, looking back at the morbid line of dead men staring skyward...yet seeing nothing.

"Well, just look at those guys," Marcy said, waving his hand at the group. "Do you see anything in particular about them?"

Fumai looked the group over yet again...trying to discern what had caught his assistant's attention. *They all got big feet,* he thought to himself, *but that can't be it. What am I missing?*

"Y'all give up?" Marcy asked, grinning slyly.

Fumai's silence was his answer.

"Well, we've been placing the enlisted men to the left...and the officers to the right. There are five dead officers here...and they all have something in common," Marcy said, pointing their way.

And that's when it hit him: all the dead officers had a binocular's case strapped across their chest. "I got it...the binoculars...right?" he said confidently.

"Yup. A sniper's dream. Takes all the guesswork out of it," Marcy replied, and added, "I bet they wish they had thrown those things away now."

"I was told that the Nips also target corpsmen since we're considered so valuable. They wait patiently and watch to see who comes to help the wounded...and then they shoot them down too. They know it depresses the other guys to see a corpsman get killed...since they know we're one of the few guys that can save them when they get hit bad," Fumai explained.

"Yeah, I considered that," Marcy said, "but I'm not afraid. When your times up, it's up."

Fumai looked at Marcy to see if he could sense any false bravado in the boy's demeanor...but there wasn't any. "Well, I'm glad you decided to help me out. I know

Captain Williams ordered you to do it…but you've given me your all…and I appreciate it."

"Thanks," Marcy stated seriously, "I just hope there aren't too many snipers left…so we don't have to drag anymore dead bodies down this tank trap. I'm gettin' real tired…just like you are."

"Amen to that," Fumai said agreeably…and he patted the young marine on the shoulder…wishing for the same thing.

"Speak of the devil," Marcy said as Captain Maxie Williams and another officer…a second lieutenant… walked past them…heading towards the eastern end of the tank trap. The captain noticed Fumai and his assistant and nodded to them…pleased with the performance of the two men over the last twelve hours. "How's young Marcy holding up?" the B Company commander asked Fumai lightly.

"Oh, he's doing just fine, sir. You couldn't have given me a better helper," Fumai…who remained seated out of his fear of snipers…yelled over to the captain.

"Keep up the good work, son," Captain Williams replied with authority.

The private began to stand up in response to his commander's compliment…but Fumai grabbed Marcy's shirt and held him down. "You tryin' to get him shot? He knows you heard him. Any hint of authority around here will draw a sniper's bullet. Just nod back," Fumai whispered sternly.

The Butcher's Block

The private did as he was told, and the captain smiled in response...and turned away.

"Did you hear that? The captain knew my name!" Marcy said excitedly.

"The captain's got eyes in the back of his head," Fumai offered up, and added, "and he already knew about the great job you've been doing. I told him so last night...when he came by checking on us. You were catching some winks when he made his rounds. He just wanted you to hear it from the horse's mouth...since you're one of his boys. He's proud of you...so he made it a point to remember your name."

"Wow...he remembered my name!" Marcy repeated... as happy as any marine private could possibly be on Betio Island on D + 2.

Captain Williams and the lieutenant then walked a few feet and stopped beside the line of dead officers. The second lieutenant pointed down at one of the men and said, "That's Bob Harvey. When was he brought in? I didn't see him here yesterday."

"Fumai and Marcy must have found him late yesterday afternoon...sometime after you got here. Did you know him?" the captain said.

"Yeah...I knew him...not well...but I knew him," the second Lieutenant answered sadly. "He was from Kalamazoo, Michigan. You don't forget anybody who says they're from that place. He was a platoon commander in A Company…in our battalion. He was married to a girl from there too. Did you know him, sir?"

"Not really. I knew he was in A Company…and Bray liked him. That's about all I knew about him. We got so many new lieutenants in the battalion while we were in New Zealand…it was hard to get to know all of them," Williams said.

The neat hole in Harvey's forehead explained how he had been killed…and it reminded the lieutenant of the advice Captain Williams had given him the afternoon before…right after he arrived in the tank trap.

Walt Yoder had experienced combat before…on Guadalcanal. While there, he had shown enough leadership potential that he had been promoted from the rank of warrant officer…or gunny as it was called…to his current rank of second lieutenant. And then he had managed to wrangle his way into staying in the same unit that he now commanded: a machine gun platoon in D Company…which was the Heavy Weapons Company of the First Battalion in the Second Regiment. Like the rest of the 1-2, Yoder and his men had experienced the horrors of D Day…and then they had fought their way across the northwestern taxiway and the main runway with Captain Jim Clanahan's C Company on D + 1.

Captain Williams had latched on to him and his powerful machine guns the minute he arrived…and in leading him and his men to their new position, they had passed by the group of dead officers and enlisted

The Butcher's Block

men that Fumai had been placing in a line. That's when Captain Williams had pointed out that all four officers in the line were carrying binoculars...just like Second Lieutenant Yoder was. No fool, Yoder had immediately tossed his sniper bait...his binoculars and their leather carrying case...off to the side. "I rarely used them," he said unapologetically, and he quickly positioned his men and their potent .30 caliber machine guns where Captain Williams wanted them.

Now the two officers were heading towards the eastern end of the long trench...where the attack against the Japs would commence at 0800 hours on the morning of D + 2.

Major Wood Kyle, the battalion commander of the 1-2, had received his marching orders from Colonel Edson a few hours before...and there was no mistaking what he wanted done. Major Kyle was to attack eastward out of the tank trap near Black Beach 2 and attempt to link up with the units of the 3-8 which would be pushing their way southward out of the logjam that had defined the Red Three beachhead for the past two days. If the link up could be made, a firm line of marine infantry would then run from the northern coastline at the eastern end of the Red 3 beachhead to the southern coastline for the first time during the battle...and the tail of the island would be completely cut off from the body of the parrot that made up the western end of the island.

Major Kyle had then given the mission to Captain Williams in turn. To complete his task, Captain Williams had a hodge podge of units to work with... including a platoon-sized group of one officer and thirty-nine men from his own B Company and another twenty-six marines from Captain Bray's A Company. Captain Jim Clanahan was able to add an officer and another fifteen men from C Company to the mix...and Williams also had two machine gun platoons from D Company...both of which were placed under Lieutenant Yoder's control. Finally, Kyle added the only officer he had from the Second of the Second, First Lieutenant Konstanzer, and the thirty marines from the 2-2 as well. All told, Captain Williams would be leading a company-sized unit of nearly one hundred and eighty men into the teeth of the Japanese defense that had stymied him and Major Kyle for the last thirteen hours. But he would also have more support this time around...which put the odds of victory in his favor for the first time in a long while.

"I sure wouldn't want to be on the receiving end of one of those planes," Private Marcy said as the squadron of Navy Curtiss SB2C Helldivers from the carrier *Bunker Hill* roared overhead.

The Helldiver was the latest model of dive bomber that the Navy was using...and it had replaced the much-venerated Douglas SBD Dauntless dive bomber...the plane that had sunk four Japanese carriers during the

The Butcher's Block

Battle of Midway in June of 1942 and the troop-carrying transports during the Naval Battle of Guadalcanal in November of the same year. While the Helldiver was larger than the plane it had replaced...and faster too... it was also much harder to control...and the pilots who had to fly it hated doing so.

The planes that Private Marcy had spotted were carrying a five-hundred-pound bomb under each wing... and they were swooping down to drop their payloads along the beach just east of where Captain Williams' men were about to attack.

"That'll give those Nips something to think about," Fumai chimed in...the explosions reverberating only four hundred yards away.

Marcy whistled in appreciation as he saw a huge column of smoke and sand rise up in the distance as one of the bombs found its mark...and then said, "You gotta hand it to those Japs. They've been fighting us tooth and nail for the last two days...and they keep doing so... even after getting bombed like that. How are any of them living through it?"

"Makes you wonder, doesn't it," Fumai responded.

"But it seems that no matter how much bombing we do, there's always a Jap with a rifle or machine gun still hiding out in a bunker or pillbox over there. We're gonna have to dig them out one by one I guess...and take casualties doing so," the private pointed out smartly.

"Which means we're going to be real busy in a little while...since our attack is going to kick off as soon as those planes disappear I would think," Fumai advised... and he realized that he needed to conduct a quick inventory of his aid bag so he would be ready when the casualties started piling up.

"You got any water left in your canteens?" Fumai asked, pulling open his kit bag. The first thing he spotted was a bottle that contained atabrine tablets… which were used to combat malaria. The risk of catching malaria on Betio was slim at best…so these tablets were not that important. But right next to it was a bottle of Halazone pills…and these pills were used to purify the men's drinking water. These pills were more important…to a degree…since the marines were parched… and they had consumed the water they came in with in no time at all. If the men found additional sources of water on the island, they were supposed to put a tablet into each of their canteens before filling it up with the new water…and especially before they drank from it. These pills had been very important on Guadalcanal… where a lot of the water the men consumed had come from small streams and rivers. Any water the marines found on Betio, however, was also being consumed by the Japanese…so it was considered safe by most of the marines…but they were supposed to use the Halazone pills anyway.

"No…I drank all mine on the first day. Stupid…I know…but I was dying of thirst," Marcy answered honestly.

"Well, there's no malaria out here…so you won't need to use any atabrine anyway. So, what have you been doing for water over the last two days? You must be dying of thirst," Fumai asked…wondering how he had avoided getting heat stroke due to his lack of hydration.

"To be honest…I didn't have any…until the captain assigned me to work with you. I feel really guilty about this…but I've been scrounging some off the dead we've been bringing in. I would check to see if they had any water left…and if they did…well, I drank it. I'm sorry," Marcy said dejectedly…knowing what he had been doing was wrong.

"Everyone's doing it, kid," Fumai said, offering forgiveness.

"But I knew what I was doing was wrong…and I've been tearing myself up inside over it," the guilt-ridden private suddenly confessed. "I knew if you caught me, you'd have me court-martialed…or worse."

"Marce, we're out here in the middle of the Pacific Ocean on some God-forsaken island that no one knew about until now…and we're fighting for our lives. You think I'd really try to punish you with a court-martial. Come on, kid. We've all done some things we're not proud of…you…me…everyone out here. Now that you've got what you were doing off your chest…just don't do it anymore. From now on, if you find any extra water…give it to me. We'll share it with the wounded…and whoever else needs some. Case closed…as far as I'm concerned, okay," Fumai said, consoling his assistant and restoring his self-confidence all at once.

Marcy nodded appreciatively…the millstone he had been carrying around his neck for the last few hours finally removed.

Fumai then turned back to his kit bag and continued counting the items inside. The two boxes that had contained the ten morphine syrettes were empty…since

Fumai had already used them on the badly wounded he had encountered along the way. But there were still three sulfa packets left...which was a good thing...since he could use them to disinfect whatever wounds he was going to be treating in the future. The pair of scissors...which was used to cut away a wounded man's uniform so the injured area could be exposed...was there...as well as his shiny steel forceps...which were used to pull out any pieces of shrapnel that he could see in an injured marine. And since he hadn't had the opportunity to sew anyone up yet...the suture kit for stitching wounds was inside and unopened. Then, he noticed the Navy-issued tourniquet...which was a braided rope attached to a thin piece of wood that was tapered at both ends...and he remembered Corporal Wilson...whose legs had been blown off in the amtrac that he had ridden in on. *I really need to carry more of these, next time. Wilson would've needed two of them alone to stem all the bleeding from his two shattered limbs,* he thought...but he had bled out so quickly that he didn't even get a chance to use the one he did have in his medical bag.

When Fumai was almost done, the private reached into his shirt pocket and pulled out two sealed dressings and threw them over to him. "I found these on the two guys we brought in last night," he said.

"Excellent," Fumai replied, and he dumped the two dressings into his bag. "That makes five dressings and three bandages. Plus, I have all my safety pins and casualty cards too. We're loaded for bear, Marce," Fumai said satisfied...and he closed the bag back up and tightened down the straps.

"What are those safety pins actually used for," Marcy asked innocently. "They probably told us about it in boot camp, but I guess I forgot...or I wasn't paying attention during that part of the class. I was so darn tired all the time that I was always nodding off. If the drill instructors caught us sleeping, they would punch us awake or torture us in some medieval way. It was brutal."

"The pins are used to secure the casualty card to the wounded man...and it shows how much morphine the guy was given. You give too much morphine to a guy and it can put him into shock and kill him," Fumai explained.

"Oh...now I remember. Can the pins be used for anything else...like pinning up a bad wound?"

"In a pinch, they can be...but that's what the sutures are really there for," the corpsman explained...and he pulled out the kit and opened it up.

Marcy looked at all the shiny instruments inside and whistled again. "Geez...you could be a doctor with all that stuff in there. I guess that's why all the guys always call you *doc*."

Fumai removed each item from its sleeve and let Marcy examine it as he explained what it was used for... and then he shoved it back in place.

"I never realized that corpsmen could do all these things," the private said mesmerized. "I might ask and see if I can be trained as a corpsman when this is over with. I think I like this job better than just being a rifleman. I like saving lives more than I do taking them... and I think I've killed a few Nips already...so I know I can do that and still live with myself. I just wonder if I can get a transfer...since you guys are Navy and all."

"It can't hurt to check it out," Fumai replied encouragingly. "I think you'd make a great corpsman. Look at the way you've helped me out. I'll put in a good word for you...if it ever gets that far along."

"You'd do that for me?" Private Marcy responded... thinking once again that he was the luckiest marine on Betio Island.

"Of course, I would...just make sure to stay in touch with me...and then we'll take it from there," Fumai said affirmatively.

Hearing the good news, Marcy's face broke out in a grin that went from ear to ear...a rare sight indeed... especially on Betio Island.

After the Helldivers peeled away to return to their ship, the F6F Hellcats from the *Essex* came in...their duty of providing top cover for the slower and more vulnerable dive bombers no longer needed.

Lieutenant, Junior Grade, or J.G., Valencia rocked his wings and rolled into a dive to begin his gun run. His wingman, Lieutenant, J.G. Basnett, watched him peel off and then he pulled the googles down over his eyes... getting ready to begin his own gun run as well. He glanced at his instrument panel to make sure that the big radial, eighteen-cylinder, air-cooled, two-thousand-horse-power Pratt and Whitney engine in front of him was running smoothly and that everything else was in proper order. *Oil pressure good...engine temperature normal...fuel tanks full...gun sight turned on*, he murmured as he read the dials one at a time...his training kicking in. And satisfied that all was in proper condition, he pushed the stick to the left and forward which caused his plane to roll over and dive down as well.

Neither of their planes were armed with any of the deadly assortment of bombs they could carry...the single one-thousand pounder...or the two five-hundred pounders...or the eight two-hundred-and-fifty pounders...since their mission had been to provide topside cover for the dive bombers that were tasked with bombing the enemy emplacements down below. And once the dive bombers had dropped their bomb loads and were safely headed home, the two pilots shifted their focus to a ground attack mode...since their six fifty caliber machine guns were still fully loaded with four hundred rounds a piece.

Five Japanese *rikusentai* were sitting in a trench several hundred yards east of Black Beach Two staring skyward. They had just endured another earth-shattering bombardment by the American dive bombers...and now they saw two smaller planes in the distance...fighters no doubt...getting ready to wing over and rain death and destruction down on them yet again.

Will this ever end, one of them thought forlornly. He looked at his fellow sailors and could see the fear in their eyes…while two of them trembled uncontrollably. They had managed to survive two full days of this madness so far…with hardly any food or water to sustain them. And now they were beginning to crack. The man could see it…but he could also smell it as well…since one of the men had defecated in his pants…and their desperation drove him to act.

I will do something about this, he seethed under his breath, and he hefted his Type 99 Light machine gun up out of the trench. Reaching down to the end of the barrel, he quickly extended the bipod legs…and then he ordered his friend to sit on the edge of the trench in front of him.

"You want me to do what?" the friend stammered.

"Sit on the edge of the trench and face me," he ordered once again…this time more forcefully.

"Why must I do that," he pleaded. "The marines will shoot me for sure once I expose myself. Are you trying to kill me too?"

"Of course not. The marines are too far away for any of them to shoot you. I need you to hold on to the bipod of my machine gun. I am going to place the legs on your shoulders…so I can fire on those damn planes that will be coming down at us shortly. I am sick and tired of just sitting back and taking it…and I will not stand for it any longer. These flyers are going to see what it feels like to get shot at…and if we die…at least we will die like men. Now do as I say…or I will shoot you and save those two pilots the trouble," the leader of the group spat out… deadly serious.

The Butcher's Block

"We're all going to get killed anyway so what's the difference how it happens," the friend said, resigned to his fate...and he sat down and took hold of the bipod's extended legs and placed them on his shoulders.

"Okay...just sit steady," the leader said calmly...and then added, "here they come."

―――

Basnett watched from behind as his flight leader roared over the island from the southern coastline to the northern coastline at close to three hundred miles an hour... his wing guns blazing. His speed was not quite as fast as the Hellcat's maximum speed of three hundred and eighty-five miles an hour...but he wasn't in a dogfight, so it wasn't necessary to push the aircraft to its maximum limits. The slower speed also allowed Valencia to see the ground below better...but an actual target was still hard to find since the Japanese had camouflaged their bunkers so well.

Basnett throttled back...to keep pace with his leader... and then he commenced his own gun run as well. Like Valencia, Basnett tried to pick out a decent target to fire on...but he found it just as hard as Valencia did...so he fired at anything that resembled a bunker or pillbox... hoping his rounds were causing some worthwhile damage while doing so.

As they emerged on the other side of the island, both pilots pulled back on their control sticks and stamped on the right rudder pedal...causing their fighters to rise and circle to the right. When they reached eight thousand feet, they leveled off...not far from their original starting point.

"Did you hit anything of value?" Valencia radioed to his wingman.

"I'm not sure. I saw some trench works down there... but I didn't see anyone in them. I just sprayed the area over real good...hoping I'd hit something," Basnett radioed back.

"I don't think I hit anything but sand down there. I still have plenty of ammo left...so I'm going to give it another go. I'm gonna take it a little slower to this time... so I can see something worthwhile to shoot at."

"I'll be right behind you...the last thing I want to do is to head back with some ammo left. Even if we don't hit anything...maybe we're keeping their heads down with our passes," Basnett acknowledged.

"Why didn't you fire on them," the man holding the bipod asked incredulously.

"Because I want them to be confident when they come back the next time. Don't worry...I know what I'm doing," the leader said coolly.

"I certainly hope so...since our lives depend on it, my friend," the other man answered warily.

"Just sit there like a rock. The steadier you are, the better my aim will be. This time we're going to make them pay," the veteran *rikusentai* guaranteed as he sighted down the barrel of the machine gun that was resting just above the head of the man who was acting as

The Butcher's Block

the weapon's firing platform. Then, in a smooth, steady motion, he reached up and made sure the curved, detachable, top-mounted, thirty-round-box magazine was seated properly into the receiver of his machine gun. Feeling it locked in place, he withdrew his hand slowly and placed it back on the stock of the weapon right in front of his chin. "Now...let them come," he said confidently...and he breathed out slowly to steady his aim.

The plane that Basnett and Valencia were flying was a vast improvement over its predecessor...the F4F Wildcat... since it flew much faster...and its six fifty caliber machine guns packed a bigger punch than the four fifties the Wildcat had. But the Hellcat had also been designed to keep its pilot alive...and to that end, it had a new bullet-resistant windshield and far better cockpit armor. And the engine...and the gas tank...which held two hundred and fifty gallons of aviation fuel...had been given more protection as well...which insured that the plane would keep flying even if it got hit multiple times in a dogfight with a Jap A6M Zero fighter.

Despite all these improvements, flying an F6F Hellcat fighter in combat was still an inherently dangerous business...and losses occurred whenever a gaggle of Zeros was attacked in the air or whenever ground targets on enemy islands were strafed from above.

"Got your six," Basnett radioed as Valencia began a gentle descent towards the target below.

Valencia rocked his wings slightly in acknowledgement and then pushed the control stick fully forward... dropping the nose of his fighter into a steeper dive. As he got closer to the island, he eased back on the throttle...shaving a few miles per hour of speed off his descent...and allowing him to see somewhat better what he was attacking.

When he got within range, he pressed the red trigger button on the control stick in front of him and puffs of white smoke emanated from the edges of his wings... leaving a distinguishable trail behind each wing...which made the plane easy to track.

Basnett looked around the sky sharply...saw no enemy fighters to tangle with...and nosed over as well.

"Steady now...here they come...just like I told you," the *rikusentai* machine gunner said as he watched the first of the two enemy planes nose over and head towards them.

The man holding the bipod legs braced himself as the sound of the aircraft's engine grew louder and louder in his ears...hoping its machine guns missed him yet again...like they had in the plane's last pass.

Before long, the second plane dipped down too... so that both planes were now coming at the two men... just like the machine gunner had anticipated. Instead of tracking the first plane down through its descent however, the veteran gunner picked a spot several hundred yards out ahead of its nose and he squeezed the trigger…hoping that the plane would fly right through the area where he had concentrated his fire.

Lieutenant, J.G. Basnett could feel the straps holding him to his seat digging into his shoulders as the g-forces started taking effect in his dive…a nagging distraction which all fighter pilots eventually got used to. Luckily, it didn't require much effort to keep an eye on Valencia since the two planes weren't trying to evade anything and their route down was almost in a straight line. When the flight leader had almost reached the point where he would begin firing, Basnett noticed pink-colored tracer rounds coming up from the island…something they had not experienced in any of their other previous gun runs against the Jap defenses down below them.

Basnett was sure that Valencia was aware of it, but he called out just to make sure. "Ground fire coming from directly ahead, V," he yelled into his mask excitedly and Valencia began to dodge back and forth to throw off the gunner's aim. Then smoke began trailing off his wings as Valencia began returning fire with his wing guns… and Basnett could see small explosions erupting on the ground as his rounds slammed into the area where the pink tracers were coming from.

It took incredible discipline for the gunner's assistant to remain seated on the edge of the trench...exposed from the waist up to whatever ground fire might come his way...and especially so when the fighter began firing back at them as well. The fact that he couldn't see the plane approaching...since he was facing the gunner...or see the edges of its wings blinking as its guns fired was certainly helpful. But discipline had its limits...and the assistant began to shake when he felt the enemy fighter's rounds striking the ground nearby...which caused his buddies to cower in the trench beside him. His shaking caused the bipod he was gripping to move slightly as well...and these miniscule vibrations then made their way up to the barrel of the machine gun too...which threw off the gunner's aim just enough to cause his tight cone of fire to widen out substantially by the time the first plane flew through it.

The *rikusentai* gunner grunted momentarily in disapproval as the first plane seemed to make it through unscathed since it flew right over them and then banked away to the west...in the direction of the carrier it had come from. But the second plane was on its way in now, too...so he focused his attention on that one...hoping his luck would improve...and it did.

Basnett watched Valencia pull out of his dive and head west...safe and sound. But it didn't appear that his flight leader had hit anything either...since those pink tracers were now coming up at his plane as well. To dodge the

The Butcher's Block

incoming fire, Basnett tapped on his left rudder pedal for a second which caused his plane to slew to the left a few feet...and then he tapped on the right one...which brought his plane back to the right...a jinking maneuver that was used to spoil the enemy gunner's aim. He did this for a few seconds...and then he straightened out again as he got closer to the island and within the range of his own machine guns. As Basnett was about to fire, he felt a thump out ahead of him in the engine area... and then another...along his right wing. He glanced sideways and saw a jagged hole in his wing, but the plane continued to fly as if it had not been hit. *Maybe I can finish what I started*, he thought hopefully, but his optimism was quickly dashed when a thin stream of oil began to seep out of his engine and splash against his windshield, obscuring his view. His gun run now over, Basnett pulled back on the stick to gain height...and then he punched the left rudder pedal and the plane reacted well...rising and turning to the left...just as he had intended. A check of his oil pressure gauge told him what he already knew...but the needle was nowhere close to the red danger mark and the engine was humming smoothly so he knew he had time to reach home and then he would have to decide whether he was going to land the plane or ditch it in the sea beside the carrier.

"I hit it!" the *rikusentai* machine gunner exclaimed proudly as the Navy fighter whisked by overhead... its windscreen darkened by the oil that was streaming out of a nicked oil line that ran alongside the engine housing.

"I guess it was worth risking my life then," the assistant gunner added as he ducked out from underneath the machine gun and sat back down inside the trench... happy to be alive.

"Yes, it certainly was. And if I get another chance to shoot down one of those evil planes, you'll be right back up there doing your duty like the good sailor you are. In the meantime, rest and take pride in knowing that you have served the Emperor well this day...and if we make off this island alive...I will put you in for a promotion!"

"I'll trade that promotion for a sip of water," the assistant proffered, "or a bite to eat."

"I wish I could give you all three...but for now I can only promise you a promotion. The food and water have run out...and you know it. Hopefully, we'll be resupplied with what we need once our Navy gets here. We just have to hang on until they do...and then they'll blast their ships out of the water."

"Tell that to the marines out there," the assistant replied dejectedly...and he waved his hand in the direction of the marines who were west of them in the tank trap. "They don't seem to be too worried about our Navy showing up. They just keep on coming no matter how many we seem to kill. And if our Navy doesn't show up soon, they'll have to blast the American Navy first...and then this island...since the marines will own it."

"Keep those thoughts to yourself," the senior man said, shushing him. "That kind of talk can infect the others. There are rumors that some men are beginning to take their own lives out of despair...instead of fighting the enemy." He nodded towards the three other men in the trench who were peering over the lip of the trench...more concerned with the advancing marines now that the planes were gone than with the subject of their conversation.

"I'm just being realistic," his friend answered back while lowering his voice in obedience to his leader's order.

"We have plenty of men left. There are hundreds of us in this area alone. And we have plenty of reinforcements to draw from to the east of us. All we must do is hold out for another day or two, and then our Navy will surely arrive, and all will be well. I do not want to hear you speak so negatively anymore. It is not good for you...or the rest of us. We must continue to trust that Admiral Shibasaki and his staff are aware of our situation...and they are doing everything possible to bring us help. Our job...our duty...is to hold on...as long as possible."

"Shibasaki? He is dead, my friend, just like we heard."

"I do not believe that rumor. And that is all it is. If he is dead, we would not be receiving reinforcements from the east like we have been. It is obvious to me that he is still in command and that he is aware of our situation here. He continues to funnel troops to us as we need them. The admiral is orchestrating this battle brilliantly...and I continue to have confidence in his leadership."

"I will try to think more like you do...and I will continue to do all I can to bring honor to myself, to you, and to our Emperor," the assistant replied, caving to the senior man's wishes.

"It will make the task ahead of you easier…and serving the Emperor should be done without complaint…as you well know. I am glad that you have thought it through and that you have made this decision. Thank you, my friend," the *rikusentai* veteran said encouragingly. Then, looking skyward, he smiled and said, "See…now there are no planes to bother us since we have driven them off. This day has begun wonderfully!"

"It has indeed…it has indeed," his assistant gunner said as he too scanned the empty sky above, and smiling, added, "maybe this will end up being a good day for us after all!"

"I'm in trouble, V," Lieutenant, J.G. Basnett broadcast over his radio.

Basnett's section leader glanced over his shoulder immediately when he heard the transmission, trying to see if he could tell what was wrong with his wingman. *Did he get jumped?* he wondered, but Basnett's plane was flying in a straight path directly behind him and his voice had no hint of urgency in it, so he dismissed that notion right away. "What's the matter," Valencia answered back, and he began a sharp turn to the left to come back around so he could get a better look at Basnett's plane as they flew by one another.

"I got hit by some ground fire during my pass," Basnett replied as he reached over and he hit the canopy release and slid it back, exposing the cockpit to the air rushing by. "I took a round in my right wing and somewhere in my engine. I've got a small oil leak, but the pressure's okay so far. My engine is running smoothly. The problem is that I can't see out of my windshield."

As Valencia eased off the throttle and flew by, he could see the darkened windshield of Basnett's plane and then Basnett himself sitting in the pilot's seat inside the open cockpit. His wingman waved his gloved hand at him and Valencia responded by giving his buddy a thumb's up with his own gloved hand. "How's your wing holding up...is it stable?"

"She's handling fine, but I haven't tried to take her into a steep dive yet," Basnett answered, and he waggled his wings up and down to confirm his assessment.

"Well, there's no need to put her into a dive. All you gotta do is make it back to the carrier. You confident you can get her back there?"

Basnett looked at the oil gauge once more, saw that it was still in the normal operating range, and then glanced down towards the ocean below. He was just passing over the outer destroyer screen...which indicated that the carrier was close, and he said, "As long as my oil pressure continues to hold up, I should have no problem reaching her."

"Okay, I'll ride in with you and help you down. You know you can ditch her too...if you think it's necessary. We have plenty of airplanes so losing her is not an issue," Valencia offered.

"Thanks, V, but I think I can land her successfully. As much as I like to swim, I'd rather feel that good old deck underneath me than some ocean waves when I put her down," Basnett replied, happy to have his section leader alongside in case he ran into some unforeseen problem while he was trying to land his injured Hellcat on a pitching carrier deck.

In moments the two planes had reached the USS *Essex*, and then the pilots began to fly around the ship prior to entering the landing circle. Basnett asked for permission to land and his radio crackled right back, giving him the authority to do so. "Red Tango Two has been given permission to land," the unknown radio operator on the *Essex* replied, using the call sign that referred to Basnett and the flight that he was in.

Lieutenant, J.G. Basnett acknowledged the call and then dropped down into the space of air around the carrier that was reserved for planes coming in to land. As he came even with the carrier, he began a series of moves to put his airplane in the proper position and attitude for a successful landing. He reduced his speed and then he began a gentle turn to the left as he came up downwind of the rear of the carrier. He lowered his flaps…which slowed his plane…and then he pulled back on the control stick…which drew the nose of the plane up…slowing it even more. Basnett then poked his head out the side of the cockpit and he felt the air rushing by his face. Little bits of oil began to pelt his face as well… but this did not distract him in the least and he spotted the carrier's landing-signal officer, who was stationed on the left side of the fantail. The man was holding a paddle in each hand and he had them extended out from his side in a parallel position…which indicated that Basnett's plane was coming in straight and level. If the LSO had lowered or raised the paddles, Basnett would have had to react accordingly, either raising or lowering his nose to counter the warning the LSO was communicating to the incoming pilot. In this case, Basnett came in perfectly...and the LSO made a throat-cutting move with his right paddle...the sign that every pilot hopes to see. In seconds, Basnett's fighter hit the deck and its tail hook caught the arresting wire which was stretched across the deck to slow the arriving airplane's forward movement. Basnett's head jerked forward as his plane slowed quickly...going from eighty miles an hour to zero in the space of seventy feet. Basnett took a deep breath and felt the energy drain out of his body...the exhilaration of the dangerous flight suddenly over. *Thank you, God*, he thought to himself, and he felt safe enough to finally relax. He removed his flight helmet and laid it in his lap...but then, incredibly, the engine in Basnett's trusty plane caught fire...and angry flames began to creep into the cockpit near the pilot's feet. Basnett scrambled to release his seat belt and shoulder straps so he could get out of the plane...but the fire spread quickly...and he began choking on the thick smoke that enveloped the cockpit in a matter of seconds.

Luckily for Basnett, Petty Officer Russell Sykes of Pittsburgh, Pennsylvania was positioned near the island of the carrier and he was ready for just this sort of contingency. Sykes was part of the carrier's crash team, and he was armed with a powerful fire extinguisher...so he could fight off both shipboard and carrier deck fires...and he was no rookie. Ignoring the flames and heat they gave off, Sykes rushed up to the plane, jumped up on its right wing, and edged his way up to the cockpit. Thankfully, it was already open...since Basnett had slid the canopy back prior to landing...and Sykes placed the nozzle inside and squeezed the handle at the top of the extinguisher bottle. The fire was knocked down immediately and this gave Sykes enough time to reach down and unbuckle the pilot's seat belt and shoulder straps. The pilot made no move to get out however; instead, he sat there limply...having passed out from lack of oxygen. Sykes was a big man and his size and strength enabled him to save Basnett in one fell swoop. He put the extinguisher off to the side and reached under the pilot's arms and pulled him up and out of his seat. Sykes then pulled him sideways and began to drag him out of the cockpit. One of Basnett's legs got caught on the seat, however, so Sykes pulled all the harder and the leg finally freed. In seconds, Sykes had the pilot's entire body out of the cockpit, and he lowered him down to two other sailors who had rushed up to assist him. They placed the inert pilot on a stretcher and carried him below to the sick bay...where the ship's doctor was already waiting to check him out.

Petty Officer Sykes' eyes stung from the smoke that continued to drift out of the cockpit as he watched the pilot and the two sailors disappear through a door in the island...and then he got back to work. He turned around, retrieved his extinguisher, vaulted down to the deck, and sprayed the rest of the fire extinguisher's contents into the engine housing...killing the fire once and for all.

Marines under Major Lawrence Chamberlin and First Lieutenant Alexander Bonnyman storm the bombproof on D + 2. One of the T-shaped ventilation shafts can be seen on the right of the bombproof. Major Chamberlin might be the marine standing next to the broken coconut tree in the photo.

Marine dead still lying along the Red 1 beachhead after the battle has ended. The tank in the photo is *Cecilia*...which ran into a shell hole as it was firing on the Japanese defenses in the *Pocket* during the afternoon of D + 1. The wooden structures in the background are the privies...or outhouses...that the Japanese used for sanitary purposes. Colonel Shoup determined the number of Japanese *rikusentai* on the island by the number of privies that existed throughout the island.

An overhead view of the Bird's Beak. Disabled amtracs can be seen throughout the length of the Red 1 beachhead. The large, rectangular area on the northern end of the main airfield and the aircraft revetments on the northern side of it can also be seen.

First Lieutenant Bonnyman leading the attack against the bombproof on D + 2. Bonnyman won the Congressional Medal of Honor for his heroic actions during the assault on the bombproof.

Photos of First Lieutenant Alexander Bonnyman before he enlisted in the Marine Corps.

First Lieutenant Alexander Bonnyman sitting in a shell hole on Red Beach 3. This photo was probably taken on D + 1 of the battle. He is the one marine not wearing a camouflage cover over his helmet in the middle right of the photo.

Marines advancing on the bombproof in the background on D + 2. The marine in the center of the photo appears to be carrying two boxes of machine gun ammunition.

Corpsmen working on a marine who has been wounded in the head.

Marine giving water to a kitten that survived the battle and was hiding under a destroyed *Ha-Go* tank. Notice the marine is wearing a binoculars case over his shoulder. Japanese snipers targeted marines that wore these since it was assumed that only officers would carry them.

First Lieutenant Bonnyman with some of his fellow engineers from the 18th Marine Regiment prior to the battle for Betio Island. Bonnyman is the one kneeling to the right.

Chaplains performing a burial service on Betio Island.

Two marines helping a buddy who has been shot in the legs to the rear.

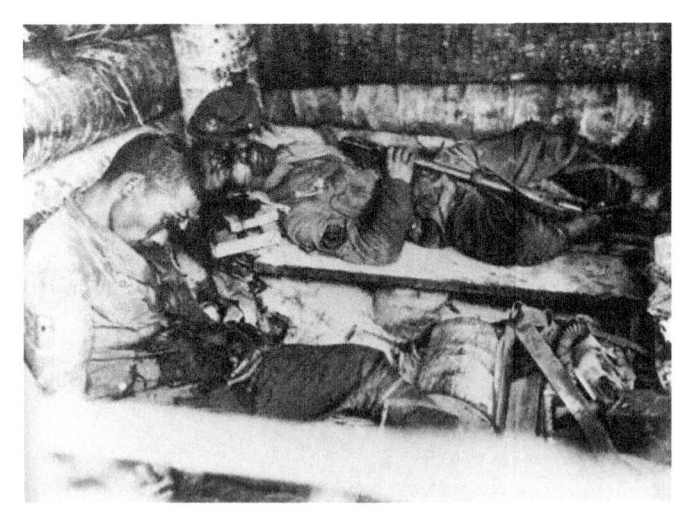

Japanese *rikusentai* who have chosen to commit *hari kari* as the marines closed in on their position.

Marine humor at its finest. The white bomb probably indicates the location of an unexploded shell that is buried in the sand.

Bringing in the marine dead for burial after the battle was finished. Two marines are wearing gas masks since the smell was so bad all over the island.

An LVT-2 coming in under fire. The marine standing up is manning a .50 caliber machine gun. Concrete tetrahedrons can be seen to the left.

Japanese prisoners awaiting questioning. Note the man on the left has a wound on his left arm and the man next to him appears to have a wound on his neck.

Major Crowe leading the marine attack on Red Beach 3 on D Day. Major Crowe was adored by his men.

Marines watch as two F6F Hellcat fighters strafe Japanese positions ahead of them. The marines in this photo are on the far eastern end of Red 3.

A photo taken from somewhere along the pier. This photo was probably taken early on during the battle...since the marine is walking casually up top. At this point, he might not realize the danger he is putting himself in. Other marines have begun to take cover along the pier...and a destroyed Japanese tank lighter can be seen up ahead...angled towards the pier just like this Higgins boat is. Many marines gathered behind the tank lighter before making their final push to the beach.

Four haggard marines heading back to their transports after the battle was over. This photo was probably taken on D + 3.

Four marines providing cover for another group of marines that are surrounding a bunker they have cut off. Two of the marines are armed with Thompson Submachine guns. The sunbaked sand was extremely hot, and many marines suffered minor burns from lying in it.

Marines digging in along the beachhead on Red 3. These men are probably from F Company of Major Crowe's battalion. The marine directly in front appears dead…and another marine is pulling machine gun ammunition off a marine who has been killed as well.

A marine with an M-1 rifle checks out the turret of one of the fourteen Japanese *Ha-Go* tanks that were on the island. This one was dug in for protection and its 37mm cannon probably damaged several amtracs that tried to land on the beach in front of it before it was knocked out. A dead *rikusentai* lies off to the left.

Marines near the boat slip unloading supplies coming in from the end of the pier. Other marines are helping get some wounded marines off the island by loading them on a rubber raft in the background. The rubber rafts proved their worth in this regard… since they were perfect for the job. The tetrahedrons that were built by Japanese engineers to defend against tank landings can be seen off in the distance.

A marine pioneer...denoted by the two white stripes on the back of his helmet...takes a Japanese bunker under fire with his M-1 carbine.

Two marines making themselves at home in a Jap pillbox after the fighting was over. The sign says: "The Lousy Lousy Lounge."

Marine dead...covered by ponchos...being laid to rest in a ditch before burial.

Marines loaded on Higgins boats heading to the island that is obscured by smoke and dust from the naval bombardment and air strikes that have already taken place.

The steel-reinforced, conical bunker that prevented the marines of F Company from advancing eastward down Red Beach 3 on D Day and D + 1. This bunker also protected the right flank of the bombproof that Major Chamberlin's force defeated on D + 2. Major Crowe's CP would have been a few hundred yards down the beach to the right. A dead *rikusentai* lies at the lower left of the photo.

A marine...possibly a corpsman...inspecting a pile of dead Japanese after the battle. Three other marines look on in the distance to the right.

Part of the L-shaped fence that Major Chamberlin used to advance against the bombproof on D + 2. The marines on top are charging after the Japanese who have abandoned the building for good.

Dead Japanese scattered about the battlefield.

Dead marines awaiting burial.

Marine throwing a grenade at an enemy target. It looks like the bombproof is off to the right. The marine on the right is taking a break from the fighting.

Supplies piled up on the end of the pier…waiting to be brought to the island. This photo was probably taken around D + 2 since there are two marines standing towards the right of the photo…no longer under fire. The smoke seems to be drifting from the left… where the attack on the tail of the island was taking place.

More marine dead being laid to rest. The two men in the ditch are probably chaplains.

A marine reloads his BAR amidst the smoke and dust that has been churned up during the battle.

Marine dead entangled in the barbed wire that was strung around the island.

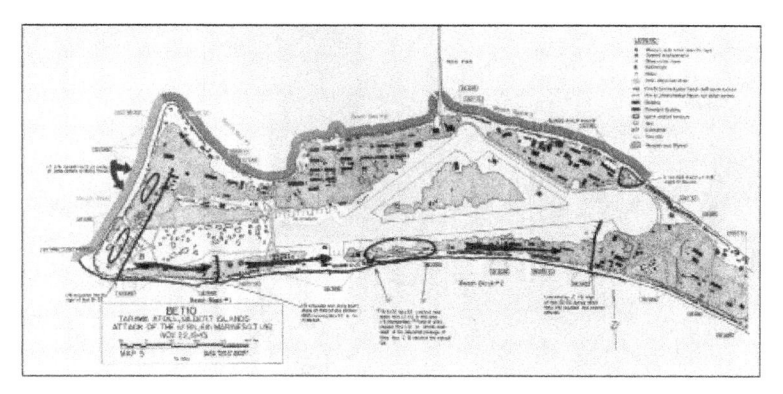

A map of the fighting that the First of the Sixth conducted down the southern coastline on D + 2 on Betio Island.

Japanese *rikusentai* sharpening their skills with their machine guns prior to the battle.

Marines taking cover behind the seawall along Red Beach 2. The pier can be seen in the distance to the left of the photo. These men are probably from the Second Battalion, Second Regiment and they met fierce resistance as they came in on D Day.

Getting ready to rise the Stars and Stripes. This ceremony took place during the morning of D + 4 and the marines loaded up on their transports after it was over.

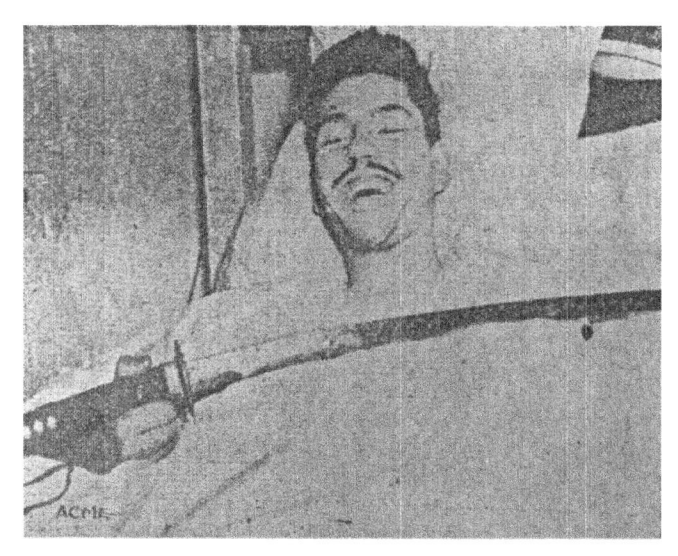

A wounded marine showing off his captured *Samurai* sword to a news correspondent after the battle was over.

Marines swarming over the bombproof on D + 2. Major Chamberlin…supervising the attack…may be the marine at the lower left of the photo. The Japanese are beginning to wage their counterattack at this point from the other end of the bombproof.

Colonel Shoup…a map case hanging off his shoulder…explaining his plans to another officer. Lieutenant Colonel Carlson is seated at his feet…and Major Culhane…the operations officer…is standing to the left in the photo. He isn't wearing his helmet…apparently unconcerned with enemy snipers. Colonel Carlson carried messages back and forth to the island because of the communications problems that plagued the operation right from the start. Colonel Edson… who took over the battle from Colonel Soup…is standing with his hands on his hips to the right of Major Culhane in the photo.

Inspecting an enemy pillbox was fraught with danger...so the marines approached them with caution...even after the battle was finished.

A lone marine with two destroyed Japanese guns in the distance behind him.

Marine dead awaiting burial. Some of these men had been lying in the open for three days...and they were no longer recognizable.

Marines under Major Chamberlin and First Lieutenant Bonnyman fighting off the Japanese counterattack on the top of the bombproof on D + 2.

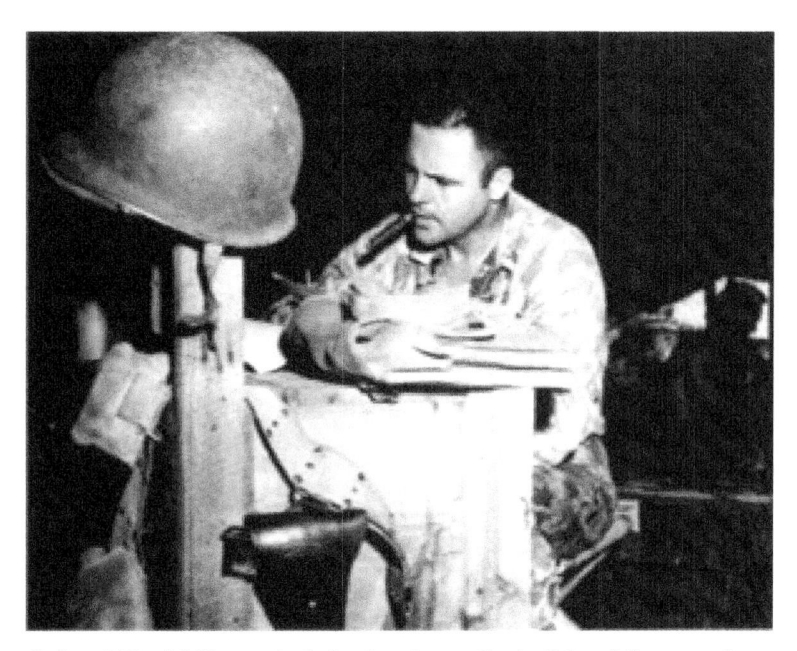

Colonel David Shoup led the battle on Betio Island for two days. He was awarded the Congressional Medal of Honor for his leadership and efforts.

Salvaging parts from the remains of a Japanese aircraft that had been destroyed along the airfield...probably from the allied bombing effort that had been waged several months before the invasion.

Getting ready for battle on the transport before the landing. The two marines are loading magazines for the marine on the right who will be carrying a BAR...while the other marine has an M-1 Garand rifle beside him. A cleaning rod and oil can...along with a canteen and bayonet...are also part of the marine's gear. The marine behind them might be reading a Bible that he had received from Chaplain Willard.

Marines from the 3rd Battalion, 6th Regiment land on Green Beach on D + 2 around 0900 hours. They were able to walk in from the reef since Green Beach had been won the day before by Major Ryan's orphans. These were the first marines that were able to land with all their weapons and special gear intact...which included flamethrowers and demolitions equipment.

Four marines carrying a wounded buddy to the seawall for medical attention. Their postures indicate how tired they were...and that they were still looking out for snipers.

One of the M4 Sherman tanks that was knocked out by Japanese anti-tank fire. The nickname for this tank...like the others...was written in white on its left side...but it is hard to read from the angle of the photograph.

Marines appear worried as they ride aboard a Mike boat and look shoreward...knowing the landing won't be a cakewalk.

A marine squad watches as a flamegunner unleashes his deadly fire on a Jap position.

Marines...one of whom is wearing a gas mask...gathering marine dead for burial.

A section of Black Beach 1 that Major Jones' marines had to fight through on the morning of D + 2 as they tried to link up with men from the 1st Battalion and the 2nd Battalion under Major Kyle in the tank ditch which was located to the right of this area in the photo.

One of the M4 Sherman tanks from the 3rd Platoon under First Lieutenant Lou Largey that ran into a fuel dump and got stuck on D Day. The fuel dump was later set on fire when a Navy fighter plane strafed the area…and the tank was destroyed in the ensuing fire.

Siwash…the 1st of the 10th mascot…and intrepid duck…that fought off the Japanese rooster along the seawall on Red Beach 2 on D Day.

Siwash's defeat of the Japanese rooster along the seawall on Red 2 rallied the marines who saw the famous fight and Siwash was later awarded a medal for his gallantry.

PICTURE OF THE WEEK

Siwash, a duck, is mascot of the First Battalion of the Tenth Marines. A year ago he attached himself to that battalion and has been with it ever since. At Tarawa Siwash landed on the beach under fire and was cited as follows: "For courageous action and wounds received on Tarawa, in the Gilbert Islands, November 1943. With utter disregard for his own personal safety, Siwash, on reaching the beach, without hesitation engaged the enemy in fierce combat, namely, one rooster of Japanese ancestry, and though wounded on the head by repeated pecks, he soon routed the opposition. He refused medical aid until all wounded members of his gun section had been taken care of." This heroic portrait of Siwash was sent to LIFE by the commanding officer of the First Battalion, Lieut. Colonel Presley M. Rixey. He reports that Siwash's favorite sport is drinking beer.

Siwash taking a drink of his favorite beverage.

The twelve pack howitzers under Lieutenant Colonel Rixey provided artillery support to the 1st Battalion, 6th Regiment marines as they fought off the *banzai* attack during the early morning hours of D + 3.

The Japanese *Ha-Go* tank that was parked outside the entranceway to the Japanese Command Post that finally fell on the afternoon of D + 2. First Lieutenant Elrod's men fired on this tank with their 37mm cannon on the afternoon of D + 1 and disabled it for good when its engine was damaged.

The Japanese bombproof...that housed the island's power station...was covered by sand to protect it from being destroyed by naval gunfire or from aerial attack and aerial bombs. Dead *rikusentai* can be seen lying around it after it fell to the marines on D + 2. A corner of the concrete building can be seen in the photo. First Lieutenant Bonnyman was later awarded the Medal of Honor for leading the attack against this position.

Chapter Twenty-Three

Major John Semmes, Jr. took his eyes off the big sergeant in front of him and glanced at the two F6F Hellcats that were heading west...seeking the carrier that they had launched from earlier that morning. "Do you think those planes have done us any good?" the officer asked, knowing that the sergeant had been fighting for the past two days. "You'd know better than me...obviously...since we just got here," he added respectfully.

Platoon Sergeant Roy...who had left the tank ditch and made his way northward a few minutes ago...looked ruefully at the two planes and said, "Not as far as I can tell. But to be fair, they've been hammering the tail of the island while me and my men have been down here on the Beak the whole time. They might've killed a few Japs at the other end for all I know. They certainly didn't kill enough of them before we landed though. And neither did the Navy's big guns for that matter."

The Butcher's Block

The major, the executive officer of the First Battalion, Sixth Regiment, considered the sergeant's answer for a second and then shook his head in agreement. "Yeah, we're definitely going to have to work on that. Air support and naval gunfire support will have to be studied far more diligently to see how it can be used more effectively in our future landings...as you have pointed out."

Now it was Roy's turn to nod in agreement...and he did so.

"So, you want to attach yourself to us as we attack up the southern coastline...is that it?" the major said, returning to the point of their original conversation.

"Yes, sir. We've been fighting under Major Ryan's command since we landed. But the dope is that our battalion...the Second of the Second...or what's left of it... is holed up in a tank trap near Black Beach Two. Major Ryan told me it would be alright to ask if you would let us head up that way with your guys...so we can link up with our own boys. I have a little less than half a platoon with me. I haven't seen my platoon commander or our company commander since we left the transports on Saturday morning. I would appreciate it if you would let us tag along...and we'll stay out of the way...I promise... unless you need us, of course."

"I see no reason at all why we can't accommodate that, sergeant," Semmes replied easily.

"Thank you, sir," Roy said, adding, "and my men will really appreciate it as well. We wanna get home."

"No problem," he responded in kind...and he went on to explain his battalion's order of attack. "Major Jones has designated C Company to lead our advance.

Since we're attacking on such a narrow front...we figure it's no more than a hundred yards wide from the beach to the inland side of the airstrip...we're going to use one company at a time at the head of our column. B and A Companies will follow up in line...and D Company will provide its special weapons...flame throwers and demolitions...in support. Plus, we have an M Four and two Stuart tanks that are going to be helping us out too. Our Headquarters and Service Company will bring up the rear...and you can attach yourselves to them. I'll let them know to watch out for you since the last thing we want is to end up having a friendly-fire incident. Sound good?"

"Yes, sir," Roy answered, and then added, "is Lieutenant Bale in command of that M Four by any chance?"

"As a matter of fact, he is," the major responded. "Do you know him?"

"I watched his tanks try to come ashore on D Day, sir," Roy answered. "They had a hell of a time trying to get in...just like the rest of us. He started out with six tanks and only two of them made it in. I got a chance to meet him later on at a meeting Major Ryan had that first night. We had to figure out what we were going to do to keep the Japs from running us off the island... and his tank, *China Gal*, was instrumental in helping us advance down Green Beach yesterday morning. We were able to secure the whole beachhead by noon thanks to that tank. It's seventy-five really comes in handy when you're going up against these hardened bunkers...which are everywhere out here."

The Butcher's Block

"In that case," the major said, "I have a proposition for you."

"What's that, sir?" Roy asked.

"Well, Lieutenant Bale has asked me to provide a sort of escort for his tank as it maneuvers down our left flank. He's gonna stick to the solid ground of the airstrip instead of getting down in the weeds with us where the soft sand can bog him down."

"That makes sense," Roy said, interjecting.

"Plus, he's worried about Jap sappers rushing the tank and taking it out with a mine. He says that several tanks have been knocked out of action that way already... which is where you come in. I need a group of marines to basically be a bodyguard element for that tank...and the two lights that will be operating with him. You want the assignment?"

"Of course, sir," Roy answered right away.

"Perfect. All you need to do is stay nearby them as they advance down the airstrip. It's an important assignment. He told me that there is only one other M Four besides his that is still up and running and that one is over with the Eighth Marines on Red Three. We can't risk losing his tank...since there aren't any backups."

"We can handle it, sir."

"Good. I'll coordinate it with him. You just need to link up with him as we begin our advance," the major said, satisfied.

"No problem, sir. And just so you know, you'll probably be passing right through our position when you begin your attack since we're holding a tank ditch just north of Temakin Point. To get to the south shore, you must pass through that area. We've cleaned it out already…but the Japs have a way of materializing out of nowhere as you'll soon find out. It's the damndest thing. Just when you think you've killed them all, one more pops up and takes a shot at you with a machine gun. Have you been able to check out any of these bunkers on Green Beach yet…so you know what you're going up against on the south shore?"

"I have. And I can see why we've suffered so many casualties in trying to take them out. No one thought the Japs were this good at engineering. I got to hand it to them. They were ready for us…if nothing else," the major said…and he shook the sergeant's hand…signaling an end to the meeting.

"Thanks again, sir, and we'll keep an eye out for your men and the tanks as they come down. Good luck," Platoon Sergeant Roy replied…and he turned and headed back towards Temakin Point where his twelve men were eagerly waiting to hear the dope he was bringing about the morning's plan of action.

Thirteen sets of eyes were riveted on Platoon Sergeant Roy as he began to speak. There was the platoon guide, Sergeant Flockerzi, and the two runners, PFC Mudd and PFC Rickard, who made up Roy's headquarters section. Then, standing next to Sergeant Flockerzi, was Corporal Oliver, the Second Squad Leader, and beside him were the three remaining men from his own squad: PFC Kevin Lewis…a BAR-man…and his assistant…Private Terry McGowan…and his last, lone rifleman…Private Doug Tuchmann. The rest of the group included Sergeant Varner, the Third Squad Leader, and his assistant squad leader, Corporal Derek Hullender, and the four men under them: the squad's two BAR-men…PFC Reisman and PFC Paul Rampley… an assistant BAR-man…Private Tyler Smith…and the squad's one remaining rifleman…Private Nelson.

Roy had called the whole group together so he could give the good news to them all at once. "Okay, listen up. There's been a change in plans," he said, and the men's ears perked up even more than they already were. "Instead of working with Major Ryan's men to take out the *Pocket*, we're going to accompany the One Six as they attack down the south coast. Our job is to provide cover for the three tanks that will be working with them. Their goal is to link up with the guys who are holding a tank ditch that is located just east of the Black Beach Two. And if you haven't heard yet, the guys in the tank ditch are supposedly what's left of our battalion. The One Six is going to pass through us here and then spread out as they—"

"It looks like they're already here, sarge," Sergeant Flockerzi said, interrupting Platoon Sergeant Roy.

Roy turned around and saw the lead elements of the 1-6 quickly approaching their position…and he looked down at his watch and saw that the time was 0815 hours. "Yeah, that's them alright…and they're only a few minutes behind schedule. I thought it would take them a little longer to get organized…but Major Jones has them raring to go," he said, and he waved to the men to make sure they knew that he and his small force were friendlies. A wave back indicated that they had been seen... and were not going to be fired on.

Before long, a young lieutenant came over and asked who was in charge. All thirteen men looked directly at Platoon Sergeant Roy and two of them even pointed at him. This caused an eruption from Roy who shouted out, "Put your hands down, damn it! You tryin' to get me killed!"

The young lieutenant was taken aback by the sergeant's harsh demeanor...and he looked at him quizzically for a second.

Roy saw the look and said, "No offense, sir. But there are still Jap snipers not a hundred yards away from here. All they live for is to shoot someone in charge...so the last thing I need is to have my men pointing at me as if I'm some big kahuna over here. I managed to survive for the last two days and I want make sure I finish this day out above ground, too." Roy then pointed to the complex that housed the two big eight-inch naval cannons in the distance and said, "We cleared this area out yesterday...right down to Temakin Point. But we pulled back to this tank ditch and revetment last night since it's as good a defensive position as there is in the area. The Japs might have infiltrated some snipers back down there during the night for all we know. There's plenty of bunkers left...and they could be hiding out in any one of them...as you'll soon find out. You'll encounter more resistance once you reach the Point and swing left. It's uncharted territory beyond there. How many Japs are still holding out between the coastline and the airfield is anyone's guess. The only good thing is that the ones there are trapped, and they haven't been able to get any reinforcements up from the tail of the island that we know of. I've been told that the Second of the Second is holding a tank ditch on the other side of them…just east of Black Beach Two. So, they're hemmed in by us and by the Second. But I wouldn't count them out just yet. These Japs are diehards…and they'll fight right up until the bitter end."

The lieutenant thanked the sergeant for his thorough analysis of the situation and then he began feeding his men forward…one squad at a time…into the ruins of Temakin Point. Heeding the sergeant's warning, he yelled out, "Keep your eyes out for snipers, boys. No tellin' how many Japs could be hiding out in this rubble."

Sergeant Flockerzi noted the lieutenant's warning and he looked over at Roy and said, "That one has potential. He listened to your advice…and put it into action. There's hope for us all, I guess."

Roy considered the platoon guide's statement and remembered the conservation that they had had when they first moved into this position. "Yeah, he seems to have the makings of a good officer. It's the ones who think they know everything and lord it over you that really rub you the wrong way. Thankfully, I haven't run into too many of them in my time in the Corps."

"Amen to that," Flockerzi replied…and he, Roy, and the other twelve men watched avidly as the rest of the lead company from the 1-6 filed past them.

The lightheartedness and give and take that had been going on among the men when they first moved out from the north end of Green Beach was now gone... having been replaced by a solemnness as they realized what they were about to do. Roy and the others...Betio veterans now...could see the tension etched on their faces...especially the young privates...and they knew the feeling...could empathize with them...since they had dealt with the stress of combat for two long days. Several "good lucks" were shouted out to the men of the Sixth as they continued by...Roy's men hoping their encouragement would buck them up. As they got closer to Temakin Point, the men in the lead platoon...the tip of the spear... began fanning out...to protect their flanks. And then, on the order from their young lieutenant, they wheeled left and began their attack up the coastline.

The rumble of engines and squealing of treads in the distance announced the arrival of the three tanks that were assigned to support the advance of the 1-6 up the southern coastline.

"Let's go, boys," Platoon Sergeant Roy announced, "they're here." Without hesitation, Roy and the thirteen other men jumped out of the tank ditch and began making their way towards the tanks that were coming south down the dirt road that ran between the tank ditch and Temakin Point. When Roy reached the road, he signaled to the lead tank and the M Four and the two Stuarts behind it came to an abrupt halt. Within seconds, the hatch on top of the turret swung open and First Lieutenant Bale popped out. "Good to see you again, sergeant," he said as the dust that the tank had kicked up swirled around him. "How can I help you?" he added, swatting the dust away from his face.

"Good...to...see...you...too, sir," Roy coughed out. When the dust had finally settled, Roy said, "We've been detailed to protect your tank and the two Stuarts. Any suggestions?"

"Yeah. Stay close. Don't let any Japs get near us. And if you see a target that we don't, point it out to us. We're going to be buttoned up most of the time...and we can't always see what's out there. Just bang on the hull and I'll stick my head up. Point out what we should shoot and leave the rest to us, okay."

"You got it, sir," Roy responded.

"We're gonna stay on this road as long as we can. According to the maps, it curves around Temakin Point and then it runs parallel to Black Beach One all the way down to that large rectangular area on the western end of the airfield. Once we reach the runway, we'll hug the southern side of it and fire on targets we can see from there. If we start taking anti-tank fire from the east, we'll pull off the runway and get down into the woods and brush. We'll just play it by ear and see what happens. I also told the two sergeants in charge of the Stuarts to leave the bunker busting up to us. I want them to keep an eye out for us...just like you are. You guys are our first line of defense. If we get attacked and they get past you, then the Stuarts are going to blast the Japs that are swarming over us with their machine guns. Unless they're tied up themselves. Then we just ride it out...until you guys kill the rest of the Japs."

"We'll try to stay clear if that happens. Hopefully, it won't. We'll do our very best to keep the Japs off your tank," Roy replied.

"Okay then. Let's get moving," Lieutenant Bale said brusquely, and he lowered himself back down into the turret and slammed the hatch cover shut.

It didn't take long for the three tanks to catch up to the lead element of the 1-6 since the Third Platoon of C Company had begun moving cautiously as it began to butt up against the Japanese defenses that dotted the beachhead along Black Beach 1. After a while, the men estimated that were about six bunkers per every hundred yards of beach...and there was about a thousand yards between them and the men of the 2nd Regiment that they were trying to relieve...which meant they would have to destroy nearly sixty bunkers to accomplish their assignment. Luckily however, the bunker system had been set up to defend against a seaborn attack...so most of the gun ports of the bunkers overlooked the beachhead...which left their sides and rear openings susceptible to attack. And this is precisely how the men of the 1-6 and the tanks decided to go after them. When the men spotted a bunker, they would point it out to the tanks which were moving down the road to their left. Once the tank gunners acquired the target, they would begin firing at its side gun ports...if they had them...or at the rear entrance of the bunker to pin its occupants down inside it. Then a combined arms team of riflemen and engineers would advance on the bunker and the bunker would be destroyed by the engineers who got close enough to use their satchel charges or Bangalore torpedoes. Bunkers that resisted these attacks were left behind…to be incinerated by several teams of flame throwers operators who were attached to the lead company as well. This system was proving to be very effective…and the men of the 1-6 were making good progress as they took out one bunker after another.

Despite the rumblings of the powerful engine behind him, First Lieutenant Bale heard the hammering sound reverberating inside his tank. "Hold it up, Josefson," Bale commanded sharply. PFC Eugene Josefson, *China Gal's* driver, pulled back on the directional levers and slowed the tank to a crawl and then a full stop…just like he been ordered to. "Anybody hear what I'm hearing," he asked the other five men inside the tank…one more than normal since he had joined this crew the day before without forcing anyone else to leave. It made the tank even more crowded than it usually was, *but they could live with it*, Bale had reasoned.

"Someone's hitting the hull of the tank on my side, sir," the gunner, PFC Jack Tansil, shouted up behind him.

"I thought that's what it was," Bale yelled back down, and reaching up, he pushed the hatch above his head open and stood up on his seat so he could see out. He spotted Platoon Sergeant Roy immediately…since he was standing close to the right side of the tank…and he was holding his helmet in his hand. "I hope you didn't dent it," he cracked, knowing how hard Roy must have been banging it against the side of the tank.

Roy ran his hand over the outer shell of the helmet, and it felt fine...no depressions or dings in it whatsoever...and he smiled up at the tank lieutenant. "Just like new," he said in reply...and he instantly thought of his own lieutenant...who was wearing a helmet with a jagged hole in its side. *I wonder how he doin'*, he thought to himself, *if he's alive at all.*

"What's the matter...cat got your tongue?" Bale yelled down at him.

Roy looked back up and quickly gathered his wits about him. "Nah...just thinking of someone for a second...that's all," he answered, and then he pointed off towards the beach in a direction slightly ahead of them. "Can you see it?" Roy asked.

Lieutenant Bale placed one hand over his eyes to shield them from the brilliantly-shining sun overhead and squinted in the direction Roy was pointing. He scanned the ground...trying to discover what Roy had found...and then, finally, he noticed it. A long, sandy rise...not really a hill per se...but something that didn't really fit in with the rest of the terrain. "That thing must be forty feet long," the tank TC said, dragging a finger along its full length.

"Probably closer to fifty," Roy countered.

"I don't see any rear doors to it from up here," Bale shouted down, and added, "they must be on the ends."

Platoon Sergeant Roy was about to answer him when he saw a metal door on the side of the bunker closest to

The Butcher's Block

them suddenly swing open...materializing out of nowhere. Neither he nor Bale had seen it...since it was so well-camouflaged...but it banged loudly as it reached the limits of its arc and hit the concrete-reinforced wall of the sand-covered bunker. In seconds, a long line of *rikusentai* emerged and split into two groups. The first group... comprising ten men...dashed straight ahead and fanned out into a trench that ran perpendicular to the long bunker. These *rikusentai* began firing at the C Company marines who were coming up the beach...trying to pin them down. The next group...fifteen men in all...made a beeline straight for Lieutenant Bale's tank. The armored monster with its big gun could wreak havoc on them... and the *rikusentai* defenders inside the bunker knew it... so they considered its destruction a bigger prize...and they had allotted more men to accomplish that specific task. And the attack had been timed perfectly...since the two Stuarts that could have helped the Sherman tank had lagged behind when they were called over to assist the C Company men destroy another bypassed bunker.

A perfect setup, Roy thought, taking the scene in. *The one tank they're really after is up ahead...isolated and all by its lonesome. They must've been watching it come up from vision slots we can't see from here...and probably gun ports too.* The sharp rattle of a Jap machine gun confirmed his assumption and the C Company men dove for cover... initially stalling their advance and then walling them off completely from the M Four that was up ahead and inland from them.

That left Roy and his thirteen men to take on the Jap contingent of fifteen determined *rikusentai* who were now advancing on Lieutenant Bale's tank...and the gap between the two adversaries closed quickly.

Ordinarily, the odds would've favored Roy's group over the Japs who were on foot...since Roy's men had sought cover as soon as they saw the Japs charging out of the bunker. But when a second Jap machine gun in the bunker took them under fire, the situation changed dramatically. Now Roy's men...who were strung out in a line several yards behind *China Gal*...were pinned down too...just like the C Company marines were. And the Jap machine gunner in the bunker was positioned slightly higher than they were...giving him a decided advantage...since he could see them moving while Roy and his men couldn't see him at all. To top it off, the Jap machine gunner was well-trained and thus accurate with his fire...making any move above ground hazardous and dangerous to say the least.

Roy suddenly heard Sergeant Flockerzi yell out, "Ah damn," to his left, and a quick glance confirmed his worst fears. His two runners, PFC Rickard and PFC Mudd, had taken up a position behind a felled coconut log not far away and Rickard had lifted his head to see what they were up against. In an instant, a burst from the Jap machine gun had hit him squarely in the neck and now a pulpy mess was all that remained above the runner's shoulders. To make matters worse, Rickard's helmet, with the remains of his blood-splattered head strapped inside, had struck PFC Mudd in the leg, and Mudd had reached over picked it up and he was now holding his friend's head...which was still in his helmet...in his bloodied hands. Seeing this, Flockerzi

The Butcher's Block

began to crawl over to Mudd, and in doing so, he was stitched across the back of both of his legs and in the butt by the Jap gunner as well. "Ahhh, hell, he got me too," the platoon guide screamed out.

"Put that damn thing down, Mudd, and help Flockerzi!" Roy ordered.

Mudd put his friend's helmet down gently and then carefully slid his way over to Flockerzi...who was lying behind the base of the coconut tree...where it was thicker...and began dressing the guide sergeant's wounds...just like he had been ordered.

Suddenly, Flockerzi began to thrash around and moan all at once. Mudd tried to hold him down...but Flockerzi's movements became more violent as he did so. And then his thrashing stopped...just as suddenly as it had started. And in mere seconds, Flockerzi was dead.

Roy watched it happen...but said nothing. He knew his friend was dead since he had seen men die that way before…the seizing a dead give away…back on the *Canal*.

Betio was not a place where you could grieve very long however, and Roy knew it. Looking back up, he saw that the Japs had kept on coming and that they would be on the tank in seconds. At this point, his only hope was that the men who were on his right...and nearest the charging Japs...would meet the challenge. And they did exactly that.

Corporal Derek Hullender was the assistant squad leader of Third Squad of First Lieutenant Robert Hackett's platoon and his squad leader was Sergeant Jeff Varner. Both men were combat veterans...each having served on Tulagi...and then Guadalcanal when the Second Battalion of the Second Regiment was called over from Tulagi to give the 1st Division marines a break from the jungle fighting that defined their *Isle of Death* campaign. On Guadalcanal, Hullender had proven himself again and again, always going beyond the call, and his superiors had taken notice. There wasn't an assignment he wouldn't volunteer for...or a job that was beneath him... and before long, he had earned a reputation of being a tenacious fighter.

Towards the end of the campaign, he had come down with a bout of malaria, as so many men had, but he never left the platoon. He simply endured the wracking chills and delirium in the jungle along with the men who were suffering just like him...fighting off the illness just like he had the Japanese. A brief stay in the hospital in New Zealand while the Second Division was on R&R had seemingly taken care of the malaria though... and Hullender had told everyone he was as good as new when he reported back to the company. No one would ever learn that he had checked himself out of the hospital early...that he had forged a doctor's signature on his Fit for Duty form...and that he had snuck out of the military hospital on his own accord.

Later, Lieutenant Hackett had approached him and asked why he liked the fight so much. Hullender's answer was straight forward and to the point. "It's in my blood, sir," he said unabashedly. "For some reason, instead of worrying about what can happen to me, I shunt it aside and get real focused like...and energized too. This might sound cocky...but I also seem to be able to do it better than almost everyone else around here... save for Platoon Sergeant Roy of course. So, I just keep at it, sir. That's all there is to it. Pretty simple actually."

Hackett had then paid him the highest compliment possible as far as the young squad leader was concerned. Hackett said, "You remind me a lot of someone else I recently met."

Hullender had looked at his platoon commander with interest...since he respected him...and replied, "Oh, and who is that, sir?"

Without missing a beat, Hackett said, "Lieutenant Hawkins, the leader of the Scout Snipers. We've crossed paths a few times since we got to Wellington...and we had a few drinks the other night. We talked about how the Japs fought on the *Canal*...and he gave me some great advice and insight into how the Japs operate. As far as I'm concerned, there's no better small unit leader or fighter in this whole division!"

"I remind you of him, sir?" Hullender had responded, astonished, since everyone seemed to know about the heroics and tenacity of the lieutenant who led the vaunted Scout Snipers.

"Yes, you do, Hull, and you're built like him too," Hackett had answered matter-of-factly...and a huge grin broke out across Hullender's angular face as he accepted the complement.

Not long afterwards, Hullender had received his sergeant stripes...a coveted promotion...and a squad of twelve men to go along with it. Naturally, he had jumped into the role of squad leader with both feet and he trained his men hard…so hard that some of them had asked for…and been given transfers out of the company. They were replaced by other men who had heard about this tough squad leader…men who welcomed the challenge to see if they could cut it with him. In the end, the ones that stayed became tough and hardened…and extremely competent in their jobs…and before long it was said that his squad could match up against any squad in the Second Division.

Sadly though, this sort of notoriety could have its drawbacks…and one of them was that it strained the already difficult relationship between the commanding officer of E Company…the much-disliked Captain Walter Turlinger…and Hullender himself.

Turlinger had become the E Company CO during the latter stages of the Guadalcanal campaign…after the much liked and respected Captain Tom Murphy had come down with a virulent strain of scrub typhus. Murphy had been so weakened by the disease that he was immediately evacuated off the island so he could receive better care in one of the military hospitals at Noumea…a port city on the much larger island of New Calidonia to the southeast that served as the staging ground for the naval forces involved in the Guadalcanal campaign. Unfortunately, the PBY Catalina flying boat that was carrying Captain Murphy and a bunch of other casualties had been lost in route to Noumea when it developed engine trouble. No one on the flight was ever heard from again…and the E Company men had taken the loss of their revered leader quite hard.

As his replacement, Captain Turlinger had tried to fit into Captain Murphy's shoes as best he could...but the two men were completely different individuals...and they also had two very different styles of commanding men in combat. Murphy had come up through the enlisted ranks...attaining the rank of platoon sergeant...and then becoming a "Mustang" officer...which enabled him to far better identify with the men he was leading. Turlinger, on the other hand, was a college boy, having graduated from the University of Massachusetts in the spring of 1937. To his credit, he had voluntarily joined the Marine Corps after that...and he had become a second lieutenant while the country was still at peace. Promotion to first lieutenant had come quickly...mostly because he was a good administrator...which was a valued commodity during peacetime. But that had all changed after December 7th, 1941...when the Japanese had bombed Pearl Harbor in Hawaii...and the Marine Corps had suddenly found itself in a shooting war with the Japanese military forces that were running roughshod over the entire Pacific region.

Sadly, the war had also intruded on Turlinger's future plans for advancement...since his skills and temperament were far better suited for peacetime service and working behind a desk. Now a captain, Turlinger tried to adapt as best he could however...but his northeastern pedigree and sense of entitlement...which had worsened as he achieved higher rank...never set well with those under him. Try as he might, he never seemed capable of meshing with his men or achieving a solid working relationship with those under his command... and he...and everyone else...knew it. Before long,

Turlinger's leadership failures and incompetence were on full parade…and to deal with it, he began directing his anger and anxiety at his charges instead of looking in the mirror…and trying to fix himself. And Captain Turlinger reserved his strongest vitriol for the men who seemed to fit in the easiest…which placed him at odds with the strong leadership team that had been assembled and forged under Captain Murphy.

That is why Sergeant Hullender stuck out like a sore thumb…as did Sergeant Endres and Platoon Sergeant Roy…and First Lieutenant Hackett for that matter. But Hullender seemed to grate on the CO the most however, and most of the men seemed to think it was because of Hullender's background. "He hates you cause you're a country bumpkin, Hull," was the refrain that the men had stressed repeatedly.

"Y'all think that's it, huh?" Hullender had answered distractedly, not really caring about the reason for the enmity between him and his commanding officer.

"Of course, it is!" the men had stated with certainty. "It drives him crazy to think that you're just as smart as he is…even though you're a redneck hick with no college in your background."

"I'm no hick…even though I did grow up in Dalton, Georgia. Trust me…I grew up with plenty of them peckerwoods from the mountains…and I ain't no redneck."

"Well, how about trying to act like you're really stupid…or dumb…just once," they suggested. "That might get him off your back."

"Oh, I don't pay him no mind. I can deal with anything he throws my way so long as he leaves my squad alone. My job is to train these boys hard...since combat...and fightin' the Japs...is hard business. So far, he's stayed outta my hair and that is all I'm concerned with for now. If he comes down on my boys though, he and I are gonna have a real problem. That's what'll get my dander up," Hullender had answered.

"Just keep an eye on him...that's all we're sayin'" the men replied, "since he's out to get you...one way or another."

Hullender had taken their advice lightly...and it came back to bite him later on...when the sergeant had been brought up on charges by the captain for failing to look out for the welfare of his men during a rigorous training exercise.

The sergeant had scheduled an arduous twenty-mile route march in full gear for his squad through the hills surrounding Wellington...ten miles out...and then ten miles back. And to up the ante, each man was to carry and extra twenty pounds in his pack...which added to the misery. To make it even more challenging, Hullender had then stipulated that the men were to begin the march with their two canteens empty. At the ten-mile mark, a water-filling station had been set up...so each man could then decide how much water he wanted to carry back with him.

As the march was about to begin, Captain Turlinger had pulled up in his jeep and gotten out. His driver was not there...which seemed strange...but no one really paid much attention to the man's absence. The captain then stood arrogantly to the side...his pressed uniform spotless...and watched as the men ambled by...their spirits high despite the rigors they would be facing over the next several hours. This seemed to trigger the captain's anger yet again…but the men were used to it by now, so they ignored him and kept on jostling each other as if he weren't there. When Sergeant Hullender finally marched by, he snapped a smart salute at his commanding officer…which was one of the captain's pet peeves… just like he was supposed to. But Turlinger made sure to turn his back to Hullender just in time so that he didn't have to return it…and Hullender let his raised right hand drop to his side without a thought about it.

The squad made great progress on the way out… marching much faster than Hullender had even thought possible. When Hullender questioned the men why they were going so fast, they had told him that there was a big dance scheduled that night in town…and none of the men wanted to miss out on the opportunity to meet the young eligible women who were sure to show up. The sergeant, who was single too, said, "Well, let's step it up then, boys," and they began to jog to get to the ten-mile mark that much quicker.

Hullender and the men were parched and worn out as they approached the halfway point of the march. They had maintained a fast pace for the first ten miles… and it showed…the uniforms they were wearing soaked in sweat. The men also anticipated a fifteen-minute smoke break…and the opportunity to fill up with as much water as they wanted. The only stipulation was that they'd have to carry it back with them on the return trip…adding more weight to their load. The men were also expected to remove their boots so they could check for and bandage any blisters…the marching soldier's nightmare…that they might have on their feet.

According to the plan that Sergeant Hullender had worked out, Platoon Sergeant Roy was responsible for erecting a hanging water bag at the road junction that marked the ten-mile mark the night before the march. The green bag was made of military canvas…so there would be no mistaking it for what it was…and its insides were layered with a rubber coating that prevented any leakage. It would also be suspended from three stout wooden poles and the bag had four spouts built into it so that several men could draw water from it simultaneously.

As expected, the bag was right where it was supposed to be…hanging off to the side at the prearranged road junction. And the sight of it caused the men to swallow hard in anticipation of gulping down some of the delicious water that was surely inside it…and thus quenching their throbbing thirst.

As usual, Sergeant Hullender…the fittest man in the squad…was the first one to reach the bag…but he did not take any water from it. Instead, he waited on the rest of his men to catch up…thus allowing the four fastest men in the squad to have the access to the water spigots first. "Drink up, boys! You earned it," he said, obviously proud of the effort his marines had shown so far.

"What the hell," one of the men yelled out.

Then one of the other men who was trying to fill up pulled his canteen away and threw it to the ground. "There ain't no water in this damn thing!" he shouted out in frustration.

"Whatta ya mean...no water in it," Hullender stammered, his mouth just as dry as theirs.

"Just what I said, sarge. The bag's empty. The spigots were left open...and whatever water that was in it has drained out!" The man then pointed to the ground below the bag and they could see that the area was damp and darker where the water had leaked out and seeped into the dirt.

At that point, the man who had arrived last...a corporal and Hullender's assistant squad leader...took his pack off and dropped it to the ground. He swore and sat down cross-legged. The look on his face reminded Hullender of the look a petulant child would make when it didn't get a toy it wanted...and the man continued to mumble obscenities under his breath.

Hullender quickly grabbed the bag and shook it. The two men were right...the bag was mostly empty...but there was still a small amount of water left below the spigots. "All's not lost, men. There's still a little left for all of us. We just gotta share it and make do. We're marines... we adapt and overcome!" Hullender then ordered the men to line up and he divvied up what water remained among them. After the last man received his portion, Hullender pulled out his canteen and went through the motions of pouring the last of the water into his own canteen. None of the men knew that the bag was empty of course, and that Hullender had sacrificed his portion so that each of his men could get a little more.

"How could this have happened?" Private Tyler Smith...an assistant BAR-man and one of the men who had made it to the water bag first...complained. A pained look was etched on his face and he shook his canteen up and down to show how little water was in it.

"This ain't right. It just ain't right," he added for effect.

"Shut up and make do," PFC Paul Rampley...a BAR-man...snarled back. "Ya think everything's gonna go perfect all the time. You volunteered to get into this squad...so act like it. No one promised you a bed of roses. Suck it up and make do."

Smith glared at Rampley, but he held his tongue...since Rampley outranked him and Rampley was considered a Hullender protege.

Hullender watched the exchange unfold but said nothing...and then he smiled when Rampley jumped in and handled it. But he could also see the dejected looks and sour countenance on the faces of the other men who were gathered around him...so he decided to buck them up. "Look, men. Things like this are gonna happen in combat. We're gonna get promised things all the time...and nothing's gonna come of it. It's just the way the military works. Hell, the Japs nearly ran us off Edson's Ridge on the *Canal* because we were so short on ammunition. You'd think that's the one thing we'd have the most of...ammo...but we ran short...and no one resupplied us...even though the beachhead was full of the stuff. The veterans already know this...but you new guys...just get used to it. It's the way it is...and it's the way it's always gonna be. The sooner you learn that lesson...that you don't get your hopes up too high...the better off you'll be. And like I said before, we're marines. We adapt and overcome. Got it!"

A chorus of *Got Its* came back and Hullender knew he had achieved his goal…that the men…save for one… understood the situation and that they would handle it as best they could…even though they had gotten a raw deal.

"Alright then," Hullender said moving on, "anybody got any blisters?"

The matter concerning the water bag and the road march had seemed to be forgotten…until a week later. That's when First Sergeant Mike O'Toole called Sergeant Hullender over to his office…and Hullender had learned that he was up on charges. "You're kidding me," was all Hullender could say at first.

"No…I'm not, Hull," O'Toole stated dryly. "How come I wasn't made aware of this when it first happened," he added, shaking his head.

"Because I thought nothing of it, First Sergeant. I asked Platoon Sergeant Roy if he remembered leaving the spigots open…and he nearly bit my head off for suggesting something so dumb. I still have no idea how it happened," Hullender answered honestly.

"Well, it seems your assistant squad leader ratted you out…to the CO no less…and the Old Man wants charges put on you."

"You're not serious," the sergeant replied contemptuously.

"I'm dead serious," O'Toole said, and the first sergeant reached into his desk and pulled out a sheaf of paperwork…and he shoved it at Hullender.

Hullender stared at the papers...and said nothing... while wondering how it had been pushed through so fast. *It's almost like the CO had this stuff drawn up before it even happened*, Hullender thought wryly...but he kept quiet.

"There is a solution out of this of course," O'Toole offered up.

"Oh...and what's that? That I consent to be shot at dawn," Hullender replied sarcastically.

Mike O'Toole laughed heartily and said, "Yes...that would work, of course. But I do have some pull around here, so I've managed to cut a deal for you...if you want it."

"What's the deal you have in mind?" Hullender asked, curious now.

"Okay, we both know the CO has it in for you. Your dedication and success as a leader apparently drive him batty...and we both know why. But he's also a vindictive SOB...so I used that to my advantage. And yours, too. I also want that chicken-shit assistant squad leader of yours transferred outta here as soon as possible. A guy like that can ruin a unit overnight...so he's gotta go. To that end, I'm having him moved over to F Company... and we're getting Sergeant Varner in return. The first sergeant over there is my buddy, and I gave him a heads up on the situation. He'll destroy that guy the first chance he gets...and no one will be the wiser. And we get a stellar guy in Varner...so we win all around."

Sergeant Hullender continued to nod as he followed along with the first sergeant's strategy while waiting for the axe to fall.

"So, what do we do with you?" the first sergeant asked rhetorically.

"That's the million-dollar question, isn't it," Hullender answered.

"Yes, it is. And here is what I came up with. Look, I wanna keep you here...in E Company. But now we're short a corporal and an assistant squad leader all in one. So how about you take a demotion from sergeant to corporal...you lose just one stripe...and I move you back to assistant squad leader. That way you stay with us...and you keep half your old squad. We deep six the paperwork...no trial...and the CO...that miserable bastard...gets his pound of flesh from you."

"Is the CO okay with this?" Hullender asked, intrigued.

"That bum loves the idea. This way he gets to rub it in every time you two see each other. He's sick...you know it...I know it...but I can't kill him...so we live with him while we have to."

Hullender thought it over for a second, and he accepted the deal.

"Good. I'll have the orders cut. All you end up doing is moving a few spots down the squad line."

"And I lose a stripe...don't forget that part. I worked my damn tail off for that stripe. Don't forget that part of it," Hullender quickly pointed out.

"Just bide your time, Hull, and you'll have that stripe and your old job back. Trust me on that. Turlinger won't last much longer," O'Toole emphasized, and he shook the newly-demoted corporal's hand and the meeting came to an end.

The Butcher's Block

In the end, First Sergeant O'Toole had been partially right...since Captain Turlinger's days as the E Company CO were in fact numbered. Just like O'Toole had anticipated, Captain Turlinger had screwed up the assignments that were given to him during the pre-invasion training exercises that were conducted at Mele Bay on the island of New Hebrides...and he had been relieved of his company commander duties on the spot by Lieutenant Colonel Amey, the 2nd Battalion CO. The new company commander, Captain John Ring, was welcomed with open arms by the men in E Company... and in the short time he had to work with them, he proved to be worthy of their respect.

Like Captain Murphy, Ring came from solid Irish stock...so fighting was in his blood too...just like it was in his father's...who had joined the Army and fought against the Germans as an infantryman in the trenches during the Great War in 1918. And Ring's warrior spirit had endeared him immediately to Hullender...and vice a versa. But time had run out before Hullender could be restored to his previous rank...and thus he hit the beaches of Betio as a corporal and the assistant squad leader of Sergeant Varner's 3rd Squad.

The fifteen *rikusentai* who were charging the *China Gal* were taken under fire by the six men that Platoon Sergeant Roy had placed on the right side of his line almost as soon as they had cleared the bunker door. These six men included Sergeant Varner himself...and the remaining five members of his squad: his assistant squad leader…Corporal Hullender…the squad's two BAR-men…PFC Rampley and PFC Mike Reisman…the squad's remaining assistant BAR-man…Private Smith… and the last remaining rifleman in the squad…Private Chris Nelson.

Just as soon as they began firing however, the Japanese machine gunner shifted his line of fire from the left of Roy's line to the men on his right…and he began raking Varner and his men with deadly accuracy. But the opening volley from Varner's men had been extremely accurate too…and three of the *rikusentai* had been killed as a result. Then, just like PFC Rickard had done before, Sergeant Varner stuck his head up to try and see where the Japs were…and he received a bullet right through the temple for his efforts. Varner's head rocked back from the impact of the bullet and then he slumped over…dead.

Corporal Hullender saw his squad leader get hit…and he knew he had to act. "Everybody stay put!" he yelled out…hoping they heard him above the racket of the incoming fire and hoping that they would obey his order if it was heard. Then he jumped up from the hole he had taken cover in and he ran right at the line of the twelve remaining *rikusentai* who were only twenty-five yards away. This bold act shocked the *rikusentai*…that a lone marine would be so brave. But it wasn't going to stop them from doing what they had to do…and they continued to advance in the direction of the American tank, nonetheless.

The Butcher's Block

As Hullender ran ahead, he began firing from the hip with his M-1 Garand rifle, and he scored a hit on one of the advancing enemy soldiers. Snarling like a dog with rabies, the Jap dropped like a stone when the bullet struck him in the middle of his chest. And then Hullender was in amongst the remaining eleven *rikusentai* and he began fighting hand-to-hand with the ones nearest to him.

Luckily for Corporal Hullender, the Japanese machine gunner in the bunker was forced to shift his fire back to the men on Roy's left...since he would hit his own men if he continued to fire in the same direction. And sensing the change, PFC Rampley and Private Smith chose to ignore their leader's last order...and the two of them immediately jumped up and charged into the pack of Japs too...just like their assistant squad leader had done.

Two more *rikusentai* were hit on the outskirts of the scrum as the Japs and the three marines engaged in the tenacious and brutal fighting that defined hand-to-hand combat. Who had killed the other two *rikusentai* was anyone's guess...but it was probably from a rifle shot that came from Private Nelson...or a burst from PFC Reisman's Browning Automatic rifle...since they had gotten up and fired from the hole they were in once they didn't have to worry about being machine gunned in turn.

That left Hullender and his two charges battling against nine *rikusentai*...but then the odds got even better for the marines when two of the Jap soldiers suddenly bolted from the group and headed straight for *China Gal*...which was sitting only fifteen yards away.

Using the cover of the Jap machine gunner, the two men made it to the tank safely...and then one of them reached inside his shirt and produced a magnetic mine while the other man ran to the back of the tank. The *rikusentai* veteran with the mine armed it quickly...since he had practiced the movements repeatedly...and then he threw the mine up at the front of the turret. His aim was accurate...and the mine hit the rounded section of the turret that encased the 75-mm main gun...and it bounced harmlessly off. The mine then rolled down the front slope of the tank...past where the driver and assistant driver sat...and dropped to his feet. The brave *rikusentai* looked down at the mine with shock and stood stock-still...since he knew what was about to happen. In a second, the mine detonated and he ceased to exist... his body blown completely apart and vaporized by the power of the mine's blast.

The force of the blast also dazed the crew members inside the *China Gal*...and several steel rivets whizzed throughout the tank like bullets as they broke free from the hull. Luckily, no one was wounded inside though... and in seconds the tank crew had recovered their wits, and the tank was back in business.

The other Jap...the one who had run to the rear of the tank…was trying to open the steel doors that protected the engine when the mine exploded...and he had been knocked down and wounded by shrapnel that had traveled underneath the tank's belly. Undaunted, the *rikusentai* then got up and returned to the front of the tank...limping on bloody legs the whole way. He looked around and finally found a plank of wood...and

The Butcher's Block

he began banging it against the hull of the tank where the tank driver...PFC Josefson...sat. Josefson heard the noise...and he looked out of his vision block to see what it was. When he saw the Jap standing right in front of the tank, he engaged the transmission and he drove the tank forward... which knocked the man down. Then...to make sure he got his adversary...he spun the tank ninety degrees to one side...and then ninety degrees to the other side as well. In doing so, the tank treads ground the Jap into a bloody pile of meat.

Platoon Sergeant Roy had watched the action around the tank unfold...and he breathed a sigh of relief when he saw that *China Gal* was still safe and sound and able to move under its own power. He then swung his attention back to the fight going on between Corporal Hullender, PFC Rampley, and Private Smith and the seven *rikusentai* who were still alive. Unfortunately, the marines and their enemy were so intermingled that the two other marines nearby...PFC Reisman and Private Nelson...were forced to hold their fire...lest they hit one of their own men while trying to kill the *rikusentai* who were fighting with them. Plus, the Jap machine gunner in the bunker was still alive and well...and his accurate fire continued to pin down Roy and the five men to his left...which made them bystanders so to speak. This group included PFC Mudd...who had finally let go of his buddy's head...but who seemed to be in shock...since he was lying there motionless. Next to him was Private Tuchmann...the rifleman. Every so often, Tuchmann would rise up and fire a few shots at the bunker with his M-1…risking his life in hopes that he would hit the machine gunner with a lucky shot.

Then came the last three. They were in a separate foxhole, and they were the farthest away from Platoon Sergeant Roy. There was Corporal Phil Oliver…who was the 2nd Squad leader…and two other men who were from his own squad: PFC Kevin Lewis…who was a BAR-man…and Private Terry McGowan…his assistant.

Oliver, Lewis, McGowan, and Tuchmann were chafing under the circumstances…since they wanted to help their buddies out…but they had also seen what had happened to Flockerzi and Rickard…who were lying dead next to them…so they sat this fight out and hunkered down in their holes…lest they end up as casualties themselves.

The frustration of not being able to help his squad mates out was driving PFC Reisman nuts…so he decided to do something about it. As he charged out of his hole, he remembered the admonition his fiancée had given him before he shipped out for Operation Galvanic. *Don't do anything stupid*, Tammie, a pretty blond New Zealander, had told him. *And make sure you come back to me…or else!* And Reisman, the squad comedian, had been following her advice for the last two days as best he could…and so far, it had worked…since all he had suffered up to this point was a twisted ankle. But the sight of his three

The Butcher's Block

squad buddies battling for their lives against a force that outnumbered them was more than he could take...and his anger had finally boiled over.

Seeing PFC Reisman limp into the fight, Private Nelson...who had fought beside him throughout that long first night...got up and joined the fracas as well. Now it was five marines against seven *rikusentai*...and in short order, the fight came to an abrupt end.

As Reisman and Nelson approached the melee, two more enemy soldiers turned away from the scrum and they charged the newcomers instead. Intending to club both Reisman and Nelson down, the two *rikusentai* raised their rifles...which were out of ammunition... over their heads and charged at them while screaming fiercely. Neither Reisman or Nelson had any intention of letting their adversaries get close enough to fight hand-to-hand...and both *rikusentai* were shot down before they got anywhere near the two marines. Reisman hit his man with a string of bullets along his belly...and the powerful BAR rounds tore that *rikusentai* nearly in half. Nelson, a crack shot with his M-1 rifle, had to fire only one round to finish off his opponent...who went down with a neat bullet hole in his forehead.

Corporal Hullender, PFC Rampley, and Private Smith were exhausted. The incredible heat and the lack of sleep had taken its toll to be sure...but having had little to eat or drink over the last forty-eight hours had finally caught up to them as well. And the hand-to-hand fighting that they had just engaged in had really drained them of any energy they had left. But luckily, all three were still alive. Cut, nicked, and bruised...but still alive... and taking a much-needed break in the shade of a coconut tree that stood near the sandy road that the tank was using as it moved eastward.

The odds that any of them would have survived the fight was astronomical...since the three men had recklessly taken on twelve Japanese soldiers all at once. And their adversaries were not your run-of-the-mill soldiers. These men were *rikusentai*...the best the Japanese had to offer. They were essentially the Japanese military forces equivalent of the U.S. Marines...and the ones on Betio were even more vaunted than normal...since they were seemingly bigger in physical stature than the average Japanese soldiers were.

None of this had been on Corporal Hullender's mind when he initiated his one-man charge, however. *If it had been, I probably wouldn't have done it*, he thought wryly, while wondering how he had managed to survive the close-call affair.

The only thought that had crossed his mind...he remembered now...was that it was his job to protect that tank...and the crew inside it...and that it was worth risking his life to get the job done. And he and his men had accomplished their role spectacularly...since *China Gal* was now several hundred yards up the road...almost at the airfield...and still blasting away at the Jap positions that were being pointed out to its crew by the marines in the 1-6...who were continuing their attack up the beach.

I gotta hand it to old Ramps and Smith, Hullender thought proudly, *and Reisman and Nelson too. I'd be a dead man for sure if it weren't for them.*

When Hullender charged out of his foxhole, he didn't expect anyone to join him. In fact, he had ordered his men to stay where they were. But they had disobeyed his order...and in seconds they had charged right into the fray along with him.

Those two coming in behind me really saved my ass though. As the gap between Hullender and the twelve *rikusentai* had closed, the corporal felt several bullets cracking right past his ears...which meant they were very close to hitting him. But his aim was even better...and he had been able to drop one of the men with a shot from his hip... which left only eleven to deal with. Then, when Rampley and Smith had raced over to help him, some of the Japs who were firing at him had shifted their fire over to them...since these two newcomers represented a greater threat to them than one crazy marine did. But whoever had fired at Rampley and Smith were poor marksmen, because those shots missed their mark as well...and the three marines had crashed into the oncoming line of eleven *rikusentai* all at once. *Thank God we didn't have to fight all of those big suckers at once though*...since Hullender remembered seeing two more *rikusentai* who were on the fringe of the fight get hit as well. He had learned afterwards that these two had been dispatched by the sharp shooting of Reisman and Nelson. And then two more suddenly left the fray...heading off in the direction of the tank...which left Hullender, Rampley, and Smith in a duel with the remaining seven *rikusentai*.

For some reason, two *rikusentai* had taken on Hullender…two had gone after Smith…and three others had chosen Rampley. It had probably worked out that way since Rampley appeared to be bigger than the other two men. Not by much…but just enough that the Japs had allocated one more man to take on the stouter marine.

The two men that Hullender ended up battling were just as tall as he was…so there was no advantage to be had by either the corporal or the two Japs as far as their physical attributes were concerned. And the fight began when one of the Japs lunged at Hullender directly in an attempt to skewer him with the long, menacing bayonet that was attached to the end of his rifle. Hullender knocked the man's rifle away with a downward sweep of his own rifle and then he came back across with a quick butt stroke move that just missed the Jap's chin. But the metal-plated butt of Hullender's rifle did connect with the Jap's left collar bone…and the solid crunching sound it made as it hit home, and the scream from the Jap told Hullender that he had wounded his first adversary significantly.

While this was happening, the other Jap circled around behind Hullender, looking for an opening to attack. This man was also carrying an *Arisaka* rifle…and it was equipped with a deadly bayonet as well…and he stabbed at Hullender's waist in hopes that he would puncture the marine's liver. But Hullender's body rotated as he followed through with his butt stroke and this caused the Jap's bayonet to graze Hullender's side instead. The razor-sharp bayonet cut through the marine's utility shirt easily and it left a deep laceration four inches long on Hullender's side…but the wound was far from fatal.

The Butcher's Block

When Hullender felt the blade cutting him, he spun around and in an eyeblink he changed the hold he had on his rifle by flipping it around...which enabled him to use it as a club. In a flash, Hullender brought the butt down on the helmet of the Jap behind him... who was now trying to recover his balance after striking Hullender's side. The heavy butt of his M-1 rifle caved the *rikusentai's* helmet in...and the head inside it too... and Hullender watched as a gusher of blood cascaded down his enemy's face. This man immediately tumbled over and his body hit the sand with a dull thud; instinctively, Hullender's knew that he wouldn't have to worry about this man anymore...that this *rikusentai* was dead for sure.

The corporal then swung around with cat-like reflexes to confront the other Jap he had wounded. This man was sitting on the ground still...nursing his left shoulder...which was probably broken...or dislocated at the very least. Either way, the man was out of the fight... and he looked up at his tormentor with a plaintive expression...hoping the marine might show him some mercy and spare him his fate. But Hullender never considered it. Instead, he simply slammed the butt of his rifle down on the *rikusentai's* other shoulder...breaking it as well. As the Jap squirmed in the sand below him, the marine corporal then bashed his head in with one final blow...killing him as well. *War's hell,* he thought coldly, and then he turned around quickly to see how his other two men were handling their fights.

Private Smith…one of the squad mates who had come to Hullender's aid…was on the ground and wrestling with one of Japs that had come after him. His fight had started out unevenly too…with two *rikusentai* circling around him and looking for a way in. Smith was smart though…and he had tipped his now empty rifle with his bayonet prior to the fight…and this gave him a slight advantage over his adversaries since neither of their rifles were so armed. Smith had been managing to fend off both men…one at a time…since neither of them wanted to come too close to Smith and that gleaming bayonet of his. Then, suddenly, one of his adversaries had dashed off…leaving Smith in a one-on-one fight.

Like the two men that Hullender had faced off with, Smith's *rikusentai* was just as big as he was…maybe taller even…and he was just as fast and as good a grappler as the American he was up against. So, this fight ended up being a longer affair…since both men were evenly matched.

Their fight began with Smith using his rifle as a stabbing instrument…and he made several lunges at his adversary…but the *rikusentai* countered these moves easily by batting away Smith's rifle with his own rifle each time. As the distance began to close between the men however, their rifles became too cumbersome to use as weapons…and both men dropped them in unison…as if they had planned it that way. It was probably because both men were experienced wrestlers…and they felt more comfortable using their hands and legs to fight with than an actual weapon.

The two men immediately rushed at one another and they became locked in a tight embrace…each one looking for an advantage that might turn the fight in his favor. Both men were grunting and groaning as they struggled…their strength equal to the task…and neither man gave in an inch as they swayed one way and then the other. Eventually, the men fell to the ground…and that's where Smith had an edge…since the Japanese wrestler had been trained to use *Sumo* techniques…which were better suited for grappling while standing on your feet. Smith's experience came from the American…or ancient Greek…style of wrestling however…which was more oriented towards ground moves…and Smith took advantage of his opponent without thinking about it.

The Jap soldier quickly sensed that the momentum of the fight had suddenly swung in the American's favor… so he struggled that much harder…and eventually he ran out of gas from his efforts to untangle himself from Smith's tight grasp and get up. With no strength left, Smith got him in a hold that was almost impossible to get out of while also pinning the *rikusentai's* arms back with one of his own. And Smith used the opportunity to finish him off. The marine looked around and saw a coconut laying nearby…and close enough to grab. Using his free hand, he picked it up and crashed it into the side of his opponent's head. Smith felt the man go limp and he struck him again and this blow hit the *rikusentai* on the side of his chin. Smith released his hold on the unconscious man and rolled out from under him. Huffing from the exertion of the fight, Smith then picked up his rifle and drove the bayonet into the center of Jap's chest. The Jap let out a muffled groan as the blade penetrated him…and he was dead before Smith could pull the blade back out.

His fight over, Smith then looked to his left and right to see how his squad mates were faring in their individual battles with their own *rikusentai*.

―――

PFC Paul Rampley was one of the two marines who carried a BAR in the 3rd Squad. These two coveted positions had usually been assigned to the larger men in the squad…since the BAR was a heavy weapon to carry. But Rampley was not that tall really. In stocking feet, he was only five foot eight inches tall…which put him at the shorter end of the stack in the platoon as far as height was concerned. But Rampley…like Corporal Ingunza… had a wider frame than the average guy…so he carried just as much weight as a taller guy did. However, what really set Rampley apart from his bigger counterparts was his strength…which was deceptive…since it didn't appear that a guy his size would be as strong as he was. And where that strength came from was no mystery…. since he been raised on a farm in the mountains near Chattanooga, Tennessee. As a young boy…and then a teenager…Rampley had acquired "*farm strength*" while performing all the jobs that were necessary to keep a farm up and running all year long. If he had been asked, Rampley would have said that it was the job of lifting and stacking hundreds of hay bales in the barn from sunup until sundown that had really built him

The Butcher's Block

up…and given him tremendous grip strength. And no one would have argued the assertion with him…especially after shaking hands with him…since he was…pound-for-pound…as strong as any man in the platoon.

This quality came into play when he was confronted…initially…by two *rikusentai* who had chosen him as their adversary as he charged into the melee with Private Smith.

Initially, Rampley had been able to hold off each *rikusentai* by swinging his rifle around like a farmer would swing a scythe to cut down grass. But then one of his adversaries had run off to help another buddy *rikusentai* when they had seen PFC Reisman and Private Nelson joining the fight. This left Rampley with only one *rikusentai* to deal with…but this stroke of luck didn't last long at all…since the BAR-man spied another Jap heading his way. To make matters worse…the man approaching now was a Jap officer…and he was wielding a vicious-looking *samurai* sword in his hands.

As this new adversary got closer, he raised the sword over his head to deliver a chopping blow which would have decapitated Rampley had he done nothing to avoid it. Seeing the officer coming though, Rampley quickly dropped his rifle and lunged at the other man in front of him. The speed of the move caught this *rikusentai* by surprise…and before he knew it, the marine had locked both his hands on each of his shoulders. Then…without the ability to stop it…the marine spun him around so his back was now facing the Jap officer who was approaching them.

The Jap in Rampley's grip...who was tall and lanky...continued to struggle with him...but the strength of the marine was surprising...and try as he might...he couldn't get out of marine devil's grasp. Then...suddenly...the marine had slung him to his right and let go of him...and that's when the pain hit.

Dropping his rifle was not the smartest of moves, but given the circumstances, Rampley decided it was his best option possible since the Jap officer was getting closer with each step he took. The tactic had even surprised the man in front of him...who was now locked in his grasp...and when the officer made his move... Rampley made his. Using his strength, Rampley slung the *rikusentai* towards the left...and right into the path of the downward arcing blade of the *samurai* sword. In an instant, the razor-sharp blade had cut a deep path right through *rikusentai's* shoulder and come out below the man's armpit...severing the left arm cleanly free of the *rikusentai's* body. At first, the Jap had felt nothing, since the sword had sliced through so quickly and effortlessly. But then the man's countenance changed as the pain began to register in his brain...and he grimaced as he looked to his left and noticed that his arm was now missing. Seeing the arterial blood squirting out, the *rikusentai* let out a horrible shriek and he fell to the ground... out of the fight.

The Butcher's Block

The Jap officer...a captain...felt nothing for the man whose arm had just been severed from his body. *He was just an enlisted man who was doing exactly what he was called to do,* the rikusentai officer thought coldly, *and death is lighter than a feather...while duty...ahhh duty...is as heavy as a millstone.*

PFC Rampley watched the man's arm drop and he reacted immediately. Reaching down, he picked up his M-1 rifle and took up a stance to parry the Jap officer's next move.

The energy exerted in the swing of the sword had carried the officer past the American...but he recovered quickly...and he turned back to face his adversary. The American marine...a gangster by all accounts...was fast too though...since he had been able to pick his rifle back up and he was now facing the Jap officer as well. Without thinking about it, the Jap officer drew his sword back up and raised it over his head...just like before. He had chopped the heads off of plenty of Chinese soldiers and peasants alike in his day...and this American was about to taste his sword's blade...just like they had.

This guy's as cocky as all get-out, Rampley thought scornfully...since the Jap officer was using the same tactic that he had just used. *Well, how'd that work out for y'all, Bud. He must think I'm stupid or something*...and this got Rampley's dander up even more.

"Come and get it, you SOB!" Rampley yelled over to the Jap officer...and though he didn't understand what his enemy was saying, the *rikusentai* officer caught the drift of Rampley's message clearly.

The officer then shouted out something in Japanese... which Rampley couldn't understand either...and he charged the American gangster and brought the sword down with all his might.

Rampley saw the move coming...had anticipated it... and he extended the rifle over his head while holding on to it with both hands. The sharp blade of the officer's sword then crashed into the wooden stock of Rampley's rifle...cutting off the pinky and ring finger of Rampley's left hand. But the blade had also penetrated the stock so deeply that it became stuck in the process.

Rampley could feel the Jap officer yanking on the sword to pull it out so he forced himself to ignore the lightning-like pain that shot up his arm, and he gripped the stock even tighter with the three fingers he had left.

The fact that the Jap officer couldn't free his sword frustrated him to no end...and he began to grunt and groan as he put more effort into freeing it.

Rampley, meanwhile, continued to hang on to his rifle as if his life depended on it...and it did...since the two adversaries had begun a dance that could only end with one of them dying. And that's when an idea on how to end it quickly crossed the marine's mind.

Without a second thought, Rampley...a tobacco chewer...hacked up some phlegm and then he spit it and a huge gob of dark tobacco juice right into the Jap officer's face...which shocked him since he didn't know what had hit him squarely between the eyes...and obscured his vision.

"It's Redman, you Jap bastard," Rampley screamed at the officer, and added, "and there's more where that came from!" Then the marine lobbed another big stream of the sticky juice at his adversary...and this time it hit him right near his mouth and chin.

Shocked and repulsed, the Jap *rikusentai* officer finally let go of his sword so he could wipe the goo from his eyes and see again.

Rampley, smiling now, took advantage of the moment...and he let the rifle fall to the sand. Then he reached down and grabbed the hilt of the Jap officer's sword. A quick tug freed the weapon...and the last thing the Jap officer saw before his head hit the sand was a smiling face of a marine farm boy and the sun glinting off his own samurai sword...which was aimed right at his neck.

"How's that hand doing," Hullender asked his protege as he shifted over a little so he could stay in the shade.

"Oh...I'll live I guess...which is more than I can say for that Jap officer I just decapitated!" Rampley answered...and he held his bandaged hand up to indicate he was alright.

"How about you, Smith? You doin' okay?" Hullender asked, turning to Smith in turn.

"I'm alright too...just burned up my back a little while I was wrestling with that guy of mine. It's so damn hot out here that I might have gotten a first degree burn while I was lying on my back in that damn sand."

"Will you three please shut up. And stay still so I can take care of this wound of yours," a corpsman from the 1-6 pleaded as he examined Hullender's wound. "But just so you know...the private's right. We're seeing a lot of burns on the guys out here. They're being burned from lying in the sand...and they're getting sunburns too." The corpsman then probed Hullender's wound... to see how deep the cut was and if any of the muscle had been damaged.

Hullender yelled out, "Ouch...that hurts!"

"Baby," Smith said, deriding Hullender as he grimaced.

"That bayonet seems to have missed everything important, so it looks like you're gonna live, corporal," he said, "just like that buddy of yours who I just patched up. But at least you'll be able to play the piano someday... if you want to...but your buddy there," and the corpsman pointed at Rampley, "will have to find something else to play. Those two fingers he's missing aren't going to grow back anytime soon...so I would recommend he take up the drums if he has any plans of becoming a musician after this war's over."

Rampley laughed at the suggestion...knowing that he had never wanted to be...or would be...a musician. "I won't miss those fingers as long as I can still drive my

The Butcher's Block

tractor back home. If I can do that, I'll be just fine," he answered hopefully.

"Well, you'll definitely be able to do that, private," the corpsman assured him and Rampley breathed a sigh of relief.

Then Rampley and Smith watched as the corpsman applied a dressing to the long laceration that ran across Hullender's side. "This wound is pretty nasty...so I recommend that you and the one missing the fingers there get to Green Beach and catch a ride out. If either of you stay on, those wounds you got can get infected... and that's the last thing you want happening out here. The scuttlebutt is that this thing is gonna be over real soon anyway...since we're making good progress down that southern shoreline. They say the lead unit of ours is nearly at Black Beach Two...which means we've cut the Japs off from this end of the island. It looks like the One Six was needed to wrap this thing up...wouldn't you say," the corpsman said triumphantly.

"That's a bunch of horseshit," Hullender replied angrily, "and you know it. The Sixth has always been... and will always be...a chickenshit outfit. They wear those ugly braids on their shoulders so they can look important too. Everyone knows that only jerks would stoop to wearing something so stupid."

That stupid green-and-red-threaded braid that Hullender was referring to was called the *Fourragere of the Croix de Guerre*...and the Fifth and Sixth Marines had been awarded this prestigious symbol of bravery by the French Government for being decorated three times with the *French Croix de Guerre*...a medal that was issued

431

for bravery and effort…during the First World War. Since its issuance, any marine serving with the Fifth or Sixth Regiments had been authorized to wear the braid on his Dress Blues and on the Dress Green uniform as well…and the men of the Sixth had been wearing it proudly ever since…which irked the rest of the men in the Second Division.

"And another thing," Hullender said, just warming up, "the Sixth is just a bunch of bogey-bait-eating misfits who arrived late to the game on the *Canal*, and then they tried to pull the same crap that they're pulling now…claiming that they're the ones who won the battle. Hell, by the time the Sixth got ashore, there were no more battles left to fight…since we took care of the Japs after the First headed home."

In this outburst, Corporal Hullender was referring to the Sixth Regiment by their nickname and then mocking their service up until that point in the war.

The *Pogey-Bait Sixth* nickname had been dogging the unit since the tail-end of the 1920's…and it had acquired the moniker during their duty in Shanghai, China. The Sixth had gotten to Shanghai in late 1927 and then stayed there until they had been ordered home in January of 1929. Nothing of note had occurred during their time there…but a rumor had begun circulating that the Sixth Marines had ordered $40,000 worth of supplies from the Post Exchange: $1 of which was for soap…while the remainder was spent on bogey-bait…which in this case was candy…a non-essential food item to say the least!

And the Sixth's World War Two wartime experience had begun in Iceland of all places…which is where the

Sixth Marines were stationed when the war had started. After successfully defending Iceland from a German invasion that never happened, the Sixth had then shipped out for the Pacific...and they had arrived on Guadalcanal in early January 1943. By that time, most of the hard fighting had tapered out...but the Sixth had consoled itself by securing the rest of the island...and the Guadalcanal campaign had finally ended six weeks later when the Sixth had taken Cape Esperance...the village that sat at the northwestern corner of the island.

Their duty on Guadalcanal over, the Sixth had then shipped over to New Zealand...where it rejoined the other two regiments of the Second Division...the Second and the Eighth...that were already recuperating there.

"And you know what we did before you guys got to Wellington?" Hullender asked the corpsman slyly.

"No idea," the corpsman answered back casually...feigning disinterest...but deep down he really wanted to know.

"We made sure to tell every girl we met that if they saw a marine wearing a braid on their uniform...they were to steer clear. And you know why?" Hullender continued...torturing the corpsman.

"No...why?" the corpsman answered...browbeaten.

"We told them that the marines who were wearing those cheap-assed braids were forced to do it. That they had been deemed undesirable...since they were infected with gonorrhea or syphilis...and any other venereal disease we could think of. I think the crabs scared them the most. Then we told them that the Marine Corps higherups were worried that these guys would sleep with the girls on the island and give them their diseases. So, the generals made them wear those braids so the girls would know who they were…and stay away from them." Hullender, Smith, and Rampley were laughing themselves sick by this point…and the corpsman looked ill…since this was the first time that he had heard a story like this.

"Ever wonder why the girls seldom showed up at your parties," Hullender asked, guffawing the whole time while slapping Rampley on the back.

"No…I never did wonder why…but you're right…we did have a hard time filling the dance hall whenever we organized a party," the young corpsman…a lobsterman by trade from Portland, Maine conceded. Rubbing salt in the wound, the three Second Regiment marines just kept laughing until he had finally gotten up and left to rejoin his own platoon…dejected…and astounded that the young women of New Zealand had swallowed their outlandish story hook, line, and sinker!

In short order, Hullender and Rampley had followed the chastened 1-6 corpsman's advice and they made their way back towards Green Beach…where they were evacuated off the island so doctors on the transport to which they were being taken could better treat their wounds. As they rode an amtrac out, Hullender looked back at Betio and shook his head. "We made it, Ramps. We could've been killed many times…as a lot of our buddies were…but somehow we made it."

"Yeah," Rampley replied, "we made it off alright. I just hope Smith survives too. Anything could happen as those guys make their way up that southern coastline. The Japs still have a lot of fight left in them."

"Y'all make me wanna head back in," Hullender said in a low voice…feeling guilty now.

"Our fights over, Hull. We did our jobs…and we did them well. It's time to let the other's finish it up," Rampley said consolingly…and Hullender relaxed… which was Rampley's intention.

The two men sat quietly while the three crewman of the amtrac had an animated conversation about the merits of the LVT-1…the model they were riding in…and the LVT-2…which some were saying was way better…since it had a lower profile, a better engine, and more armor. There were several other wounded marines on board, but none of them seemed to be in a talkative mood… so the churning of the amtrac motor and the waves lapping against its sides were the only other sounds that Hullender and Rampley could hear as they made their journey out.

"Pretty quiet now, huh," Rampley finally said.

"Especially after what we've endured for the last two and half days," Hullender replied, and added, "I wonder how long it'll take our ears to get back to normal?"

"I've spent a lot of time operating tractors, and the ears readjust pretty quickly. At least that's what I've experienced." Then Rampley swallowed and a serious look came over his face. "Let me ask you a question, Hull, since I trust you."

"Shoot," Hullender said.

"You know I was never a religious guy, right. Which is kinda surprising…since my dad is a preacher," Rampley admitted for the first time to anyone in the platoon.

"Your old man is a pastor?" Hullender replied, genuinely surprised.

"Yeah. He's a part-time pastor of a small Baptist church up the hills near our farm. His congregation is about thirty people or so…the locals who live near us…that's it. Nothing big. But there was a lot of spirit in that church…let me tell y'all. And I was a member of it from the time I was a little boy. But then I ran into some trouble…and I got thrown out of the church."

"What the hell did you do?" Hullender asked, and he slid over a little closer so he could hear Rampley's voice better above the engine noise…since the story was getting interesting.

"Oh, nothing crazy like. I was just arrested by a local cop for riding my cousin's horse while I was drunk."

"Were you really drunk?" Hullender asked…trying to look serious and not laugh…since he wanted Rampley to continue his story.

"Oh, I had had a few beers, of course. I had been working my butt off all day long and my cousin called me over to his farm to chase a few beers and see if I could break a horse that he was having trouble riding. Was I really drunk? I don't think so…but the cop was a little older than me and he had a crush on the girl I was dating…the very same girl I intend to marry when I get back home. Her name is Whitney. The end of the story is that I had to spend a night in jail. And when word got out about what had happened, my father and a bunch of the guys at church called me in to explain why I had been drinking. That's a big no-no in our church...and when I wouldn't repent over what I had done, they kicked me out. I was angry about it for a long time...since that cop had it out for me...and I was still mad until we shipped out and Chaplain Darling got a hold of me."

"I can see why you were mad," Hullender stated emphatically...since he loved to drink...especially Irish whiskey. "I was raised in a Methodist home...and my folks still go to church...but I kinda fell off the wagon as I got older. It just never took hold of me the way it seemed to grip my folks. So, I have nothing against church folks mind...it's just not that important to me...that's all. Maybe I'll change someday...but for now I'm okay with where I'm at as far as the religious stuff goes. But we always thought it was funny that you Baptists thought it was a sin to drink. Just a bunch of man-made rules that create more problems than they solve. Wasn't that the message Jesus constantly delivered to the Pharisees. I mean what did Jesus do for his first miracle, right," Hullender said wisely.

"What did He do?" Rampley asked, intrigued.

"I thought all you Baptists were Bible toters?" Hullender answered jokingly.

Rampley thought of the Bible that Chaplain Darling had given him aboard ship and how it was sitting in his pack somewhere back on Red Beach One. "I never was one...since I always thought it was an older folks kinda thing...so I never read one. Then Chaplain Darling gave a service one night while we were heading here, and I decided to stop in and listen to him. What he said that night made a lot of sense to me…and it kinda changed my way of thinking. I took one of the Bibles he was handing out…a lot of guys did actually…and I started reading it for myself. But I guess I didn't get to the part about Jesus performing His first miracle."

"Well, believe it or not, Jesus performed His first miracle at a wedding feast that was being held in a town called Cana. The Jews…you know…guys like Reisman and Friedman…really did it up when it came to weddings back then. The whole event would last around a week…and the groom's family was responsible for footing the bill. The cost in shekels must have been astronomical…since the whole town came to the affair too. Y'all gettin' this so far?"

Rampley was listening avidly…and he nodded to show the corporal that he understood everything he was saying. Rampley knew that Hullender had a reputation for knowing a whole lot about a lot of things that no one else seemed to know anything about…but he also had a short fuse and didn't tolerate know-nothings, so he rarely took the time to offer his insights to them. As a result, Rampley continued to nod…to show Hullender that he appreciated what he was telling him…and that he took it seriously.

"Knock off the nodding…I get it," Hullender said dryly, and he continued his explanation. "So, Jesus and his followers…they weren't even called disciples at this point…show up at this wedding along with Mary…who was the mother of Jesus. Well, at some point during the feast, the wine runs out…and someone must have approached Mary to let her know about it…since that was a disaster. Mary probably had a reputation for being a good problem solver so that's why they went to her. At least, that's my take on it. Mary then gets Jesus...who was still a regular Joe at this point...to perform a miracle...and He asks for six big jugs that were used for ceremonial bathing...Jewish religious ritual stuff...to be filled with water. Then, He blesses them and walla...the water is converted into wine. And not your run-of-the-mill wine either. It was top notch stuff...and the wine steward knew it."

"So why do the Baptists think drinking is so bad then...if Jesus did that?" Rampley asked.

"Rules, my boy, rules. Your church folk were probably employing a line or two from one of Paul's writings. First Corinthians Chapter Five comes to mind. Most organizations exist off rules. The Marine Corps got 'em...and so do most churches, I guess. Which is why I stay away from church. I got enough rules to follow just being a corporal. I don't need to complicate my life with any more of them...at least not now," Hullender answered honestly.

"Geez...thanks, Hull. I never knew that. But it really helps...and it ties right in with what Chaplain Darling explained. Without realizing it, you might have just converted me again...like Darling did on the way here."

Hullender smiled and said, "Glad I could be of help, my boy! So, what was your question? This whole conversation started because you said you had a question for me. What was it?"

"Oh...my question. Right. I guess I was gonna ask you if you felt God's presence out there at all. You know...when we were in a bad way...and it looked like we might buy the farm. Did you feel Him at all, Hull, cause I did. And I was wondering if I was the only one."

"To be honest, no," Hullender replied...and if nothing else, Hullender was as honest as the day was long. "But that doesn't mean He wasn't. I just wasn't looking for Him...or praying to Him...as some of the other guys surely were. For all I know, He was there beside me the whole time, protecting me and nudging me this way and that way to make sure I didn't eat a bullet. Don't let my feelings influence your own. What you felt is genuine...and treat it that way. So, did you?"

"Yeah, I did. And I was wondering if it was just because of what happened to me aboard ship. Was God rewarding me...in some kind of way...and showing me that He heard my prayers...since I started praying to Him again before we hit the beach."

Hullender took his time answering. He wanted to get it right...since he knew the importance of the talk they were having and the significance of what Rampley was sharing with him. Then he cleared his throat and spoke, "I think God was with you the whole time. He was with you when you were in jail that night...and when you joined the Marines...and He was there when you were on the ship...before you listened to the chaplain. My folks used to love to quote one particular line from the Bible to me...and I brushed it off...for all the reasons I already mentioned. It was from Revelations...Chapter Three...Line Twenty. I think it's really applicable to what you're asking me...so look it up."

Rampley's jaw dropped and he sat there openmouthed. "You mean you're not gonna tell me what it says?" he stammered.

"No...I'm not. That's your homework assignment. If it's important to you, you'll find a Bible and look it up yourself...and then you'll always remember it." Hullender was obviously adamant about his decision...since he sat back and closed his eyes while waiting for the amtrac to reach the transport.

"Huh...how do you like that," Rampley said silently to himself...and like his assistant squad leader...he closed his eyes and sat back against the inside wall of the amtrac. With no further ado, he fell fast asleep...just like Hullender had...who was now snoring away...out like a light.

Private Tyler Smith, the man PFC Rampley was worried about, was making his way down the dirt road again... trying to link up with Platoon Sergeant Roy and the rest of his men who were still acting as a body guard for *China Gal*...the Sherman tank that had destroyed nearly thirty bunkers so far. He had just passed the large bunker that housed the men they had recently fought and he saw that it was now a smoking ruin...the *China Gal* having fired twenty 75mm rounds at the doors on the western and eastern ends...and then another ten rounds at the multiple gun slits that were spaced evenly along the front...or ocean...side of the bunker. The engineers that were with the 1-6 had then clobbered the bunker with multiple satchel charges...which had probably killed several more men that were still alive inside. But what really finished the bunker off...and killed whoever remained...

were the two flame-thrower operators who spewed their fiery flame into the gun slots…which caused the ammunition stored inside to explode as well. Three *rikusentai* had stumbled out of the eastern door afterwards…completely engulfed in flames…and the 1-6 marines had shot them down in turn.

Before long, Smith could see the dark plume of smoke and smell the fumes that were belching from the *China Gal's* engine along with the dust that was being kicked up by its treads in the distance…so he knew the tank was close. He smiled at the thought of seeing Platoon Sergeant Roy again when a bullet smashed into his mouth…destroying the lower row of teeth and shattering his jawbone below them. Blood immediately filled his throat…but Smith was able to cough it up and he rolled over on his side to let the blood drain out…just like he had been trained to do.

The man who thought he had killed Smith was stealthily hidden high up in a coconut tree that sat along the beach…and he had been waiting for just this sort of opportunity to come along: a lone marine who was in easy range of his *Arisaka* rifle. The *rikusentai* sniper had sewn some palm fronds into his uniform days before the invasion so he would blend in with the fronds that were still attached to the branches of the tree he was in…and he had been waiting patiently for two and a half days for the perfect shot. He had taken a small amount of food with him…and water too…which he ate and drank only at night…so that he wouldn't have to leave his perch once he got up there. And his discipline and slight movements had allowed him to maintain his vigil without alerting any of the marines from the 1-6 who had passed underneath him all morning long. Plus, the marines who were stuck in the tank ditch behind him…further up coast… were too far away to shoot at…so he had held his fire and never risked being discovered by taking an errant shot at them…even though he was dying to give the marine devils some payback for what they had done to his island and his friends who were lying dead around him.

What he didn't count on however, were the marines from C Company…who had led the original attack up the coast…coming back the other way…looking for enemy stragglers they may have missed or enemy bunkers that had been bypassed and might still be active.

Now relieved of their point duties, the 2nd Platoon marines of C Company under First Lieutenant Peter Lake had doubled back, and they saw Private Smith coming their way…and they scattered on seeing him fall.

Two veteran sergeants…both Guadalcanal veterans… had seen the way the marine's head reacted when he got hit…noting that it didn't snap back like it would've if he had been shot by someone on level ground. They had also seen the splash of blood coming off his face jet downward…and they figured…based on experience… that he had been shot from above…no doubt by a sniper in a tree. On cue, both men fired into the top of the only coconut tree in the area that had a full head of palm fronds…and the Thompson submachine gun and

BAR made quick work of the Jap sniper's hideout. In seconds, the bloody body of a *rikusentai* rifleman fell out of the tree...but it didn't hit the ground...since the sniper had tied himself into the top of it with a stout rope. Instead, he hung there in a U-shaped contortion... about twenty feet high...suspended from the rope that was tied around his waist...with his arms and helmeted head hanging down beside his long legs so that his hands were almost touching the tips of his shoes. Blood, running in rivulets, fell to the ground below him...turning the sand into a reddish pool of mush.

"Someone go check out that man that got hit," one of the sergeants ordered...and two marines ran over to Smith and began to bandage his wound...which indicated that he was still alive.

The other sergeant then turned to two other marines and said, "Hot foot it back down the beach...but be careful...and tell the CO we need a stretcher. There's no way this guy's gonna be able to make back to Green Beach on his own. And I want you two to handle that for me. Understood. Get him back to the beach. That guy is from the Second...and we need to make sure he makes it off this island alive. Got it!"

Both marines...young kids no more than eighteen... assured the sergeant that they understood their orders and they jumped up and ran east...to catch up to the C Company CO...Captain Joe Golding...so they could get that stretcher and then get that marine off the island and headed home.

The Butcher's Block

Platoon Sergeant Roy was wondering where Private Smith was. He had sent him back with both Hullender and Rampley earlier...to make sure the two wounded men made it to Green Beach safely. After that, his orders were to head back to them...since a living, breathing rifleman among the 2-2 ranks was too precious a commodity to simply write off because of a slight burn on his back. And since Smith was a fast runner...and in great shape...he just figured that Smith would've made it back by then...since it was now nearly 1000 hours...and two hours into the attack.

Roy's small force was now even smaller...since they had suffered three killed, two wounded, and one missing in their last action. That left Platoon Sergeant Roy with just seven men now...or eight if Smith made it back anytime soon. *So now I'm basically an assistant squad leader,* Roy thought wryly...and then the tank they were walking behind had come to a stop. The main gun then slewed slowly over to the right another few degrees and the gunner fired off a round. Roy could hear the empty shell casing hitting the floor of the tank after being ejected from the breech block...and then the loader shouting, "Up," as he loaded another round into the gun. The gun tube lowered a little this time...and then the 75mm main gun cracked again as the next round was fired at the same pillbox in the distance. This shot was more accurate, and a bunch of coconut logs went flying up into the air...along with the arm of a *rikusentai* machine gunner who must have caught the full brunt of the blast.

"Scratch one more Nip," Corporal Oliver said callously...the men's sense of fair play long gone.

"Good riddance!" Private Nelson...the Florida golf course builder and now a deadly rifleman...shouted out...his nerves...and hunger...since he was famished...getting the best of him.

"Okay, guys. Let's tighten things up. Lash down the yardarms and let's get this ship back in trim, right," Roy ordered...sensing the men were beginning to lose their sense of direction and focus. "I know you're tired...and I know you're hurting over the guys we've lost...but we still have a job to do...and we're marines...so let's put our best foot forward and finish this out with our heads held high."

The six men looked at Roy...realized he was right...and made the mental adjustments to get back on track.

Then the hatch cover on top of *China Gal's* turret sprung open and Lieutenant Bale poked his head and shoulders out. "How's it going?" he asked.

"We lost some men a little while ago when the Japs staged that attack against your tank. Your driver drove over one of the Japs, in fact. Was anyone hurt inside when the mine exploded?"

"No...no one was hurt. We got lucky there. So Josefson ran over someone? I had no idea. How many guys you lose?" the tank TC asked curtly.

"Three...and two wounded. One's missing. Could've been worse, I guess. We could all be dead, right," Roy answered back...wondering what Bale would say.

"Hell," was all Bale said...and he stared at Roy...who he respected.

"Yeah...hell," Roy replied...the two men understanding intuitively what they were trying to express.

Lieutenant Bale then looked at the smoking pillbox in the distance and said, "We're outta shells. We're gonna head back to the rear...wherever the hell that is... to see if we can find some more. Without those shells, we're just a roving machine gun platform. And there are plenty of bunkers left...so we need to find those shells or else."

Roy said, "Okay, sir. We'll see you soon."

Bale looked down and replied, "Yeah...see ya soon." Then he lowered himself back into the turret and slammed the hatch cover closed. The tank turned around slowly to the left and then roared off across the main airfield...heading towards the pierhead where... hopefully...a full load of tank shells was waiting.

Chapter Twenty-Four

It was a little after 1000 hours on Betio when the marines of the 1-6...now being led by B Company under Captain George Krueger...finally reached the men from Major Wood Kyle's 1st Battalion, 2nd Regiment who were hunkered down at the western end of the long tank ditch that ran parallel to the southern shoreline just east of the Black Beach 2 beachhead. Kyle's survivors had occupied the trench on the afternoon of D Day + 1...after crossing the dangerous northwestern taxiway and main airstrip...and they had managed to fight off multiple attacks that the Japanese had launched against them throughout the remainder of the day. The Japanese had then continued their attacks...and sniping...as the sun came up on D + 2...but the ferocity of these attacks had diminished over time...since the marines of the 1-6 were breathing down their necks as they attacked the Jap positions from the west. Caught in

The Butcher's Block

a vice between the marines of the 1-6 who were attacking and the marines of the 1-2 who were defending, the Japanese in this pocket were eventually wiped out, and the linkup between the two marine forces was cause for a major celebration as soon as the two groups saw one another.

Captain Bill Bray...the A Company CO...and Captain Jim Clanahan...the C Company CO...of Major Kyle's Battalion could only smile when they saw Captain Krueger's men coming into their perimeter. Their arrival meant that the shortages of food, water, and ammunition that had plagued the men of the 1st Battalion since they had arrived in the tank trap would be finally addressed. With the road back to Green Beach wide open, all the supplies they needed could be now brought up to them as soon as the stuff landed on the beach in the rear.

"Not a minute too soon," Captain Bray said wanly. He was now sporting a bloody bandage on his left arm to go along with his leg wound...and he looked dog-tired.

Captain Clanahan...who was standing right next to Bray...said, "Yup...the cavalry has finally arrived." Then, glancing at Bray's arm, he said, "When did you get hit?"

Bray looked down at his wounded appendage and said, "Oh...this. During that last mortar barrage the Japs sent over last night...right before dark."

"I was wondering if they got anybody with that one. Ten rounds alone must've hit near us if one did. It was sort of like their last harrah," Clanahan replied dryly.

"Fumai...that corpsman we got with us...dug a nice piece of metal out of my arm. It was so hot that it stung for a while when I first got hit." Then Bray reached into his shirt pocket and pulled out a three-inch chunk of shrapnel and showed it to Clanahan. "Fumai gave it to me as a souvenir. I'm gonna mount it on a stand and put it above my fireplace when I get home so my grandkids can see it."

"Great idea," Clanahan said while looking at his own arm...and wondering what it would feel like to get hit with a piece of shrapnel that big. "Did it hurt," he asked, "when it hit you?"

"It hurt like hell. It felt like someone smacked me with a baseball bat when it first hit. Then it burned too... like I said. It was so hot that I couldn't touch it at first. Fumai used a forceps to yank it out. Then he stitched it up. He said it'll look just like new...but I think it's gonna leave a scar."

"There's going to be a lot of guys with lots of scars from this op," Clanahan replied evenly and he raised his arm and waved at the fresh-looking marines of the 1-6 who were jumping down into the trench and shaking hands with the ragged-looking men of the 1-2 who were ecstatic at their arrival.

The men of the 1-6 passed quickly through the tank trap and kept going...leaving the happy marines of the 1-2 who they had relieved fast behind. And as they advanced, the lead elements of B Company began encountering the dead and wounded from the attack that Captain Williams had led out of the eastern end of the tank trap to link up with the men of the 3-8 who were trying to do the exact same thing on Red 3.

"Who's that?" Private Reed Marcy said. He had looked up from the marine that Pharmacist Mate Second Class Fumai was working on and was surprised to see a group of men advancing towards them.

"Never mind who it is," Fumai ordered, "just pay attention to what we're doing here. This man's life depends on it."

Marcy could hear the strain in Fumai's voice, and he immediately looked back down at the marine lying on his back beside him. Fumai had already torn the man's shirt open and exposed a grizzly-looking wound in the man's chest that was bleeding heavily and bubbling every time the marine breathed in and exhaled out. He had then rolled the marine on his side and did a quick inspection to see if there was an exit wound. The back felt solid and he felt no blood so Fumai rolled the man back down and began digging through his medical bag. "He's got a sucking chest wound. Put your hand over the wound and put as much pressure on it as you can." Fumai pulled out a thick dressing and handed it to Marcy and said, "Pack that dressing into the wound. Get it in there as tight as you can so no air gets in." While Marcy did as he was told, Fumai dug through his bag again...and this time he pulled out a large square bandage that had long strips of cloth hanging from each corner. "Put the bandage over the dressing and tie it off around him as tight as possible so that dressing stays in place. Do you know why that's important?"

"So we stop the bleeding as soon as possible?" Marcy replied.

Fumai watched as his helper bore down on the marine's chest and tied two tight knots with the ends of the strips of cloth to secure the bandage in place. When he was done, the corpsman complimented his work and added, "The reason I had you pack the wound was to stop the bleeding. You got that part right. But the other reason…and some of the doctors who trained us told us that it was more important…is that this marine has a pneumothorax. What that means is that air is being sucked into his chest cavity as he breathes in. The problem with that is the air going into his chest cavity acts as an obstruction…and if enough air gets in there…then the lung on the side of the wound eventually can't expand to take in air from the lungs as the man breathes. Without enough air, the body goes into shock…and then it starts shutting down important organs…and then the man dies. That's why I had you do it that way."

Marcy understood most of the explanation that Fumai had offered up…as did the wounded marine… PFC Joey Kendall. The nineteen-year-old boy had been conscious the entire time…and he had watched the two men working on him with concern and interest.

"Do you think I'm gonna make it, sir," he asked humbly…the frightened look on his face a sight that Fumai would always remember.

The Butcher's Block

"Of course, you're gonna make it. Marcy here did a wonderful job fixing you up. We've worked on far worse than this...and those kids made it...so you will too. I guarantee it," Fumai said with such authority that the kid believed every word of it.

"Thanks, guys," Kendall sighed, and he closed his eyes to rest.

Fumai then looked around to see who he could get to carry the wounded man back to Green Beach. Two other marines were huddled by another man who was down not thirty yards away. The corpsman called over to them and they looked his way...but neither man budged. Fumai yelled all the louder, but the two men acted like they didn't hear him this time... the noise of the battle in the background seemingly drowning out Fumai's pleas. Then, Fumai sent Marcy over...but he returned after having a brief conversation with them.

"What'd they say. Did you tell them we gotta get this man to the rear as soon as possible for him to have a chance to make it?" Fumai asked, frustrated now.

"They told me that their lieutenant was down...and that they were going to stay with him until the end," Marcy answered.

"Down? You mean he's wounded too?" Fumai responded.

"I don't...I don't think so," Marcy said hesitantly.

Fumai looked at Marcy quizzically and he got up and went over himself this time. "Hey, did my man tell you what we got going on over there," the corpsman yelled out as he got within earshot of the three marines. Two of them looked up at him…and then Fumai realized that one of them was cradling the one that was down. "Is he okay," the corpsman asked…concerned that he had another case to care for.

"He's dead," Private Paul Gerdis said sadly.

"Dead?" Fumai responded.

"Yes…dead," the private affirmed…and he rolled Second Lieutenant Joe Sexton's head over so Fumai could see the bullet hole in the side of his head.

"We got the sniper that got him," the other marine said, "so we evened the score…but it wasn't worth it."

"Our lieutenant was the best. He didn't deserve this," Gerdis added as tears flowed down his cheeks. "He took care of us during the landing…and he risked his life for us dozens of times over the last two days. And then a lousy sniper up and gets him…when it's almost over."

"I'm sorry," was all Fumai could manage to get out…the very love the two men showed for their officer affecting him, too.

Private Gerdis laid the officer down gently and patted him on his chest. Then he said, "Thank you, sir, for all you did for us. We're gonna miss ya." Then he looked up at Fumai and asked, "Do you need help?"

"I got a marine who's got a sucking chest wound over there…and I need to get him back to Green Beach as soon as possible or he'll end up dying too," Fumai stated as forcefully as he could manage under the conditions.

"Me and Denny will help ya get him back," Gerdis said, and he got up and the three of them headed back to Marcy and the wounded marine.

The Butcher's Block

PFC Kendall looked at the three men plaintively as they approached...and Fumai said, "These two men are going to take care of you now, okay."

The wounded marine nodded and then closed his eyes again.

Fumai looked over at Gerdis and said, "He's weakening. You gotta get him back as quickly as possible or he won't make it."

"I'll make it...I know I will," Kendall eked out, obviously listening to their conversation while appearing out of it.

Gerdis smiled and turned to PFC Dennis Smith... who was tall and broad-shouldered...and said, "Denny here will pick him up and carry him as far as he can. Then we'll switch over when he gets tired. We'll get him back."

The corpsman thanked the two men and without further ado, Denny reached down and picked up the wounded marine and draped him over his right shoulder.

"Let's go," Gerdis said, and the two headed off on their new mission...the next stop Green Beach.

The corpsman would never know that Private Paul Gerdis...a rifleman in C Company of the 1st Battalion, Second...was a good friend of one of the men in his very own platoon...Private Johnny Scott...and that the two had grown up together in the very same town in New Hampshire. Or that the two had hoped...had dreamed even...that they would end up in the same battalion after getting to New Zealand. That wish had not been granted however...thanks to an irate admin pogue... and Scott had ended up in the 2nd Battalion, Second instead of the 1st Battalion, Second...where Gerdis had been assigned.

Chapter Twenty-Five

Captain Maxie Williams' one-hundred-and-eighty-man *ad hoc* force had left the tank trap at 0800 hours and made good progress as they pushed their way down the coast...but casualties began to mount as the morning dragged on...and before long the entire attack had stalled out as they hit a solid wall of Japanese resistance.

"I don't think we're going to be able to reach the airfield circle without tank support," First Lieutenant Ken Konstanzer stated. The F Company executive officer in the 2nd Battalion, 2nd Regiment was talking to Second Lieutenant Walt Yoder...the commander of a machine gun platoon from D Company in the 1st Battalion, Second. The two officers were lying next to each other in a deep shell hole along with several other marines who had followed them when they jumped into it. "Do you think you can get your machine gun teams up here? Just in case the Japs decide to stage a counterattack."

"I can try," Yoder responded…and he turned around and waved his arm in the air…signaling his men to move up. But as soon as they tried to advance, several enemy machine guns opened up on them and they were forced to take cover…only yards from where they had just been.

"Leave them where they're at. Until we get some support, we're not gonna risk getting anyone else killed just to advance a few more yards. Unless we get some help, we're here to stay," Konstanzer said…and Yoder agreed. Then Konstanzer turned to a young marine lying beside him and asked if he'd be willing to deliver a message to Captain Williams who was organizing the men behind them.

"What do you want me to tell him, sir," PFC Joey Shoemaker replied…undaunted by the task.

"Tell him we have reached the limits of our advance. The ground ahead of us is loaded with Jap bunkers and machine gun pits. A fly couldn't make it through here without getting hit. Tell him that we're stuck unless we can get some help from a tank or two. Did I leave anything out?" Konstanzer, a tireless worker that everyone liked and admired, said.

"I think you covered all the bases, sir," Shoemaker responded…impressed that the officer had asked for his help in describing their predicament.

"Okay, take off then…but don't get killed along the way. I need that message to get through," Konstanzer said with a light heartedness that characterized everything he did.

"Got it, sir. I'll do my best to follow through with that part of your order," Shoemaker said in jest...while hoping that he actually would...and he disappeared into the smoke that was drifting across the ground behind them.

⋈

First Lieutenant Ken "LT" Konstanzer had started Operation Galvanic out in a foul mood. He had not slept well the night before the landings...even though it was his second operation...the Guadalcanal operation almost a year prior having been his first. Then, after he had finally fallen asleep, the younger...and inexperienced...officers had woken him back up with their laughing and jostling as they psyched themselves up to meet the challenges of the day ahead. But what had really got his goat was the fact that the berth he was in had been very dark during the entire journey...since a blackout light had burned out or was broken as the voyage began. Despite the complaints they had sent to the ship's maintenance officer, nothing was ever done about it...and he and the other officers with him just endured it as best they could. Sadly though, he had forgotten or misplaced his favorite knife as he was getting his gear ready on the morning of the landings...and since it was so dimly lit, he had not noticed that it was missing until it was too late. By then he was riding in an amtrac that was headed for Red Beach 2...and knife or no knife...the landings were turning out to be an unmitigated disaster.

As shell bursts exploded in the air above and waterspouts erupted to the left and right of the amtrac he was in, Konstanzer thought back to that calendar that his friend, First Lieutenant Robert Hackett, had pinned to the bulkhead opposite his bunk. He had admired the page above it, of course. *I mean who hadn't,* he thought. It had pictured an attractive, dark-haired, dark-skinned, twenty-something-year-old female lying on a beach with a wave washing over her. The girl had reminded him of Jennifer, his Kentucky-born wife, who was waiting for him back in Patchogue…a town on the eastern shore of Long Island…in New York…where he had grown up.

He had met Jenny…as her friends called her…at a dance sponsored by the USO in New York City while he was home on leave after being promoted to second lieutenant in December 1941.

Prior to that, he had been an enlisted marine… having joined up in 1937. He had reached the rank of corporal by 1940…which was faster than normal…and then he had been stationed at the naval air station in Montauk…which sits at the very eastern tip of Long Island. How the young enlisted marine had been able to secure that billet had astounded everyone…since it was considered a plum assignment…but secure it he did…and the legend of the "Konstanzer magic" had begun to take hold.

Trained as an aircraft engine mechanic, Konstanzer then began working on Navy seaplanes that were conducting anti-submarine patrols in the Northern Atlantic to assist the British Navy…which was on a war footing with Germany. While the duty was demanding,

The Butcher's Block

Konstanzer excelled at it...and the naval officer in command of the station noticed it...as did the men whose very lives depended on his work: the pilots and crew who were flying in those planes out over the cold Atlantic Ocean in hopes of spotting a German U-boat.

Glowing efficiency reports followed...and before long, Corporal Konstanzer had been called into his CO's office for a meeting.

"Do you know why I called you in here," the naval lieutenant asked him when he arrived at his office.

"Not a clue, sir," Konstanzer answered, and added, "I hope I didn't do anything wrong, did I?"

"Do anything wrong? No, of course not," his CO said laughing. "Your record is as clean as a hound's tooth."

"So why exactly am I here, sir...if you don't mind me asking, sir," Konstanzer replied.

"You're here because I'm considering recommending you for the Marine Corps' Officer's Candidate School. Are you interested in going?" the lieutenant asked.

"I'd love to have a shot at it, sir," Konstanzer answered enthusiastically.

"Good...then I am going to submit your file."

"Thank you, sir," Konstanzer answered. "I'm kinda speechless...which I'm told I never am," Konstanzer added, smiling.

The lieutenant stood up and extended his hand to the corporal...and Konstanzer took it and shook it. Then his CO asked, "So, there's one thing I would like to know. How did you manage to get yourself assigned to this station? You're a marine...and the only one here that I know of. Did you pull some strings to get here?"

"How I got here is a long story...a real long story, sir, and you'd be bored to death after I got done with it. But why I did it is more important, so I'll tell you that part of it...if you want to hear it," Konstanzer offered up.

"I'm all ears," the lieutenant said, interested.

"The reason I picked this place is because it's as close to home as I could get. My mom is disabled...nothing horrific...just disabled. She has a hard time getting around now...so I head home as soon as I get off duty to take care of her. That's why I came here," Konstanzer replied.

Dumbfounded, the lieutenant stared at the corporal at first...and then he glanced down at the paperwork that he would be submitting for Konstanzer and said, "I am going to include my personal recommendation along with your file. Begin making plans for attending OCS...cause I guarantee you'll be accepted after what I have to say."

"Thank you, sir," Konstanzer said, and he saluted the lieutenant smartly and turned on his heel...beaming.

True to his word, the lieutenant had written a wonderful recommendation...and Konstanzer had been accepted into the OCS program...which was designed to transform motivated enlisted marines into capable officers. And true to his word, Konstanzer had given it his best shot...and he had graduated in the middle of the pack...the academic portion of the course being a little more difficult than he had anticipated. But graduate he did, and then he had rushed home to Long Island to show his mom his brand-new lieutenant's bars...and he had bent over and she had pinned the gold bars on his shoulders while sitting in her wheelchair.

The following Saturday, Second Lieutenant Konstanzer had decided to head into New York City...an hour's drive away...with Mark...a high school friend who had joined the Army and who was home on leave at the same time.

When Mark arrived, he held up something in his hand and said, "I got 'em cheap. Four tickets to a Broadway play. We'll use them as bait so we can meet some girls at the USO dance we're going to. They're all the rage now...no booze mind you...but they sell cigs if ya wanna smoke. Plus, the place is usually loaded with girls. You'll probably do better than me though...decked out in those Marine Greens and with your shiny lieutenant's bars. I'm just a private...but I've always had the gift of gab...so that'll make up for it. Let's go!"

Jenny, meanwhile, had recently arrived in New York City. She was there with hopes of securing a job in a company in the growing pharmaceutical industry...which had openings now since all the men were in the service. Before she had left home, a good friend of hers who knew she was headed there had given her the phone number of a friend who lived in New York City. "Call her when you get in...and she'll show you the City. She's really sweet and you'll have a great time with her."

Jenny had done as she said, and she called the friend after she got settled into her hotel room after taking a long cab ride from LaGuardia Airport. Happy to hear from the girl from Kentucky, the friend had cabbed it over to her hotel and the two of them were now headed to another hotel that was hosting a USO dance to see if they could meet some eligible bachelors.

"Let me do all the talkin'" the friend said confidently, "since I've been to a few of these dances…and I know my way around…trust me."

Despite her lilting accent, Jenny wasn't quite the demure Southern belle that the friend had taken her to be. Jenny, full of confidence herself, replied, "When these boys see me in this dress of mine, they'll take notice…trust me!"

And Jenny was right…since Second Lieutenant Konstanzer had noticed her the minute he walked into the hotel ballroom. "I know my target for the evening," he said to Mark as soon as he spotted her.

Mark, looking around, replied, "Ken…are you crazy. Look at how many girls are in here. Take your time and enjoy them all. The last thing you wanna do is tie yourself down to one girl. What happens if you put all your time into one girl and then she doesn't like you in the end. I'm keeping my options open and I'm gonna play the field."

"You do that, Mark. Good luck," the marine lieutenant said…and then he made a beeline over to the auburn-haired raven from Kentucky.

Kenny and Jenny seemed to be hitting it off...at least Ken thought so...when Mark and a cute blond found them. He held the four tickets aloft and said, "Well...is she going?"

Kenny looked at Jenny and with a pleading look said, "That's Mark. He's my buddy from home. We grew up together...and he's on leave...just like I am. Those tickets he's holding in his hand are for a Broadway show. It's not too far from here. Would you like to go with us... with me...I mean?"

Jenny scanned the room for her friend...couldn't see her...and looked back at the most handsome man she had ever met. "Of course, I'd like to go. It's every girl's dream to see a Broadway show with her knight in shining armor."

Thrilled, Kenny turned to Mark and his date and said, "Let's go...we don't want to be late."

On the way over, Jenny slipped her arm around Kenny's elbow...and two of them walked to the theatre as if walking on air...each knowing they had met the person they intended to marry and be with for the rest of their lives.

Now First Lieutenant Konstanzer was wondering if he would ever see his Jenny...the girl he had married three weeks after he met her...again. Everywhere he looked, he saw devastation. Fifty yards ahead of him, an amtrac got hit and exploded in a fiery red ball and several marines were flung into the air...their uniforms on fire.

The scene reminded him of that damn calendar again… only this time he remembered the number 20…the day's numerical date…circled in red. *I knew that was a bad omen the second I saw it,* he thought. *Why would anyone circle the date of an invasion in red ink? It was just asking for trouble.*

As the executive officer of F Company in the 2nd Battalion, First Lieutenant Konstanzer was scheduled to land with the initial attack wave on the left side of Red 2. This was because Lieutenant Colonel Amey, Konstanzer's battalion commander, had planned it this way.

According to his plan, two of his companies would land first…since he had divided Red Beach 2 in half. F Company was slotted to go in on the left…closest to the pier…and E Company would land on their right. The third company…G Company…would come in right behind them…down the middle…in reserve…and go wherever they were directed as the two lead companies advanced across the island. Most of H Company…with its engineers and special weapons and equipment… would land last…and go where they were needed as well.

Unfortunately, the officer ranks of Amey's three lead companies were decimated…with almost every one of the officers from captain on down being killed or wounded before they ever had a chance to affect the battle. And Amey himself would be killed before reaching the island as well. To make matters worse, Amey's executive officer…the number two man in the battalion…never

The Butcher's Block

made it to Red 2 either. The fire coming from the *Pocket* along the beachhead boundary line between Red 2 and Red 1 was so intense that it drove the amtrac that Major Howard Rice was riding in over to the Bird's Beak...and he fought with Major Michael Ryan's orphans for the rest of the battle.

When First Lieutenant Konstanzer hit the beach, his first instinct was to seek out his commanding officer... Captain Warren "Lefty" Morris. But the twenty-five-year-old Morris...who had grown up in Arkansas and graduated from Oklahoma University in 1941...was nowhere to be found. Like so many others, his amtrac was hit by a large shell as it was approaching the beach and only four men survived: Morris...Staff Sergeant Bill Bordelon...and two other engineers with the 18th Engineer Regiment who were assigned to support F Company. All four of them would make it to the seawall alive...despite the fire that was sweeping the beach... and Bordelon would go on to win the Medal of Honor for personally attacking and knocking out several Jap bunkers before being killed himself. Morris...likewise... would head inland...but he was wounded and knocked out of action later that morning.

In the absence of his company commander, First Lieutenant Konstanzer took charge that morning and he assembled whoever he could find beneath the seawall. Unfortunately, with all the casualties F Company had taken coming in, there weren't that many men left however…at least not in the lieutenant's vicinity. But that didn't stop him…and he led a small force of fifty or so marines into the airfield triangle. Taking casualties along the way, forty men eventually made it to a deep trench that ran parallel to the northern border of the main runway…and that's where they held up for the time being.

"Whatta we do now, sir?" It was a young private who had made the dash over with Konstanzer…and he was clearly frightened.

"We sit tight…and wait for the reinforcements to show up…that's what," the XO said confidently…the sound and authority of his voice reassuring the private. Before long, one of the men had lifted his head over the lip of the trench…trying to see if any help was coming. The marine…a corporal…first looked right…in the direction where E Company should have been…but saw nothing. He then glanced to the left…where somebody from the Eighth Regiment should be…and he was nailed by a sniper's bullet.

As the man's body slid down the slope of the trench, Konstanzer yelled out, "Everybody stay down…and I mean everybody. If ya get antsy and wanna take a peek out to see what's gonna on, then take a look at this man right here. He's as dead as he's ever gonna be because he couldn't sit tight…like I said. Everybody got it now?"

The Butcher's Block

All the men looked over at the dead marine...who's handsome...but bloody...face was now wearing a look of shock that had registered when the bullet hit...and they quickly nodded their assent.

The young private then echoed the rest of the men's feelings when he turned to the private next to him and said, "I'll sit here 'til kingdom comes if I have to, so I don't end up looking like that."

Konstanzer sensed the men's apprehension though... and to counter it and said, "So, here's what we're gonna do. The Japs certainly know we're here...and they might mount a counterattack against us. So, we gotta stay sharp. Make sure your weapons are clean and functioning. You senior men...get in the game and keep up a vigilant watch. Keep your eyes glued to the top of the trench and be ready to react immediately if the Japs show themselves. That's the only trump card we can play right now so let's make it work in our favor."

As the men nodded again, Konstanzer smiled and thought, *Not a bad little speech. Hackett would've liked my sport's analogy...and that inveterate gambler Staggs from E Company certainly would've liked my reference to a trump card.*

As the hours dragged by and nothing happened, Konstanzer realized that he had to get word back to the beachhead that his small force was out there...looking to fight...but unable to move.

And this is when the "Konstanzer magic" came into play...yet again. "Alright, I've decided to make the trip back to the beach so I can let 'em know we're here." When the lieutenant then asked if they needed anything, a chorus of "we can use more water, sir," echoed back at him.

"Okay...water it is. How are we fixed for ammo?"

"We got all we need...since we've hardly fired a round," a senior sergeant...who appeared to have risen to Konstanzer's earlier challenge and taken charge... shouted out.

"What about food?"

Several men who were still wearing their backpacks held up their cans of C-rats...which they were sharing with the others...and Konstanzer nodded this time.

"Okay...don't do anything stupid. Just sit tight...like I said before...and I'll be back," Konstanzer ordered before leaving.

"Sir?" It was the young private again...but this time he sounded more confident somehow.

"What?" the XO answered, eager to start his journey back.

"Do you want me to come with you, sir. Just in case somethin' happens to y'all along the way."

"You really wanna risk it," Konstanzer asked him... while marveling at the courage these young marines had.

"Heck, sir, you're putting yourself in the Jap crosshairs. The least I can do is lend a hand...if you end up needing one."

"You're hired, Private..."

"Von Rosenberg, sir. Private Randy Von Rosenberg. Or just V as the boys in my platoon call me," the young private said without a trace of fear in his voice.

"V it is, son," Konstanzer replied...and the two sprinted out of the trench...headed for the rear.

As they made their way back, Jap bullets began whipping past them...so they started zigzagging to throw the Jap gunfire off. The tactic seemed to work, since neither of them were hit...and within fifteen minutes the two had reached the beachhead safely.

Major Culhane...the Regimental Operations officer... looked Konstanzer over and said, "You look like crap. Where ya been?"

Konstanzer wasn't intimated by the tough major one bit. In fact, they were good friends...since Konstanzer and the major were close in age. "Me and my F Company boys have been sitting in a ditch just shy of the main airstrip. We've been there for over three hours...and no one has shown any interest in getting to us. Do you have any help for us, major," Konstanzer responded boldly.

"Help...are you serious. Look around. Those bodies lying in the sand down there by the pier aren't reinforcements, Ken. Those guys are dead. We're holding on for dear life now. Crowe is stuck behind the seawall over on the left. He thinks he might have two groups out forward...somewhere to your left. One group is being led by a sergeant...McBride's his name...and the other one has First Lieutenant Edmonds in charge. Edmonds might be closer to you by the sound of it. Have you seen either of them?"

"We can't risk sticking our heads up for a second. Jap machine guns and snipers are a dime a dozen out there. One guy I had got his head shot off in three seconds when he tried to see what was going on around us. Edmonds or McBride are probably in the same boat... maybe worse off even...since they're further east then my boys are."

"Okay. Just hang on as long as you can. We got A and B Company from the First Battalion trying to fight their way into the airfield triangle as well. They'll be coming up on your right...so look out for them...if that's possible. I'll try to get word to Maxie and Bill that you are over on their left," Major Culhane advised.

"The First has been committed already," Konstanzer replied...amazed.

"Yup...and the Third Battalion has been over on Red Three. Kyle and Rudd got slaughtered too...just like your company did."

The F Company XO then looked around and saw Colonel Shoup addressing another officer not far away. "How's the Old Man holding up?"

"Tired...like the rest of us...but fit as fiddle. He's got some mortar fragments in one leg...but it hasn't affected him...at least as far as I can tell."

"Give him my best, okay," Konstanzer said.

"I will that," the major said...and then he turned away from the lieutenant in a flash and began barking an order out at some unfortunate who had incurred his wrath.

The lieutenant and Von Rosenberg found each other easily after the meeting...since they had agreed to meet near the pile of supplies that were being stacked near the end of the pier. The private had spotted the lieutenant and waved him over when he saw him headed that way.

"Find any water?" Konstanzer asked hopefully.

"This place is as dry as a bone," the private answered back, and he swung his arm to encompass the entire supply area. "They say the water is stored too deep in the bowels of the transports...and that it is taking way too much time to get to it. It'll be coming in later is what they told me."

"Great. Well, let's grab some ammo instead. You can never go wrong bringing back some ammo is what a wise sergeant once told me," Konstanzer advised.

"Already have as much as I can carry, sir," Von Rosenberg replied...and he showed the lieutenant his pockets...which were bursting with hand grenades. And then he got up and showed him the bandoliers of rifle ammo that he was sitting on. "I think this stuff weighs more than I do," he said jauntily.

Konstanzer reached over and began picking some of the bandoliers up. Then he draped them over his head, and he let them fall across his chest. "Ready when you are," he said to the private.

"You can stay back here if you like, sir. I mean...this is officer country and all. I have enough ammo on me alone to fit out a full company. If you think you can do more good being here...than back out there...than by all means stay back. I'll let the guys know," the private offered up encouragingly.

Konstanzer's admiration for the boy was increasing the more time he spent with him. "No. My place is out there with the company. I appreciate your offer...but I would rather die up front...with guys like you...than ride it out safely back here. But if you mention that to any of the boys when we get back...I'll shoot you myself and save the Japs the trouble."

Von Rosenberg laughed out loud and said, "Your secret lives and dies with me, sir. Nobody'll find out about it, okay."

"For your sake, you better hope not," Konstanzer said easily...and the two began their journey back to the ditch across hell's half acre.

Incredibly, Konstanzer and Von Rosenberg made the trip to the rear and back four more times over the next twenty-four hours...and neither man sustained so much as a scratch while doing so. In the end, the F Company men were convinced that the "Konstanzer Magic" was as strong as it ever was...but if they had asked him... Konstanzer would've told them that it was his guardian angel working the magic...and protecting him as he traveled in harm's way.

"I've got some good news for you," the lieutenant breathed out...exhausted after his final trip to the rear. It was late in the afternoon of D + 1 and the men quickly gathered around their XO to hear what he had to say.

"You got us some water finally," one of the men yelled out...his thirst getting the best of him.

"Yup...water's on the way," Konstanzer answered... and the men let out a shout. "Lieutenant Colonel Jordan is bringing it over in an amtrac. He's on his way now. And food too."

"Who's Jordan?" one of the other men yelled out.

"Lieutenant Colonel Jordan is an observer from some other outfit. He decided to tag along on this operation...and now he's running the show over here on Red Two," the lieutenant explained.

"Why's he running the show? That's Lieutenant Colonel Amey's job, sir," another marine pointed out.

"Our colonel's dead. He didn't make in. I was told that he was machine gunned in the water. I should've told you earlier...but it just slipped my mind. So, Jordan is in charge...and he's on his way over now. When he gets here, half of you here are going to ride over with him and me and join the boys from the One Two who are holding out in a tank ditch...just like we are. Only they're on the other side of the runway...near Black Beach Two...over to our right. Major Kyle...the One Two CO...will be along shortly after that...and he's gonna pick the rest of you up and bring you over. The higher ups want that ditch held at all costs...and they want us over there to help the One Two do it. Anybody got any questions?"

"How much water is he bringing, sir? I hope a lot," the thirsty marine asked.

"The stuff just made it in to the pierhead. The water's in five-gallon cans...and there's plenty aboard that amtrac. You'll get your fill," Konstanzer answered, and added, "anybody else?"

"Did anybody bring in the colonel's body, sir?" another marine asked.

"Yes, they did. They carried him in...and he's lying near the cemetery site that is near our regimental HQ. Chaplain Willard is in charge of tagging and burying the dead...so you should be able to see him...or where he's buried...after this is all over," Konstanzer told the man...who revered his battalion commander.

"Thank you, sir. I intend to do just that...just as soon as this is over," the crestfallen marine responded. He had worked as a runner for the battalion staff and then been assigned to F Company after being promoted to corporal. But Lieutenant Colonel Amey had treated him like a son while he was his runner...and the corporal never forgot it.

"Okay then. Everybody keep an eye out for that amtrac... and then let's go help the One Two hang on to that tank ditch. Is everybody with me," Konstanzer shouted out in the best leadership voice he could muster up.

The men let out a raucous cheer...and Konstanzer knew immediately that they'd follow him anywhere... which was the best feeling in the world!

Now he and those very same men were stymied once again as they tried to advance down the coastline. And just like before, the men could barely lift their heads out of their foxholes without receiving a burst of machine gun fire in turn. And by the sound of it, it was just one machine gun team that was responsible for most of the fire that was coming their way.

"Anybody got a fix on that gun?" Konstanzer yelled out to his men who were holed up around him.

When nobody answered him, Konstanzer glanced over at Von Rosenberg who was bravely peeking out of his own foxhole. The lieutenant yelled over and signaled him with a wave of his hand.

Von Rosenberg took a big gulp...tensed...and then flew out of his hole like a bird being chased by a cat. The Jap machine gunner was a touch slow this time...and the private dove into the hole occupied by Konstanzer. The lieutenant waited a while...letting him catch his breath, and then said, "You ready for another assignment?"

"Are you serious, sir?" Von Rosenberg asked.

"As a heart attack," Konstanzer replied right back.

"What is it that you have in mind...if you don't mind my asking...since it looks like I'm gonna be one carrying out this desperate assignment."

"That you are," Konstanzer replied, and added, "so here's what I need you to do. Get a hold of Captain Williams and let him know what we're up against here. Without a tank, we're never going to be able to move forward. Now look to your right."

The private did just that...and off in the distance... beyond the reef...was a lone destroyer cruising on an easterly tac. "You want me to see if he can raise that destroyer, right," Von Rosenberg said, smiling.

"You're starting to think like an officer," Konstanzer replied, and he patted him on the shoulder and added, "now get going...and bring Shoemaker back here if you run into him."

"Aye aye, sir," the private answered, and he dashed back in the direction they had come...trying to find Captain Maxie Williams...and hopefully...a functioning radio.

Like his lieutenant, Von Rosenberg seemed to be living a charmed life as well...because he was able to make it back to Captain Williams...just like he was supposed to. And he delivered his message word for word...just like he was supposed to. And sadly, he had run into Private Shoemaker as well...but he wouldn't be making the journey back with him...since he had passed Shoemaker's dead body on his way to the rear. Shoemaker's gallant dash back had been cut short by a Jap sniper and he had been killed while trying to do the very same thing that Private Randy Von Rosenberg had been able to accomplish.

The five-man *rikusentai* machine gun crew could sense the end was near. The pressure from the marines out in front of them was increasing by the hour...but so far, they had been able to hold the marine devils off...which was a miracle in itself. And the four other *rikusentai* had taken delight in watching their leader gun down a marine who was obviously a runner...since he had bolted for the rear a little while ago. The marine had been husky...and slow...and it had required little effort on the part of the *rikusentai* leader to nail him after he had gotten fifty yards or so away. But their joy had turned to sadness when another man...obviously another runner... and far quicker...had managed to scamper back without being hit. This...they knew...was not a good omen...and a cloud of doom had settled over the four men as soon as the marine had disappeared into the smoke that was hanging over the battlefield from several fires that were burning across the island.

"Don't lose heart, men," the leader said, trying to encourage them. "All is not lost. We have plenty of ammunition remaining...and our comrades behind us are depending on us. We will hold out for as long as possible... and take as many of these devils with us before we suffer a warrior's death. And what a glorious death it'll be."

Three of the men nodded their assent...but the fourth...who was slightly older than the other four... wore a look of gloom that shook the other three to their core. And then the shells began hitting...a few at first... but then a tumult as the American destroyer that was visible off to their left beyond the reef got the range down pat. The ground shook violently as 5-inch shells exploded all around them...and one of the young men began to scream as his nerves fell apart. Another man... cowering in the trench...began to dig into the sand...trying to get away from the shelling...but to no avail. Their leader though...who seemed to be nonplussed by it all somehow...continued to kneel and rail against the devil Americans as if nothing was happening...striking the very image of a mighty Japanese warrior.

And then a sharp crack...closer to home...went off... causing the four other *rikusentai* to flinch. Looking around, they saw their older friend lying at the end of trench all by himself. In an act of desperation, the man had removed the shoe on one of his feet and then placed the muzzle of his *Arisaka* rifle in his mouth. Saying a brief prayer to himself, he had then placed the big toe of his shoeless foot into the trigger housing and depressed the trigger...committing *hari kari*.

As more and more shells continued to rain down around them, two more *rikusentai* broke. In panicked terror, they left the cover of the trench and headed east...towards the tail of the island and safety...or so they thought. Leaving their weapons behind, they ran as if their lives depended on it...arms and legs pumping... trying...it seemed...to outrun the shells bursting around them. But within seconds, both men were obliterated into nothingness as a shell hit directly above them.

That left the *rikusentai* leader and his assistant machine gunner on their own, and before long they too recognized the utter hopelessness of their situation. "Are you ready, brother," the leader shouted to his friend... whose fingers were now bleeding from his failed effort to dig his way to safety.

"I am ready, my sage friend," he yelled back over the deafening noise of the shells impacting around them... and the two jumped up and ran directly at the marine line in their final act of warrior bravado.

Their charge did not go unnoticed however, and the F Company marines...who were up and watching the effects of the destroyer barrage...dispatched both *rikusentai* before they had gone ten feet.

The effectiveness of the destroyer barrage could not be overstated since it allowed Captain Williams' force to regain the momentum of their attack...and they began advancing once again into the teeth of the Japanese defensive system in the area just beyond Black Beach 2. In addition, the intense shelling had taken the sting out of the Japanese machine gunners as well...since many of them were now dead or wounded...and this allowed the marines to advance and occupy more ground at a quicker pace than they had beforehand.

And then it happened. At 1100 hours another key event occurred on D + 2 which had a dramatic impact on the battle. That's when the marines of the 1-6 under Major Willie Jones finally caught up to and passed through the men of Major Kyle's *ad hoc* force under Captain Maxie Williams. All told, it had taken the 1-6 three hours to complete the first part of their mission... and they had killed over two hundred and fifty Japanese along the way.

After a brief pause of thirty minutes or so, the 1-6 charged ahead to complete the second part of their overall mission...which involved linking up with the marines of the 3-8 who were pushing their way southward from Red Beach 3. And in an hour or two that link up would also be achieved...which cut Betio in half...just as Colonel Edson and Colonel Shoup had envisioned the night before. With that task accomplished, the Americans now owned the western half of the island...while the Japanese continued to occupy the eastern half all the way down to Takarongo Point. And the Japanese in the tail would continue to fight as long as there was air for them to breathe.

"Did you ever see a more beautiful sight than that," First Lieutenant Konstanzer said to Captain Maxie Williams...who was now wearing a bloody bandage on his left forearm.

"I can think of a few girls I dated...but other than that...no," he replied as the two officers watched the men of the 6th Regiment enter their perimeter.

Konstanzer glanced at the wounded arm and said, "So, how did you get hit?"

The captain didn't even bother to look down at his arm. "Some sniper must have figured out that I was the one in charge. He must've been a bad shot though. The bullet went right between my arm and my side. The arm got nicked...nothing to write home about...and we killed the sniper...so it was worth the price of getting hit. Couple of inches over and he would have got me in the gut. Lucky me, right."

"Ahhh...Lady Luck. She's made her presence known more than a few times today. So, any idea whose company that is," Konstanzer asked...since he knew a few of the officers in the Sixth.

"That's B Company coming up. A Company is behind them...and C Company is bringing up the tail... since they started out in the lead this morning."

"B Company, huh. That's George Kruegar's company. He's a good friend of mine. Ya mind if I go look him up, Maxie," the F Company XO asked.

"Kruegar's gone, Ken," Williams said softly.

"Gone...as in dead?" the rattled Konstanzer asked.

"Not dead. No. A Jap sniper shot him in the throat. He's paralyzed from the neck down. At least that's what our corpsman...Fumai...told me. He worked him and saved him...and they got him to Green Beach fairly quick...so there's a good chance he'll make it," the captain answered matter-of-factly.

"Damn," was all Konstanzer could muster up.

"At least he's alive...for now anyway," Williams said... and then he told Konstanzer about the other big event that had occurred on Green Beach earlier that morning.

"Are you sure...the Three Eight is here now too," Konstanzer said...his confidence quickly returning at the announcement of this good news.

"Yup...the whole battalion landed at oh eight hundred this morning. Came in on Green Beach...just like Jones and the One Six did. Supposedly walked in from the reef without a shot being fired at them. Biggest danger was twisting an ankle, I guess."

"How about that," the amazed Konstanzer replied.

"That's two complete battalions ashore now...with all their gear...and special weapons. And no fouled radios...which is why we were able to get in touch with that destroyer. I sent a runner back to coordinate it with

Jones earlier when I saw that DD show up. His radios weren't waterlogged like ours…and he was in touch with that destroyer captain in no time. The gun captain did a beautiful job walking those rounds right up the coastline as we advanced. We sure could've used one of them on D Day. Think of how many bunkers it could've knocked out on Red Two instead of us having to do it. Would've made a big difference. At least I think so anyway."

"Yeah…a lot of men would still be with us that's for sure," Konstanzer agreed. "So, what do we do now? Are we gonna follow the Sixth up the coast?"

"No. We stay here for the time being…secure the area…and then as the battle winds down I'm sure they'll release everybody so they can reunite with their own units. What's left of them anyway," Captain Williams explained.

"Roger that. Stay here until told otherwise. I can live with that," the lieutenant said…and he glanced down at a dead *rikusentai*…one of the two hundred or so that had been killed by Williams' force. "I wonder who he was… and what he was like," he said absentmindedly…and then he left to go brief his own men on the great news.

Chapter Twenty-Six

Major General Julian Smith was standing inside the bridge of the USS *Maryland* with several of his staff officers...and everyone seemed to be in good spirits...since the battle had finally turned their way. Without saying a word, the commander of the Betio operation then walked outside and leaned against the steel bulkhead that protected the bridge area while he looked at the island through his binoculars. "What time is it?" he yelled...and an officer inside the bridge looked at the ship's clock and yelled back, "Just after eleven hundred, sir. Eleven oh seven to be exact, sir."

"It's time we got ashore. This bucket of bolts has served us well...but it's outlived its usefulness. Call us an amtrac and let's head in," the general ordered.

His staff scrambled around...issuing the orders to make the trip to the beach happen...and before long an amtrac was pulling up beside the old battleship.

"Your ride is here, sir," a staff officer bellowed out.

"Wonderful. Now who's coming with me?" he asked while looking over the members of his staff.

All the officers appeared eager to go...and several expressed their desire to do so...even Brigadier General Hermle...who was the only senior officer who had already been to the island so far.

"No," Major General Smith said sternly, "you stay back. You'll oversee things here while I'm gone. You can handle that assignment, right."

"Yes...I can do that for you, sir," Hermle shot back... his curt tone indicating that Hermle understood the veiled slight his commander had leveled against him. "Is there anything else you will be needing from me then," the deputy commander added.

"No...nothing," Smith replied dourly...and Hermle turned on his heel and left the bridge.

The bad blood between the two officers had developed as a result of Brigadier General Hermle's first trip to Betio...which Major General Smith considered a complete bust. Instead of assuming command of the battle as Smith had ordered on D Day, Hermle...unaware of

The Butcher's Block

the order...had planted himself at the end of the pier and he used his expertise and rank to better organize the landing of supplies and reinforcements that were making their way in from the transports and supply ships. And then...sometime before daybreak on D +1... the brigadier had left the pier and made his way over to a destroyer that was operating inside the reef...and he transmitted a message concerning the landing of the 1st Battalion, 8th Regiment under Major Larry Hays. Sadly, his message had left out the most important aspect of the landing...that the First was to come in as close to the left side of the pier as possible. To Colonel Shoup's consternation...and General Smith's when he learned of it...the First had instead landed right in the middle of Red 2...and directly under the guns of the *Pocket*...and a slaughter ensued.

Fuming, General Smith had then ordered Hermle to return to the *Maryland*...and the chastened deputy commander had arrived back sometime after dawn on D + 1.

One of the officers who volunteered to go in...and who the general had picked...was Major Paul Millichap. The Second Division's Ordinance officer knew what he was getting into when he put his hand up...since he had already been to the island...having accompanied Brigadier General Hermle ashore on D Day.

The steely-eyed Millichap was from Hartsville, Pennsylvania...and he had graduated from the University of Pennsylvania in 1940. Then he had set his sights on the Marine Corps…and he had been commissioned in May of 1941…several months before the war began.

Millichap was assigned to the 2nd Division while it was recovering on the island of New Zealand. And like a lot of the new officers, Millichap was not a Guadalcanal veteran…which was a strike against him…so he had desperately wanted to get ashore and prove his metal.

And luckily for him, Millichap was good friends with the officer who had been chosen to lead the first jaunt into Betio. Dutch Hermle had even pushed through the paperwork to allow Millichap to get married early while they were stationed on New Zealand…and Hermle had attended Millichap's wedding to boot. Their familiarity with each other and friendship had led to his being picked for the first trip to Betio…but now his relationship with Hermle was a cause for alarm. *It'll probably end up hurting me in the end*, Millichap thought dourly, *since the general seems to have his knives out for good old Dutch*, and he had given up any hopes of heading in again. But Smith had surprised him…and he was chosen along with eleven other men to accompany the commanding general to Betio that morning.

"Steer for Green Beach," the general ordered…and the amtrac driver altered his course by a few degrees as they entered the lagoon. The course correction took them away from the pierhead…which ended near the reef… and put them on a line that would keep them away from the Bird's Beak by several hundred yards. The driver would then turn left...head down the coastline for a minute or two...and then land them on the middle of Green Beach...hopefully safe and sound.

And this is exactly how it played out...right to the letter. At 1205 hours, the amtrac pulled into Green Beach and the general and his staff jumped down...no worse for wear.

Welcoming them to the island was Major Michael Ryan...the officer who had led the desperate fight for the Bird's Beak on D Day and who had conquered Green Beach on D + 1...which made their trip possible.

"Welcome aboard, sir," the weary officer said...his blood-caked uniform making an immediate impression.

Major General Smith put both of his hands on the major's shoulders and squeezed them tightly. "You did a wonderful job over here, major. What would we have done without you? You're a reserve officer, right."

"Yes, sir, I am," Ryan acknowledged proudly.

"Well, reserve or not, you performed tremendously. We couldn't have done it without you," Smith reiterated.

Ryan accepted the backhanded compliment graciously and said, "If you'll follow me this way, sir, I'll show you what we were up against when we landed."

"Of course, major. Lead the way," the general said agreeably...and then added, "has it smelled this bad the whole time?"

Ryan began walking and glanced back over his shoulder. "Oh...the smell," the hardened officer replied casually, "is part of the ambience of the place. All kidding aside, I'd like to say that you get used to it...but you don't. It started around noon on Saturday...on D Day...and if anything, it has gotten worse by the hour.

And that reminds me...there's lots of dead bodies and remains around here...so just watch your step."

At the warning, the general and the men following him looked down to make sure they hadn't stepped in anything disagreeable...and so far, they hadn't.

Ryan led them over to a bunker that was overlooking Green Beach. It sat about twenty feet from the beach and right behind the seawall. It was made of coconut logs...which were stacked on top of each other...and the whole affair was held in place by metal angle irons. While the major stood back, the general and his staff walked around the bunker...so they could see it from all sides. Spying a set of stairs at the rear of the bunker, the general headed that way and began descending them... but Major Millichap rushed up and gripped him firmly. "Let me check it out first, sir. Just in case," the major cautioned.

The general thought about it for a second and made a wise decision. "Be my guest," he said to Millichap...and the major slid past him and cautiously pushed against a rickety door that was made from coconut log scraps. As the door swung open, a large swarm of flies flew out and the stench coming from inside the bunker was so strong that it nearly knocked the major over. Knowing the other officers were watching, Millichap peered into the bunker and then stooped his way in...while holding his nose. The interior of the bunker was spacious enough to allow four men to work in it comfortably...and that's the number of *rikusentai* bodies that were in it. But there were two other bodies as well...and these belonged to two dead marines. Millichap could only imagine what

The Butcher's Block

had taken place when the two marines had charged into it and confronted the four Japs...but it didn't take that much imagination to piece it together. It looked like most of the fighting had been done with knives...since one of the marines was still grasping his K-Bar knife in his hand. And one of the Japs was still slumped over his machine gun...with several big stab wounds across his back and a huge pool of coagulated blood at his feet.

Millichap backed out slowly...and turning to the general said, "You don't need to see this, sir. But two brave marines died fighting four Japs...so the guys coming in behind them wouldn't have to."

The general nodded in appreciation and said, "Why don't we go check out the Three Six. Let's see how they're faring up."

No one objected...especially Millichap...and the group made their way south to the area where Lieutenant Colonel Kenneth McLeod's Third Battalion was setting up.

"You take care, sir," Major Ryan said as he handed the group off to Lieutenant Colonel McLeod...and the reserve officer headed back north...to see to the needs of his own men.

After spending one hour on Green Beach, the general had seen enough...and he decided that he wanted to head over on Red 2. "Let's go see what Edson and Shoup have to say, Tom," General Smith said to Brigadier General Thomas Bourke...who was one of the twelve men traveling with the general. Bourke was the commanding officer of the 10th Marines…the artillery regiment that was assigned to the 2nd Marine Division.

"Sure, sir," Bourke answered, and added, "I want to see how old Rix is doing."

"I was told that Rixey's pack howitzers have really had an impact on the battle," the general replied…referring to the Lieutenant Colonel Presley Rixey's 1st Battalion…which was part of Bourke's 10th Regiment. Rixey's men had done yeoman's work while manning their twelve 75-mm pack howitzers inside the Red 2 perimeter.

"I believe they have, sir," Bourke answered…an old artillery man himself…who was convinced that his big guns were the King of Battle.

And in no time at all, the thirteen men were back aboard their amtrac…and heading over to Red Beach 2. This time though, the driver made a mistake and cut the corner around the Bird's Beak a little short…to save time…and this put the amtrac within range of the enemy guns in the *Pocket*.

In mere seconds, the amtrac was taken under fire by a Japanese gunner who knew his business. Though parched and famished, the gunner was still serving his Emperor loyally…and his heavy machine gun rounds found their mark. Incredibly, the amtrac carrying the division commander was knocked out…its engine disabled when an oil line was severed…and the driver was badly wounded as well. Just in time, the assistant driver coaxed the amtrac northward…out of the line of fire…and everyone aboard began hailing another amtrac that was nearby.

The other amtrac driver...seeing the emergency...headed their way...and he reached the smoking vehicle before it sank.

Once everyone had transferred over to the new amtrac, it got underway again...but instead of heading out, it reversed course and headed towards the pier. In short order, it reached the middle of the pier and swerved to the right and made a beeline for the island.

As the amtrac reached the boat quay near the end of the pier, the driver yelled out, "Get ready to bail out...we're almost there!"

On hitting dry land, everyone jumped out of the amtrac without being told to do so...the terror of the machine gunning fresh in their minds. Yet the joy of being alive was thrilling too...and the men couldn't contain their enthusiasm.

"Well, that was a close call," Brigadier General James Underhill...and observer from the 4th Division...said breathlessly as he patted one of the other men on the back.

"Close calls are for hand grenades," another staff member joked...the adrenaline kicking in and fueling his bravado.

"The Japs couldn't hit me if I was wearing a bullseye," one of the more junior staffers proclaimed boldly and he began loading his M-1 carbine...convinced he could take on the whole Jap Army if he had to.

"I'd advise using a different strategy of getting ashore when you're with your new division, General Underhill," General Smith said lightly. Then he added, "Hell, we're lucky we weren't all killed out there." His effort to dampen down their excitement apparently fell flat however…since the men continued their joking.

"That'll be in my report…trust me," Underhill replied seconds later since he was preoccupied with brushing himself off…having fallen when he jumped out of the amtrac. Covered in sand, he was laughing easily now…since he knew he had survived.

And then the exuberance of the moment came to a screeching halt.

"Knock it off, fellas," Major Millichap said tersely. The major…unlike the others…had been under heavy machine gun fire already…when he was helping Brigadier General Hermle get things organized at the end of the pier. This latest brush with death had not fazed him…and to emphasize his point, he added, "just take a look around."

Following his prompt, the men stopped joking…and looked around. And that's when the unbridled horror of what had transpired over the last two and half days became readily apparent to everyone there.

Behind them…about twenty yards away…were the bodies of the dead men that had been laying on the beach behind the seawall for the last two days or so. Sadly, they were now floating in waist-deep water…since the tide had come in higher that morning than it had on the two previous days.

And beyond them were the bodies that were still entangled in the barb wire fencing that ran around the island. Most of these men had been dangling there for over forty-eight hours…and the saltwater and heat had corrupted their bodies completely.

And to their left and right were more dead bodies… or parts of bodies…of the brave men who had been gunned down in front of the seawall…and those who had died while leading the initial forays over the seawall.

"Don't forget what you see here, gentlemen," the major stated stoically as they took in the devastation around them. "War's a serious business…and these men did everything they possibly could to carry out the plans that you came up with…tried with their very last breath to carry out the plans you devised…to win this battle. War's no game…as these brave men certainly found out."

General Smith…a wizen leader…took a step back and was listening to the major…just like the rest of the staff was…and he tried to gauge the reaction the men would have when he was finished. *Would they be insulted… or would they take it in the right vein,* he wondered.

The silence that followed told the general all he needed to know.

"Thank you, major, we needed to hear that," the general said graciously…the tone of his voice and the look in his eyes clearly indicating that he was on board with what the major had said.

Major Millichap nodded at the general and whispered, "Thank you, sir."

"You're one of Dutch Hermle's boys, aren't you?" Smith replied.

"Oh, I don't know about that, sir. But, yes, I do respect him. And I like him too…enough to have invited him to my wedding back on New Zealand."

"Well, congratulations are in order. Is your wife a New Zealander?"

"Yes, sir, she is."

"Well, I hope it all works out for the both of you. It seems like a lot of our men got married while we were there…given all the marriage licenses I had to approve." Then the general swept his hand out to encompass the dead laying around and added, "I hope to God that none of them got married…if that means anything."

"It does, sir, and these men came here knowing you had their backs. Every one of them believed in you…and the ones that are alive still do."

The general looked at the major and said softly, "Old Dutch got a good one when he got you, son. Now let's go see what the colonels who are running this show have to say."

Everyone nodded this time…eager to get on with the job at hand…and the whole group headed over to the bunker that was serving as the battle's CP.

As usual, Major Culhane…whose head was always on a swivel…spotted him first. "Heads up, everyone! General Smith is on the way over," he said hoarsely…his mind and body exhausted after being on edge for over fifty-five hours straight.

Everyone in the CP from Colonel Edson on down stopped what they were doing and looked up to see the general and his entourage heading in…and Colonel Edson walked over to greet him. "Damn, sir! I wish somebody

The Butcher's Block

would've told me you were coming by. I would've tidied the place up for you," he joked...and he pointed the general towards a map that was hanging from one of the coconut logs that made up the back wall of the bunker.

"How's it going, Mike," the general said...and he took his helmet off and wiped his brow. "I thought it was hot down in Nicaragua...but this place has it beat by a country mile."

"That it does, sir. And the smell's nothing to write home about either," Edson replied. "We got a few chaplains working on that though...but there's only so much they can do. I don't know what we would've done without those guys. Kelly, Willard, Darling, and the rest of them."

"Kelly? I know him...he's from Upper Darby. It's right outside of Philly," the general...who was from Maryland... and not too far away...said casually.

"Yes, sir. He's one of the Catholic chaplains. He and Darling are assigned to the Second Regiment. Lieutenant Willard's the Eighth Marines' chaplain. Good men...all of them. Kelly asked if he could start a cemetery for the boys yesterday...and he's been at it ever since. We gave him a bulldozer...and he's been using that to dig grave sites for our boys and for the Japs, too. Our boys are getting buried with markers at least...so long as we can identify them. It's an overwhelming task...but thank God he's willing to do it."

"Yes...thank God for that," the general replied. "So, what's the situation now? Has it improved any?"

"You got here too late, sir. I just had a meeting with all the commanders I could get a hold of and I gave them their marching orders for the rest of the day. I dismissed them about thirty minutes ago and they're on their way back to their commands as we speak. The good news is that we finally got the Japs on the run, sir!" Edson said while cracking a slight smile. Then he pointed at the map and added, "Here, let me show you."

Using his finger as a pointer, he circled the area that sat on the cove just west of the boundary line between Red 2 and Red 1 and said, "Colonel Shoup's Second Regiment along with Larry Hays' First Battalion, Eighth has the mission of eliminating the *Pocket* for good. We've got the damn place surrounded finally and it's just a matter of time before that position collapses."

General Smith nodded in agreement…allowing Edson to move on to the next phase of the operation… which involved Colonel Elmer Hall's Eighth Regiment. This time his finger traced out a large square…with the lower right corner of the square anchored on the pier. "Major Crowe was finally able to knock out that large bunker complex that had stymied his own Second Battalion for two and a half days. I told him to keep pushing east…with the goal of reaching the main runway turning circle before dark. At the same time, we've got Major Rudd's Third Battalion attacking southward out of Red Three. Their job is to get across the northeastern taxiway in strength and then to push out as far south and east as they can. I would love to see them get across the main runway…but I'm not making any promises there."

Smith leaned in closer and marveled at the large bunker complex that had been protecting the concrete, two-story Japanese Command Post building that sat on the eastern side of Red 3. "That must've been one hard nut to crack," the general said, "no wonder it took them so long."

"Crowe and Chamberlin...his XO...did everything under the sun for two days trying to take that place. And if they couldn't do it...well, then nobody could. I even talked to Crowe last night about it and he said the place was a real bitch. But they took the damn place today... and that's what counts. And don't forget that they nailed down our left flank for two days...which bought time for Shoup and the rest of us when we needed it most."

"What about the Sixth Regiment? I just met with Lieutenant Colonel McLeod over on Green Beach and they seem to be raring to go over there," Smith interjected.

"That brings me to my last point," Colonel Edson replied, and he used his finger once again as a pointer. Starting at Temakin Point, he dragged his finger along the southern coastline and didn't stop until he reached the area that was directly south of the turning circle for the main airfield. Then he described how the 1st Battalion under Major Willie Jones had made great strides as it attacked eastward down the coast. "They've already met up with the Second Regiment boys who were trapped in that tank ditch near Black Beach Two and now they're beginning to push past them as well. Jones himself was just here and I told him that I want him to keep heading east and go as far as he can go until dark sets in. Hopefully, the One Six and the Three Eight will meet up and then we'll have a solid line from the north coast to the south coast. I told Colonel Hall to coordinate this part of our plan. He's responsible for the linkup between Rudd's Third Battalion and Jones' First Battalion."

"What supporting arms are available?" Smith questioned...aware that the division had both artillery and tank units assigned to it.

"I've assigned Rixey's twelve guns to support Jones as he attacks south...and I told Major McCoy to send whatever tanks he has left over to Jones as well."

"Why McCoy? What happened to Lieutenant Colonel Swenceski?" Smith asked...since Lieutenant Colonel Alexander Swenceski was the CO of the 2nd Tank Battalion and Major Charles McCoy was his XO.

"Sir, no one has heard from Colonel Swenceski since Saturday. We think his amtrac got hit...but no one is certain of it. McCoy took over when he went missing."

"Understood," Smith replied...picturing all those dead bodies on the beach and in the water...and dreading the thought that Swenceski could be one of them.

"Anything else, sir?" Edson asked...confident that he had covered everything about the plan that he and Major Culhane had drawn up in the last few hours.

"That should do it, Mike," the general replied...and he backed away from the map...indicating that he was satisfied with the briefing. He then turned around and spotted a man he recognized. "Isn't that Sherrod...the correspondent?"

"That it is, sir. He's been hanging around the CP for a while to see what he can pick up. He's a good man...

The Butcher's Block

even if he is a press guy. I bet he'd love to talk to you. Do you want me to call him over?"

"No. I'll just shock him and go over and say hello."

"Sir, that guy's been here since the get-go. He landed with Amey's boys over on Red Two on Saturday...and he's seen as much action as anyone else has. These correspondents have been incredible as far as I'm concerned. They're willing to take the same risks our riflemen are so they can tell their story. With that being said, I don't think seeing a general is gonna really shock him at this point."

"Touché," General Smith replied...and thinking about it...he added, "you know, that reminds me of a story I once heard about Julius Caesar...when he was a Roman general. Back in those times, they would have enormous parades when the Roman Army returned to Rome after waging a victorious campaign or winning a big military victory. And as great as those parades were for the citizens, Caesar also knew that all those parades could falsely inflate his own view of himself...and that his ego was his own worst enemy. So to keep that ego in check, he would have a little slave boy always walk beside him as he came into the city...and while the crowds were worshiping him...the little boy would whisper in his ear, 'Remember, Caesar, you are just a man...and all fame is fleeting.'"

Colonel Edson looked at the general and said simply, "Sound wisdom, that," and the general nodded and went over to see how Bob Sherrod was doing.

"How's your day going, Bob!" the general said as he walked over to Bob Sherrod and extended his hand.

"Why hello, sir," the surprised Sherrod replied, "I'm amazed you remembered me!" Sherrod extended his hand as well and the two men shook hands. "My day is going wonderfully. Thank you for asking!"

"That's good to hear. Have you gotten any good stories for your magazine?" the general asked.

"Of course, sir. Several. I think those editors of mine back in New York will like the stuff I send back… and the Marine Corps will too. One of my stories is going to be about Chaplain Willard. I just spent some time with him, in fact. He's not too far away from here," and Sherrod pointed to an area behind the CP. "He's helping two other chaplains out." Sherrod then reached into his satchel and pulled out his notebook. He flipped through several pages and stopped. "Here they are. Chaplains Francis Kelly and Malcolm MacQueen. Kelly's with the Second Regiment…and I wrote here that MacQueen is with the Eighteenth Engineers. Nice guys…both of them. Real men of the cloth. They established the Second Division cemetery yesterday…and they've been hard at work at it ever since…unfortunately."

Smith stared in the direction of the cemetery but said nothing…deep in thought.

Sherrod sensed his uneasiness and stopped talking as well.

After a minute had gone by, Smith turned back to Sherrod and said, "So what are you going to write about our wonderful chaplains?"

"Oh, I'm going to write about their connections with the men in their regiments. A lot of men began to take their faith very seriously as the landing date got closer. All the chaplains told me that. Nonstop confessions and communion all week long...especially on Friday. I'm also going to do a personal piece about Willard. On one hand, I found him very complicated, but down to earth on the other. I spent an hour with him...and he gave me the whole scoop about himself. I found it very interesting...so I think my readers will. For instance, did you know that he hangs two dud hand grenades from his utility shirt. He calls them *Ike* and *Mike*...and he says he wears them to frighten the Japs. He doesn't want to kill 'em mind you...just scare them away!"

"He certainly sounds like a character," the general laughed. "Your readers will love that story. What else about him struck you as interesting?"

"Don't get me started, sir. I could on and on...since his life's story was so fascinating. Do you have time to listen to it or do you wanna just read about it when it hits the newsstands?"

"Who do you write for again...remind me."

"For *Time* magazine, sir. I figure the story will hit sometime next year...probably around May or June...maybe sooner. It's up to the bigwigs in New York to decide which stories they like best and when they get published," Sherrod explained.

"So, what's he like...this Willard. I love learning about the men under my command. If I didn't know anything about them, they'd just be numbers to me...and I'd be less inclined to consider their needs when I make decisions. Any good commander knows his men… as much as he can anyway. At least, I think so."

"Well, sir, since you asked, here's what I've managed to scribble down so far. I'd give you the cliff notes version of it…but I think it would lose something in the translation. So here goes:

Wyeth Willard was born in Massachusetts in July of 1905… which meant that he was 38 years old and far older than the young marines that he landed with on Betio Island. Raised in the Baptist religion, Willard was way too young to participate in the First World War…but he remembered enough about it to know that he was a pacifist and wanted no part in any future wars…or so he thought.

His convictions about the subject were strengthened while attending Brown University in New Hampshire…where he majored in theological studies…and then especially so after he received his Master of Divinity degree from the Princeton Theological Seminary in New Jersey…which was the second oldest seminary in the Country.

At this point, Willard's achievements could have landed him a plush assignment at any number of prominent churches in the Boston area…but Willard struck out in a different direction and chose…to the consternation of many…a pastoral position at a small Baptist church in Forestdale, Massachusetts with twenty-one congregants and a lofty salary of $10 a week.

As with most Americans at the time, Willard's life was progressing just fine…or so he thought…until December 7th, 1941… when the Japanese launched their sneak attack on Pearl Harbor in Hawaii. Like the rest of his countrymen, Willard found the idea of a sneak attack to be so repugnant that he couldn't wait to do something about it...to get even so to speak...which was contrary to the beliefs he had held since he was a little boy. But Japan's actions trumped his passivity towards war...and he reversed course completely and he applied to be a chaplain in the Naval Reserve the very next day!

At this point, General Smith cut Sherrod off. "Are you telling me that one of our chaplains was an inveterate isolationist." The very idea left a bad taste in the general's mouth...since he had lived through the anti-war animus that gripped the country in the early stages of his career.

Sherrod considered the general's accusation and said, "Well, sir, if he was as serious an isolationist as you put it...he probably wouldn't be one of our chaplains right now...would he?"

Smith thought it over and conceded the point to Sherrod. "No...he wouldn't. Please go on."

"What I like about Willard the most is that he represents most of us. Deep down, none of us really want to go to war...at least none of us out there in the civilian world did. You military guys might have wanted it... looked forward to it even...but war is nasty...and at some level, even the people know it. I don't mean any disrespect by that, sir. I hope you know that," Sherrod said directly.

"No disrespect taken," the general said easily...so Sherrod continued.

"So, Willard attends the Chaplaincy School in Norfolk and gets assigned to your division after he passes muster. And next stop...you guessed it...is Guadalcanal. He was even a tent mate of First Lieutenant Hawkins...the leader of the Scout Snipers of all people...at one point. He told me that Hawkins wasn't afraid of anything... that he was the bravest man he had ever met...which fits given what Hawkins did while he was here. You know about Hawkins, right, sir."

"Yes, I do. First man on the island. Led the initial attack down the pier. I am well aware of his exploits. I wish we had a thousand of them."

"Colonel Shoup told me that he'll probably recommend him for the Medal of Honor. I hope he gets it too...after doing what he did to clear the way on Red Two."

"I heard what he accomplished was quite extraordinary...and I am looking forward to seeing that recommendation as well."

"So back to Willard. For this operation, he was assigned to the Eighth Marines...and Colonel Hall placed him with Larry Hays' Battalion. Now get this... Willard was supposed to go in with the later waves...with the HQ group I guess...but Willard asked Hays to put him in the lead wave. He told Hays that the best place he could be was with the boys who were going in first...with the ones that were going to meet the enemy head on. He felt that those boys were going to need his help the most...since a lot of them might get hit. And he wanted to be there if they did...to console them if that was possible. He was willing to put his own life in jeopardy to lend a hand to the men who were doing the same. In my book, that takes a lot of guts...and I want the people back home to know we have guys like this out here."

The Butcher's Block

"This'll make really good copy...for our Country...and for the service," Smith said...considering the implications and knowing that the people back home wanted to hear... and needed to hear...about some of the good things that were happening out here in the Pacific Theater.

"I told you this was a good story, sir. I know it in my bones. But it gets better. Before he got to the Second Division, he met a pastor in San Diego who had an extra two thousand Bibles that he wanted to donate to someone. Who better to give them to than the military... and the Marine Corps especially. So, Willard tells him that he'd take them...and Willard ended up passing out nearly every one of them to your boys before they hit the beaches. Well, I ran into one young marine yesterday who showed me the Bible that Willard had given him... and he had kept it in his backpack. After he landed, he pulled it out to read a passage of Scripture...to buck him up...and he discovered a hole in his pack and a bullet embedded right in his Bible. He'd be dead if it wasn't for that Bible! And I'm dead serious...I'm not making this stuff up. These are the kinds of stories I am hearing from every guy I talk to."

The general...a religious man himself...nodded and said, "That's not the first miracle I have heard about on the battlefield. They happen more than you think."

"I have no doubt that they do, sir. I bet I could write a whole separate book about all the miracles that have occurred out here alone."

"So how do you think this chaplain of ours squares what his faith teaches and what he has experienced out here?" the general asked...scratching the scab of a deep theological paradox. "Can the Lord be served while all this killing and maiming is going on?"

"I think Willard would say that war is the ultimate expression of evil. Yet plenty of wars were written about in the Old Testament. Heck, David was a warrior king… and God still loved him despite it."

"But He did punish him for it," Smith cut in, "by denying him the right to build His temple."

"You know your Bible, sir. I'm impressed. And so does Willard…and he still believes that taking a man's life is a sinful act…which is why he's a chaplain…and why he hates war. He told me that he couldn't kill anyone… even a Jap. But he realizes…or he's convinced himself anyway…that God may condone the taking of human life in a war if defeating evil is the purpose of the act. There's plenty of that in the Bible, too. Who knows… maybe he's right…but he said that he was going to be here nonetheless…so he could share Jesus with the boys who were forced to fight…and who might be seeing Him sooner than they thought."

"I find nothing wrong with that logic," the general said…and looking at his watch, he said, "I have certainly enjoyed this Sherrod. I don't think you'll have much trouble with the censors when you send your material up through channels. And I think you'll become a famous author, too. You write well…and I think the public will really appreciate your eyes-on rendition of this battle."

"Thank you, sir!" Sherrod exclaimed and the general nodded and made his way back to his staff.

Sherrod put his notebook away and then realized that he had forgotten to tell the general about another

The Butcher's Block

great idea he had come up with…and one the general had touched on as well. Instead of writing short magazine articles about individual marines he had run into, like Chaplain Willard, for instance, he was thinking about writing a book about the entire battle for Tarawa. He certainly had enough material for one…since he had written down everything he had experienced…along with the names of the marines who were involved. He was meticulous about that…since he wanted his "rendition" of the battle…as General Smith had called it…to be as accurate as possible. *Oh well*, he thought positively, *I guess he'll find out about it…just like the rest of my readers will…when my book finally hits the shelves!*

Earlier that very day…when dawn had finally broken across D + 2, Robert Sherrod was wondering where his next story would come from. *Would it come from Red Two,* he wondered…*or maybe back over on Red Three this time?* Luckily, the action he had already experienced on the two previous days had provided enough material to keep him writing for another year or more even…*but what the heck*, he thought, *I'm still alive…so I might as well see if I can find something else that my readers would love to hear about.*

Sherrod started D Day off in a Higgins boat with Major Howard Rice…the 2-2 XO…and thirty other men who were part of the 2nd Battalion, Second's headquarters detachment. Assigned to come in with the fifth wave, they would ride in a Higgins boat for the first part of the journey and then transfer over to an amtrac if the water level over the coral reef was too low. If the tide was in... and the water was deep enough to accommodate the draft of the Higgins boats...then they would ride right in without stopping at the reef to affect a transfer.

It didn't take Sherrod and the men with him very long to realize that the landing was not going well. Geysers of dark seawater began sprouting up around their Higgins boat and then some of the amtracs up ahead of them in the first three landing waves began exploding in sheets of flame. In another minute or two, the whole landing seemed to be in jeopardy...and Sherrod wondered what he had gotten himself into.

Then their Higgins boat hit the reef...and ground to a halt. With perfect timing, an amtrac pulled up and Major Rice and half the detachment transferred over to it and it took off...churning towards the beach. Soon after that another amtrac showed up and the crew chief gave them the bad news. "It's horrible in there. Amtracs are getting hit left and right and there are dead and wounded all over the beach." Then, pointing to the *Niminoa* scuttled just inside the reef, the crew chief said, "I can take you that far. I can't risk going any further. It's just too dangerous." Since a ride in an amtrac...no matter how short... was better than no ride at all, the men agreed, and they transferred over to the amtrac...and off it went.

True to his word, the crew chief had the driver stop the amtrac when it got close to the *Niminoa* and Sherrod and the fifteen marines jumped overboard and landed

The Butcher's Block

in waist deep water. Alone now, the whole group began slogging their way in...but the heavy machine gun fire coming from the pillboxes and bunkers along the seawall on Red 2 forced the men to separate...and Sherrod made for the pier.

It took a while, but Sherrod finally made it to the beach safe and sound. But instead of heading right...towards Red 2...like he was supposed to...he changed his mind and went left...towards Red Beach 3. In his mind, it was a prudent decision: there seemed to be more order over there... and fewer dead bodies than there were on Red 2.

After a while, he made his way down the seawall and eventually ran into the legendary commander of the 2-8...Major Jim Crowe...who was standing behind a damaged amtrac that was stuck on the seawall.

He remained there for the rest of the morning and early afternoon...recording everything he saw in his notebook so he could reference it later when he wrote his stories. Then, as the day wore on, he decided to find out how things were faring for the 2nd Battalion, Second...since that was the unit he had been assigned to originally. But the 2-2 was over on Red 2...on the other side of the pier...a little over two hundred yards away. Undaunted, he backed up his notebook and headed that way...the snipers be damned...to see what he could dig up before dusk set in.

Robert Sherrod...the *Time* magazine correspondent... spent most of the morning of D + 1 in a foxhole just behind the seawall and about fifty yards to the right of the pier. His companion was Bill Hipple...a war correspondent like himself...and they had been huddling there since daybreak. Those cursed Jap snipers...as dangerous as ever...were still shooting at anyone who stuck their heads up too high. But their Red 2 location did have its advantages...since it wasn't too far from Colonel Shoup's CP...which was about fifty yards or so past the seawall...and it had given them a front row seat when the 1-8 made its landing in the middle of Red 2 at first light.

Sherrod and Hipple knew how bad things could get when making a landing...since both of them had personally come ashore with the Second Battalion, Second nearly twenty-four hours earlier. But to watch another battalion get slaughtered with your own two eyes took the experience to a whole new level...and just like that, Sherrod had a few more stories to add to his burgeoning collection. Scribbling in his notebook as quick as he could, Sherrod wrote: *Now one of our mortars discovers one of the machine guns that has been shooting at the Marines. It is not back of us, but is a couple of hundred yards west, out in one of the wooden privies the dysentery-fearing Japs built out over the water. The mortar gets the range, smashes the privy, and there is no more firing from there.*

Sherrod put his pencil down and stopped writing for a moment...watching the debacle unfold...too close for comfort. Wincing at what he was forced to watch, he picked up his pencil again and jotted down what he was seeing so he'd never forget it. He wrote: *But the machine guns continue to tear into the oncoming Marines. Within five minutes I see six men killed. But the others keep coming. One rifleman walks slowly ashore, his left arm a bloody mess from the shoulder down. The casualties become heavier. Within a few minutes more I can count at least a hundred Marines lying on the flats.*

He took a deep breath and wiped what might have been a tear from his eye...and continued writing: *0730: The Marines continue unloading from the Higgins boats, but fewer of them are making the shore now. Many lie down behind the pyramidal concrete barriers the Japs had erected to stop tanks. Others make it as far as the disabled tanks and amphtracks, then lie behind them to size up the chances of making the last hundred yards to shore. There are at least two hundred bodies which do not move at all on the dry flats, or in the shallow water partially covering them. This is worse, far worse than it was yesterday.*

Putting his pencil down, Sherrod turned to Hipple and said, "I wonder if the people back home have any idea what's really going on out here. I'm sure they think these boys have it rough...being away from home and all...but can they really imagine for one second how bad it really is."

The erudite Hipple...who worked for the Associated Press...said plainly, "They won't...and they can't...unless we tell them. It's to protect their own sanity. They know their loved ones are over here...but they don't want to think for one second that it could be this bad for them. The alternative is too rough. Knowing what it's really like would only increase their anxiety over the whole deal. So, they bury their heads in the sand and hope for the best. Your job...and mine...is to let them know what's really happening out here to their sons, brothers, and fathers...and how brave these men are. And hopefully we'll be able to do just that...and truthfully...as long as we stay alive. If we don't...I hope it's because we were both killed, of course."

Sherrod looked at Hipple with admiration and said, "Amen to that, Brother. It's an important task... the reporting end of this business. Some would say it's almost as important as the fighting itself. I'm not willing to go that far just yet. But I'm thankful that I've been given the chance to tell these boy's stories...and I'm gonna do it the best way I know how."

"You're a good writer, Bob. Everyone knows it. Just write what you see. No fairy tale stuff. You do that and the story will speak for itself."

"Thanks, Hip. And the same goes for you. You wouldn't be with the AP if you weren't one of the best. You know that as well as I do. And it's an honor to be here with you," Sherrod replied.

Now it was Hipple's turn to brush a tear from his eye...or was it a speck of sand...and the two men turned their attention back to the water...where the massacre of the 1-8 continued to unfold.

Sherrod eventually made his way up to Colonel Shoup's CP later that day...and that's when he got a tip about D + 2.

"If I were you," Colonel Shoup advised, "I'd head over to Red Three. Crowe's men are going to be attacking that big bunker complex sometime tomorrow...and

The Butcher's Block

there's gotta be a good story in there somewhere. The damn place has frustrated Crowe for two days now...but my gut instinct tells me it's ready to fall. I'd wanna be there to see that happen. Hell...you can write an entire book on Crowe alone and become famous. There's my two cents...take it or leave it."

And like any good writer with a nose for a story, Sherrod had taken the colonel's advice...and he had struck out for Red 3 at first light.

"Well, well. Look who's back," the legendary Jim Crowe exclaimed to the marines around him as the correspondent made his way over to the abandoned amtrac that was serving as the 2-8 command post. Looking at his watch and seeing that it was 0610 hours, the cocky major added, "I hope we didn't upset your breakfast schedule," for effect.

One of Crowe's men who was cooking his meal above a sterno flame decided to get into the act as well...and he held up his C-ration can and yelled out, "You can have my corned beef and potatoes if you write a good story about me!"

"You tell him, Mac!" Crowe boomed out...and the marines...who idolized their leader...cracked up laughing.

Major Henry Pierson "Jim" Crowe was indeed larger than life. As the commanding officer of the 2-8, Crowe had forged a reputation as one of the most feared…yet well-liked…officers in the Marine Corps…and it was said that his men would easily follow him to hell and back… if that's where he wanted to go.

Crowe was born in Boston, Kentucky in March of 1899…but his parents moved soon thereafter, and he and his three sisters were raised on a small farm in Mount Pulaski, Illinois. In 1916, the seventeen-year-old teenager had tried to enlist in the Army…so he could head south with General "Black Jack" Pershing and fight the Mexicans…but his parents didn't like the idea and they refused to sign his enlistment papers. Undeterred and patient, Crowe waited two more years and then decided to enlist again…since World War I was in full swing. But instead of going the Army route, Crowe decided to check out the Marine Corps…since the marines were grabbing all the headlines while fighting in France in places like Soissons and Belleau Wood. Then, while on a trip to Chicago, Crowe ran into an impressive Marine recruiting sergeant who was resplendent in his Dress Blue uniform…and that sealed the deal. Crowe enlisted in October 1918…and he reported to Parris Island eleven days before the war in Europe ended. The young recruit found the training challenging…not brutal…and he adapted easily to the rigors of the day. Years later he would say, "Our drill instructors were thoughtful men… and they taught us discipline…which stuck with me all my life."

His first combat experiences…which were more like Old Western gun fights…came when he was stationed in the Dominican Republic in 1921…and then in Nicaragua in 1928...during the *Banana War* years of the 1920s. Instead of waging all-out war though, the marines acted more like policemen during this period as they preserved order and protected the burgeoning American business interests and growing commercial enterprises in the region.

Crowe was also a gifted athlete...and in 1923 he discovered football while he was stationed at Quantico, Virginia. Now a sergeant and working as a military policeman, Crowe was recruited to play a sport he knew nothing about by the commanding general...Smedley Butler. The athletic officer in charge of the team was Major Alexander Vandegrift...who would later command the 1st Marine Division on Guadalcanal...and the civilian coach was Hugo Bezdeck...who had previously coached at the University of Arkansas...where he coined the term *Razorbacks* to describe the tough demeanor of his team. Bezdeck had also spent ten years leading the *Nittany Lions* at Penn State...and Crowe later characterized him as the meanest man he had ever met.

Though not as big as the other linemen, Crowe tried out for guard...since that was the position he had played in basketball...and he made the team. This was quite an achievement...since it was the same *Devil Dogs* program that had defeated the Army's Third Corps team in 1921 that was coached by an up and coming Army major named Dwight Eisenhower...who had been a football legend himself when he was a cadet at West Point a few years earlier.

The game had been played in front of 16,000 rabid fans in Baltimore, Maryland...and the *Devil Dogs* team won 21-0. The Marine team was led by Lieutenant Frank "Big Moose" Goettge…a bruising running back who would later rise to the rank of lieutenant colonel. Walter Camp…the genius coach and founder of American football…had watched the game…and he described Goettge's performance this way: *Today, for today at least, I saw my greatest all-time football player; for today at least greater than Jim Thorpe on a good day.*

Twenty-one years later, Lieutenant Colonel Frank Goettge would lead an intelligence expedition on the island of Guadalcanal to investigate the potential surrender of the Japanese forces there. Tricked into thinking the Japanese were whipped and wanting to parlay, he and the rest of his party of twenty marines had taken a boat ride several miles westward…and then debarked.

The Japs waited until the boat had taken off and the marines had moved inland…and then they sprang their trap. Hidden in the jungle, they opened fire and killed several marines with their first volley. Goettge and the survivors pulled back to the beach and continued to fight back…but the Japanese picked them off one by one…until there was one man left. Out of options, the man had run into the surf and swum as far out as he could and then headed east…back towards the marine lines. Luckily, he was a good swimmer…and he made it back alive before the sharks got him…and he would report the massacre that had occurred on the beach several miles west of the Henderson Airfield perimeter in early August 1942.

The Butcher's Block

Jim Crowe ended up playing football for nine years... from 1924 until 1934...and for many of those years he played on the All-Marine team out of Quantico, Virginia. The only year he didn't play was 1928...when he was stationed in Nicaragua...and many of the teams he played on won the President's Cup...an award that was created by President Calvin Coolidge in 1924. The award was designed to recognize *"good clean healthy recreation for the people of the entire country and to encourage and stimulate athletics among the enlisted men of the Services."*

During those years, the lineman Crowe had opened up holes for two great running backs. The first one was Frank Goettge...who had excelled in the 1921 game... and these two men's paths would cross many times over during the next several years.

The other back who Crowe would always remember was First Lieutenant Harold "Indian Joe" Bauer. They played together in 1931 and 1932 for the Quantico Post team...which was different from the All-Marine team... and then again on the San Diego post team in 1934... their most memorable game being a 57 to 6 thrashing of the Baltimore Firemen during the 1931 season. That same 1934 team would also go on to win the President's Cup...just like the teams that Crowe had played on in 1925, 1926, and 1927 did.

Sadly, Bauer...like Goettge... would end up losing his life during the battle for Guadalcanal as well. By then, Bauer was a lieutenant colonel and the squadron leader of VMF - 212...a Wildcat fighter squadron that was part of the Cactus Air Force that flew out of Henderson Field.

Bauer had shown up during the dark days...when the Japanese appeared to have the upper hand in the fight for the island. Usually outnumbered, Bauer had become an ace nonetheless...racking up nine kills... downing both bombers and fighters alike. His first kill had been a Jap bomber which was threatening a ship off Lunga Point...and then he got eight more during two separate sorties...four per mission. On his final sortie on November 14th, 1942, Bauer shot down two more Jap planes...giving him eleven kills...before his plane was hit as well. He ditched his plane successfully in the *Slot*... and he was able to get out...since he was later observed wearing his Mae West life vest and floating along fine. But Bauer went missing thereafter...quite possibly the victim of a shark attack...or he may have succumbed to an unseen wound and drowned. Whatever the cause, Bauer was never seen again...and he was posthumously awarded the Congressional Medal of Honor for displaying incredible leadership during the most challenging period in the air war over Guadalcanal.

On top of being a wonderful athlete, the Marine Corps also found out that Crowe was a phenomenal marksman. In 1927...while stationed at Quantico...Jim was not only promoted to gunnery sergeant...but he also gave the sport of match shooting a try as well. He was so good at it that he won a spot on the twelve-man Marine team that came in second in the National Matches to the vaunted Army team that finished first. That year he also

The Butcher's Block

earned the Marine Corps' Distinguished Marksman Badge for winning a medal in a division rifle match and then getting two more awards in other top-level competitive matches. And one of Crowe's teammates on the 1927 team, First Lieutenant Merritt Edson, also shot so well that he too…like Crowe…qualified for Distinguished Marksman.

Jim Crowe's football and competitive shooting careers were put on hold in 1928, however. That year Gunnery Sergeant Crowe was sent to Nicaragua with a company from the 5th Marines. Their primary mission was protecting the Guaymil Fruit Company…and Jim would often lead patrols deep in the Nicaraguan jungle along the Guiraguas River to keep the local revolutionaries in check.

By 1929, Jim was shooting again…and he made the Marines' National Match team that was captained by a young major named Julian Smith. As a marine, Jim was also required to re-qualify with his rifle and he shot a score of 344 out of a possible 350 points…which was the best re-qualification score achieved by any marine that year.

Jim was then transferred back to Quantico in 1930… and he was assigned to the Rifle Range Detachment. That same year, the Marine National Team…with Jim holding down one of the ten enlisted man slots on the team…won the "Dogs of War" Rifle Team Trophy…the award given to the best shooting team in the Country.

Crowe would continue his competitive shooting as his career progressed…and he won the regional President's Match in 1934…shooting an incredible score of 144 out of a possible 150 points. Then…in 1936…Jim won the Wimbledon Match…and broke a rifle accuracy record that was set back in 1923 while doing so. Not to be undone, he also won the Browning Automatic Rifleman award when he served as part of a seven-man squad that ended up winning the Infantry Trophy for the event.

In 1934, Crowe was promoted to the rank of Marine Gunner in order to keep him in the Marine Corps. According to Crowe, the Coast Guard had approached him as he neared the end of his enlistment…and they used the carrot of promotion to entice him over to their branch of service. If he joined them, Crowe would be given the rank of chief boatswain…the equivalent of a warrant officer…which meant a pay raise…and he would become the head coach of the Coast Guard rifle and football teams as well.

Crowe might have accepted their bold offer but Captain Elmer Hall…his company commander at the time…found out about it and nipped it in the bud. When he learned of the plot, Hall told Crowe that he should consider applying for a Marine Gunner's rank…which was the equivalent of a warrant officer in the other services…and that he'd support him if he decided to do it. Despite the odds, Crowe threw his hat in the ring…and Hall made good on his promise as well. Crowe…along with nine other candidates…a very select group…made the list and they were allowed to compete for the available openings for Marine Gunner.

The Butcher's Block

Crowe took the written and oral exams that were required for the Marine Gunner position in March 1934 while he was serving as part of the marine detachment aboard the USS *Pennsylvania*...one of the mighty battleships that was part of the burgeoning US Navy. His results were then sent to Marine Headquarters in Washington... and he waited...hoping that his test scores and board performance were high enough to do the trick.

Gunnery Sergeant Crowe received his answer a few months later...when his detachment commander, Captain Goettge, and the other officers on the ship called Jim into the wardroom. As Jim stood before him, Goettge cut Crowe's chevrons...which marked him as an enlisted man and non-commissioned officer...off his uniform and handed him a Sam Browne belt, a gleaming officer's sword with its pearl-white hilt, and the bursting bomb insignia of a Marine gunner.

Jim Crowe was officially promoted to Marine Gunner on September 1st, 1934...and it would take him another six and half years to garner his next promotion to Chief Marine Gunner. Prior to that though, Crowe would spend three years...1936 to 1939...in China serving in the Chinese capital with the American Embassy Guard. He loved the duty and during his time there he was also able to observe the Japanese Army up close...just like a mentor of his...Major "Red Mike" Edson...was doing.

Upon his return from China, Crowe was assigned to the 6th Marines...and one of the officers who came under his tutelage was Second Lieutenant Willie K. Jones…newly assigned to the 6th Marine Regiment himself. As with most second lieutenants, Gunner Crowe saluted the young lieutenant with his left hand…but since Jones was a reserve officer…Crowe went one step further and extended his pinkie finger at an exaggerated angle…to ram the point home.

Crowe ended up serving with the 6th Marines until the 8th Marines…a regiment that had been inactive since 1925…was reactivated in April 1940 and based in Southern California. Almost a year later…in February 1941…he made the rank of Chief Marine Gunner…an extraordinary…and rare…achievement…since there were only five other men who held that rank in the entire Marine Corps!

Crowe's first assignment with the 8th Marines was establishing and running a Scout-Sniper School…and anyone who attended the fledging school would never forget it. Physical drill under arms started two hours before dawn…and that was followed by a one mile run. The rest of the long day was spent learning the intricacies and art of sniping…and anyone who survived the course was never the same. Of those that did, it was said, *"They were leaner, harder, and had a haunted look. But they were also more confident, and certainly more competent Marines. They were devoted to violent exercise and they were completely uninhibited on liberty."*

Crowe could've written that last line about his snipers himself…since he had played an extremely violent sport...American football...for nine years...and he trained his men to think and act along those lines. And Crowe liked to drink as well...and he considered his ability to hold his own liquor one of his most formidable qualities.

One of the stories the feisty major liked to tell about himself occurred when he was in China. It seems a lot of their duty...as embassy guards...centered around ceremonial activities and social outings...which suited Crowe just fine. But one function…in particular...stuck out in Crowe's mind: a birthday celebration for Emperor Hirohito...which was held at the Japanese Embassy in the Chinese capital. Crowe was detailed to attend the party...and he wound up being the only marine there.

Tension was heavy in the air when Crowe arrived... since Japan had recently invaded and overrun Northern China...and the rest of the foreign delegations that were invited were comprised of diplomats that were far senior in rank and age to the lowly marine. Crowe didn't let it bother him one bit though...and he strode around the party as if he owned the place. In his mind, he was equal to...if not better than...the British, French, and Italian envoys in attendance…and no one was going to tell him different.

Towards the end of the evening, the toasts began... led by the senior Japanese officer there...a full colonel... and his aide...a major. *Saki* was the drink of choice...and before long one toast began blending into another... especially after several *gombei*...or bottoms up toasts... were declared and downed.

According to Crowe, only three participants of the drink fest were still standing...or sitting upright in their chairs actually...when the party ended: the Japanese colonel...his aide...the major...and the Marine enlisted man and gunnery sergeant...Jim Crowe! To reward Crowe's endurance, resilience, and honor, the Japanese colonel presented the gunnery sergeant with a pass that allowed Crowe to travel anywhere he desired in the areas that the Japanese Army held in Northern China...which was quite a gift. Then the colonel called out the Japanese guard force and they saluted Crowe as he left the embassy in a rickshaw...no worse for wear!

Crowe's next assignment with the 8th came in late 1940...when he was given command of the anti-tank platoon in the regimental Headquarters and Service Company. At the time, the platoon was equipped with four small, World War I era 37mm cannons...but they didn't fire them all that much. Instead, the training was centered around physical endeavors...and since the division was stationed outside of San Diego, long marches were the order of the day. And that's when Chief Marine Gunner Crowe heard that the *Desert Fox*...General Erwin Rommel...the commander of the German forces in North Africa...had bragged that his *Afrika Corps* could still fight after moving forty miles in a single day. Not to be outdone, Crowe took up the challenge...and then went one step further: he decided his unit would be able to go fifty miles in a day...and still fight to boot! Taking turns pulling their two-wheeled anti-tank guns, the crews alternated between running and walking in order to meet the new standard set for them by their indomitable platoon commander.

But as the winds of war began to blow harder in America, the Marine Corps began to expand with them...and in the fall of 1941, the anti-tank platoon was phased out and replaced by a company-sized unit that was called the Regimental Weapons Company. The new company was made up of three platoons that were equipped with four newly designed...and far more accurate...37mm guns each and a machine gun platoon to protect them.

Naturally, Marine Gunner Crowe was given command of this unit...and the promotion to Chief Marine Gunner came with the greater responsibilities as well. Then in February 1942, Crowe was promoted directly to captain...bypassing the lieutenant ranks in one fell swoop...which suited Crowe's temperament perfectly and confirmed his lowly opinion of the lieutenant ranks altogether.

Captain Crowe's distain for lieutenants had supposedly developed when he was young recruit in boot camp in 1918. New to the rules and regulations, the flustered Crowe had failed to salute an approaching lieutenant correctly. Instead of using his right hand to render a proper salute, the green recruit had begun the salute with his left hand...but switched to his right when he realized his mistake. According to the story...the arrogant lieutenant made the most of the opportunity...and he mocked Crowe by saluting him with both hands...first his left...then his right...mimicking the young recruit's error. The lieutenant walked on by without saying a word...leaving the chastened Crowe red-faced and utterly embarrassed.

Crowe never forgot the slight apparently...and he took it out on the future lieutenants...or trainees as he called them...that he encountered by saluting them with his left hand...and sometimes...if the mood struck him... with both hands at the same time!

In January of 1942, the 8th Regiment...along with the rest of the 2nd Marine Brigade...participated in its first wartime assignment: the ground defense of the Samoan Islands. Located 2,500 miles southwest of Hawaii, the islands were important since they were located along the line of communications linking Hawaii with Australia...and the islands appeared to be a prime target for the Japanese as they expanded their hold on the Southwest Pacific region. As it turned out, the islands were never threatened...but it did give the 8th Marines a perfect jump off point for its next wartime assignment: Guadalcanal.

Captain Crowe and the rest of the 8th Marines arrived on the *Island of Death* at Lunga Point in early November of 1942 as part of the Second Division's effort to relieve the worn-out First Marine Division. And for the next three months, Captain Crowe and his

The Butcher's Block

men would engage the Japanese forces on the *Canal* along the Mantanikau River and further west as the marine perimeter began to expand beyond Henderson Airfield. And it was during these jungle engagements that Captain Crowe's reputation as a fearless leader and ruthless fighter emerged.

At one point, after an attack had stalled out, Captain Crowe jumped out of a half-track and rushed over to a group of marines who were taking cover in a shell hole. Frightened by the intense level of fire coming at them, the marines had no intention of advancing any further... or so they thought. Standing over them, the six-foot-tall Crowe yelled down at them from the lip of the shell hole and cajoled them to fight. "Damn it," he said, "you'll never get the Purple Heart hiding in a foxhole! Follow me!" And follow him they did...despite their fear...and they took out the Japanese position and restored their pride at the same time.

Later...in mid-January...the 8th marines were waging an attack towards Point Cruz...west of the Mantanikau River...along with two Army regiments...the 164th and the 182nd. As the attack advanced, a Jap artillery position in the 164th's zone of action played possum and the 164th Regiment soldiers bypassed it...since it was too difficult to locate in the dense jungle. Before long, the Jap artillerymen were firing again though...and shells were landing among the marine and army ranks alike. Relying on his instincts, Captain Crowe decided he could find the troublesome site...and he told his Army counterparts that he was going to destroy it. With nothing more than a shotgun and a gunnery sergeant and three other marines, Crowe entered the jungle and stalked the enemy position...waiting for the artillery pieces to fire...and then orienting and adjusting his movements to the sound of the artillery shells as they traveled in the air above them.

Captain Crowe's team eventually found the Jap artillery site...and they ended up killing twelve men who were manning two 77mm field guns. And for this action, Captain Crowe was awarded the Army's second highest award...the Silver Star. His citation read a little differently from the captain's take on the fight: *With 8 men he rushed and captured an enemy emplacement containing a 77mm field piece, located behind the advanced lines. His group killed five enemy in the gun emplacement and destroyed a large ammunition dump.*

The Army also took note of how valuable Captain Crowe and his men had been in assisting the Army troops during the overall engagement...and they awarded him the Bronze Star...for displaying bravery under combat conditions...as well.

Captain Crowe's superiors wasted little time when they learned of his meritorious actions on Guadalcanal and he was given a battlefield promotion to major on the spot.

Major Crowe and the rest of his company left Guadalcanal on January 31st, 1943. They traveled to New Zealand aboard the USS *Crescent City*...or APA 40... an attack transport...and during the trip, Crowe shaved off the thick red beard that he had grown while on the *Canal*. But he left his mustache...which was red...like his beard had been...and it eventually grew to eight inches in length from waxed tip to waxed tip. This mustache would become his legendary trademark...as were his swagger stick and shotgun...and all three...along with his trusty cigars...would make the trip to Betio when the 2nd Division left New Zealand in October of 1943.

Now...on the morning of D + 2...the major was watching Bob Sherrod...one of the correspondents assigned to cover the Tarawa invasion...slink his way over to his CP on Red Beach 3.

Sherrod, in an effort to follow Bill Hipple's exhortation about staying alive, was crouching as he worked his way past the marines lying behind the seawall. As he passed the marine holding out his C-ration can, he said, "Keep the corned beef...but I'll take the potatoes off your grimy hands!" This brought a chorus of laughter as well...just like Crowe's comments had seconds ago.

"You can stand up straight now, Sherrod. We've cleaned out most of the snipers since you were here last. And if one does pop up...he doesn't last very long," Crowe said confidently. Then he added, "Isn't that right, boys!" for effect.

Most...if not all...of the men in this sector were strictly 2-8 men by now...Crowe's boys...and they responded accordingly. Several men let out a whoop at the major's comment...and one marine...a young boy who recognized Sherrod…yelled out, "You tell 'em, sir! If y'all come for a story, Mister Newspaperman, y'all come to the right place. The 'ol Two Eight is the toughest battalion in the whole dang division…and probably the world too! And ain't nobody gonna say any different."

Sherrod smiled at the boy…and wondered what grade he had made it to before dropping out. Another marine…slightly older…drawled, "Y'all tell 'em, Lestor. We ain't afraid of no Japs…or newspapermen neither!"

Everyone laughed at the interchange, and Sherrod… who took a seat beside the amtrac…said, "Well, I can certainly see that your boys are fired up for today's work… that's for sure."

"They're the best fighting force in the entire world… just like Lestor there said," Crowe stated proudly, "and I pity those poor Jap bastards out there. They're gonna find out what the Marine Corps…and especially the Second of the Eighth…is capable of this morning."

The men let out another cheer…the pride they had in their commander clearly evident.

"So, what's on tap for this morning, sir," Sherrod asked…getting down to business.

"Here…let me show you," Crowe replied, and a junior officer…one of his staff…unfolded a map and laid it out on the sand. Crowe knelt down and Sherrod scooted over to get a better look at it. Crowe then pointed what looked like a swagger stick at the area on the map that indicated their location along the seawall…and then he pointed to the Jap complex located to the southeast of them. He described the layout of the Jap defenses and how they had failed to take it after attacking it for two

The Butcher's Block

days. "I've got my XO...Major Chamberlin...and several other officers working up a plan right now," Crowe said.

"Why do you think you'll be successful this time," Sherrod asked...wondering what had changed.

"That engineer officer from the 18th--"

"Bonnyman, sir. First Lieutenant Bonnyman," the staff officer said, cutting in.

"Yeah, Bonnyman. Well, Bonnyman came up with a good idea this morning. He told me that he noticed several T-shaped stove pipes sticking out of the sand near the top of the bunker...or bombproof as he's calling it. He thinks they're ventilation pipes...which means they're supplying air to the Japs inside. And if they are... that's its weak spot. He thinks it's possible to blow the thing up by placing some explosives down the shafts."

"How come nobody noticed these things before," Sherrod asked...a logical question.

"We had the *Dashiell* and the *Ringgold*...those two destroyers out in the lagoon...firing at that bunker all day yesterday. Their fire was mostly ineffective though... since the sand that's covering the bunker absorbed most of the shells' impact. We might as well be throwing marshmallows at it...for all the good it did. But Bonnyman thinks the shelling actually blew enough sand away to uncover those shafts...which could've happened. Anyway, they're there now...and Bonnyman's gonna try to get some explosives into them."

"When is the attack supposed to kick off, sir?" the correspondent asked...sensing a story.

"Chamberlin, Bonnyman, Palopoli, and Elrod are putting the finishing touches on it right now. They'll let me know when they're done and then we'll go ahead with it. I'm hoping before oh nine hundred anyway."

"So, two or so hours from now," Sherrod said, looking at his watch.

"Yup. If all goes according to plan. But when has that happened over the last two days," the major answered wistfully.

"Do you mind if I stick around to watch?" Sherrod asked.

"Go right ahead," Crowe answered, and added, "you can team up with Hatch and Kelliher. They're already over that way."

"Norm Hatch…from the division's Photo Section? And Bill Kelliher…his assistant, sir?"

"Yeah…that's them. They're carrying that big camera around with them. Too bad it doesn't shoot bullets though. If it did, they could've knocked off a bunch of Japs with it by now," Crowe replied smartly.

"Norm started out as a photographer for *Leatherneck* magazine after he got out of boot camp," Sherrod said, "and he did such a good job there that they recommended him for field work."

Crowe laughed and said, "You should've seen him when he came to my office to ask permission to head in with us."

"You mean with your battalion?"

"Yeah. He specifically volunteered to go in with the Two Eight. He said I was the embodiment of the Marine Corps…all in one man no less! He got that part right at least…so I cut him a break and I asked him what he did.

He says, 'I'm a motion picture cameraman,' and I nearly strangled him. You know what I said to him?"

"I can only guess," Sherrod offered up.

"I screamed, 'I don't want a damned Hollywood Marine with me! I want only fighting marines around me!'" Crowe laughed again...picturing the scene...and he remembered how Hatch had defended himself effectively by saying, "Sir, I already have over four years' service in the Corps...and I've been through all the training...and I shot expert with the M One."

"So, you let him stay obviously," Sherrod pointed out.

"Yeah...I told him he could stay. But I made sure to tell him to stay the hell out of my way!" And Crowe laughed again...knowing that Hatch had followed through on his end of the bargain. "And the same goes for you...if you're gonna stay over here," Crowe added for good measure.

"Well, sir, the fact that Hatch is here...and is ready to film whatever takes place...puts me in sort of a bind. I don't want to try to steal their thunder, so to speak. And if I've learned anything over the last few years...it's that the written word has a tough time competing with a movie version of an event. It makes a big difference when you can see something with your own eyes as opposed to just reading about it. Plus, Hatch and Kelliher are my friends... so I'd rather see them get the credit for this one."

"I get your point," Crowe replied.

"Plus...I don't want to step on their toes. Hatch and Kelliher have been here the whole time. I'll just let them have this one. Sound good?"

Crowe looked at Sherrod with respect and said, "You're a good man, Sherrod. Hopefully, we'll all get a chance to read your stories about this place someday… just make me look good in the story you do about me!"

"That's a deal, sir," Sherrod replied…and he turned on his heel and walked straight back to Red 2…leaving a smiling major behind him.

Chapter Twenty-Seven

"That lieutenant's back...and he's talking to that sergeant and corporal next door," Private Rolf Jorgenson pointed out.

It was a little after eight in the morning on Red Beach 3 and Jorgenson was wide awake...the shelling from the two destroyers in the lagoon ruining his morning nap.

Corporal Staggs stirred...the mention of an officer always triggering alarm bells. "Is he just talking to them...or does it look like something more than that?" Staggs asked...sitting up and wiping the cobwebs from his eyes.

"Hard to say," Jorgenson answered, his eyes glued to the three men in the shell hole across the way. The private watched the two NCOs nodding at whatever the officer was saying...and then he looked over their way. "Uh oh," Jorgenson said as the officer made eye contact with Jorgenson and waved him over.

"What is it?" Staggs asked with trepidation...his instincts kicking into full alert.

"He wants me...I guess us...to come over there," Jorgenson replied...and he waited to see what Staggs would do.

"Well, if he's callin' us over, we'd better go," Staggs said, and he grabbed his M-1 rifle and crept over to Jorgenson's side of the hole. "I'll go first. If I draw any fire, try to see where the fire is coming from...so we can nail the sniper."

Jorgenson took a quick glance at the tops of the coconut trees in the distance and said, "Okay...I'll follow you over."

Staggs looked at Jorgenson for a second and then took a quick look at the men in the shell hole nearby. "Ready," he added.

"Whenever you are," Jorgenson shot back.

"Okay, here goes," and Staggs scampered out of their hole and ran through the soft sand as fast as he could... trying to outwit any Jap snipers in the area. When he got close, he leaped into the hole that First Lieutenant Bonnyman, Sergeant Andre Owens, and Corporal Todd Wilbanks were sitting in...but he landed awkwardly. Losing his balance, Staggs then smashed into Wilbanks... who was sitting on the far side of the hole...and the strong corporal pushed Staggs off him without much effort.

"Nice landing...good thing you're not a carrier pilot," Wilbanks said lightheartedly.

"Thanks for the cushion," Staggs joked right back, brushing himself off.

"There's two of you, right," the lieutenant said, smiling as well.

"Yes, sir. The other one is getting ready to head over right now. I told him to keep an eye out for snipers. You never know if you're really safe around here," Staggs replied.

"You got that right, corporal," First Lieutenant Bonnyman replied. "I was in a meeting this morning with Major Chamberlin and two other lieutenants behind the seawall and out of nowhere a Jap sniper up and shoots one of us. Killed the guy instantly. So, you're right…there's nowhere safe out here."

"Who was in the meeting, sir?" Staggs asked.

"It was me, the battalion XO, and Lieutenant Elrod. He's the officer in charge of the four thirty-sevens that made it ashore. The officer that got killed was First Lieutenant Palopoli…the F Company XO. He was hit right in the heart. Great shot, I guess. He was going to lead the F Company boys in their attack this morning. Someone else will have to do it now."

"F Company?" Staggs said. "They're the guys that are all around us over here."

"Yes, they are. Second Lieutenant Bussa…one of their platoon commanders…led an attack on Saturday against the bombproof…and he got killed doing it. All their other lieutenants are out of action too…wounded. That leaves Captain Barrett…their CO…as the only officer left. He's wounded too…but not bad enough to knock him out of fight, I guess. He told me that when he landed, he managed to get up against the seawall… and then a Nip grenade suddenly landed on his back. It was a dud…or it would've killed him…or so he thought. Because within seconds another grenade plopped right down on him...and that one went off...but it only wounded him in the legs. He's still walkin' around somehow. I guess he'll lead the attack now...since he can."

As Staggs nodded, Private Jorgenson jumped into the shell hole and landed cleanly...to the chagrin of Staggs...who noted it with a look of nonchalance.

"Now that guy could be a carrier pilot," Wilbanks said, seeing Staggs' look and ribbing him.

Staggs smirked at Wilbanks and turned back to the lieutenant. "So, there's going to be an attack, sir."

"Yeah...it'll probably kick off in an hour. You want in on it," Bonnyman replied...hoping the corporal would say yes...since the more men he had going on it the better.

Staggs, ever the poker player, said, "Well, sir, I would never reveal my hand without knowing what I'm up against. Tell me what y'all got and maybe I'll push all my chips in."

"We're going after that bunker complex one more time. And this time we're gonna take it out. The key to the place is the ventilation shafts...which I saw yesterday afternoon for the first time. The destroyer salvos must have blown the sand away and revealed them to us. That's what I'm going after. And I'm putting a team together do it."

Staggs' interest was tweaked...and it showed. "Go on, sir. I'm likin' what I'm hearin' so far," he said...and he punched Jorgenson in the arm...his exuberance getting the best of him.

The Butcher's Block

First Lieutenant Alexander Bonnyman, Jr. was thirty-three years old and a shore party officer with F Company of the 18th Marine Regiment when he landed on Red Beach 3 on D Day. If everything had gone right...like Captain Joe Clerou...his company commander...had wagered prior to the landing...then Bonnyman's duties would have involved organizing and issuing the supplies to the front-line units as they were delivered to the island. But things had not gone right...and the engineer platoon that was supposed to provide grenadier support...the explosives and demolitions side of the business...to the 2-8 had been decimated during the landing. As a result, Bonnyman and his men...the pioneers...were pressed into action as grenadiers since they had been cross trained in the use and handling of many of the demolitions that the engineers used... especially TNT. But the accurate fire coming from the bunker complex had prevented Bonnyman's men from getting anywhere near it...at least for the first two days of the battle.

"So, here's what we came up with," First Lieutenant Bonnyman said...and he explained the plan that he, Major Chamberlin, and First Lieutenant Elrod had designed. "I'm gonna tie three or four sticks of dynamite together and arm them with a black powder fuse and blasting cap. I'll make six bundles...two for each ventilation pipe that's up there. Sergeant Owens and Corporal Wilbanks will each carry one of the bundles...

and they will go after the ventilation shaft on the left. Me and another one of my Eighteenth engineers...Corporal Niehoff...will carry the other four bundles and we'll go after the shaft in the center and the one on the right. It's that easy."

"How are you going to set the fuses off, sir?" Staggs asked.

"I'm going to use my cigar to light mine off," Bonnyman replied, and then added, "and Owens and Wilbanks can use a cigarette or a cigar...whatever they like...to set theirs off."

Owens glanced at Wilbanks and smiled. "We'll use my cigar on ours too," Owens said, and he patted his shirt pocket where several cigars were resting comfortably.

"So there you have it. Cigars it is," Bonnyman said confidently.

"And where do we fit into this plan of yours, sir?" Staggs asked again, still interested.

"I could use two more men up there with us...just in case one or more of us gets hit. It's no more complicated than that," Lieutenant Bonnyman replied.

"Well, I gotta hand it to you, sir. You don't mince words...and your honesty won me over...so I'll go," Staggs answered and he looked at Jorgenson who was nodding to indicate that he wanted in as well. "Make that...we'll go," Staggs added...and he gave Jorgenson a wink.

"Thanks. I don't anticipate being up there that long. We go up...arm the bundles...toss them into the shafts... and get the hell off the thing. And while we're doing that, we'll have F Company attacking on our left…with G Company supporting them…and K Company attacking to our right. K Company's gonna have two of those thirty-sevens firing in direct support of them and we got several sixty-millimeter mortar teams throwing shells at a coconut-log bunker to the right of the bombproof. F Company has the job of taking out that steel pillbox and the bunker beside it. They've been holding them up for the past two days…and they'll have that Sherman tank for help as well."

"The *Colorado*?" Staggs asked.

"Yup…that's the one. First Lieutenant Largey's commanding it. He's trying to find ammo for it right now," Bonnyman replied.

"His gunner's a buddy of mine. Kingrey…a good man," Staggs said.

Lieutenant Bonnyman shook his head as though he knew the man…but he didn't know Kingrey at all. Then he glanced down at his watch and said, "Okay. So that's it. We're supposed to begin the attack at nine. That gives you about forty minutes to get ready. We'll launch our attack from the seawall…so head over that way as soon as you can."

All four men shook their heads this time…and the lieutenant acknowledged each of them in turn. Then he took off towards the seawall to finalize the details of the attack with Major Chamberlin…who was standing in the open beside Major Crowe and amtrac #23 in the distance.

Major William Chamberlin had been the biggest surprise of all to the men of the Second Battalion, Eighth Regiment. While all of them knew what they were getting when it came to their larger-than-life and hard-charging CO...Major Jim Crowe...very few of them would have anticipated the job that Major Chamberlin was pulling off on Red Beach 3.

No one doubted what Major Crowe stood for or what he wanted done on their next operation. In New Zealand, he had called a meeting to introduce his officers to the new arrivals...both officers and enlisted men alike...to the Second Battalion. When the introductions were over, Major Crowe turned to the new men and issued a challenge: if anyone of them thought he was better than the major, he could join him in the woods outside... where the matter would be settled with a bare-knuckled brawl right then and there. No one took the major up on it.

One correspondent who had spent time with the 2-8 on New Zealand even wrote this about the major: *His men spoke about him reverently, in subdued whispers, as one worthy of the highest respect of man and God.*

Then, in route to Betio, Major Crowe had issued another challenge to his beloved marines: his 2-8 men were going to be the first marines to reach the southern coastline of Betio after they landed on D Day. And he was so sure of it that he bet Lieutenant Colonel

Amey...the battalion CO of the 2-2...a case of whiskey on the outcome of the race.

◈

Major Chamberlin, on the other hand, had been an enigma to the men of the 2-8.

Born in Chicago in 1916, Chamberlin had enlisted in the Marine Corps Reserve in 1936 while he was attending Dartmouth College in New Hampshire. Sensing a higher calling, he took officer classes at Quantico, Virginia for the next two years...and he received his commission while he was graduating as Dartmouth's valedictorian in 1937.

Not to be undone, Chamberlin had then studied for and received a master's degree and a doctorate in economics from Columbia University in 1940...which led to an economics professorship at Northwestern University in Chicago.

Then, in November of 1940, the Marines had called him in...and he gave up his lucrative teaching position and reported for active duty. After serving for a short while as an intelligence officer in Iceland with the Sixth Marines, Chamberlin had served on Guadalcanal where he performed admirably as a staff officer. He had been promoted to major as a result...and in June of 1943 he was transferred to the Eighth Marines... where he was soon teamed with the feisty Major Crowe.

◈

As a former college professor, the reticent Chamberlin seemed to be out of place in the Eighth Marines...and especially so during the voyage to Betio. Aboard the USS *Heywood*...or APA 6...many of the men were silently worrying that their XO wouldn't cut it once the bullets started flying. Based on what they saw, it appeared that Chamberlin was far better suited for the dignified environs of a college classroom than the harsh reality of a modern battlefield.

Tight-lipped by nature, Chamberlin rarely spoke to the men...and when he did, they found him irritating... as if he were teaching students instead of leading men... and teenage boys...who were about to storm an enemy beachhead. He was also a stark disciplinarian...and he enforced arcane rules that no other officer did...like forcing the men to wear their utility shirts while they were out in the open on deck in the oppressive heat. This drove the men crazy...but to Chamberlin's way of thinking, the men were at risk for getting sunburned... and that would lead them to remove their packs to alleviate the pain of the straps cutting into their shoulders instead of keeping them on when they landed on the island. It made perfect sense to him...since that's when the men would need their packs the most...but to the men of the Eighth, he was nothing more than an annoying mother hen and micro-manager whose staunch rule-following was making their lives miserable. And before long, many of his men had taken to calling him *The Old Maid* behind his back. The others... the less sympathetic ones...called him things far worse.

The Butcher's Block

All that changed on D Day, however. Major Chamberlin was slotted to go in with the first three attack waves of the 2-8...while Major Crowe would come in as part of the fourth wave...just like the other two battalion commanders were doing. And it was during the initial landings that Major Chamberlin's warrior side finally emerged.

Unable to catch an amtrac ride in from the reef, Major Chamberlin began wading in...undaunted...just like hundreds of other marines were doing all across the lagoon. In no time at all, Chamberlin began encountering young marines from the 2-8 who were so scared that they refused to move...frozen with fear from the unrelenting Japanese fire coming at them. While machine gun bullets lashed the water around him, the major would make his way over to these paralyzed marines and threaten to shoot them with his .45 caliber pistol if the men remained where they were and didn't begin to advance. This display of bravado shocked the men into action...since they didn't expect it...and they headed in...lest their XO shoot them with his own weapon. But the major didn't stop there; incredibly, he kept right on going with them... willingly exposing himself to all the dangers that they were subjected to as they slogged their way towards Red Beach 3.

And once ashore, the major showed the same distain for the Japanese bullets that were headed his way. Instead of slinking around, Major Chamberlin walked around boldly...issuing orders and positioning the men where he needed them most. Rarely...if ever...did he duck for cover…and in that instant, the men of the 2-8 knew they had a true combat leader in their midst. His fearlessness was catching even…and before long the men around him began vaulting over the seawall to engage the Japanese up close…in their bunkers…where it really counted.

Now the man who had fooled them all on the *Heywood* was standing right beside Major Crowe…and the two of them…the college professor and the barroom brawler…were putting the final touches on their morning attack plan. Both men turned suddenly at the sound of a revving engine and they watched as the *Colorado* churned down the beach towards the Burns-Philip pier.

"It looks like Largey found some ammo," Major Chamberlin noted.

"Yup. I guess he's using some of the same ammo that the pack howitzers are firing," Crowe pointed out.

"Is that possible. Can they fire the same stuff?" Chamberlin asked…never having seen or heard of it being done.

"Yeah. Largey said he could make it work last night after they came up empty looking for their regular tank ammo at the pierhead. These tanks have been really churning through their own ammo trying to destroy these bunkers and we can't get it into the beach fast enough. Largey's incredible though. He knows that M

Four inside and out. He's a mustang officer...like me. We make the best officers," Crowe crowed.

"Aren't you being a little bit full of yourself, sir," Chamberlin shot back...never one to mince words.

"It's not bragging if you can back it up," Crowe answered right away...the confidence he had in himself never an issue.

"Are the artillery rounds just as effective when a tank fires them?" Chamberlin asked. He was confident too... but in a different sort of way: he was extremely competent...but he also knew that he didn't know everything... and he didn't try to fake it when he didn't know something. And it didn't bother him when he didn't know something...since there were always more things to learn. To him, acquiring knowledge and solving problems correctly...based on what you learned from asking... was far more important than being judged by others for revealing your hand when you showed a lack of knowledge about a particular subject.

"Largey says there's a slight drop off in the muzzle velocity of the round...but it blows stuff up just like it's supposed to when it hits whatever it's aimed at."

"Well, that'll definitely help Captain Barrett out," Chamberlin said...knowing that the wounded F Company commander was going to be leading the men he had left in their attack against the beachside steel bunker that had bedeviled them for the last two days.

"I told Barrett to commence his attack at oh nine hundred sharp. Largey's going to head in first." Crowe then glanced at his watch and added, "It's eight thirty-five now. Twenty-five minutes early…but still pretty good timing considering."

"My gut is telling me that this place is finally going to collapse today. I can just feel it in my bones," Major Chamberlin blurted out confidently…caught up with emotion.

"I'm glad you feel that way, Bill…it's about time we put this place to bed. As soon as we're done here, then we'll go after that command bunker further east. Shibasaki's supposed to be in it. I'd love to capture him…if that were possible!"

"He's not gonna let himself get captured…and he certainly won't surrender. And if he's wounded, he'll just have some assistant shoot him…or cut his head off…or run him through with his sword. They pay a much bigger price than we do when they fail at something," Chamberlin asserted…having read a book about Japanese customs on the way to Betio.

"I'd still love to present him as a gift to General Smith if we could capture him. Imagine what that would look like…kind of like when General Cornwallis surrendered to General Washington after losing Yorktown in our revolutionary war." Crowe smiled widely, picturing the scene in his mind. "We've got a couple of cameramen around here that could film it too!"

Crowe's XO frowned instead. "The only problem there, sir, is that Cornwallis didn't surrender to Washington. He sent one of his lackey's out to the surrender ceremony with his personal sword. He didn't have the guts to do it himself. The idea of turning his sword over to that farmer general was so repugnant to him that he stayed behind in his headquarters and wrote letters back to London."

Now it was Crowe's turn to frown. "I thought you were an economics guy. Not a history buff. How'd you know that stuff about Washington and Cornwallis?"

"I read a history book, sir," Chamberlin replied glibly...and the dig drew a laugh from Crowe...which was what Chamberlin intended.

"I like to say that I went to the school of hard knocks...since I've knocked a few heads silly on the football field...and knocked out a few teeth when I needed to too," Crowe replied proudly. "And that reminds me... why don't you get those two cameramen to film your attack on that bunker. It's what they're here for...and they'd probably jump at the chance to do it."

"Great idea, sir," Chamberlin replied...and he ended the meeting saying, "I'm going to head over that way now. I'll probably run into them...and I'll see what they want to do. I'll also check on our right flank. I gave First Lieutenant Elrod the job of coordinating the attack on that end. Let me go see how he's doing."

"Great! I'll manage Barrett over on the left. Elrod was one of my old platoon commanders...when I was a captain in charge of those thirty-seven-millimeter cannons. He'll get the job done on the right. Straight up fighter that one. And we'll meet you in the middle...and then take out that bombproof together!" Crowe then slapped the thin major on the arm...jarring him.

"You got it, sir," Chamberlin croaked out while rubbing his arm...and he made his way back down the seawall...trying to locate Staff Sergeant Hatch and Private

Kelliher...the two combat cameramen who were about to get the offer of a lifetime.

During the next few minutes, Chamberlin was able to find Hatch and Kelliher...and they were thrilled at the idea of filming a marine attack from start to finish. The major then told them to head over to the amtrac...which was the jump-off point for the center attack. Next, he continued down the seawall and found Lieutenant Bonnyman and the five-man team he had put together getting ready. He instructed them to head over to the amtrac as well...and to be ready to go by the time he returned.

He retraced his path...and as he got near the amtrac he hesitated. Now came to dicey part of his mission. He leaped over the seawall and dashed inland about seventy-five yards or so without drawing any fire...a minor miracle if there ever was one. *The Japs must be getting lazy*, he mused, since very few men had been able to cross the taxiway without getting shot at. Winded, he finally stopped at a point along the fractious marine line where First Lieutenant Elrod had positioned two of his thirty-seven-millimeter cannons. These two guns were facing east...in the direction of the bombproof...and a short distance away...where the marine line angled back towards the beach...were the other two 37s. Both of these guns were facing south...in the direction of the main airstrip...and they were commanded by Elrod's platoon sergeant...Staff Sergeant Louis Ramsey. Chamberlin could see other groups of marines strung out along this line... which ran parallel to the beach and it ended near the area where the pierhead reached the island. These were the marines from Major Ruud's Third Battalion...and they had been pinned down for two days as well...just like Crowe's men were along the beach.

"Good to see ya, sir," First Lieutenant Roy Elrod said. "I can't believe not one single Jap took a shot at you on your way over. Maybe they're finally running out of ammunition."

"That would be nice," the major stated, but doubting the suggestion all the while. "So how are things going on this side of the world," he added...since this was his first trip inland.

"Oh...not bad. The Japs we killed on D Day are startin' to stink up the place though. When the wind blows right, you can really catch it from the ones in that tank over there." Elrod then pointed out a derelict Jap *Ha-Go* tank that one of his guns had knocked out on the first day of the battle. Its hull was scorched black near the turret and back deck...where a fire had broken out after it had been hit by two 37mm rounds that had been fired by the cannon commanded by Staff Sergeant Ramsey. "The three crewmen probably didn't make it out. Their bodies must still be inside it...and the sun is basically making the tank an oven...and cooking them up really good. I wasn't here for it...but it doesn't take a genius to figure it out."

The major grimaced at the thought of it...and he almost got sick to his stomach...so he looked away. "Anything else?" he said...trying to compose himself.

"We were able to knock out another one yesterday too...at least it hasn't gone anywhere since we hit it," Elrod said, and he pointed to the two-story, concrete Jap command post building way off in the distance. One of my boys saw it moving around yesterday afternoon and we were able to get several shots off at it. We didn't see anyone get out of it...so they may be dead inside it too... just like the other one out there. You can see it if you look real closely. It's parked right underneath the stairs that lead to the top of the building. It looked like they were backing it in when we started firing at it."

Major Chamberlin squinted since the sun was directly in his eyes. "Oh, yeah. I can see it now. That's some damn good shooting...make sure you congratulate your men on their fine work, lieutenant."

"I will certainly do that, sir. These cannons are deadly accurate when they're zeroed in...and when the crew is well-trained. And my guns are. And my men are the best...every one of them," Elrod said, beaming at the major's compliment.

"Glad to hear it. Now...let's talk about the attack we're going to conduct against that bombproof again. Just so we're on the same sheet of music. F Company and G Company are going to hit its left flank from the beach...down near the Burns-Philip pier. We'll go in as they attack those two supporting positions...the steel-reinforced pillbox nearest them...and then the log bunker in between it and the bombproof. F Company also

The Butcher's Block

has the responsibility for taking care of that machine gun that's on top of the bombproof as well. The one that is firing to the east. Your job is to pin down the Jap machine gun on the other end of the bombproof... the one that is covering the southern side approaches. K Company's got the job of taking out the other log bunker to the right of the bombproof. As soon as we get up there...shift your fire to the right...to assist K Company and to keep any reinforcements from reaching the bombproof. Don't let any Japs get near it from that direction. Once they see that it's under assault...and this time we're going to really mount a serious attack against it...the Japs near the airfield circle are sure to mount a rescue operation. You can't let them succeed if they try. I'm going to have about ten men with me when I head up there. First Lieutenant Bonnyman is responsible for destroying those ventilation shafts that he talked about earlier. We have no idea how many Japs are inside that thing...but we gotta figure there's a lot. When the air shafts are ruined, the men inside will have no recourse but to leave it. And when they do, your next job is to block their escape route to the south. That's it."

Elrod...a serious man to begin with...was listening with keen interest. "We've got enough canister rounds with us to keep kingdom come away from that bunker...if it comes to that. And we'll use it on anyone that abandons it too. And I've already talked to the K Company riflemen that are around us. They're read in on it too. I'll make sure none of your guys are hit by them...trust me."

"Well, good luck then, lieutenant," Chamberlin said, and added, "and don't forget to tell your men what a fine job I think they've done over the last two days. Do that for me…will you."

"I will, sir. Count on it," the steely-eyed Elrod said… and he meant it.

Major Chamberlin slapped the lieutenant on the arm…mimicking his CO…and he headed back to the seawall feeling just as confident about the outcome of the attack he was about to lead as he had felt before giving his doctoral dissertation to the professors at Columbia University in 1940.

Major Chamberlin got back to the seawall with minutes to spare. "Sorry…about…that," he said as he jumped down…huffing and puffing away. The exertion of avoiding Jap snipers on the way back from Elrod's position was…like on the way over…exhausting…and it showed.

Hatch and Kelliher said nothing. They were busy organizing their camera gear and paid scant attention to the major. First Lieutenant Bonnyman noted the XO's condition though and said, "Take a break, sir. We can handle this part of the plan. We got everyone here… and we know what you want done."

"Thank you, lieutenant. I'm fine. I just need to catch my breath. I was just tying up some loose ends with Elrod out there," and the major jerked his thumb over his shoulder…in the direction of Elrod's position.

As he rested, he scanned the group of men Bonnyman had assembled…to see if he recognized any faces among the five of them...but he came up empty. Then...harkening back to his professor's days...he said, "So tell me who we have here, Bonnyman. I like to know the names of the men who are risking their lives with me."

"Oh...of course, sir. Sorry. I just thought we were pressed for time...so I didn't think it mattered," the pioneer officer replied defensively.

"It does matter...at least to me anyway. So fire away," the major answered...schooling the officer gently...but effectively.

And starting with the man farthest from the major, Bonnyman worked his way down the line towards Chamberlin...introducing each man in turn. "This man here is Sergeant Owens...and next to him is Corporal Wilbanks, sir. They're with the Eighteenth Engineers... from my own platoon in fact."

The major nodded at each of them and Bonnyman continued, "That one there is Corporal Staggs. He's with the Second Marines...so he's just visiting us...as is the next man...Private Jorgenson. We're letting them join us on this one so they can go back and tell the rest of their buddies with the Second Marines what a heck of a job the Eighth Marines did over here on Red Three."

The major cut in and said, "We're glad to have the two of you with us. I'm sure the Second could use your help too...but for now...you're with the Eighth."

"We wouldn't wanna be anywhere else, sir," Staggs replied...and for the moment he truly felt that way...while Jorgenson smiled from ear-to-ear...proud as a peacock.

"Last but not least comes Corporal Niehoff...or just Harry...as I call him. He's with the Eighteenth

Engineers...a demolitions man. He helped me rig the charges. He assures me they'll go off...just like they're supposed to...since he's blown up several bunkers with them over the last two days."

Corporal Niehoff touched the brim of his helmet with his index and middle finger of his right hand in a casual salute...and the major nodded right back... acknowledging it.

"That's your team," Lieutenant Bonnyman said... finishing up. "These are the men that have volunteered to storm that bunker with you," he added proudly...the sheer magnitude of what they were about to do lost on no one.

"Thank you, gentlemen. I hope this won't be the last time we're all together. Now let's go get that damn bunker once and for all," the major said, rallying the men one final time before they charged their way into history.

First Lieutenant Bonnyman glanced down at his watch and said, "Eight fifty-five...five minutes to go, boys."

Staggs looked at this own watch and saw that it read eight fifty...five minutes behind. *Probably due to the water damage*, he thought, and he pulled out the pin and adjusted the hands five minutes ahead... to synchronize with Bonnyman's. Then he slid over to the lieutenant...who was sitting next to Sergeant Owens...and said, "So how did you get here, sir? You seem to be a little older than most of the lieutenants I've run in to."

"That's a long story," Bonnyman replied, laughing.

"Well, we've got five minutes or so…you might as well fill me in. At least I'll have a good story to tell my grandkids when this is all over with, right."

Bonnyman looked at Staggs and Owens and said, "You really want to know it…my story?"

"Why wouldn't we?" they said in unison.

"Well, I grew up in Tennessee…near Knoxville."

"No kidding, sir. I'm from Tennessee too. From Columbia," Staggs said, cutting in.

"Another gyrene from the Volunteer State…how about that," the lieutenant replied.

"So how old are you, sir, if you don't mind me asking?"

"I'm thirty-three…which seems a bit odd…since it makes me a lot older than my contemporaries. But there's a reason for that. You see my dad was the president of a big coal company…which means we had it pretty good growing up."

"My dad dug coal for a living too," Staggs threw in…but he decided to leave out the part about his dying from black lung disease…an occupational hazard.

"My dad's company employed a lot of guys…from all over east Tennessee…from middle Tennessee…and from as far away as West Virginia. As I got older though, I wasn't sure what direction I wanted to go in…so I went off to college…to Princeton University of all places. I ran into some pretty smart guys while I was there too. Real geniuses. But I ended up playing football…and

I did pretty well. I made the starting team even...and became a star...but I never finished school. I dropped out after my sophomore year...and then I bounced around a little. After a while, I got it into my head that I wanted to be a pilot...so I joined the Army and I was sent to the Air Corps' pre-flight training in Nineteen Thirty-Two. That didn't work out either...I washed out...and so went my dream of being a pilot. I got discharged...and then decided I'd better head home and see if my dad could use me. I ended up working with him for several years...and I used my experience there to strike out on my own yet again. This time I headed out west...to New Mexico and Colorado...and I ended up prospecting for all sorts of metals...and that led me to buy a copper mine near Santa Fe. That was around Nineteen Thirty-Eight."

"A copper mine?" Staggs asked...and added, "is there good money in that?"

"Great money. Copper's being used in everything nowadays. I can't dig the stuff out fast enough," Bonnyman explained. "And I could have opted out and stayed home...instead of signing up with the military...since I was running a company that was producing what the military called vital material...or strategic material...I can't remember which one they called it. But I couldn't take that route and live with myself. With so many others willing to go off and fight, I figured I had to do my duty as well...which was tough...since I have a wife and three daughters back home."

"You left your family...a wife...and your daughters...to do this?" Staggs asked incredulously.

"Crazy, right! My wife went ballistic when I first told her what I was gonna do...but she eventually understood my decision. That's why I married her in the first place. She's always has my back...which is why I love her so much."

Staggs looked at the lieutenant like he had two heads. "Well, if you were crazy enough to do that...then I'm just crazy enough to tackle this hill with you...and whatever else happens along the way...well, so be it."

Bonnyman smiled...and Staggs could see that this officer had never had a problem attracting the ladies... which made his decision to get married and settle down even more impressive. Then he took a cigar out of his shirt pocket and lit it with a lighter that he pulled out of his pocket as well. He snapped the lighter's cover closed and put it back in the same pocket he took it out of...so he would know exactly where it was if he needed it in a pinch. Then he said, "Well, let's get this show on the road," and he turned and looked for the major...but he was already gone!

"Where'd he go?" the lieutenant yelled out...and the other four men he had picked for his team looked up surprised.

"You mean the major?" Sergeant Owens responded.

"Yes! Where's the major?" Bonnyman yelled again... only louder this time...the sharp crack of the *Colorado's* 75mm main gun echoing off to their left...competing for their attention.

"He got up and left really sudden like. And he took the two cameramen with him. I think he went out on a scout," Owens answered...and he pointed over the seawall.

Bonnyman looked that way...and there...on top of the bombproof was Major Chamberlin and Staff Sergeant Hatch...all alone. Kelliher was below the crest...kneeling and fiddling with a camera stand. "What the hell," Bonnyman mumbled...and then the major and Hatch scrambled back down the hill. In mere seconds, the three men jumped down below the seawall...wild-eyed and out of breath.

"What were y'all doing up there, sir?" Bonnyman asked...the confusion evident in his voice.

"What were we doing? We were attacking the bombproof! That's why we're here. I gave the order to go...and I expected it to be obeyed. When I got up there...the only men with me were these two cameramen...and neither one of them was armed. And neither was I! I gave my rifle away...during the landing...and I left my damn forty-five back here by mistake!" With that, the major reached over by the edge of the seawall and picked his .45 caliber pistol up from the ground. "It must have fallen out of my holster," he said sheepishly.

"Nobody here," and Bonnyman pointed to his group, "heard you give the order to go, sir."

"Oh, what the hell. I thought everybody was ready...so I gave the order. When we got there, the top was clear. Then about twenty Japs came out of a door and they just stared up at us. I guess they were as shocked to see us as we were to see them!"

The Butcher's Block

"Well, we're ready now, sir," Bonnyman said confidently. "Just give the word!" he added, and then a huge explosion rang out...from the vicinity of the bomb proof...and the men could see a cloud of thick, dark smoke rising in the air...not far away.

First Lieutenant Elrod could hear the mortar crews cheering behind him...so it must've been one of their rounds that caused all the damage...or at least they thought so. The smoke that was boiling up in the distance supported their contention...so he waved to one of the crew...and he came hustling over. "What happened?" he asked.

The 60mm mortarman from K Company...Corporal Guy Reidel...broke into a big smile and said, "We were dropping our rounds all around that log bunker...the one on the right...and damned if we didn't obliterate it. Johnny Rutherford...my tube man...thinks he hit an ammo dump near it...or maybe a fuel dump. Whatever it was, when it went up, it took the bunker right along with it! That clears the way for the rest of the boys to finally circle around the bombproof from the east now!"

The man's excitement was contagious...and even Elrod smiled now. "Okay, go tell your CO to be ready to go at my signal!"

"You got it, sir," the corporal said...full of energy now. Incredibly, it was ten minutes after nine when he dashed away to carry out his new assignment.

Over on the left...near the Burns-Philip wharf, the *Colorado* was having the same kind of success. With the F Company men providing covering fire, the tank clanked down the beach and pulled to the right...its farthest advance yet. Under the cover of the seawall, the tank gunner...Corporal Ed Peterson...began pumping armor-piercing rounds directly into the steel-covered pillbox.

"Keep it up, Ed!" First Lieutenant Lou Largey yelled over the tank intercom, "we got 'em now!"

As smoke began to pour out of the conical structure, a group of engineers rushed up and heaved several satchel charges against its sides. The resulting explosions caved the sides of the pillbox in and the Japanese defenders inside were killed before they could retaliate. Seconds later, the small bunker next to it was destroyed with hand grenades by the marine engineers as well. Incredibly...at fifteen minutes after nine...the western approach to the bombproof that had been so troublesome for two days was finally free and clear as well.

The only structure left was the sand-covered bombproof in the center...the very same one that had blocked the marine advance for the last two days. And the very same one that Major Chamberlin and his six cohorts were about to attack. "This is it, men," Chamberlin said sternly...the moment of truth finally at hand.

"Say when," Lieutenant Bonnyman stated...ready this time.

Then, out of nowhere it seemed, a marine...PFC Joe Lucas...came scrambling over to them from the right. "Sir!" he screamed, "Major Crowe wants you to hold up!"

The major looked incredulous...as if he had seen a ghost. "He wants me...to hold up? For God's sake why?" he stammered.

"The major wants you to know that both the left and right flanks around the bunker have fallen. He's ordered Captain Barrett to advance F Company beyond the bombproof...to cut it off from the east. And he's got K Company under Captain Odom doing the same on the other side of it. He thinks you'll have an easier go of it if the place is surrounded."

Major Chamberlin considered what the man was telling him, and he relaxed slightly...knowing the order made sense. "Okay," he said, "tell the major that we'll wait...like he wants...but make sure he knows that we're all set to go over here. We can go whenever he wishes... but the sooner the better. Tell him that."

The private first class nodded and dashed off...kicking up sand in his wake. Running upright now, Lucas made good time...and in a minute he was back at the pierhead...where Major Crowe was now. He quickly relayed Major Chamberlin's message...and then he headed out towards the taxiway...so he could tell Captain Odom to keep pushing east...just like Major Crowe wanted.

Three hours later, Major Chamberlin's patience had just about worn out. "Damnation," he uttered to no one in particular...totally frustrated. And that's when Major Crowe's runner showed up again...but this time the news was less favorable. "Major Crowe wants you to know that Captain Barrett is having trouble moving down past the bombproof on the left. There's a whole tangle of foxholes and bunkers...and the Japs aren't budging. Captain Odom has had more success on the right, but he's starting to take flank fire from his right...so he held up too. The major says that you can go ahead with your attack...if you think it's advisable."

"If I think it's advisable, huh," Major Chamberlin said, repeating Major Crowe's words...as the runner had stated them.

"Yes, sir. Those were his words...or that's what he wanted me to convey to you at least."

"Okay, go back and tell the major that I find it advisable...and that I will be attacking in about five minutes," the XO said sharply.

The other six men had listened to the exchange expectantly and they began checking their weapons yet again as the runner turned and sprinted off.

"Change of plans, men," Major Chamberlin said quickly...his mind at work.

The men stopped what they were doing and eyed the major suspiciously...wondering what he was thinking.

"Listen up. Instead of attacking the bunker from here...head on...we're going to move down to the left about fifty yards. I've been down that way before...with F Company...and there's a wood fence that runs up to the base of the bunker. It's about seven feet high...and it's held in place by coconut logs...like everything else around here is. It's L shaped…and it offers decent cover and concealment…even from the machine gun nests up top. And it's only about twenty feet from the seawall…so we won't be exposed for that long as we approach the bunker…like we would be from here. Sound good," the major said…and everyone nodded in agreement.

"I know the fence you're talking about," Lieutenant Bonnyman acknowledged. "We couldn't get to it before… but we can now since F Company has taken out that pillbox near the beach. All we'll have to deal with is those machine guns on the corners. It's perfect."

"Then that's the plan…so let's go," the major ordered…and everyone began heading down to the left along the seawall. They passed several dead marines lying on the beach along the way…by the Burns-Philip pier…and then they stopped when they reached the tall, wood fence that the major had mentioned.

"Hey, check this out," Sergeant Owens said suddenly, and he pointed to two men wearing bulky-looking, cylinder-shaped tanks heading their way. They were coming from the direction of F Company…which was further down the beach.

"Is Major Chamberlin here," one of the men said as they slid in and took a knee along the seawall…sweat dripping from his face.

"I'm Chamberlin," the major said, his lack of rank and haggard look making him hard to identify.

"Sir, Captain Barrett sent us back. He's thinks we can do better here than up ahead with him. He said you guys are going after that bombproof…and you could probably use our flame throwers when you attack it."

"Captain Barrett's right. We can definitely use you. How are you fixed for fuel?" Chamberlin asked.

Both men smiled. "We're almost completely full, sir. No worries there," PFC Borich…a flamegunner from the 18th Engineers replied confidently.

"Good to see y'all again, Johnny," First Lieutenant Bonnyman said, slapping his fellow engineer on the arm.

"We thought you were dead, sir. We saw your boat get hit and thought no one made it out." Borich looked both shocked…that he was alive…and happy…that he was alive…all at once.

"Me, Wilbanks, and Owens here are the only ones that made it out alive. Sheer luck, right!" Bonnyman said jauntily…and the men exchanged pleasantries… glad to see one another finally.

"Well, me and Ski here are ready to help out. Show us what you want blasted and we'll do it," Borich said, and he patted Private Andrew Ruszkowski…who was from a different unit…on the shoulder. Both the men's uniforms were soaked with sweat and covered in dust…a result of having hauled the duel-tanked, seventy-pound flame-thrower weapons around on their backs for the last two and a half days.

Now Wilbanks spoke up…and the men looked towards the pier…where he was pointing. "We got some more reinforcements comin' in, sir."

Jogging down the seawall was a squad of eleven marines…a welcome sight indeed. As soon as they pulled up, the squad leader spoke up. "Captain Odom sends his compliments. I'm Corporal Harris…G Company…at your service, sir."

The Butcher's Block

"Don't that beat all. I've got myself a small army of here now," Major Chamberlin said happily. The major then explained how he intended to storm the bombproof...and when he was done, Harris turned to a private first class and barked out, "White...you go right with your four guys...I'll take my five to the left."

The major then looked the assembled group of marines over one last time...and he knew some of them might not be coming back. *What men,* he thought to himself, *and what an honor it is to lead them*...and with that, he jumped up on the seawall and screamed, "Follow me, men!"

All twenty-two men rushed forward...with Major Chamberlin leading the way. They dodged through the debris littering the ground ahead of them and then they squeezed themselves up against the wood siding of the fence...wondering if the Japs above had seen them. This part of the fence ran parallel to the bombproof...and when no fire came their way, Major Chamberlin peeked around the corner and scanned the top of the bombproof. Incredibly, the top appeared clear...empty of Japanese...at least for the moment. "Let's go, men," the major yelled...and he ran down the section of the fence that pointed directly at the bombproof. He stopped when he reached the base of the bombproof...near the end of a wooden foot ladder that ran up the side of the sand-covered bunker...and he turned quickly around to face the oncoming marines. He pointed up the slope...and

PFC Borich...along with Sergeant Owens and Corporal Wilbanks...began drudging their way up the sandy hill. As Borich neared the top, he saw two *rikusentai* scrambling across the roof of the bunker towards him. In a flash, they were gone ...having vanished as if they were ghosts. Then Borich saw the muzzle of a machine gun swinging his way from the corner of the building...and he let out a blast of fire from his flame thrower.

Although Borich couldn't see it, the two *rikusentai* had slid into a two-man hole that they had fashioned on the rooftop at the northwestern corner of the bombproof for just this kind of emergency.

Months before, the Japanese engineers on the island had worked around the clock to camouflage and protect the building - it held the island's power plant - from the preying eyes...and bombs...of the American heavy bombers that had suddenly appeared overhead. To that end, they had piled tons of sand on top of and around the concrete building...which made it resemble a small hill instead of an actual building. And since the sand was deep enough to dig through...the gunner and his loader had scooped out shallow holes at the corners and piled excess sand around the building's edges...thus creating a rampart of sorts...and four effective fighting positions at the corners of the bombproof. The ramparts were thick enough to afford the men up top a decent amount of protection...since the sand absorbed most of the bullets that were fired at them as they crawled from

The Butcher's Block

one position to the next to ward off an incoming attack. And they were also built high enough around the gun positions that the men could kneel in their holes and still fire their machine gun accurately while only exposing the tops of their helmets...a small target at best. These positions had served them so well in fact that the marines had been thwarted from taking the bombproof from the north and the west sides for the first two days of the battle.

—◆—

All that changed when PFC Johnny Borich squeezed the trigger on his flamethrower, however. A liquid stream of red flame jetted out and it totally engulfed the corner of the building...incinerating everything in its path... including the *rikusentai* machine gunner and his loader. The stream of flame also touched off several small fires as loose palm fronds and empty ammo boxes began to burn along with the bodies of the two Japanese men who had been killed...and greyish smoke began to swirl around...obscuring the roof of the bunker.

Borich backed down the slope slightly...waiting to see what would happen...and then he advanced up again...with Niehoff, Owens and Wilbanks beside him this time. As he neared the top, Borich saw more Japs heading for them from the far side...and he yelled out a warning that they were coming.

Niehoff didn't need to be told what to do. Without thinking twice, he reached up and took a lit cigar out of his mouth and set it against the end of the fuse that led to one of the bundles of TNT that he had assembled earlier. The fuse ignited and he held it tightly while counting silently to himself. At three he hurled the bundle with all his might over the lip of the rampart towards the far corner of the bombproof and knelt down. Wilbanks then moved over...nudged him...and stuck his bundle out. Without a word, Niehoff lit his fuse as well. Just like Niehoff had done, Wilbanks counted the seconds off slowly as the fuse sparked, and at three he threw his TNT bundle up and over towards the corner nearest them. Both bundles exploded violently within seconds of each other...and more smoke, sand, and dust were thrown into the air...which further obscured the top of the bunker.

The double explosions seemed to galvanize the rest of the men who were assembled down below...and Bonnyman turned towards Owens and said, "Forget the pipes...we'll use the flamethrowers for that. Use your charges on the roof...and along the sides and front!"

"Aye aye, sir!" Owens shouted as he removed the cigar from his mouth...and in seconds he had hurled his sparking bundle onto the roof as well. More explosions followed...and the rest of the marines...no longer anxious...stormed up the hill like ants on a jelly sandwich. One marine, kneeling beside a wooden box of hand grenades that he had dragged up the hill with him, began handing the grenades out to the marines nearby...and they threw them towards the eastern side of the bunker and up onto the roof as well.

The Butcher's Block

As the grenade explosions continued to erupt on the bunker's roof, First Lieutenant Bonnyman began edging his way up towards the top of the slope…so he could see what the Japs were up to. When he reached the parapet, he looked over at the far side of the bombproof and he could see at least forty *rikusentai* pushing their way out of a doorway that was hidden on the southeast corner of the bombproof down below. They had been forced out of the bunker seconds before…when PFC Borich and Private Ruszkowski began spraying their liquid fire into the bunker's black, T-shaped ventilation pipes to burn up everything inside…especially the air…which the Japs needed to breath to stay alive.

Now outside…the Japs turned around and they quickly spotted Bonnyman standing up there all alone… staring back at them. Crazed and filled with a desire to kill, the *rikusentai* began charging up the far side of the bunker so they could kill the arrogant American and retake their building.

Bonnyman saw the Japs charging…and he held his ground…refusing to budge. "Here they come!" he yelled out…and he slapped a fresh magazine into his M-1 carbine. Firing as fast as he could, he was able to drop some of the enemy…and then his rifle was empty. He reached down to his web belt as fast as he could and pulled out another fresh clip of fifteen rounds from his ammo pouch as bullets whistled by…just missing him. Then he rammed the clip home and started firing again…but this time his luck changed…and a bullet slammed into his chest…killing him instantly. As he slumped over, Sergeant Owens, Corporal Niehoff, Corporal Staggs, and Private Jorgenson charged up the hill along with some of the G Company men and they engaged the Japs with their M-1 rifles. Niehoff, meanwhile, reached down and checked the lieutenant's carotid pulse to see if he was alive.

"The lieutenant's done for," Niehoff yelled out…and several more marines fell by his side…some wounded…and some dead…just like the lieutenant. Without a thought, Niehoff reached into his explosives bag and pulled out yet another bundle of TNT. He lit it and heaved the bundle into the midst of the Japs…and the powerful explosion did the trick. The rest of the Japs…the ones that had survived the blast…maybe five at best…turned around and scampered back down the slope…their ears ringing…but out of the line of fire.

Major Chamberlin was still down below…giving orders to the marines near the bombproof's base…when he saw Lieutenant Bonnyman fall. Without thinking, he charged up the slope to lend a hand to Owens and Niehoff…but he arrived too late to do any good. But looking around, he could sense that the momentum had finally swung in the marines' favor…and he called the rest of his force up. These men…and some others that had happened by and joined the fray…swarmed up the slope and they all jumped onto the roof…just as Owens, Niehoff, Staggs, and Jorgenson had done.

The Butcher's Block

"Spread out!" Major Chamberlin yelled...and the men quickly divided themselves up so all four corners and sides of the bombproof's rooftop were now covered...giving the marines the high ground...what little there was of it...for the very first time in the battle.

―✦―

First Lieutenant Elrod could see the smoke and feel the explosions erupting on the roof and along the front and sides of the bombproof and he told his gunners to get ready. His instincts were spot on...and at one in the afternoon one of the two hidden doors on the bombproof slammed open. Elrod saw about a platoon's worth of *rikusentai* pour out of it and then they reversed course and slogged their way up the side of the bombproof to attack Chamberlin's marines that must have reached the top from the other side. Seconds later, a much smaller group came scampering back down...and they headed east...and away from Elrod's cannons...towards the tail of the island...where the Japanese remained in force.

"Steady, boys," Elrod yelled out, "there may be more of them in there," as he and his men continued to eye the action taking place around the bombproof...up ahead and to their left...no more than two hundred yards away.

Then...just like he had anticipated...another group came out...only this one was larger...totaling about a hundred men in all. Instead of heading east though, these men began running towards the southern coastline...where the Japs were still entrenched as well. Their route couldn't have been worse though...since it led them right into the target lanes of two of Lieutenant Elrod's 37mm cannons...which were already loaded with cannister rounds.

These two cannons had made quick work of another group of rikusentai who had tried to reach the bombproof late in the afternoon of D Day. And they had employed the same type of ammo to do it: the cannister round...which was basically a large shotgun shell that contained one hundred and twenty-two pellets the size of a .38 caliber bullet. When the round was fired, the cannister encasing the pellets broke away and the pellets spread out...just like a shotgun round would. It was a devastating weapon to use against attacking infantry because it cut wide swathes through the group it was fired at...killing and maiming large numbers of men in one fell swoop.

At just the right time, Elrod ordered his two guns to fire...and the initial rounds did terrible damage to the Japanese trying to escape southward. Scores of *rikusentai* were knocked down...some being wounded by one pellet alone...while others were killed when several pellets hit their bodies all at once.

Elrod's two crews worked quickly...loading the cannons with ease...used to the drill...and they fired several more volleys at the departing Japanese before they were out of range. Thinking they were done, the crews relaxed for a moment...but then a lone *rikusentai* who was hiding in the brush got up and charged the two-gun position...all on his own. One of the gun crews still had a round in the chamber of their cannon...and when the Jap got within fifty yards of their position, they cut loose. Elrod watched as the round went right through the man's mid-section...separating his upper body... his head, shoulders, and chest...from his lower body... his waist and legs. The two separate parts of the Jap attacker kept coming on though...his momentum carrying the two body sections forward before they fell into the sand with a thud.

"I'm gonna have bad dreams about that one," Elrod said to the gun crew morosely...the sight of the Jap's body tearing apart fixed in his mind.

"Don't worry about him, sir," one of the younger members of the gun crew...PFC Rick Olson from Western Massachusetts...said coldly, "we just saved him from having to commit *hari kari*...that's all."

"Yeah, sir. Don't worry about it," PFC Tom Stolz...a Colorado mountain climber...chimed in. "You'll never get any sleep if you start thinkin' about all the Japs we've killed...both here and on the *Canal*," the lanky, blond-haired marine added...agreeing with his buddy.

"Old Stolz's right, sir," Olson continued...and he held up his right hand and started counting off on his fingers. "We probably knocked down about a hundred Saturday...maybe more...and there's gotta be another hundred or so right out in front of us now. That makes something like over two hundred dead. You're gonna have a lot of bad dreams if you start thinkin' that way... so don't do it." Olson then nodded at Stolz...to confirm his contention.

"Don't forget about the three dead ones in that tank over there," Stolz said, and he pointed to the disabled Jap tank off to their right.

"Stolz's right again, sir. Make that two hundred and three," Olson maintained...and Stolz nodded in agreement with a wink of his eye.

"So, no bad dreams then, right, sir?" Stolz added... protective of his lieutenant.

The lieutenant looked at the two marines...buddies... Stolz and Olson...and smiled inwardly. *Good kids these boys of mine*, he thought proudly. *They do a job that nobody else wants to do...and they do it happily...without a complaint even... and they try their best to take care of me. God bless these kids.*

First Lieutenant Elrod knew that most marines...at least the sane ones...would refuse the opportunity to serve on a 37mm gun crew...especially in combat...since the weapon was so potent. The marines had learned on Guadalcanal that the Japs trained their men to find and take out the American automatic weapons first...like a .30 caliber machine gun or a BAR...since they caused the most casualties. A 37mm cannon attracted even more enemy attention then...since its cannister shells were so devastating in the close confines of the jungle... and the Japs would try to knock it out before doing anything else.

And the gun shield that sat in front of the 37mm cannon was not that large...so it didn't really provide the necessary protection that a shield should have. Most of the time, the gunners and other crew members were forced to look over the shield to see their targets...which exposed their heads and upper bodies to the incoming enemy fire. So, nobody in their right mind would sign up to be on a 37mm gun crew...which was what made Elrod's men so special to him.

"No...no bad dreams. I promise," Lieutenant Elrod said...and he reached into his utility shirt pocket and he took out two cigars. He handed them over to Stolz and Olson and said, "I was saving these for something special...and now I want you to have them."

"Geez," Stolz said...since he loved smoking cigars. "Thanks, sir!"

Olson took his and put it in his shirt pocket. "I'm gonna save mine for when we're back aboard ship, sir. I don't want to smoke a fine cigar like this while wearing these dirty, nasty clothes I got on. A good shower...and then a good cigar. Now that's the life," Olson said...and he winked at Stolz to celebrate the moment.

A few minutes after the second group of Japs left the bombproof, another group of *rikusentai* were forced to bail out as well...the flamethrower work of PFC Borich and Private Ruszkowski having created a living hell inside the bunker. This group emerged out of the northeastern door however...and they numbered nearly a hundred men as well. And like the five men who had survived the fighting on top of the bombproof...these *rikusentai* headed straight east too...towards the tail and safety...or so they thought.

The two combat correspondents had their hands full the entire time. Standing beside Major Chamberlin,

Staff Sergeant Hatch had filmed almost the entire attack with his hand-held movie camera from the base of the sand-covered structure. While he was doing that, Private Kelliher had set up a stationary camera site back by the wooden fence...and he filmed the whole attack as well. Now...with things finally settling down... Hatch had moved back to the fence line and taken a break.

"I can't believe we got it all," Hatch said to Kelliher... and the two men embraced...glad to be alive.

Hatch then removed his reel and handed it to Kelliher. "Store this away safely," he said...and then he put another fresh reel into his camera, and he moved down the fence line towards the east...to see if he could get any good shots from that angle.

He noticed a marine rifleman kneeling at the end of the fence and he went over to him. The marine glanced up and smiled...his face smeared with dust...his uniform caked with dirt and sand after crawling around for two and a half days in combat.

"Anything happening on this end?" Hatch asked... and the man shrugged...to indicate that nothing of importance was occurring at the moment.

Then...suddenly...the two men heard a commotion of sorts off to their right...and they saw a large group of Japs coming out of a hidden door on the northeastern corner of the bunker. The Japs gathered together and stood there...as if wondering what they should do...and then they dashed in ones and twos towards the tail of the island as the marines on top of the bombproof took them under fire.

The Butcher's Block

Hatch whipped his camera up to his shoulder and sighted in through the view finder. He was standing far enough behind the kneeling marine that he had captured him in the frame as well...and then the Japanese began streaming by...some crouching over...some just hunching their shoulders...as the marine bullets whipped past them...blowing up clouds of dust as they struck the ground around them. The marine continued to fire his M-1 carbine at the Japs...his shoulder recoiling as he pulled the trigger...but none went down...at least it didn't look like it.

Breathless, Hatch lowered his camera and wiped the lense clean. "I can't believe it," he finally said...and the marine with the carbine turned around to look at him.

"Can't believe what?" the man asked...wiping sweat from around his dust-smeared mouth. He smiled now...the man's teeth gleaming despite the grit on them...and he added, "You can't believe that I missed every one of them, right?"

"No...not that all. I can't believe I got both you and the Japs in the same frame. I don't think anyone has ever done that before...having the enemy and the friendly forces in the same shot."

"I guess I woulda been famous if I had managed to hit one of them at least," the marine said dejectedly, and looking at the cameraman he added, "Oh, well...I'm alive at least."

"You're going to go down in history nonetheless, son," and Hatch patted the marine on the shoulder to buck him up.

"Yeah, sure. I can just hear the boys now. Here come's 'ol deadeye," he said, mimicking what his buddies would say when they saw him coming.

"Oh, don't worry about it. When we get back home... every girl in your hometown is gonna wanna be seen with you. You'll be the cat's meow...trust me, son," Hatch offered up...trying to make the kid see the glass half full instead of half empty.

"Ya really think so?" the marine asked expectantly.

"Think so...I know so. Women love men in movies...and you're going to be showing up in every theater across the Country once the big wigs back in New York see this clip."

"Holy mackerel," the marine replied, finally understanding the implications of what would happen once the public saw the film.

"I'm convinced the public really wants to see what's going on out here...and the stuff I've shot so far is really going to open their eyes. When they see what you boys have been through...the war will never be the same," Hatch explained...and then he bade farewell to the marine and headed for the rear...to the pierhead...so he could get his precious film off the island and into the right hands as soon as possible.

While the *rikusentai* may have dodged the lone marine's carbine fire right outside the bunker, they were about to run into far bigger trouble the further east they went. For unbeknownst them, F Company and *Colorado* had moved down past their bombproof...and the marines were lying in wait for them as they came into the open.

"Fire," Captain Barrett yelled out...and the remaining men of F Company...about ninety survivors in all...let loose with everything they had as the one hundred or so Japs stumbled into their ambush. The rifle and BAR fire of the marine riflemen was relentless enough...but then the *Colorado* began firing its cannister rounds and that really broke the back of the Japanese who thought they had escaped. After thirty minutes, it was over...and not a single Jap was left alive...the cannister rounds having done their vicious and deadly work just like they were designed to.

Major Chamberlin watched as the men...Corporal Staggs...Private Jorgenson...Corporal Wilbanks...and Sergeant Owens...brought him down from the top of the bombproof. They had slid First Lieutenant Bonnyman's bloody body onto a poncho and each man was on a corner now...struggling with the load as they gingerly made their way down the slope...the sand giving way with each step they took. The men stopped when they reached the base, and they lowered the body gently to the ground. Major Chamberlin came over and looked at the corpse solemnly...his friend's face barely recognizable now from the damage inflicted on the body as it lay defenseless in the open on top of the bombproof. The Japanese defenders had thrown a slew of grenades at the marines during the battle for the summit...and many of them had landed right next to Bonnyman when he slumped over after being hit with a rifle bullet. At one point, Corporal Harry Niehoff had actually pulled his body down and then crawled between it and a dead *rikusentai*...using them as a shield of sorts to protect himself from the grenade explosions and shrapnel that whizzed by.

"Anybody want to say anything," Chamberlin asked quietly...looking at the men one at a time.

No one replied at first...but then Private Jorgenson spoke up. "I'd like to, sir, if it's okay."

"Go right ahead, private. We're honored that you've offered to do it," the major answered, and everyone nodded their assent and removed their helmets.

The private cleared his parched throat...the dust and smoke still swirling around them...and he tried to think of a Bible verse that would apply...but his mind went blank suddenly. *You got this then, Holy Spirit,* he thought silently...and with that he spoke from his heart. "The man laying before us, Lord, is now up there with You...in Heaven...praising You with all Your angels. We were privileged to know this man for just a short while, Lord...and I am sure that You have welcomed him home, along with all our other brothers who made their glorious journey home today. May the memory of this brave man remain with us forever...and we hope and pray that we will see him again one day...and You too, Lord...who reigns over Heaven and earth. Amen."

The Butcher's Block

The men looked at each other silently...nodding their approval...and then Major Chamberlin put his helmet back on...the signal that the service was finished.

"Semper Fi, lieutenant," Corporal Wilbanks said... and he, Staggs, and the major walked away. Then Jorgenson put his helmet back and he turned and left... leaving Sergeant Owens alone with the lieutenant.

"I'll let your wife and girls know what happened, sir. Don't you worry about that, okay," Owens said sadly...and then he walked away too...as several more marine bodies were brought in and laid down beside the dead officer...their home now Heaven...just like the lieutenant's.

Jorgenson saw Staggs sitting down...his back and head resting against the side of the fence...and he sat down next to him. The corporal...whose eyes were closed... sensed it was Jorgenson...and he rolled his head forward and let his helmet drop into his lap. "Geez, I'm tired," he breathed out as he turned and looked at Jorgenson...the strain of two and a half days' worth of fighting etched across his face.

"Me too," Jorgenson replied, shifting his body into a comfortable position.

"I thought I was gonna get killed back there," Staggs said slowly, and added, "whatta 'bout y'all?" Occasionally, Staggs' southern twang would kick in...like it was now.

"I felt a few bullets go right past me...and when those grenades started exploding, I felt for sure that I'd get hit by some shrapnel...but it all missed me somehow...

just like during the landing two days ago. I gotta be honest, I prayed a lot while we were up there…silently…to myself. It was just God and me up there…and I think He took care of the both of us too…since we're sittin' here and not laid out over there." Both Jorgenson and Staggs glanced to their left…and they could easily see the line of dead marines lying near the base of the bombproof… some under ponchos…some not.

"That's what I wanna talk to you about…it's about that relationship with the man upstairs y'all have. You see…I was sort of praying too…and I felt something happen up there…and I think it's time that I got my ducks in a row with God. Can you help me with that?"

Jorgenson looked at Staggs and he could see that the corporal really meant it…that he was serious in his request. "Sure, I can help you with that. It's not that hard really…although most people think it is."

"So, what do I do?" Staggs asked…the same question that many others had asked over the last nineteen hundred years of so.

"Well, let me put it to you this way. When Martin Luther was confronted with the same problem…he searched through the Bible…looking for something that would help him with his dilemma. He was trying to figure out if the Church in Rome was right…that you could do things to remove sin from your life…like making donations to the church…for instance. He was arguing against this practice at the time…and that put him at odds with the church, obviously. Something told him this practice was wrong…but he had to have proof that his contentions were spiritually correct…that he wasn't doing this to satisfy his own ego and vanity. He found his answer in the Book of Ephesians. Chapter Two...Line Eight."

Staggs was following his every word...and he asked, "What does that line say? I never did spend enough time reading ours...the Bible we had at home...when I was there."

"It says that we are saved by God's grace...through our faith in Jesus Christ alone. This means that God gave us Jesus as a gift...and that it is up to us to believe in Him...and what He did for us on the cross and through His resurrection. We can either accept it...or reject it...just like any other gift that someone might want to give you."

Staggs made a quizzical expression and said, "You're saying that all we have to do is believe...and that's how we're saved? What about all the bad decisions I've made...and all the bad things I've done in my life. They just go away? It's gotta be more complicated than that?"

"The world thinks there's more to it than that...but it isn't...and that's the beauty of it! In fact, Line Nine says that our works...the stuff we try to do to gain favor with God...don't really work. In fact, our works...or good deeds...make God angry...if we try to use them as a bargaining chip to get ourselves into Heaven. If it did work that way, then our salvation would be left up to us...by the good works we did...and we could brag about it... instead of just accepting God's grace. And when Luther understood those two lines...his life...and mission changed. Do you see that?" Jorgenson wished he had his Bible with him...so he could show Staggs the lines...

but it was stored inside his pack...which was now lying beside the seawall...right where he had left it before the attack began.

"I sorta see it. What about John...Three Sixteen? I think that's the one. I always heard the churchgoers... the regulars...throw that line around like it was the gospel truth or something. They could quote that line without looking at their Bibles."

"That's an extremely important line too. I'll show it to you when we get back to the seawall. And another one...Acts Chapter Two...Line Thirty-Eight. That's real important too. And easy to understand."

"So, do I have to become a Bible lover like you? I mean you just threw those lines out there like you've studied it all your life. I'm not a big reader...never have been. How am I going to learn this stuff if I don't get into it like you do?" Staggs was making genuinely good points...and Jorgenson appreciated it.

"Don't worry about the details, corporal," Jorgenson replied. " Just turn your life over to God...by loving and serving His Son...and everything else will just fall into place on its own. That's basically what Matthew, Chapter Six, Line Thirty-Three says. Seek first the Kingdom of God and all His Righteousness...and all else will be added to you. It's that simple!

Listen...coming to this island...you told me to trust you...that you'd take care of me. Well, I did...and I'm still alive because I did. I'm just asking you to do the same now...but to just trust in God instead of your own instincts this time around. And if you do, just watch what happens."

Staggs smiled now...picturing their trek in...and everything else that had happened since. "Okay, kid. I'll see your call...and I'm going to push all my chips in. I never did anything halfway...and I'm not gonna start now. I'm gonna turn my life over to Jesus...just like you said...and I'll let God deal the cards from here on out. Sound good?"

Jorgenson glanced upwards now...and a wonderful feeling came over him. "That does sound good," he said confidently to the corporal, "and I'll bet ya another thing. I bet that Lieutenant Bonnyman is smiling now too...up there in Heaven...knowing that he played a role in your decision. I even bet he'd do it all over again too... so you could be saved," Jorgenson added...and he let his head rest against the wall...beaming from ear to ear.

Chapter Twenty-Eight

Once the bombproof fell, the only thing left for 8th Marines to deal with was the huge, two-story headquarters building that sat two hundred yards away...slightly southeast of where they were now.

As a bulldozer pulled up to push sand against the two steel doors of the bombproof...sealing it for good...Major Crowe's and Major Ruud's marines began circling Shibasaki's CP...anticipating a fight. But the *rikusentai* in the area had retreated inside...knowing the end was near. Incredibly, no fire met the advancing marine ranks...and they were able to get within throwing range of the building itself.

Several engineers crept up and armed a satchel charge. With the pinpoint accuracy of a big league pitcher, one of the engineers threw the charge with all his might. It hit the ground and bounced right up against the steel door that was next to a Japanese *Ha Go* tank...which seemed to be abandoned...since it never engaged the marines as they advanced against it. The charge exploded with a loud *crummmphhh*...and the door caved in...but it remained standing...dangling from one lone hinge.

"What was that?"

"It was nothing, Jinzo. Relax," Petty Officer Tadashi Koshio replied as he soothed his driver by wiping his brow...which was bathed in sweat. He continued to ignore the bullets that were hitting the steel door only feet away.

The two tank crewmen...Petty Officer Tadashi Koshio and Seaman Second Class Jinzo Yoshizawa...were sitting in the hallway inside the headquarters building... with the rest of the badly wounded...by the door that was near their tank. They had moved inside the building the day before...after their tank was hit when it returned from a mission that had taken it to the tail of the island.

Yoshizawa...the driver...had been backing the tank into position...so its main 37mm cannon faced outwards...when several rounds had slammed into its engine...located behind him...and the hull around him. Whoever had fired the rounds was very good...since the engine had been damaged beyond repair. The tank was going nowhere now...and the three crew members had been wounded as well...by the shrapnel from the explosive rounds that hit the hull of the tank. The tank had not caught fire though...which was every tanker's nightmare...but Koshio had ordered the crew to abandon it anyway...since they were all sporting wounds to some degree or another. Koshio and Yoshizawa had been riddled with metal fragments…while Kubo had been hit in his right shoulder only…a stroke of luck. None of the wounds were life-threatening…but manning a tank that couldn't move…while bleeding from shrapnel wounds and ousing sweat from every pore from the heat inside the tank…which made the shrapnel wounds sting even more…was no way to fight a war…at least to Koshio's way of thinking.

Now the two men were sitting alongside the others…men who were terribly wounded…some disfigured beyond imagination…and the longer they sat there…the worse it got.

"It sounds like the marines are getting close," Yoshizawa said…dreading the thought.

"They might be. But this building is solidly built. I imagine Commander Horii is gathering men right now as we speak. He'll initiate an attack any moment…trust me," his tank commander replied…hoping he was right.

Commander Horii…Admiral Shibasaki's Chief of Staff…had abandoned the building the night before with the rest of his senior officers so he could direct the battle from the tail of the island. Someone had said that there were nearly a thousand men still there…ready to do battle with the marines who were moving closer to them by the minute…and Horii's leadership would place them right where they were needed most.

"I hope you're right," Yoshizawa said…the wounds to his back and arms stinging…his thirst beyond imagination.

The conditions were so bad inside the building that several men had tried to commit *hari kari* even…

The Butcher's Block

by banging their heads against the concrete wall of the hallway. And that was before the ventilation fans had stopped working...after the electrical system had failed for some reason. Now the heat inside was becoming unbearable...and the wounded men...packed like sardines in the hallway...were begging for water. Koshio watched sadly as one man even peed into his hands and greedily drank the fluid to soothe his thirst.

"We just have to hang on a little while longer," Koshio said. "Remain strong...your family is depending on you to survive," he added...trying to inspire his driver.

"Koshio...you held up your end of the bargain. You made sure that I didn't burn up in our tank. And for that I thank you. I dreaded the idea of dying that way...and you didn't let me down."

"Jinzo...you were the best driver a tank commander could ask for. You knew that tank engine inside and out...the way a *samurai* knows his way around the body of a *geisha* girl. You never failed me either...and I thank you for that."

"Is Kanji okay? Where did he go?"

The tank assistant gunner...Naval Seaman First Class Kanji Kubo...had moved to another section of the building...where the less wounded were congregated.

"I'm sure he's doing fine. You know him. He'll manage to wrestle his way into the best spot wherever he's at. That's just his way. And while he did give us trouble at times...he was always honest...and he was an expert with our tank's machine gun. I watched him gun down a whole line of marine infantry coming up the beach when we were over by the cove."

"Ahhh, Jinzo. He did have a wicked tongue at times. I was never smart enough to counter his arguments. I'm sure he thought I was stupid at times. Even so, I hope he survives too…like you and me."

Koshio patted his friend on his good arm…and sighed…thinking of better times. And that's when the door suddenly blew in…the noise of the explosion deafening. In a split second, their refuge…the hallway…had become totally engulfed in smoke and dust.

PFC Johnny Borich crept up to the doorway and glanced inside. It was too dark to see anything…but he could hear a bunch of moaning. Without a second thought, he aimed at the doorway and squeezed the trigger of his flamethrower…just like he had on the slopes of the bombproof. A red-hot, liquid-burning flame shot down the hallway…incinerating everything in its path…just like it was intended to do. Releasing the trigger, he moved up closer and looked inside…to see the results of his work…but the smell of burning flesh overwhelmed him. Backing away, he heard someone else call him…a harsh voice saying that there was another entrance over on the left…and he dashed that way. Finding another door blown off its hinges, Borich repeated the process…and before long every living person that had been in the HQ building was burned beyond recognition.

The Butcher's Block

By late in the afternoon of D + 2, a solid defensive line ran across the island of Betio...the first time the marines had accomplished this in over two and a half days of vicious fighting. Facing eastward...towards the tail of the island...the exhausted Second Battalion marines under Major Crowe held the line nearest the beachhead...while Major Robert Ruud's Third Battalion marines...who were just as worn out...were positioned off their right flank...right in the middle... along the edges of the turning circle at the eastern end of the main runway. And next to them were the freshly blooded marines of the First Battalion of the Sixth Marines...under Major Willie Jones...who held the rest of the line right up to the southern shoreline. If everything had gone according to plan...this is where the marines should have been by twilight of D Day. But things had not worked out like they were supposed to... thanks to the tenaciousness of the Japanese *rikusentai*... and it had taken the marines almost forty-eight hours longer...and a lot of lives...to achieve the objectives that they had set for D Day.

Late that afternoon, Tokyo headquarters received its final radio transmission from Betio Island. The message was short and to the point: *Our weapons have been destroyed. From now on everyone is attempting a final charge. May Japan exist for ten thousand years!*

Chapter Twenty-Nine

"Ya think we'll catch a break tonight, sarge?"

Platoon Sergeant Roy considered the question thoughtfully...and shook his head no. "But what do you think?" he said...wondering if the lone squad leader he had left had suddenly forgotten what the Japs were like on the *Canal*.

"Nah...I'm with you," Oliver replied. "The Japs never let us rest on the *Canal*...so why would they do it here."

Oliver had been a private first class with the 1st Division on the Guadalcanal...so he was no stranger to combat...or to the tactics the Japanese would employ once they were boxed in and cut off.

Then...after the *Canal*...PFC Oliver had been given a break of sorts...and he had been transferred to a cruiser... but he hated the duty from the moment he set foot on the deck of the ship. A grunt marine at heart, Oliver asked to be transferred back to a line unit within a week

The Butcher's Block

of getting settled in...and since the Second Division needed men, his request had been accepted right away. With his new orders in hand, he packed his sea bag and headed over to New Zealand...where the Second was recuperating. His promotion to corporal came next...and because of his combat experience...he was handed a squad as well...which suited him just fine.

Platoon Sergeant Roy had liked Oliver right off the bat...and he had given the junior corporal a lot of leeway in how he ran his squad as a result. Oliver had excelled in return...and Roy knew that he could trust him to make the right decisions as the night attacks dragged on through the rest of the night.

"Exactly," he continued, and added, "so have your boys ready. I know how tired they are...but keep 'em sharp. This'll probably be our last night facing the Japs...so let's try to keep the ones that are still alive above ground from here on out...right."

"You got it, sarge," Corporal Phil Oliver replied...and he crawled over to his men to let them know the scoop. The men listened intently...knowing their lives depended on it...and then Oliver crawled back and nodded to Roy. "All of 'em are ready," he said confidently.

"Excellent," Roy replied, satisfied.

Then Oliver decided to go in a different direction. "I've got a question for you," he said to Roy.

"Shoot," Roy said.

"I was wondering why your records show you as T. J. Roy...but you call yourself S.T.J. Roy. When I got assigned to E Company and the First Platoon, a clerk with the battalion staff pulled your records so I could see who I'd be getting as my platoon sergeant. He shouldn't have really done it... but he was a buddy of mine, so he showed me your file. It's good to know who your boss is gonna be. So, what does the S stand for...and how come your records don't show it?"

"That's what you really wanted to ask me?" Roy answered...puzzled at the corporal's interest in his name.

"Yeah...I overheard you introduce yourself to Major Ryan...back on Saturday...and you called yourself S.T.J Roy. Call me crazy, but I've been trying to figure out why," Oliver replied.

"Well, since you asked, I'll fill you in. My first name is actually Stephen...but some records clerk along the line decided to drop the S and go with just T.J. for some reason. I have a feeling that he did it because he was a Southerner...since the T.J. stands for Thomas Jackson... after the Confederate general...Stonewall Jackson. The clerk probably felt he was doing me a favor...since most marines are Southerners...and that my new name would help me pass muster with the promotion boards. Maybe it did for all I know...since I made rank fairly quickly... despite my age."

"So, your first name is Stephen...and not Thomas?" Oliver replied...following along.

"Yup...Stephen it is...and always has been. Stephen Roy. The Thomas Jackson part came about because my dad was a teacher...and he liked old Stonewall's battlefield accomplishments during the Civil War. Not really a big mystery after all, right?" Roy answered.

"No...not really," Oliver responded...sort of disappointed that there wasn't more to it than that. "But

The Butcher's Block

thanks for filling me in just the same," he added...the mystery now solved.

―※―

Roy's original force of thirteen men had been whittled down significantly...having lost six men in their last action. But Lieutenant Bale had asked Roy to stay on...and he had consented...so Roy and his seven effectives...Corporal Oliver...the Second Squad leader...PFC Lewis...a BAR-man from Oliver's own squad...Private McGowan...his assistant...Private Tuchmann...a rifleman from Oliver's squad...PFC Reisman...a BAR-man from the Third Squad...Private Nelson...a rifleman from the Third Squad...and PFC Mudd...Roy's runner... were still assigned to *China Gal*...acting as its guard force.

The tank sat nearby...and its loader was tossing empty shell casings out of a port that was located on the left side of the turret for just that purpose. The empties were hitting the side of the hull with a resounding bang and then piling up beside the tank.

"Is that really necessary?" PFC Kevin Lewis grumbled...as another casing fell into the pile below...making a second jarring sound as steel hit steel.

"That's what that hole is designed for," Private Terry McGowan pointed out. "It must be cramped inside there as it is...since they got an extra guy riding around in it. You add all those empties to the mix and there must be barely room to move around inside that turret."

"You sound like you know a lot about those tanks," Lewis replied...still annoyed as more empties continued to crash into the growing pile.

"I volunteered for them...for the tanks...when I first came on. It didn't work out so well though. The Stewarts were way too small...and I was too big to move around inside the turret on the Shermans as well...and I was really cramped when I tried to drive it. So, they gave me my walking papers and I ended up with the grunts. That's how you ended up being stuck with me here."

"Lucky me," Lewis drawled out...his attitude softening...since he and McGowan got along famously. "I'll tell ya what," Lewis continued, "you just share some of your water with me and I'll forgive you for all the crap I've had put up with dealing with you. How's that sound."

McGowan pulled his canteen out of its pouch and unscrewed the top. He turned the canteen upside down and nothing came out. He screwed the top back on...put it back in its pouch...and then repeated the process with his other one. "Bone dry," he said, "just like yours."

These two were always thirsty...like everyone else...but for beer...more than anything else. And while water had finally managed to work its way forward to the units in the front lines, most of the men...even these two...would not drink it. Stored in old five gallon cans, the water had mixed with the enamel lining inside the cans while it was stored aboard the ships, and it made the water taste like gasoline...which is what the cans had originally carried in the first place. Only the thirstiest of men could manage to keep the stuff down...but most of the men would spit the foul-tasting water out right after they took a sip...despite their thirst.

"What I wouldn't do to get my hands on a bottle of beer right now. I might chop off a finger if you wanted to trade me for it...if you had some that is."

"Remember that stash of beer and *saki* we found on Tulagi," McGowan said...savoring the moment when he and Lewis had stumbled upon several crates of beer and *saki* that had been hidden in a cave they were detailed to search.

"Remember? Hell, it's all I've been thinking about for past two days. I've been dreaming about it for the last two nights even. It's the only thing that's kept me going. That and thinking about the good times we had back at Wellington...with the girls. You don't think we're alcoholics, do you? I mean we do spend a lot of time thinkin' about drinking...and it did cost us each a stripe, you know."

"We're not alcoholics," McGowan replied, "we just like to blow off steam every so often...and if having a good time cost us a stripe...then so be it."

"Well, you gotta admit that we might've pushed it too far every so often. It's one thing to have a good time... but we should never have let that night out with the girls cause us to be late for guard duty."

"How was I supposed to know that O'Toole would be waiting right there for us that night? How he knew we'd be jumping over the fence...at that spot...at four in the morning...is beyond me. No one in the barracks except you and me knew we'd be there...yet there he was...waiting on us like a hawk. Nothing gets by the guy.

He's got eyes in the back of his head. I guess it's a *been there done that* sort of thing with him. Trying to get one over on old O'Toole was useless…and that's where I went wrong. But I had to try…and that night was worth it…if you ask me," McGowan explained.

"Yeah…it certainly was, but our guard duty tour started at midnight…so we should have made it back on time. We compounded the problem by scaling that fence. We should've just walked through the gate and taken our punishment for being late. Trying to put one over on the first sergeant was dumb…and you know it," Lewis pointed out.

"You know O'Toole loves that nickname some of the guys gave him. Tough as a mule O'Toole…which does fit him. But some of the other guys have been saying, 'Dumb as a brick…but one tough mick.' I don't know about the dumb part…since he figured out where we would be that night…but the tough part definitely rings true," McGowan said…still admiring their first sergeant despite the circumstances.

"He's tough alright. I'm not gonna be the one to challenge him…that's for sure. So, are you going to see Jenn ever again?" Lewis asked…changing the subject.

"I hope so. She said she would write me. What else can we do at this point other than write?"

"Me and Sherri are in the same boat. We really like each other…but she's there and I'm stuck on this island for the time being. And who knows where they'll ship us next…after this one is over," Lewis said.

"You two seemed to have really hit it off though," McGowan replied, and added, " it'd be a shame to see nothing come of it…don't you think?"

"Oh, I intend to write her back, don't get me wrong. It's just the timing and the distance that's going to be a challenge. If I could, I'd go back and marry her right now…but we didn't want to do anything rash…like a lot of other guys did…so we didn't consider getting married. So, what about you and Jenn…any chance that you two will end up together?"

"I guess we're in the same boat too…that you and Sherri are. Only those letters will tell, I guess. I had a great time back in Wellington though…and I miss her already. Like you, I might end up marrying her too…if I can find my way back to New Zealand somehow. But what I'm really missing right now is a good glass of beer. What I wouldn't do for a nice cold mug of beer. I can picture it…sitting there on the bar…waiting for me to drink it. Since the Japs kept some beer on Tulagi, I wonder if the Japs stashed any of the stuff around here?"

At the thought of it, Lewis and McGowan began looking around…but there were no caves on Betio… so their hopes were dashed for the moment…but their thirst…unfortunately…was not.

China Gal was parked about forty yards behind the 1-6's line…to the south of the turning circle…just off the edge of the main runway. Major Jones…sensing a *banzai* attack…had brought up all three of his rifle companies and he placed them in one continuous line…facing east…towards the tail of the island…where close to one thousand Japanese *rikusentai* were now gathering. Over on the left...out ahead of the turning circle...was C Company. Their left flank was tied into Major Ruud's 3-8...and to its right...in the middle position...was A Company...and to their right...holding the shoreline...was B Company.

The terrain facing them...from the marine line to the tip of the tail...Takarongo Point...resembled a tapering arrowhead from above...and the land was pockmarked with shell holes and crisscrossed with anti-tank ditches and barbed wire entanglements. From end to end was seventeen hundred yards long...and at its widest point...where the marines were entrenched...was three hundred yards wide...not a gigantic piece of real estate. But the marines knew they would have to occupy it just the same...to close out the battle...and the Japs weren't about to give it up without a fight.

Pharmacist Mate 2nd Class Fumai scanned the ground ahead of him and watched as marines in ones and twos from the 1-6 helped their wounded comrades to the rear. Scattered about were other marines...but they weren't going anywhere. Their bodies were lying in the open...where they had fallen to enemy fire. An M-1 rifle with a helmet resting on its stock was stuck in the ground beside a few of them...their friends having marked the end of their valiant advance. And then their buddies had moved on...some sad...some mad...but all undaunted...as the 1-6 continued its attack eastward.

The corpsman then glanced behind him...and he could still see the three marines who had just left him in the distance. He could tell it was them since one of the men...the taller one...was still carrying another one over his shoulder...and the third one was walking off to the side...unhindered.

They're making good progress, he thought hopefully. *With any luck, they'll get that kid back to some real doctors... and they'll be able to save him.*

Then he turned and looked back down the beach again...and he made a fateful decision. "Marce," he said to his assistant, "this is where you and me part company."

Private Reed Marcy had known this moment was coming...so he wasn't as shocked as Fumai thought he would be. "Okay, Fume," was all he said in reply.

"I'm gonna catch up to the One Six. They're going to take casualties the further they go...and I can lend a hand with the wounded. You stay here...with your guys...and do the best you can to get the wounded ones back to the rear. A few of them will try to stick around...for the mop up... even though they're wounded. Take care of them...but try to get them headed back to Green Beach. They must have a battalion aid station set up there by now...so they're going to receive much better care than you can give them. Convince them of that so they'll go on their own."

"I'll do that," Marcy answered, and added, "but you be careful too up there. The Japs still got a lot of bullets left. They're not going to just up and surrender."

Fumai told Marcy he'd be careful...and then he thanked him for the great job he had done helping him out with the wounded in the tank trap.

Marcy looked at the corpsman with eager eyes and said, "And don't forget about that recommendation you said you'd pass up the chain for me. There's gonna be plenty more battles ahead of us…and I really think I wanna be a corpsman…just like you."

"Whatever you need me to do, just find me…I'm in the Second of the Second…and I'll write a recommendation or vouch for you personally. You did a great job…and I'd be proud to help you get that transfer. You got corpsman's blood running through you veins, kid. You'll make a good one," Fumai replied…and he smacked the kid on the shoulder and took off…leaving the smiling Reed Marcy behind.

Seaman 1st Class Kanji Kubo winced as he inadvertently leaned against his injured right shoulder…and he quickly shifted his position in the trench to relieve the pain.

"Are you okay," the sailor leaning next to him asked…noticing his discomfort and the blood-stained spot on his shirt. "Let me take a look at that," he added.

Kubo peeled his shirt back and the *rikusentai* examined the area around the small wound by gently pushing against Kubo's shoulder with his fingers. Kubo winced once again…and the man stopped his probing.

"It's worse than it looks," the man assured him. "You probably have a nice sliver of shrapnel in there…and deep. It's not going to kill you…but you will certainly experience a lot of pain from it."

The Butcher's Block

Kubo pulled his shirt back over his shoulder and thanked the man for his assessment...even though he had already figured that part out himself. "Should I head back...or stay here?" he asked.

"You can do whatever you like," the sailor answered, "but if you stay, you'll need a weapon. Where is yours? Did you leave it in the headquarters building?"

"I never had a weapon," Kubo explained. "I was the assistant gunner on one of our tanks. At least I was until late yesterday afternoon. That's when we got hit...and I got wounded. It's parked on the other side of the headquarters building. My commander and driver are still inside...with the badly wounded," Kubo said, and he pointed to the concrete building a short distance away.

"Why did you leave it?" the *rikusentai* asked...curious.

"Have you been inside?" Kubo replied.

"No. I have not," the man answered.

"If you had been, you'd understand why I'm out here. The smell inside is worse than it is out here...if that is possible. Plus, I could only take the moaning for so long. There are so many injured men in there that they are lying on top of one another."

"It's that bad?" the man responded.

"It's worse than you can imagine," Kubo said dryly...and that's when he noticed the marines sneaking up in the distance. As they got closer, the marines fanned out and circled the building...cutting it off from help. Then there was a violent explosion on the far side of the building...near the entranceway where their tank was parked. Next, Kubo watched as a marine carrying a weird-looking contraption on his back approached the corner of the building as well. The man stood there for a second...and then he braced himself as he directed a stream of fire from the muzzle of the weapon he was carrying right into the doorway. As far away as he was, Kubo could still hear the horrible screams coming from the building...and he knew in an instant that the men he had served with were dead.

"You should head back now," the *rikusentai* advised.

"Will you and your men come back with me?" Kubo asked...since there were just four other *rikusentai* in trench with them. "Your numbers are too small to turn back this horde," he warned.

"No. Me and my men will stay here until the end... come what may," the man answered stoically...and his men nodded their assent...their devotion to duty just as strong as their leader's was.

"Well, I wish you luck, my friend," Kubo responded... and he dashed eastward...leaving the five brave *rikusentai* to their fate.

Seaman 1st Class Kubo had trekked nearly a thousand yards towards Takarongo Point when he was finally stopped by an officer...the same one that had come over with his men when their tank was parked by the beach the day before. The officer...an ensign...recognized him as well...and he wanted to know what Kubo was up to.

"I have been wounded in the shoulder...and my right arm is nearly useless now," Kubo explained...and he

The Butcher's Block

pulled down his shirt…revealing his deeply discolored shoulder and upper arm.

"But your left arm works, right," he said, pointing to it.

"Yes, sir. It works fine…as you can well see," Kubo added testily.

"And your tank is out of action I assume," the ensign continued.

"Yes. It was knocked out yesterday afternoon…right after we returned from our mission down here in fact," Kubo stated…sensing where the conversation was headed.

"In that case, you are to join the force being formed under Commander Horii. He has instructed me to send every available man I come across to him…wounded or not…it makes no difference. You will find them gathered in the wood line just south of here…over by the beach. Anyone refusing to go will be summarily shot. There are no excuses. Is that understood?" The ensign stood there…ramrod straight…his right hand resting menacingly on his holstered 9mm pistol…daring the tanker to resist.

"I will do as you say," Kubo answered, eyeing the pistol…knowing fully well that some officers had no compunction about killing their own men if it served their purposes.

"Good…then head that way," the ensign advised.

"What will I do for a weapon," Kubo asked, "since my arm is useless…as you can see."

"You will be given a grenade…that is already armed. Even a one-armed man can take out several marines…as you will soon find out," the ensign stated encouragingly.

Kubo nodded...accepting his lot...and as he was about to head off to the right...towards the wood line near the beach where the attack force was forming...he saw two *rikusentai* pushing another man towards the ensign. The man had tear streaks running down his cheeks...and he was mumbling something unintelligible as he approached the ensign.

The two *rikusentai* were using the tips of their bayonets to nudge the man forward...and when the man was finally standing before the ensign, one of them said, "We caught this one hiding in a bunker not far from here. He's says he won't go...no matter what we do to him."

"Is this so," the officer stated casually.

The man continued to mumble...so the ensign smacked him hard on the cheek with the palm of his hand.

"My nerves, sir. I can't take it anymore," the man said...teetering from the blow.

"So, you will not fight...is that it then?" the officer asked...his voice calm and somewhat soothing.

"I...I...can't. My nerves. The shelling. When will it stop?" the broken man begged...continuing to cry.

The officer gave Kubo a sly look...and he walked behind the man and said, "Then you will serve our Emperor in another way." In an instant, he drew his 9mm pistol and he placed it right against the back of the man's head and pulled the trigger. A spray of blood shot out and the man crumpled to the sand...the point made.

The Butcher's Block

There would be four Japanese attacks that night...and all four of them hit that part of the line that the First Battalion, Sixth Marines were defending. Their line would be tested...and it would bend...but in the end it, would not break. This was an incredible achievement given how tired they were after fighting their way up most of the southern coastline during the day.

The first attack was a probing action that began at 1930 hours when a small force of fifty or so *rikusentai* left the undergrowth on the tail end of the island just after dark. Creeping silently forward...their goal was to locate a gap in the marine's defensive line...and in an uncanny stroke of luck...they found one...right between A and B Company...on the right side of the marine line. Hoping to exploit the weakness, they surged forward and fanned out in the darkness...looking for marines to kill. Sensing the marines around them, the *rikusentai* opened fire... hoping to hit anything at that point...and hoping the marines would fire back with their automatic weapons... revealing their key positions. But the marines refused to swallow the bait...and they didn't fire their machine guns or BARs at all. Instead, the enemy was met with a smattering of small arms fire from the marines wielding M-1 Garands and M-1 carbines...which thinned their ranks considerably while denying them the information they desperately sought.

When word of the breakthrough filtered through, Major Jones got on the radio and he called his battalion reserve forward to take care of the threat. Answering the call, a mixed bag of marines from the Headquarters Company and a platoon of mortarmen from D Company charged forward into the darkness…seeking out their Japanese prey with the same vigor that the *rikusentai* were seeking them. In moments, the *ad hoc* group of marines crashed into the remaining *rikusentai* and a vicious hand-to-hand struggle ensued. It was a fight waged with knives, bayonets, and fists…with no quarter given…and none asked…among men who were trying to kill each other in the most primitive fashion…all during the black of night.

Despite the ferocity of the two-hour encounter, the marine casualties…five killed…and several more wounded…were surprising light…when compared to that of their attackers. Of the original fifty or so *rikusentai* who had begun the attack…only ten…bloody and exhausted…made it out of the marine perimeter alive.

The next attack came two hours after the first one…but Major Jones had been busy during the interim.

From 2000 hours on, he was raising one unit after another on his radio…checking on their status… and exhorting them to hold on. At one point, First Lieutenant Norm Thomas…who had taken over the helm of B Company in the afternoon after the original commander had been shot in the neck and paralyzed… radioed back: *We need reinforcements. Another attack like that and the line may break.*

Jones's reply was short and succinct: *I can't give you any. You've got to hold.*

Thomas' reply gave Jones hope: *Aye aye, sir. We'll hold the line.*

Major Jones then promised additional support as well: *Water and ammunition are coming up to you on China Gal...and we're going to open with naval gunfire. Let us know how the shells are landing.* His message closed with: *They'll be pretty close, you know. Good luck!*

The shells Jones was referring to would be coming from two destroyers that were currently off the coast... from the USS *Schroeder* and the USS *Sigsbee*...and they began pounding the tail of the island with their 5-inch deck guns right after that...at 2015 hours. In a display of expert gunnery, the destroyers walked their rounds right up to within fifty yards of the marine line...providing a layer of protection to the marine line that frustrated the Japanese to no end.

And that was not all. Major Jones also contacted Lieutenant Colonel Rixey...and within minutes he had his twelve 75mm pack howitzers back on Red 2 firing in concert with the twelve howitzers on Bairiki Island as well...and before long their rounds were impacting all over the tail as well.

Despite the hell raining down on them, the Japanese still managed to get their 2130 hours attack off as well... which didn't surprise anyone...since the Japanese had been performing miracles of the same sort the entire battle. This time they started with another probing attack...and like their first one, this one had about fifty men involved as well. This attack hit the opposite end of the A Company line...the end closest to the beach... but it lacked the effort and intensity of the first attack... and the Japs quickly pulled back as soon as the marines contested it.

Platoon Sergeant Roy and the rest of the men were surprised when *China Gal's* engine coughed to a start and the tank rambled off across the main runway...heading in the direction of the pierhead.

"Where's she going?" Corporal Oliver asked out loud...giving voice to what the other men were wondering as well. "Do we go with her?" he added...since they were her escort.

"No. We sit tight," Roy stated emphatically. "No one moves at night...unless they wanna get shot. The lieutenant probably got a message over the radio. She'll either come back...or we'll find her in the morning...but none of us are going to start walking around at night. The tank'll just have to fend for itself it if wants to head off on some mission after dark. Lieutenant Bale knows that...and I didn't make it this far to go and get shot by some trigger-happy rifleman in the Sixth Marines."

"Can you imagine gettin' knocked off by our own guys...after having made it through three days of this hell," Oliver added...but it was too dark to tell if the guys were agreeing with him or not.

"That's why we sit tight. No one moves around...even to crap. If ya gotta go...go where you are...and then toss the shit away...preferably towards the Jap lines. Let them crawl through it if they want to probe our position. You saw those tracers off to the right a little while ago...that was the Japs finally hitting back. We've got 'em cornered...and they've only got one hand to play now," Roy continued...his logic making perfect sense to the rest of the men.

"You sound like Staggs," PFC Lewis said...and the men laughed at the thought of it.

Roy understood what Lewis meant...that the Japs only had one hand left to play...like in a card game...and he laughed too...since Staggs would've used a phrase like that to describe the fix the Japs were in. And then he wondered if Staggs was still alive...or dead. And the thought of it also made him recall how fickle war was...since Flockerzi had been wondering the same thing the day before...whether Staggs was alive or dead. And now it was Flockerzi...his buddy...who was dead...instead of the other way around. For all he knew, Staggs could be out there now...still alive and well somewhere...and wondering if Flockerzi or Roy were dead.

"Ya think Staggs made it this far," McGowan asked...thinking along the same lines.

"Who knows," Oliver answered. Then he added, "I just wonder if any of 'em are left alive."

That question lingered in the back of every man's mind almost as much as any other one did during the battle. Wondering how their friends were doing took an emotional toll on the men...so some of the men avoided bringing the subject up...but it was always in their thoughts, nonetheless. The only other question that may have eclipsed it was if any fresh water was ever gonna find its way to them. That question arose from their physical discomfort...which was just as strong...if not stronger...since the men needed water to literally survive and function.

"We'll find out soon enough I guess," PFC Reisman...who had been unusually quiet...offered up. He had just removed his boot to inspect his twisted ankle...which didn't seem to be getting any better...since it was hurting more and more.

"Why do you think that?" Private Chris Nelson...the sharpshooter...asked.

"Because the Japs gotta be in worse shape than us. They must be just as thirsty as we are. Their water supply must have run out by now. I ain't no geologist...but I haven't seen any lakes around here...or wells either. That means their only source of water came from collecting runoff during rain showers...or what was delivered to them on ships. And I have yet to run across a water barrel of any kind in any of these bunkers we've knocked out. So, they gotta be hurting by now," Reisman pointed out methodically.

Nelson looked at Reisman strangely...trying to decipher his thick New York accent...and said, "What's a geolokiss? Y'all are thinkin' about that Tammy gal of yours back on New Zealand at a time like this?"

Now it was Reisman's turn to look amazed...and he just shook his head...leaving the question about the Jap water situation up for grabs.

"What's that, you guys." Private Nelson had crawled around to the backside of the big shell crater they were in and motioned out into the darkness. "Somethin' is moving around out there."

Everyone's attention was immediately drawn in that direction but one. Platoon Sergeant Roy continued to look ahead...scanning the ground out in front of them.

Corporal Oliver crawled over...and as a precautionary measure...he reached down and withdrew his knife from the sheath that was hanging off his web belt. He raised himself as gingerly as he could, and he peeked over the rim of the hole...trying to see what...if anything...was moving around in the darkness beyond their position.

"If something's out there...I can't see it. It's too damned dark," he whispered...the tension of the moment increasing with every little noise that made its way back to the men huddled in the hole.

Then...suddenly...a voice called out to them from the blackness. "Corpsman comin' in."

"What the hell," PFC Lewis said, "that sounded like Fumai."

"Fumai?" Corporal Oliver sounded just as surprised. "How'd he find us out here...if it is him?"

Platoon Sergeant Roy was listening to the exchange and he lost his patience. "Are you just gonna leave him out there...or are you going to call him in?"

"It could be a trick, no?" Oliver replied...since he had heard the Japs calling out to the marines on Guadalcanal. *But they had never sounded as American as Fumai just did...so it must be him,* Oliver thought, so he called out cautiously, "Over here...we're over here."

Then another idea hit him. Just to be on the safe side, he yelled out, "Fumai...if that's you...what's your company commander's last name?"

A voice called out from the darkness, "Ring. Captain John Ring!"

Oliver looked over at Lewis and said, "If it was a Jap, he wouldn't have been able to pronounce his last name right. He would've said something like ling. The Japs have a hard time pronouncing our R's."

Lewis looked at Oliver and said, "Good idea. I should've thought of it."

Oliver wasted no time now. "Fumai...we're over here. Over here!"

In mere seconds, Fumai was sliding down into the hole...safe and sound...and a mini-reunion took place.

"So, you saw the lieutenant?" Roy asked as he continued to listen to the corpsman tell his story.

"No, sarge. I ran into Petraglia and Agresta...back at the pierhead...yesterday. The lieutenant was with the rest of the platoon over by the cove somewhere. I never did get to see him...or the others that made it in after our amtrac got hit. I was detailed by Major Culhane to help the guys that were trapped in the tank ditch back down the coastline. That's how I ended up here. But I had no idea you guys were over this way. I tried to stick close to the airstrip...since I knew the Sixth was up this way. I was looking for them...and then I find you guys at the same time. I can't believe it. What luck!"

Fumai then filled Roy and the others in on who was left alive in the platoon based on what PFC Petraglia had told him. "So that's who made it. We were hit real hard during the landing...like a lot of units were. I have no idea if the lieutenant...or Sergeant Endres...or the rest of them are still alive though. I just know that they were yesterday morning."

The men became quiet now...absorbing the news and reflecting on the loss of so many of their friends and platoon mates.

"We took it on the chin too," Roy finally said, "as you can see."

Fumai looked at each man now...and the realization that only seven out of twenty-three men that had ridden in on the *Rum Runner* with Sergeant Roy were left unscathed was mind-boggling. Fumai ran the numbers in his head quickly and said, "That's nearly seventy per cent casualties in your amtrac alone. How are we going to recover from this?"

"As bad as it is...we will," Roy stated...his confidence in the Marine Corps still rock solid.

The corpsman considered what his platoon sergeant said...and he admired him for it. "I wish I could be that positive...but seeing what I've seen over the last three days really makes me wonder."

"Don't worry about it," Roy intoned. "After you've been on enough cruises...you get a sense of these things. We'll be alright...you wait and see."

And just then a brilliant flash occurred in the distance…down by Takarongo Point. A shell fired by the one of the destroyers had landed in a Jap ammo dump… and the resulting explosions and pyrotechnics went on for hours as the ammunition continued to explode all night.

First Lieutenant Bale pushed the tank commander's hatch open and stood on his seat so he could see what was going on outside *China Gal*. He had just come from the pierhead…where they had picked up all sorts of supplies for the embattled First Battalion, Sixth Marines… which Major Jones had requested three hours ago…at 2000 hours. He called out to a marine running by and the boy skidded to a stop. "Where is your battalion commander…Major Jones?" he yelled down as he leaned out of the hatch…so the marine could hear him over the gunfire erupting up ahead.

"He's right over there, sir," the boy screamed back up at him…the noise level rising as the Japanese began their third attack of the night. This one was hitting mainly against B Company…which was holding the terrain along the coastline.

"Go tell him that *China Gal* is back with ammo and water…and all the stuff he requested earlier."

"Aye aye, sir," the boy yelled…and he dashed off in the direction of the battalion CP.

Several marines returned minutes later…and they began offloading all the supplies that were stacked on

The Butcher's Block

the back deck of the tank while the loader began handing boxes of ammo that were piled up inside turret up to the lieutenant. Lieutenant Bale slid them down the side of the turret...and some of the wooden boxes bounced off and hit the sand beside the tank. Other boxes...the heavier ones...came to a rest against the side of the turret and before long the pile was reaching up to the TC's hatch.

"Let's go, men. Major Jones told me you needed this stuff...so here it is. Come and get it!"

The men darted back and forth...straining under the weight of the boxes...and before long all the supplies were gone.

"Tell Major Jones we got him everything he asked for. Now we're going to head back to the runway...where we were previously," the tank lieutenant said to same young marine he had seen when they first pulled up...and he told the driver to move out...their nighttime resupply mission a resounding success.

The third attack of the night was larger than the first two...and it started with another probing action...which ended up being a diversion...against the right flank of A Company...which was tied in with B Company to their right. All three platoons of B Company were dug in along the beach...and they heard the action taking place to their left and got ready.

"What's happening," Major Jones yelled into his handset.

"We're hearing all sorts of yelling out to our front. The Japs think they can scare us with their death chants, I guess," First Lieutenant Norm Thomas replied back. "Other than that, nothing so far. We heard some firing off to our left. I guess they were trying to find another gap in the line. It looks like that attempt failed though… since it's turned quiet again…except for the Marine You Die chants. You don't wanna know what they think about our president either. It's some pretty nasty stuff."

"Okay. Let me know if you need anything. How is that artillery fire doing?"

"Good right now. It's hitting anywhere from one hundred yards to two hundred yards out. If the Japs can mass up for an attack in that, I'll tip my hat to them," Thomas replied…hearing the artillery rounds impacting out in front of his lines.

"Alright. Out here," Major Jones said…and he handed the handset to his radioman.

"Out here, sir," Thomas answered…and he handed his radio handset to the radioman by his side.

In fifteen minutes, everything changed for B Company and First Lieutenant Thomas. Out of nowhere, a group of nearly one hundred and fifty Japanese stormed the marine line all at once…screaming profanities, firing their rifles, and heaving grenades as they went. The marines answered back with their own rifles as well… and then they added their automatic weapons to mix…since the Japs were hitting them in force. Tracer lines crisscrossed the beach as the two opposing forces fired into one another…and in moments the Japanese *rikusentai* were in and among the marines. Like the first action earlier, a vicious hand-to-hand fight broke out as the two sides battled it out in the darkness. At one point, a Japanese sailor jumped into the foxhole with Lieutenant Thomas…and he ended up clubbing the man down with the butt of his empty .45 caliber pistol. He quickly reloaded…a procedure he had practiced over and over again while on the transport coming to Betio…and he fired two rounds right into the head of his assailant…finishing him off for good.

"Battalion's on the line," the radioman screamed… thrusting the handset at his company commander.

Thomas took it and listened while scanning the ground out ahead…trying to see through the darkness. He watched as several *rikusentai* were shot down after they had broken through the forward line…their shadowy figures collapsing after they were hit by a BAR-man who had turned around and fired at them as they ran past.

"Thomas…here," he yelled into the mike.

"How are you holding?"

"We are killing them as fast as they come at us…but we can't hold much longer! We need reinforcements!" Thomas' voice boomed over the radio…the situation clearly dire for B Company.

Jones considered the request for but a second…and replied just as staunchly, "We haven't got any to send you…you've got to hold!" Then he turned to the men around him and said, "If they don't hold, we may lose the entire battalion."

Then, turning to his fire support officer, he said, "Get those destroyers on the line and have them walk those rounds to within fifty yards of Thomas...and tell Rixey to give us everything he's got with his seventy-fives!"

Within moments, 5-inch shells from the destroyers were crashing down on what was left of the Japanese formation...breaking it apart...and the momentum swung back over to the marines...saving B Company for good.

"They're pulling back," Thomas radioed back. And minutes later he added, "We're holding the line. That naval gunfire broke their backs."

Jones breathed a sigh of relief...and turning to his staff...he said, "They did it...they held."

A burly officer came by and handed the seaman a Type 97 fragmentation grenade when he noticed that his arm was injured. "I already pulled the pin...so all you have to do is strike the primer and it will go off in four to five seconds. You can either carry it yourself after triggering it...or you can throw it at the enemy. Do whatever you like. Either way is good...and it will kill several marines if you can get it close enough to them. Does your arm work at all?"

Seaman 2nd Class Kanji Kubo winced as he tried to lift his arm. It was all but useless now...the swelling in the shoulder locking it in place. But he was able to move his fingers...so the officer placed another grenade in his pocket.

"We have plenty more of them. If you survive...come back and find me and I will give you a few more. Hold onto the grenade with your bad hand and pull the pin with your good one. Then transfer it over to your good hand...and use your good arm to throw it."

"Will you be participating in the attack, sir," Kubo asked...well aware of the answer.

"Ahhh, not this one. Probably the next one though," the ensign answered defensively.

Kubo thanked the officer with a nod of his head... but as he walked away, he mumbled, "Idiot."

Kubo then walked over and joined a large group of *rikusentai* who were armed with an assortment of weapons. Some were loading their *Arisaka* rifles with bullets they had in their pockets...while others were adding a bayonet to the tips of their muzzles. Others... like Kubo...were checking over the grenades they had been issued...making sure the safety pins were in place. Strangely, some were dressed simply in loin cloths... and they were carrying sharpened spears or swords. It was obvious that they planning to end their lives while fighting as their ancient *samurai* brethren had once done...man-to-man.

Kubo figured there were nearly four hundred men in this group...and word had been passed around that they would attack the marine line along a broad front... so that the American artillery couldn't concentrate on them all at once. The attack was scheduled to commence at four in the morning...two hours away.

"Anybody know what time it is," PFC Lerman Mudd suddenly asked. No one had heard him speak since his buddy...the other runner...PFC Rickard...had been killed by a Jap machine gun earlier in the day.

"It's oh three hundred. Why do ya wanna know?" Corporal Oliver said...checking his watch.

"I'm just wondering what time it is back home...in Kentucky...where my girl...Debbie...is."

"It must be around eight or nine in the morning in Kentucky. Everybody's probably gettin' ready for breakfast," Nelson said, trying to figure out the time differences. Then he thought about his girlfriend...Micky... who he intended to marry as soon as he got back home... just like Mudd was thinking of his.

No one spoke after that. Instead, all seven men began to reminisce about home...even the tight-lipped Platoon Sergeant Roy. He was thinking about his own wife...a petite girl named Gail...who he had married four years ago. He had met her at a USO dance in San Diego while she was serving coffee and cookies...and he fallen in love instantly...which confounded anyone who knew him...given his tough exterior. Gail's sense of humor and love of family had slain the dragon however...and the platoon sergeant was devoted to her...maybe even more than the Marine Corps...if that were possible.

"Keep your heads down!" It was Platoon Sergeant Roy... and he was warning his men since several Jap machine guns had begun firing only fifty yards ahead of them.

Five brave *rikusentai* machine gun teams had crawled through the underbrush and set their weapons up among a group of wrecked trucks that were blocking a sandy trail that wound its way down to Takarongo Point…right under the marines' noses.

And while their fire was indiscriminate, it was annoying and potentially dangerous nonetheless…and Major Jones was determined to do something about it.

"Runners comin' in!"

The eight marines and their corpsman in the shell hole turned to their right and got ready to engage the shadowy figures who were approaching their position… even though one of them had just announced their presence. When they saw that the men were actual marines, they relaxed their posture…and let the four men come in.

The one who had called out…a staff sergeant named Janos…looked everyone over and decided that Roy had to be the leader of the group…given his size and presence alone.

"Major Jones wants those machine guns taken care of…before someone gets hurt. He picked me…and my three men here to do it. But I could certainly use your help if you're up for it. Thirteen are better than four in my book," the sergeant said…explaining his mission.

"Sure, we'll lend you a hand," Roy said…and he introduced the seven others and his corpsman to the sergeant and his men. Then the sergeant did the same… introducing himself and his three men as well.

"I'm Staff Sergeant Janos...and this is Corporal Giachi...he's my right-hand man. Those two next to him are PFC Ganzenmuller and PFC Harms. We're part of Major Jones' headquarters detachment. When he asked for volunteers to go knock out these machine guns, I volunteered, and my three musketeers decided to come along with me as well. We're tired of sitting around in the rear. I led a lot of scouting raids back on the *Canal* and I'm pretty confident that I can get these machine guns too."

"So, what do you propose," Platoon Sergeant Roy asked...obviously comfortable with this junior sergeant taking charge.

"Those guns sound pretty damn close and I estimate there are three or four of them at best. You figure three or four men per gun...which means we'll be facing as many as fifteen or sixteen men. Twenty tops. I plan to creep our way up...using the sound of the machine guns as a guide. I'm hoping we'll get within a few yards of their position without being seen. Then we hit 'em with grenades. We finish the rest off with our rifles and BARs...easy." The sergeant then checked his watch and added, "It's three twenty now...and it should take us about fifteen minutes to get up there...and then we spring the trap."

"Let's go," the confident Roy stated...the thrill of the hunt energizing him.

"Okay...I'll lead off...with my boys right behind me. If I signal a stop...everybody stops...no questions asked. You bring your boys up behind us. Spacing is whatever you need to be able to see the man next to you...but

The Butcher's Block

don't bunch up...even though it's pretty damn dark out there. When I make contact, I'll signal you up...to the left or right...depending on the terrain. And nobody fires on them until I open up on them. We're gonna give them a grenade shower first. Agreed?"

Everyone nodded...and they quickly checked their gear...making sure that everything was secure...that nothing would rattle as they crawled along and thus give away their position. Then they filled their pockets with as many grenades as they could carry from a box of them that Corporal Giachi had brought up with him.

Without another word, Janos inched his way up to the lip of the crater and paused for a second...scanning the ground ahead. When one of the Jap machine guns began firing, he slithered out and crawled on...moving in the direction of the gun...like a snake silently stalking a mouse.

Everyone followed...just like he had said...and in minutes the sergeant had signaled a stop. He checked his watch...and saw that it was nearly three thirty. Then a second machine gun joined the first one...and Janos was able to see the muzzle flashes of the two guns directly ahead...only twenty yards away. Now a third gun joined the chorus...and Janos knew it was time to act.

He looked behind and signaled that he wanted his three men on his left. They quickly crawled up and fanned out to form a short line...just like he had trained them to do. Then he signaled Roy to bring his guys up... on his right...and they moved up too...positioning themselves behind anything they could use for protection.

Janos pulled a grenade out of his pocket and he held it up so all the men could see it. Everyone understood what he wanted, and they reached into their pockets and took out a grenade as well. Then he pulled the pin while holding the spoon trigger in place with his hand. The men...except for Corpsman Fumai...followed his lead and seconds later twelve grenades were sailing through the air in the direction of the Jap machine gunners. Some of the grenades hit the ground and bounced right up against the trucks the Japs were hiding around...while others landed just short and rolled to a stop. All the grenades detonated at the same time... and the force of the explosions occurring all at once knocked the *rikusentai* flat...stunning them...and killing many. Many more grenades landed now...the marines throwing them as fast as they could pull the pins...and chunks and slivers of cast iron flew everywhere...saturating the area. Several more *rikusentai* were killed in this hailstorm...cutting their numbers in half yet again.

Not knowing where the grenades were coming from, the remaining *rikusentai* fired their machine guns randomly...sweeping left...then right...trying to kill their attackers...but they failed miserably. And when the grenades ran out, the marines switched to their personal weapons...the three BAR-men...Reisman...Lewis...and Ganzenmuller...doing the most damage. The Browning automatic rifles large .30 caliber rounds tore through the trucks easily...each bullet leaving a huge jagged hole in its wake...and the remaining *rikusentai* abandoned their guns and dove to the side...trying to hide in the underbrush.

"Corpsman!"

Tom Fumai looked to his left...in the direction the cry was coming from...and strained to see who was calling him.

"We need that corpsman over here! Harms is hit," Giachi yelled out...more emphatically this time...and he waved his arm in the air to attract the corpsman's attention.

"On the way!" Fumai yelled back...but instead of crawling, he got up and ran...his desire to help the man stronger than his desire to protect himself.

"Here he comes," Ganzenmuller...who was laying a few feet away from Harms...yelled over...and he laid his BAR down and he crawled up to Harms so he could check on the wounded man himself. Reaching him, he said, "How you doin', buddy," and he patted his friend on the shoulder.

Harms gave him a worried look...and he pulled his utility shirt aside...revealing a bloody hole just below his neck...in the area of his left collar bone. "Am I gonna die," he asked weakly.

"Don't worry. The corpsman's here and he'll fix ya right up. You'll be as good as new in a few minutes...just hang on," Ganzenmuller said, hoping his encouragement would work and help keep Harms alive.

Fumai slid in and took a knee beside Harms. "Where's he hit?"

Ganzenmuller pushed the wounded man's shirt aside...like Harms had done moments ago...and Fumai quickly examined the man's wound...which was bleeding profusely. Fumai gave Ganzenmuller a dire look, and then he opened his medical bag and pulled out a large dressing and placed it against the bullet hole. Leaning forward, he pressed on the dressing...hoping that the bleeding underneath would stop. He looked at Ganzenmuller and said, "I think the bullet hit his collar bone and deflected off. Where it ended up is anyone's guess. If he's bleeding internally, there's nothing I can really do for it."

Random shots continued to fly through the marines' line as Fumai continued to work on Harms...but the wounded man's breathing began to slow...and then his face lost all its color...turning a ghostly white. Then he stopped breathing all together. Disheartened, Fumai sat back on his haunches and sighed...his lifesaving efforts over.

"Ahhhh, no," Ganzenmuller pleaded, "isn't there anything you can do for him?"

Fumai was about to say something when he was suddenly bowled over by a machine gun bullet that smashed into his chest. The corpsman landed flat on his back... the shock of the hit surprising him...and he struggled to take a breath.

"Are you hit bad," Ganzenmuller said...scrambling over to him. He had just watched his buddy die from a wound in the chest...and now the corpsman who had been trying to save him was hit in the same area of the body.

Giachi crawled over now...and he gave Ganzenmuller a imploring look and said, "Both of them?"

"Harmsie's gone, Joe," Ganzenmuller said firmly... recovering quickly...and then added, "I don't know about the corpsman though. He just got hit. I haven't been able to check on him yet."

Then...like a ghost coming out of a grave...Fumai suddenly sat up and shook his head...surprising both Ganzenmuller and Giachi alike.

"Hey, you're alive," Giachi said…surprised...and he grabbed Fumai's arm to steady him.

"I guess so," Fumai replied...and he ran his hands over his chest to see if the bullet had penetrated anywhere. He stopped at the shirt pocket over his left breast and he put his right hand into it. As Ganzenmuller and Giachi continued to watch, Fumai poked a finger through a dime-sized hole in the pocket...made by the Jap bullet that had hit him...and they both whistled in admiration.

"How'd it miss you? Was it spent?" Ganzenmuller asked...shocked.

Fumai smiled and pulled his hand out of his pocket. "Pure luck," he said...and he showed the two men a watch that had the end of a bullet protruding from its face. "I was gonna send it to the father of a kid that got killed in the landings two days ago. He saved my life."

"Holy mackerel," Ganzenmuller...a New Bedford fisherman before the war...said in awe.

"I guess I'll hang on to it now though...as a good luck charm...and I'll write a letter to that boy's dad instead. I think he'll understand," Fumai added...and he put the watch back into his left pocket again. Looking at the two men, he laughed and said, "Lightning never strikes the same place twice...right!"

The few remaining members of the Jap machine gun teams that had not been killed by Janos' party dragged their wounded back to their own lines...their forward position far too dangerous now that the marines had discovered their whereabouts.

"Stay here," Janos said to the others...and he crawled up to the truck site to survey the damage. He saw dead Japs lying all over place...victims of the grenade and the rifle fire that had saturated the area only minutes before. Janos got up slowly...his head on a swivel...and he moved to the trucks. As expected, he found several more dead Japs splayed out in the beds...the marine gun fire having made the sides of the trucks look like swiss cheese. Satisfied, he turned to go...and that's when he spied some movement in the cab of the second truck he had checked out. He pulled the .45 caliber pistol he was carrying out of its holster and he moved down the side of the truck slowly until he reached the driver's door. The window had been blown out...so he moved quickly and peered inside...his pistol up and ready.

The wounded *rikusentai* was grasping his stomach in a vain attempt to keep his intestines from spilling out of him. He had been badly wounded by one of the marine grenades early on...and one of his buddies had taken the time...despite the incoming fire...to help him into

The Butcher's Block

the cab of the truck. As his friend turned to go, his head had been split down the middle by a junk of iron from another exploding grenade…and he fell out of his sight…rolling partially under the running board of the truck.

Knowing he was going to die, the *rikusentai* had then pulled a grenade out of his pocket and placed it between his legs…hiding it…just in case.

Staff Sergeant Janos eyed the wounded man suspiciously…yet pitying him as well. The man's efforts to hold his intestines inside him had failed…and they were spilling over his lap and falling to the floor of the cab…their bluish color at odds with the bright red blood that covered his shirt and pants.

The *rikusentai* eyed the marine with contempt…and made his final move. Releasing his intestines, he reached between his legs and grabbed the grenade with one of his hands. Using the last ounce of strength he had, he banged the grenade on the edge of the window…arming it.

Janos had encountered wounded Japs on Guadalcanal, so he wasn't surprised when the Jap reached for the grenade underneath him. What really amazed the staff sergeant though was that the dying man was able to arm the thing...and that's when Janos shot him and dove to the ground.

The large .45 caliber bullet smashed into the side of the *rikusentai's* head...and the grenade fell from his hand. It bounced off his right leg and fell to the floor of the cab...where it detonated with a flash...shredding what remained of the dead *rikusentai's* body.

Janos got up and brushed himself off...the sand flecked with bits of bloody flesh from the bodies of the men who had been blown apart around the trucks...and then headed back to Roy and the others.

"How'd we do," several men said at once...as if they had practiced it.

"That group won't be bothering anybody again. We probably killed about twenty of them...maybe more. I was low in my estimate...in both men and weapons. I counted five machine guns out there...so we must have taken on about twenty-five men...maybe more."

The men nodded in appreciation...and then Giachi stepped up and told Janos the bad news. "Harms is dead," he said.

"I saw him get hit. It was that bad?"

"Yes," Fumai said, cutting in. "He got hit in the upper chest and the bullet deflected downward. He bled out internally. There was nothing I could do for him. Sorry."

"Don't be," Janos stated firmly. "Guys get killed. You did what you could...that's what counts. Thanks for trying to save him...he was a good man...and a good marine."

Roy came over and set his hand on Fumai's shoulder. "You did fine. It's good to have you back."

Fumai smiled and thanked Staff Sergeant Janos and his own platoon sergeant for recognizing his efforts. Most corpsmen took the loss of the men they had tried to help very hard...and Fumai was no different...and it was nice to know that the men he was supporting knew it.

"Well, our work is done here," Janos said, and added proudly, "so let's head back and let Major Jones know. Maybe we'll even get some medals for it!"

"Medals? Just give me a bottle of beer and I'll be happy," PFC Lewis yelled out...and all the men laughed as they headed back...their mission a resounding success.

The fourth and final attack of the night came at 0400 hours...right after Roy and his men had returned to their nighttime position. This attack started out just like the last one...with the Japanese catcalling and mocking the marines out in front of them...hoping to intimidate them while bucking themselves up at the same time. And then...when the signal was given...four hundred or so *rikusentai* warriors charged out of the darkness. They were able to maneuver their way through the ghastly American destroyer fire...whose 5-inch shells hit among them…obliterating whole swaths of men…and then they fought their way through the marine artillery fire…their ranks raked and decimated by the incoming rounds of twenty-four 75mm pack howitzers. Incredibly, scores of *rikusentai* still found their way through somehow…and the determined survivors slammed into the three companies of the 1-6 in an attempt to destroy the southern half of the marine defensive line yet again. The fighting was just as vicious as the three previous attacks were…and hand-to-hand combat broke out across all three company fronts as the Japanese pushed their way through another wall of machine gun fire…rifle fire… mortar fire…and grenade explosions. Then the fighting devolved into a series of one-on-one battles…with marines and *rikusentai* clubbing each other down with their rifles and stabbing each other with bayonets and swords. When their weapons broke…they used their fists…or anything else they could lay hold of. Men hit, bit, spit, kicked, and clawed one another until the men they were fighting with were killed…their adversaries dying in the most brutal and basic of ways known to man.

Major Jones got First Lieutenant Thomas on the radio yet again…and his response was no different than it had been earlier. "We are killing them as fast as they come at us, but we can't hold much longer. We need reinforcements," he pleaded.

Major Jones gave him the same guidance he had earlier: *You've got to hold!*

In the end, the marines of the 1-6 were able to hold their line…just like Jones had asked…and the scores of *rikusentai* dead confirmed it. When the sun finally rose on D + 3 and they were able to see, the marines counted over two hundred dead Japanese in front of their lines... while another one hundred and fifty bodies...or parts of them...were found further out...the ground a literal butcher's block of blood and guts.

Major Jones' men had suffered too...though the numbers were not as stark. The *rikusentai* had managed to kill forty-five of his marines and wound another one hundred and thirty others during the last ten hours of brutal combat.

When they were relieved that morning, one of Jones' men saw a combat correspondent that he recognized standing off to the side...observing them and taking notes...as they headed to the rear.

Taking a break from his writing, the correspondent looked up and spotted the man among the throng of marines passing by. "How'd it go last night? Was it as rough as they said?" he asked, eager to hear what the marine would say.

Without missing a beat, the marine broke into a smile and said, "They told us we had to hold, and, by God, we held!"

Chapter Thirty

The final phase of the battle for Betio Island began on D + 3 and it involved two separate actions...the first being the elimination of the *Pocket* at the Red 2 and Red 1 boundary line...and the second being the occupation of the last fifteen hundred yards of the eastern end of the island...right down to Takarongo Point.

To complete the second part, Colonel Edson had ordered the Third Battalion of the Sixth Marines...who had landed successfully on Green Beach at nine in the morning on D + 2...to move up and pass through the tired 1-6 at first light. This move had been plotted out the day before...at a noontime meeting that Edson had conducted with all his commanders at Colonel Shoup's command post. Jones had ridden to the meeting in a Stuart light tank from the vicinity of Black Beach 2... while Lieutenant Colonel Kenneth McLeod, the CO of the 3-6, had been ferried over in an amtrac from Green

The Butcher's Block

Beach. Major Jones had acknowledged the order… and then climbed back inside the cramped tank and returned to lead his battalion as it continued its fight down the southern coastline. Lieutenant Colonel McLeod received the order as well, and he returned to Green Beach and led his battalion through the same ground that the 1-6 had just cleared along the western end of the southern coastline so they could conduct the shift in positions the following morning.

Major General Smith and his entourage had arrived at Shoup's CP a short while later…and Colonel Edson had taken him aside and briefed him personally on his plans. The general concurred with everything Edson had shown him…thus casting the die for D + 3.

———

A few minutes after four in the afternoon on D + 2, Major General Smith sent the following message to Brigadier General Hermle…who was still running the division CP aboard the *Maryland*: *Situation not favorable for rapid clean-up of Betio. Heavy casualties among officers make leadership problems difficult. Still strong organized resistance…many emplacements intact eastern end of island…In addition, many Japanese strongpoints to westward of our front lines within our positions have not been reduced. Progress slow and extremely costly. Complete occupation will take at least five days more. Naval and air bombardment a great help, but does not take out emplacements.*

Chapter Thirty-One

The 1-6 and 3-6 had swapped places just like they were supposed to at daylight on D + 3...and the 3-6 launched its own attack at 0800 hours. F6F fighters had already swept the area clean for thirty minutes... from 0700 to 0730...and then two new destroyers - the *Schroeder* and *Sigsbee* had been replaced since they had run out of ammunition for their 5-inch guns - shelled the tail of the island for the next thirty minutes...until 0800. The 3-6 had also been given the two remaining Sherman tanks for support as well: *Colorado*...under First Lieutenant Lou Largey...took up a position on the left... and *China Gal*...under First Lieutenant Ed Bale...covered the right. Behind them were and additional seven Stewart tanks...which were there to provide cover for the two Shermans.

McLeod's potent force covered a front that was only three hundred yards wide at the beginning of their advance...and it got narrower the further they went. The first one hundred yards were fairly easy...since most of the Japs in this area had been killed the night before... in the artillery barrage and by destroyers' five-inch gunfire that had saturated the area all night long.

At this point, they encountered a tank ditch that extended from one shoreline to the other in the form of a shallow V...and the marines could see that the ground beyond it was honeycombed with bunkers and pillboxes...just like the coastline east of Black Beach 2 had been.

As expected, the surviving Japs took the marines under fire as soon as they had moved past the tank ditch...but their fire lacked the coordinated discipline that had marked the other areas the *rikusentai* had defended. As a result, the marines quickly figured out that they could advance on one obstacle at a time by pinning it down with direct fire. Then they were able to outflank it and destroy it without getting caught in a vicious crossfire from the other pillboxes and bunkers around it. Using this same tactic had gotten many other marines killed earlier...when they tried to destroy an obstacle that was holding up their advance on the first two days of the battle...but now it worked...and so they pressed on.

The marines continued to make good progress as they headed east...and before long they encountered one of the largest bunkers in the area. They surrounded it...just like the smaller ones they had faced...but this time the Japs inside decided to take matters into their own hands. Instead of waiting for the marines to destroy their position with explosives or a flame-thrower…at least seventy-five *rikusentai* charged out of the bunker… firing wildly at the marines who were coming up.

Colorado was positioned perfectly to intercept their move however, and one blast of their main gun took care of the problem. The *rikusentai* were met by a 75mm high explosive round that exploded in their midst and the entire group was obliterated in one fell swoop.

This charge marked the end of the main Japanese resistance for the tail of the island…and by 1300 hours the marines were standing at Takarongo Point and waving to the marines of the Second Battalion, Sixth who were holding Bairiki Island…two miles away.

Lieutenant Colonel McLeod's Third Battalion, 6th Marines had killed nearly four hundred and seventy-five Japanese in five hours' worth of fighting…while losing only nine of their own. Another twenty-five men had been wounded in the effort…a small price to pay given the number of enemy his marines had killed. They had also captured fourteen prisoners…but only two of these men were Japanese. The other twelve unfortunates were part of the forced-labor contingent from Korea…and these men considered themselves lucky indeed…since they had no desire to die for a country they hated in the first place.

The Butcher's Block

Twelve hundred yards in the opposite direction, the men of the 1-8 under Major Larry Hays closed in on the *Pocket* from the east…while Major John Schoettel…who had finally linked up with his own men…and the 3-2 marines…including Major Ryan…Captain Jim Crain… and Second Lieutenant Fawcett…did the same from the west. The two groups eventually merged near the ten aircraft revetments that were built on the north side of the large rectangular area that sat at the western end of the main airstrip sometime around 1000 hours…and the *Pocket* was finally cut off for good. To hasten the stalwart position's fall, two half-tracks carrying 75mm cannons drove out into the water and pounded the *Pocket* from the reef…their fire deadly and incredibly accurate.

Despite this, the Japs refused to surrender…their loyalty to their Emperor and devotion to duty beyond question. Even as the ring closed in around them, the *rikusentai* continued to fire at the marine invaders…hoping to put one more marine in the ground before their lives were taken from them.

Before long, an 18th Engineer team led by First Lieutenant Gordon Leslie…the very same officer who had led the attack down the pier with First Lieutenant Hawkins on D Day…approached the bunkers that made up the *Pocket* stealthily. Armed with satchel charges, grenades, flamethrowers, and Bangolore torpedoes, Leslie's men closed the range bit by bit and by noon the *Pocket* and the *rikusentai* who had defended it for three and a half days were finally overrun…the brave warriors and their position blown, blasted, and burned to kingdom come.

○○○

At 1150 hours on November 23rd, 1943...on D + 3... Major General Julian Smith radioed a message to Admiral Harry Hill...the commander of Task Force 53... that stated: *Decisive defeat of enemy counterattack last night destroyed bulk of hostile resistance. Expect complete annihilation of enemy on Betio this date. Strongly recommend that you and your chief of staff come ashore this date to get information about the type of hostile resistance which will be encountered in future operations.*

○○○

At noon...on D + 3...another significant event occurred... which brought smiles to all who witnessed it: a Navy F6F Hellcat fighter...piloted by the bandaged Lieutenant, J.G. *"Wild Bill"* Basnett...landed on the four-thousand-foot airstrip and slowly coasted to a stop. Pulling the canopy open, the cleanly-shaven pilot looked down at one of the marines who was mobbing his plane and asked, "Is it over?" to PFC Adrian Strange.

The dirty-looking, twenty-year-old marine...wearing a uniform caked and smeared with blood and dirt from three days' worth of fighting...limped closer to the plane's cockpit and removed a cigarette from his mouth. He blew out some smoke and yelled up, "You better hope it is…or your scalp's gonna be hanging off a Jap sniper's belt in about a minute or two!"

And at 1305…a little over an hour later…General Smith sent another message to Hill that stated what every marine had craved to hear…and what every marine had been fighting for since they left their transports seventy-six hours earlier: BETIO HAS FALLEN.

Chapter Thirty-Two

As word spread that the battle was over, the marines from the 2nd and 8th Regiments who had become separated from their own units...and there were scores of them...were given permission to head home to their own units. Specific areas were selected as rallying points for each unit...and the men began making their way there...so they could see who was still alive...and who wasn't. Then they would begin making their way to the ships the following day...and leave the island for good on D + 5.

Colonel Hall...the regimental commander of the 8th Marines...choose Bairiki Island as the rally point for his Second and Third Battalions...and the marines from those two battalions headed that way on the morning of D + 4.

The First Battalion...under Major Larry Hays...had permission to remain near the *Pocket*...since it had been

The Butcher's Block

fighting with the Second Regiment since it landed on D + 1. Hays would take up his rollcall there...all while hoping that the results would not be as grim as he first suspected.

Colonel Shoup, meanwhile, chose the area just inland from his own CP on the Red 2 beachhead as the rally point for the First and Second Battalions of his own 2nd Regiment...and his survivors began streaming in from all three sectors of island where they had been fighting for the last three days as soon as commanders they had been fighting for let them to go. And like Colonel Hall had done with his 1-8, Shoup allowed the 3rd Battalion under Major Schoettel to reform on the Bird's Beak... where they had spent a good majority of their time during the seventy-six hours of the battle.

The Sixth Regiment...which was still relatively fresh and had suffered the least amount casualties...was picked to secure the entire island and to hunt down the few remaining *rikusentai* diehards who were still hiding out in bunkers here and there and who refused to surrender. This duty would keep them on island slightly longer...for another two months or so...until the garrison troops...who would run the island permanently... arrived from the States.

Corporal Staggs and Private Jorgenson were walking near the pier on the afternoon of D + 3 when they ran into two marines escorting a Japanese prisoner to Colonel Edson's CP. Major Chamberlin had shaken their hands moments ago…and then let them go…their duty with the Second Battalion of the 8th Regiment finally over.

Looking the two marines over, one of the guards asked, "Are you guys with the Second Marines by any chance."

"Who wants to know?" the ever-alert Staggs shot back…his instincts still keen.

"Me and my buddy here are with the Third Battalion, Sixth. We ran across this guy this morning…as we attacked down the tail. He was knocked out cold when we found him," the one marine said…and he pointed to the lump on the prisoner's forehead to confirm their story. "Well, he came to pretty quickly after I kicked him…since I could see that he was breathing. He hasn't given us any trouble at all. Not like the other one did."

"You mean you had two prisoners? Where's the other one?" Staggs asked…and he glanced at Jorgenson skeptically.

"Scotty here took care of him. He wasn't like this one. The other one was the biggest Jap we've seen on the island so far. The guy was really big…at least bigger than either one of us. And this guy cops an attitude with us right away. We caught him trying to hide out in a bunker we had knocked out. He was probably gonna wait 'til we passed and then come out from hiding and shoot us in the back after we moved on. But we found him…so that didn't happen. On the way here, he starts some kind of weird chant…maybe a death song or something…and then he lowered his hands and folded them across his chest like he had a say in the matter. You would have thought he was the emperor the way he locked his arms.

The Butcher's Block

Then he starts smiling at us...like we were kids...and he sits down...and refuses to move. Well, me and Scotty are tired...we've been up all night...fightin' these crazy Japs...and this guy is stretching our patience real thin. Scotty finally had enough though...and he just hauled off and bayoneted the guy. Drove his bayonet into his chest...right up the muzzle on his M One...and wiggled it around to finish the job. You should have seen the look on that arrogant Jap's face. He was probably trying to goad us into doing it anyway...so he wouldn't go home in shame. Well, he got what was coming to him...and he won't be making the trip home...just like he wanted."

"So, what do you want us to do?" It was Jorgenson this time...cutting in.

"Could you take this one off our hands...since you're headed that way anyway?" Scotty said...jumping into the conversation.

"Sure...no problem," Corporal Staggs replied...and Scotty edged the prisoner over to them with the tip of his bayonet...which was still streaked red with the blood from the *rikusentai* he had stabbed earlier.

"Thanks, guys," Scotty said...and the two marines turned around without another word and walked off... glad they were rid of the cooperative Nip and happy to be heading back to their own unit.

Naval Seaman 1st Class Kubo rubbed the lump on his forehead and realized what had happened. He had moved forward during the attack...with the rest of his comrades...

like he was supposed to...and he had thrown his grenade at the marine lines...just like he was supposed to. Then he had taken the other grenade out of his pocket and just dropped it to the ground...unarmed. And that's when the shells hit nearby. The ground had erupted all around him...the noise deafening...and he had been knocked senseless by a chunk of wood that had been blown into the air by the force of the explosion. *I'm just lucky to be alive,* he thought, and then he looked at his two new captors and hoped they'd be more lenient than the last two marines were. He had watched the other man...who he did not know...antagonize the other two marines... and he ended up being stuck on the end of a bayonet. He had no intention of provoking these two either...any more than he would've the other two...since the marines seemed to be fair...unless you did something to rile them up. His mission now was to survive as long as he could... despite the rumors that had been passed around that the marines liked to torture and then kill their prisoners. *But what if those rumors were wrong...and the Americans were kind and understanding?* This seemed impossible given the fight that had just taken place...but stranger things had happened...and maybe he was in for a surprise. *These crazy Americans have already given me a drink of water...hadn't they. They wouldn't have wasted their precious water on me if they were just going to kill me later,* he thought, considering his options. *Maybe...just maybe...I'm going to survive this battle after all...and if I do...then my next goal is to eventually make it home...and to see my wonderful family yet again.*

Staggs and Jorgenson marched the prisoner on... towards the CP...and then they handed him off to a military police unit that had come ashore that vey morning. They took Kubo to an interrogation area not far away... and his clothes were cut away by a marine wielding a razor-sharp K-Bar knife. Then he was asked questions by a marine who spoke fairly good Japanese...which surprised him too. He was also given some food...which he ate ravenously...and after that he answered some more questions about where he had been during the battle and what he had done. He didn't think he was giving away any military secrets...since he was a lowly member of a tank crew...and the information he was giving was basic to say the least. But he also thought it was a fair thing to do...since the marines were treating him fairly... and he was just returning the favor...which is what civilized people did.

Staggs and Jorgenson continued on...heading inland...to the area where their individual battalions were forming up. Seeing a sign posted for the 2nd Battalion, Staggs turned to Jorgenson and said, "This is as far as I go this time, partner."

Jorgenson stuck his hand out...but Staggs knocked it away and hugged the private tightly instead. "Thanks for everything," Staggs said, backing off and looking Jorgenson in the eye. "I learned a lot from a kid from Wisconsin...and I hope I taught you some things that'll keep you alive on your next operation. Deal?"

Jorgenson wiped a tear away...not at all ashamed that he was crying...and said, "You promised me that you'd do me a big favor, right?"

"Of course...but what did I promise to do?" Staggs asked...and then it hit him...as he looked at Jorgenson.

Jorgenson turned slightly and he glanced at his back...which was bare.

"Oh yeah...about that backpack of yours. I remember what you wanted me to do. You're still worried about that squad leader of yours...Trackman...and what he'll do when you show up without your pack," Staggs said confidently.

"Exactly," Jorgenson replied. "He's gonna bite my head off when I tell him that I forgot it at the seawall on Red Three. He's a real stickler for the rules...just my luck."

"Well, don't worry," Staggs said assuredly. "I'll come by when we get back to the rear and square it all away for you. I'll vouch for you...and tell him that you carried that dang thing around for nearly two and half days."

"Thanks, Staggo...or should I say corporal," Jorgenson eked out...the emotional aspect of leaving Staggs...who he had fought beside for the last seventy-six hours...getting the best of him. "And remember... don't ever let God get too far away from you again...no matter what happens. He put the two of us together for a reason...and if I never do anything worthwhile again...at least I shared the Gospel with you. There's nothing more important than that...so thanks for letting me share it with you."

The Butcher's Block

"I won't let you down, Clutch...or the man upstairs either. Thanks again," Staggs replied...and the two separated...their joint ordeal on Betio now over.

Over by the *Pocket*...or what was left of it...First Lieutenant Robert Hackett...the platoon commander for the 1st Platoon of E Company of the 2nd Marines was resting inside one of the aircraft revetments that sat on the northwestern corner of the main airfield complex. The high log wall provided a good amount of shade...which was a sought-after commodity on the island at this point. Besides the sickly-sweet smell of death that seemed to hang over everything...and the hordes of flies that seemed to be everywhere...the oven-like heat was just as bad as it had been on D Day...and the marines did anything they could to lessen its impact.

Most of the other men who had been with him since the landing on D Day were there too...attempting to cool off as well. Sitting next to him was Sergeant Endres...his first squad leader...and next to him was Private Scott...his erstwhile sidekick. Then came Corporal Ingunza...who was not in his platoon...or his company for that matter...since he was from F Company...and PFC Petraglia and Private Agresta...who were. Then came PFC Wykoff...an amtrac driver...who was stretched out on the ground and snoring loudly...fully asleep. He was not a member of Hackett's platoon...nor were any of the men laying in a row after him...who were out too...just like Wykoff was.

The first man in this group was PFC Ed "Harry" Mornston...who...despite his rank...had served as one of the squad leaders in Hackett's *ad hoc* platoon. Next to him was Private Kevin McCaffrey...a third battalion man...and then came two privates...Beach...a radio-man...and Poffineger...a BAR-man...who were from G Company. These last three were in the same battalion as Hackett was...and they had landed on the right beach on D Day at least...only too far to the right...which is how they had ended up serving with Hackett.

Last of all came PFC Martin Mychale...an assistant amtrac driver...who...like Wykoff...was a member of the 2nd Amphibian Tractor Battalion. Martin...while extremely competent...had not said much the entire time...which was strange...but not unheard of. The other guys had quickly labeled him a loner...so they had left him largely alone over the last three days...which suited Mychale just fine.

Only one man was missing...and he showed up shortly. "Knock, knock," PFC Sean Feeney...one of Hackett's rifleman...said loudly as he came up to the revetment.

Everyone stirred at the sound of Feeney's voice...especially Wykoff...who seemed to sleep with one eye open even though he was snoring the loudest.

"What did you find out?" Hackett asked...lifting his head up off his chest.

"The Second Battalion is forming over by Shoup's CP. The Third is staying on the Beak. You amtrac boys are gathering near the pierhead. They want us to start heading that way as soon as possible. We're not gonna hang around here very long. They want us back aboard the *Zeilin* by tomorrow afternoon tops. The Sixth is going to stay behind. They drew the short straw as Staggs used to say," Feeney responded...a font of information as usual.

"Alright, boys," Hackett said, "let's saddle up. You heard Feeney...so let's make it happen...sooner rather than later. Is everybody good on where they gotta go to find their units?"

Everyone nodded that they knew...and then they got up in ones and two...stretching as they did so.

Hackett took out his black notebook and scanned the entries...making sure he had every man's name and unit written down. When he was satisfied that all was well, he turned to the men one last time and thanked them for all they had done.

The men clapped each other on the back and shook hands...knowing that they might not see one another again for quite some time. Some hugged even...while Mychale stood quietly off to the side...watching but not participating in the camaraderie.

PFC Wykoff slid over next to Private Scott and said slyly, "Watch this."

Scott...not knowing what he was going to do...just stood there...waiting to see what would happen.

"Hey, LT," Wykoff said.

"Whatta ya got, Wykoff," the lieutenant answered, wondering what the amtrac driver wanted.

"Are you just gonna leave Scott here in the dark?"

"Scott in the dark? What do you mean?" Hackett replied…confused now.

"Well, you kinda left Scott hanging since you never finished your story about what it means to be Black Irish. You started to tell us on Saturday…but you never finished your story. Those mortar rounds hit, and they cut you off. Remember now?" Wykoff said, poking Scott in the side.

Hackett bit his lower lip…thinking about it…and then said, "Oh yeah…I remember now. You're right, Wykoff. I never did finish that explanation, did I."

PFC Petraglia rolled his eyes now and said, "Seriously, another history lesson? Now?"

"Well, I can't really leave Scott hanging, can I? And since Wykoff wants to know too, I might as well finish what I started, right."

"Right, sir," Scott and Wykoff echoed.

"If I remember correctly, I told you about the Spanish Armada encountering that storm while they were heading home to Spain. Well, it just so happens that the storm caught their ships in the sea between Ireland and England…and a lot of ships were destroyed outright…but some were forced westward…and they sank close to the Irish coastline. Luckily, a large group of Spanish sailors survived…but they ended up shipwrecked on Ireland itself…and then they decided to stay there for the rest of their lives. Naturally, the sailors met and married Irish gals…so their kids had both Spanish and Irish blood in their veins. Those kids…by virtue of their Spanish fathers…were a little darker in countenance than the average Irishman…

and hence…they were called, 'the Black Irish.' Make sense, now?"

Wykoff looked at Scott and Scot smiled…the mystery finally solved. "That's a great story," Scott said, "I never heard of such a thing…but I know now. Thanks, sir."

"That was a great story. Thanks, sir," Wykoff added…satisfied.

Petraglia looked at the two of them and shook his head. "Now that class is over, can we get going, sir?"

"Of course. Class dismissed," Hackett replied…and the men began hugging again…knowing their time together had finally come to an end.

Then, their good-byes finished, the men left the revetment and walked into the bright sunshine. The heat was just as oppressive as it had been on D Day…and the two days thereafter…since it was now 1400 hours…and the hottest part of the day.

As everyone stepped off, Feeney yelled out one more tidbit. "And there's plenty of fresh water waitin' on us too…not that gasoline-fouled stuff we've been forced to drink since yesterday," and everyone sped up…the news of fresh water too enticing to ignore.

Corporal Tom Bosco was sitting beside a bunker that his make-shift squad had destroyed earlier that morning in route to the *Pocket*.

He and his men had isolated it on their very own after they attacked it…and they had used grenades to finish off the four occupants inside. The fifth man in the crew had obviously killed himself though...since he was lying on a cot right beside the entranceway to the bunker. The *rikusentai* had placed the muzzle of his rifle against his forehead and he pushed the trigger with the big toe on one of his feet. When Bosco looked inside, he saw that the man was still grasping his rifle barrel with both of his hands...and he had a large, bloody hole right in the middle of his forehead.

He had inspected the bunker from top to bottom right after they knocked it out...just to make sure that everyone was dead inside...and that no one was trying to hide himself. The last thing he wanted...at this point... with victory so close...was to have someone get shot in the back by a Jap who had been hiding in a bunker that they thought had been destroyed.

Once the *Pocket* had fallen, Bosco had released the men that he had gathered up the day before...on D + 1...right after the 1-8 had tried to land on Red 2. His decision allowed them to return to their own squads and platoons...so their own leaders could get a handle on the state of their own units.

His own squad had been nearly wiped out though. Two of his men had been wounded...that he knew...and several others were dead...which he knew as well. But one...the kid...was still missing...his whereabouts a mystery. Bosco had not been able to confirm whether he was dead...or hopefully...still alive...and the thought that he might never know what happened to him had begun to nag him. *I was his squad leader damn it,* he thought dejectedly, *and if I can't account for him...well...then who can?*

And that's when he spied a small figure walking up the beach. As the marine drew closer, Bosco started to think it might be him...and his hopes soared. Then... as he got closer still...Bosco saw that it was him...and he ran up to him and hugged him...the mystery finally solved!

"What the hell happened to you?" Bosco shouted out... releasing him.

"Geez...I've been worried that you'd want to kill me the whole time I was gone," the kid replied...relieved that his squad leader was happy to see him.

"So, what happened? Where'd you go?" Bosco pressed.

"Well, you were gone for a while...and the guys sent me off to get some more ammo. So, I went down to the pierhead...and I ran into a major who was running the show there. He was one mean SOB...and he told me that I had to stay there...to help his crew out. He said he was short men...and that no one wanted to volunteer any... so he just hijacked me and sent me out to the end of the pier. I ended up carrying boxes of ammunition in for two days and nights. It was horrible...and I'm beat to the bone. I think my skin is gonna fall off from walking in the water beside the pier for so long. Back and forth... back and forth...it seemed like it would never end...and every time I tried to get away...the major was right there...

daring me to try. He only let me go a little while ago." The kid turned around and looked back down at the pier in the distance and he just shook his head. "Well, I'm glad to be back...as you can see! So where are the rest of the guys...are they okay?" he added while glancing over Bosco's shoulder...looking for them.

"Casto and Harper were wounded," the squad leader said hesitantly.

"So where are the rest of them?" the kid said.

"Dead," was all that Bosco could get out.

"All of them?" the kid emphasized.

"All of them...except you and me," Bosco stated...his voice drawn and haunting.

Neither of them said anything for a while...and then Bosco spoke up...and said, "Well, let's go see our lieutenant...so we can tell him you made it. No sense makin' him worry about you any longer, right. Just knowing you made it will make him feel better...since you became our mascot from the time you showed up in the platoon."

"Mascot? I'm no mascot," the kid countered.

"Oh really? How many other outfits got a sixteen-year-old as one of their riflemen?" Bosco asked...and he patted the small kid on his back.

"Oh..." the kid replied...thinking about it. Then he added, "But I'm gonna be seventeen in six months...so I'm no mascot after that...okay?"

"You got it, kid. No more mascot after you turn seventeen," Bosco replied agreeably...and the two walked off...to let their lieutenant know the kid had made it.

Platoon Sergeant Stephen T. J. Roy and his men had returned to their nighttime position…near the airfield turning circle…after their successful raid with the four headquarters men of the 1-8. They remained there for the next two hours or so…wiling the time away until the sun came up. And that's when *China Gal* arrived.

First Lieutenant Bale jumped down onto the ground and steadied himself…not used to feeling solid ground under his feet. "I'm glad to see that you survived the night," he said matter-of-factly.

"We had another little dust up," Roy replied, "around three or so in the morning. But we made it through alright. It sounded like all hell broke loose against the Sixth right after that," he added…hungry for information.

"Yeah, the Japs hit the One Six with everything they had. Jones did a great job and his line held. Now they want me to team up with another one of my tanks…the *Colorado*…and we're going to support the Three Six as it heads down the tail. The One Six is going into reserve… directly behind them. No sense you following along," Bale replied. "I think we broke the Japs' back for good last night. The Three Six can take care of me and good 'ol *China Gal* from here on out."

"So, we're relieved of our duty?" Roy asked.

"Yes, you are, sergeant. And you're to head back to the Red Two beachhead. The Second is reforming there. You're done it seems. And I don't have to tell you…at least I shouldn't have to…that I'm personally grateful for your support. And my crew thanks you for all you and your guys did for us too. I know you lost some men doing it…

just like I did. That's war…but it doesn't mean we don't appreciate it. So please let your guys know that."

"I certainly will, sir. Now you be careful from here on out. Just because the Japs seem to be finished is no excuse to let your guard down. They got a few crazies left…and any one of them might want to take a crack at a tank before heading off to Valhalla…or wherever they think they're going after they blow themselves up."

"Head's on a swivel," Bale answered…moving his head right and left…showing Roy that he was ready for whatever might come his way.

"Alright, sir. You take care…and we'll see you when this is all over," Roy said.

"Semper Fi," Bale responded…and he climbed back up on his tank and lowered himself inside. He gave one last wave to Roy…and then he disappeared without another word.

"What's the deal?" It was Reisman…the thorn is Roy's side…speaking out of turn…as usual.

Roy glared at him for a second…and then broke into a grin…as much as he could. "We're done. We got orders to head back to Red Two. The Second is reforming there…to see who made it…and who didn't."

"So that's it? The battle's over?" Lewis asked…seeing the bigger picture.

"Yup. That firing we heard last night…after our little engagement…was the Japs' stagin' a *banzai* attack. They do it when they're desperate…and out of options.

The One Six held them off…and broke their backs doing so," Roy explained. Then he added, "So we're heading over to Red Beach Two…where the Second is gathering up."

Private Nelson looked over at PFC Reisman and said happily, "So it looks like you're going to get to marry that girl that's waitin' on you back in New Zealand!"

Roy…in a deadpan voice…cut in and said, "Tammy… oh she's probably got her claws hooked into some other marine by now. Why would she wanna hang around and wait for somebody like Reisman?"

"How'd you know her name was Tammy?" Reisman asked…amazed that Roy knew it.

The platoon sergeant looked at him with a wary eye and said, "I know everything Reisman…and don't you ever forget it!"

Riesman turned to Nelson and said, "Don't ever cross that man…or you'll end up dead. That guy knows everything!"

As the men began to head back…towards the Red 2 beachhead…Nelson said in a voice loud enough for everyone to hear, "I bet he doesn't know the name of my girlfriend!"

"Micky!" his platoon sergeant shouted back over his shoulder…and everyone broke out laughing…their long ordeal on Tarawa finally over.

First Lieutenant Ken Konstanzer walked down the long line of bodies lying in the tank ditch on Black Beach

Two and stopped beside one of them. A marine was kneeling close by…going through the men's pockets…trying to identify them…if their dog tags were missing. "Do you know this one," the marine asked randomly…the task overwhelming.

"Yes, I do," Konstanzer answered sadly. "That's Shoemaker. PFC Joseph Shoemaker. He got killed trying to deliver a message I gave him. Treat him respectfully, okay."

"I will, sir. There's just so many of them." The marine then wrote Shoemaker's name down on a list he was compiling…and he moved to the next man.

"I know…and there will be many more…so just do the best you can…and give them everything you can…as they did here."

"Thanks, sir. For understanding…" the marine said…and he rolled the next body over to see if his name was written on the back of his utility shirt.

Konstanzer didn't envy the man…but somebody had to do it…and he walked off across the airstrip…to the area where the Second Battalion was gathering.

The sun was beating down on him…just like it had the day before…and the day before that…fueling his desire…and need…for water. His wounds had stopped hurting long ago…but now…as he laid there in the open…his bloody bandages had become covered with flies…so thick in fact that he could no longer see the bandages underneath them. But what he wanted most of

The Butcher's Block

all was water...but he had no way of getting any...or so he thought.

"Hey, this one might be alive," a marine said...and his buddy came over for a closer look. The two marines had been scouring the area near the *Pocket* for souvenirs...a precious commodity now that the battle had finally wound down.

"Yup...he's breathing alright. Roll him over...and see if he's conscious," the other marine said...a K-Bar knife in his hand and a bag of gold teeth-fillings hanging off his web belt.

The marine who had spotted him knelt down and eyed the sword with relish. *I'll be able to trade that for a month's worth of cigarettes,* he thought greedily...and then he casually scanned the Jap's bloody body for any sign of booby traps. There didn't appear to be any...so he rolled the Jap over deliberately...having done it many times already.

The *rikusentai* officer had waited for this opportunity for hours. He knew he was badly wounded...and that he would never make it off the island alive. The Americans tortured their prisoners...of that he was sure...and he doubted he could withstand such a thing without disgracing himself. So, he placed his sword beside him... knowing it would attract attention...and then he had pulled his 9mm pistol out of its holster and hid it underneath him…where he could get it when he needed it.

The sound of the American voices alerted the *rikusentai* that his moment had arrived. He felt some hands grab his shoulder and hip and thrust him over. As his body rolled over…he came up firing…hitting the marine who was standing up first…and the one who was kneeling beside him next. He put another bullet into each of them after they were down…ensuring that they were dead…and then he turned the gun on himself. Now he would die the death worthy of a *samurai*…the killing of the two marines just icing on the cake…and smiling…he pulled the trigger.

Chapter Thirty-Three

The reunion was joyous...yet sobering at the same time. First Lieutenant Hackett and his five men - Endres, Scott, Agresta, Petraglia, and Feeney - arrived first...the rally point for the Second Battalion a short distance away from the aircraft revetments where they had finished the battle.

Corporal Staggs walked in next...and men's jaws dropped...since all of them had ridden together in the same amtrac on D Day...and they had seen his body lying on the coral shelf...apparently dead.

"I thought you were killed," the lieutenant said defensively...covering for the others.

Staggs shrugged his shoulders and made light of it. "Don't worry about it, sir. I'm like a cat that's got nine lives...the Japs can't kill me. But if anyone thinks they can, I'll offer you two-to-one odds on it," he said cockily, morphing right back into his old self. Then, looking around, he added, "Where are the others? Is this all that made it?"

"I have no idea what happened to Platoon Sergeant Roy's amtrac," the lieutenant said. "I never saw it after we boarded ours...and none of the guys that we ran into after we landed saw them either. Fumai...the corpsman... made it in, though. Petraglia ran into him two days ago. Fumai told him that he was able to get Thompson...who was wounded when you got blown out of our boat...back to the ships. So, Thompson made it too. Whether Fumai is alive now though is anyone's guess."

"I was over on Red Three the whole time," Staggs explained, "and I didn't run into any of our guys either. It doesn't mean they're dead though...just missing. Anybody wanna bet that they made it?" Staggs asked slyly...but no one took up his offer.

Roy and the eight others arrived around three in the afternoon. They had stopped at the pierhead along the way...to fill up on water, food, and ammo...and then... and only then...did they move on. When they finally arrived at the rally point, another celebration broke out...just like before...only bigger. Friends who had not seen each other in three and a half days embraced one another...happy to see that they all had survived. Then they took turns explaining what had happened to each of them...telling their own stories repeatedly...and no one seemed to tire of it.

After a while, First Lieutenant Hackett had left… to report the 1st Platoon's status to his company commander…so the captain could then report E Company's status up to battalion.

He returned an hour later…and the look on his face said it all. "Gather up, boys," he said quietly, "so I can fill you in on what's happened."

The men did as he asked…assembling around him in silence…their mood suddenly changing…reflecting their lieutenant's attitude.

"Here's what I got from First Sergeant O'Toole. Lieutenant Colonel Amey is dead. He got killed during the landing. Major Rice…the XO…is now the battalion commander. As far as our own company goes…I'm the only officer left alive. Captain Ring…our CO…was killed the day after we landed…trying to get across the same taxiway that held us up. First Lieutenant Reichel…our XO…and Lieutenants Beck, Culp, and Dahlgren are all dead too. I'm it, boys. I'm the only officer left in the company…so I've been bumped up to company commander. Platoon Sergeant Roy will take over as your platoon commander. As far as our own platoon goes… Private Thompson was wounded…but he's alive…thanks to our corpsman there…Fumai. He got him evacked on D Day…just like I ordered him too." At this point, Hackett stopped talking…and he glanced over at Fumai and nodded to him…acknowledging the great job he had done.

Fumai returned the nod…feeling a foot taller now.

Then Hackett continued. "On another good note… Private Hennessey made it too. He got hit in the arm while he was helping Grasso…who was already wounded himself. Both of them got evacked out on D Day…but Grasso didn't survive. He died of his wounds on the transport. So, Hennessey will be waiting for us on the *Zeilin*. And Corporal Hullender, PFC Rampley, and Private Smith have been accounted for as well. They were evacked to the *Monrovia*…which was off Green Beach…and they're alive. Wounded…but alive."

"So, Smith went and got himself wounded. I was wondering what happened to him," Roy said…since Smith had never returned from his escort mission to Green Beach.

"Yup. Smith is with Hullender and Rampley. Smith got his jaw shot off…according to the medical report coming from the docs on the *Monrovia*. It doesn't sound good…so Smith is probably gone for good. Hullender and Rampley will be back as soon as they're healed up. First Sergeant O'Toole's rollcall shows that the First Platoon had twenty-three men killed in action…with another five wounded. That leaves sixteen effectives…all of whom are standing right here. All told, twenty-one of us made it out alive."

Staggs whistled and said, "Twenty-one, huh. Why that's the same number of guys that made it off the *Canal*, sir. What are the odds of that happening twice!"

Chapter Thirty-Four

The casualty figures for the Battle of Tarawa were compiled and released several months later and they were as grim as first suspected. Although these figures would change slightly over time, the number of marine dead...those that were killed outright...and those that would also die of wounds afterwards...came in at nine hundred and sixty-one...fifty of which were officers of various ranks. The wounded in action were two thousand one hundred and ninety-six.

The Japanese casualties were just as sobering. Nearly the entire garrison was wiped out...with four thousand six hundred and ninety being killed in action. Only seventeen...most of whom were wounded to some degree or another...were taken prisoner.

James F Dwyer

On a brighter note, one hundred and twenty-nine Koreans laborers who were forced to work on the island under their Japanese masters survived the battle...an incredible number given the violence that enveloped the island for seventy-six hours.

Epilogue

Many of the marines who survived the seventy-six-hour ordeal spent the last few hours they had left on the island searching for their buddies who had been killed. Because of the sheer number of dead, and because the Japanese had fought right up to the end, it was impossible to have buried all of them in a timely fashion…so many of the marines were still lying right where they were when they had been killed.

This ended up being a particularly brutal task…since the marines they were looking for had been lying there dead for quite a while…some as many as seventy-six hours or more by now. And the heat and equatorial sun had been baking them the whole time…so their bodies were stiff with rigor mortis…and bloating…then turning black…and in some cases…bursting open.

Other men had been blasted apart when they got hit…and the marines found their body parts strewn all over the place…a leg here…an arm there.

A dead marine could be identified by his dog tags…but if they were missing…by a piece of jewelry… or by some other form of identification he may have carried in one of his pockets. If they knew who he was, then a crude marker was made with the marine's name on it and the marine was buried where he was… in a shallow grave…or simply covered over with sand. Some markers said nothing more than what was buried there: *A Marine leg lies here…owner unidentified…24 Nov '43.*

Several marines were chosen from certain units to remain a few days behind…to serve on the burial detail. Their job was to complete the task that the friends of the dead marines had already started…and they went about the island as well…identifying and burying the dead marines they encountered.

PFC Bob George…the small, eighteen-year-old machine gunner from the hills of Oklahoma…was one of the marines who was detailed for this unenviable job…and he was wondering if he could complete it without throwing up. He had just completed the most onerous task of all…dragging in the one of the bodies that had been hung up in the barbed wire entanglements just off Red Beach 2.

The Butcher's Block

He had sloshed out into the waist-deep water and untangled one of the three bodies that were there…a challenging job to say the least…since the smell alone was almost too much to bear. Now freed of its restraints, George got hold of the man's body and he began to pull on one of his arms…the goal being to get the marine ashore so he could be identified and buried.

George was making good progress…until he tripped over a jagged piece of coral. He did not fall though…he just stumbled…and then he caught his balance. But while doing so, he had also yanked on the arm of the dead marine who was trailing behind him. The small marine…who had watched Lieutenant Hawkins earn a soon-to-be-issued Medal of Honor not far from where he was now…heard a pop…and the dead marine's arm and shirt sleeve tore completely loose from its body. Then the lifeless body began to drift away in the current…like it had a mind of its own. George did not let it get away though…like it apparently wanted. Instead, he chased it down…and while holding onto the single arm with one of his hands…he grabbed the marine with his other and dragged the soggy body ashore with as much dignity as he could muster. Since the marine's face was long gone, George rolled the body over…to see if he had written his name on the back of his utility shirt…like a lot of men had done. George could see where the marine had done so…but the ink and lettering were now smeared…the saltwater having washed it out…so the man's name…like his face…was unrecognizable. George then patted his pockets…seeing if he could feel a wallet or anything else that could i.d. him…but he came away empty again. Then the bubbling noises started…as the gases inside the dead marine found an exit…and that made the whole process intolerable…the smell too much to take. George fashioned a small cross from bits of wood that lay scattered about…and he scooped some sand over the dead marine…enough to cover him completely. Next came the sign…and it read: *Unidentified Marine. Died in the wire off Red Beach 2. Nov 24, '43.*

That gruesome task done, George looked offshore and saw the other two brave marines who had tried to get ashore…and he knew what he had to do.

Now inland on Red Beach 2…near the *Pocket*…PFC George turned to the marine behind him and signaled him to remove his gas mask.

"What is it?" he asked…worried. The threat of hidden snipers was still very real…and the marine was scared that George may have seen one.

"See that Jap body over there," George said, pointing to it. It was obviously a Jap…since it was dressed in a Jap uniform and the man was wearing those peculiar Jap leggings…at least on one leg. The other leg…which was torn up…was covered with flies…a fairly common sight by now.

"Yeah, what about it?" the other marine answered, making a face. The gas mask was riding high on his head now, exposing his nose to the horrible smell of the dead bodies all around them.

The Butcher's Block

"Well, that one moved," George replied, and added, "at least I think it did."

"Go check him out then. Just don't get killed doing it. Two guys got killed yesterday souvenir hunting. If it was up to me...I'd just bayonet the guy and be done with it."

"I don't have it in me to just up and stab a guy. It might sound crazy...but the Japs are sorta just like us. They were just trying to survive...most of them. There were some bad apples in the bunch...I know that, too. Don't get me wrong...I'm not naive. I just think everyone deserves a chance...until proven otherwise," the young PFC said.

"That attitude...might get you killed...so be careful... just the same," the other marine replied gagging...yet still cautious.

George approached the Jap slowly...eyeing the body closely. Sure enough, the man's back was rising and falling slowly...as he was taking in air and exhaling...trying to stay alive. George moved closer...and he kicked the man in the ribs...and nothing happened. The man continued to breath though...so he was still alive. "I'm gonna risk rolling him over," George said...and the other marine pulled out a .45 caliber pistol and got ready to shoot if the man made any sudden moves.

"Here we go," George said, staring up at the marine... and George grabbed the Jap quickly and rolled him onto his back.

James F Dwyer

Petty Officer Saburo Okagi felt his body being rolled over…but he had no strength left…so he didn't fight it… not that he would've tried had he been able to. He was so thirsty at this stage that he could think of nothing else. As the sun beat down on his face, he lifted his two arms slowly…an inner voice telling him to do so. All he could see were shadows as he tried to look up…the sun so bright…and he asked for water…hoping whatever or whoever was standing there would appreciate his condition. "Please…give…me…some…water," he managed to ask again…before fainting.

George looked at the Jap and then at the other marine. "Is that what I think it is?" he asked.

"I don't know. I never went to church much before this. I will now though…trust me," he said honestly.

George leaned in closer and the object the Jap was holding in his hand was exactly what George thought it was. "It's a cross!" George stated. "This guy must be a Christian."

"Whatever you say, Mac," the marine replied, and added, "like I said…I didn't go to church much…so I'll take your word for it. I wouldn't know a Christian from a shoe salesman…but I'm gonna fix that as soon as we get back on the ships. I'm gonna be a regular attendee at Chaplain Willard's services from here on out!"

The Butcher's Block

Saburo Okagi felt the delicious taste of water running into his mouth for the first time in three days...and he thought he was in Heaven. He coughed suddenly... the water flowing faster than he could drink it...but he reached up and held onto the canteen so the man...or angel...would keep the water flowing. When he had had his fill, he nodded...and said, "Thank you, whoever you are...for saving my life."

Bob George looked down at the Jap and said, "I have no idea what you just said...but I think you meant it...so this is your lucky day." Then he and other man placed the badly wounded Jap on a large piece of corrugated tin - it must have come from the roof of a building that had been blown up nearby - and the two men carried the Jap all the way back to the medical station at the pierhead. They left him there...in the care of the Doc Brukhardt... who immediately examined him.

"We can save this one," the doc yelled out confidently...and his assistants scrambled around the man... peeling the dirty bandages away and cleaning his wounds.

George and the other man watched for a second or two...and then they headed back out. There were other ones still out there...marines who had died fighting for the Country they loved...and they needed to be buried properly. Bob George had been raised that way...to help others who could not help themselves...and Bob George knew intuitively that he was the best marine to do it…so he did it…without complaint.

Corporal George left Betio two days later. He was one of the lucky ones. Nearly a thousand other marines would not be leaving…they were there for good.

The End

Printed in Great Britain
by Amazon